FALLING

– A novel inspired by true events of 9/11 –

J.R. Van Buren

D1296455

VB Publishing, LLC

Library of Congress Control Number: 2016900326

ISBN: 978-0-9970251-0-1

Book Design by Dawn Mitchell at G4G Interactive

www.JRVanBuren.com

This book is dedicated to those who have lost their lives at the hands of terrorists. It's for their families, friends, and other loved ones left behind, and for those who have been witnesses to terrorist acts.

———•◦•———

A portion of the proceeds of this novel will be donated to 9/11-associated charities.

Contents

Prologue   1

PART 1: THE CONSEQUENCE

Chapter 1:   Risking It All   11

Chapter 2:   Opulent Dealings   27

Chapter 3:   Becoming One of Them   55

Chapter 4:   Spires to Heaven   71

Chapter 5:   Veil of Sultry Shadows   83

Chapter 6:   Fanning the Flames   99

Chapter 7:   Hell's Kitchen   117

Chapter 8:   Assorted Dealings   133

PART 2: THE FALL

Chapter 9:   A Beautiful Day   151

Chapter 10:   Awakening from the Fall   159

Chapter 11:   Dinner in Hell's Kitchen   175

Chapter 12:   The Next Morning   195

Chapter 13:   The Afternoon After   201

Chapter 14:   Driving Home   213

Chapter 15:   A House, But Not Home   229

Chapter 16:   Finding Speed and Home in Movement   247

Chapter 17:   Going Back   255

Chapter 18:   Resignation   271

Chapter 19:   Leaving   293

PART 3: THE SEARCH FOR TRUTH

Chapter 20:   Living to Ride in the Mountains   307

Chapter 21:   Curly's Place   321

Chapter 22:   Finding Doc   343

Chapter 23:   Confrontation   353

Chapter 24:   Searching Backward for the Fork in the Road   367

Chapter 25:   Meditation for Warriors   379

Chapter 26:   Om and Touching Eternity   391

Chapter 27:   Falling Again   413

Chapter 28:   Love and Fear   437

Chapter 29:   Too High and Too Fast   447

Chapter 30:   Carrying Things   469

PART 4: THE SURRENDER

Chapter 31:   The New York Gravesite   491

Chapter 32:   Day of Days   505

Chapter 33:   Back to Ground Zero   515

Chapter 34:   Racing in the Streets   537

Epilogue: The Final Veil   549

Judy,

I hope you

enjoy!

I hope you
enjoy

[signature]

Acknowledgements

It is with deep love and gratitude that I acknowledge my father—my best friend. He listens to me and really hears, accepting me as I am and supporting my dreams. He is a devoutly spiritual man and an avid reader whom I respect immensely. Without his vote of confidence and approval, this book would never have been made public.

Also, it is with a grateful heart that I acknowledge the contribution and hard work of my editor, Corrie Lisk-Hurst, without whose help this book would not have been possible. The words that best fit what she brought to this project are: encouragement, reassurance, and professional advice.

Prologue

Early Spring 2008

Michael put down his book and stared across the small, square room, not focusing on any of the small, shiny instruments, the jars holding balls of cotton, or the broad, flat wooden sticks and cotton swabs. He had the sensation that everything around him was falling slowly. He felt he could perceive one bad cell transferring bad information to another cell, just as one bad thought transfers bad information to another thought. If continued unabated, the process leads to death of the body and the mind, and the darkness of the mind shading the heart from light. One mistaken man from one village sees darkness and finds blame, cries for death, and the information is passed to another and another until darkness covers the heart of an entire village. Michael's thought stream was broken when the door to the examination room opened slowly and a man wearing a white lab coat walked in, looking down at his clipboard. The man stopped, raised his head, and looked at Michael over his glasses.

X-rays of Michael's chest were clipped over the top of large, backlit white plastic boxes neatly trimmed in bright reflective chrome. The gray and black shadows on the x-ray exposed, by the contrast of light and various shades of darkness, images of his ribs and breastplate and outlines of lungs and muscles. At locations across Michael's left lung were three dime-sized areas of darkness. The oncologists had already reviewed the images, and Michael idly wondered if the doctor had put them up for reference or to forewarn him, making the coming conversation less a shock to Michael and easier for the doctor.

"Please, Michael, get dressed and join me in my office across the hall. We need to sit down and talk." His smile intended to reassure Michael, but the expression failed in its intention.

"Doc, are you breaking up with me?" Michael quipped halfheartedly. The doctor did not look up or respond as he exited the room. Michael slid off the examination bench. He was standing in his underwear as a nurse walked in to pick up a file. Before walking out, she looked up at Michael with a manufactured smile. Michael met her eyes with his intelligent, engaging gaze that, when reciprocated, had always allowed him to communicate with others long before words were ever spoken. But she did not lock eyes with Michael, her non-communication communicating something nonetheless.

The door swung closed, and Michael began dressing. He was tall, lean, and slightly muscular for a man in his forties. His build and fitness were not born of ego, but of habit and his constant need for stress relief. He was always searching, always moving, trying to know something, figure things out, be something. Exercise was like a meditation, a break from the mind.

Michael began to cough; he bent over slightly and went from one cough directly into another. He sat on the chair across from the examination table and slid his trousers on both legs at the same time, and chuckled as he thought to himself, *No, he does not put his pants on one leg at a time.* He took a slight break between putting on his pants and his shirt. He slumped slightly, then, as he straightened, he began coughing again. It was a hearty, meaty cough this time, with a bit of a spasm at the end. He controlled the urge to cough again and could feel burning in his lungs. The skin of his stomach itched.

"Damn," was all he said. He reached over to the tissue box, and pulled two out so he could wipe away a small amount of fluid from the side of his face. He looked into the wadded, wrinkled tissue and could see streaks of red. "Just great," Michael sighed as he continued dressing, letting his mind wander again. It occurred to him that most people in his situation would be worrying about the deterioration of their bodies, the first visible stages of cancer. Beyond that, though, Michael realized he was headed for an experience that he just did not want to have. It was like accepting someone else's opinion of his life. He was not going to let someone else judge him and write the ending for him. He was not arguing with the inevitable, just how the inevitable would play out.

Michael finished dressing and walked out of the room. A nurse motioned him to the doctor's office, which was in complete contrast to the small white room from which he had just come. The carpeted room was large, with dark wood furniture and bookshelves lining the walls, which were painted dark green. There was a massive desk, more suitable, Michael thought, for the CEO of a large company. Michael sat in the square chair facing the giant desk, angled just slightly.

On the desk was a book with a glossy cover. Michael picked it up—it was heavier than he expected—and read the title: "Getting Your Affairs in Order." The words of the title bounced around awkwardly in his mind and made no sense. "Affairs," he began to laugh to himself, knowing what it meant, but feeling as though there was no relevance to him.

"Order." Now there was a word. Michael had bought into that word hook, line, and sinker for years, following the advice and guidance of his school teachers, of friends, of his father. "Getting things in order" was exactly what he had been doing for most of his life, accepting that life strategy without challenge. He had learned the importance of "order" as a child from adults: If you do this, this certain way, then the world will give you that...and the rule-followers and hard workers are always rewarded.

For Michael now, though, getting his affairs in order was the last thing he wanted to do; instead, he wanted to break out, break through. Then again, he chuckled wryly to himself, *I'm not really sure that there was much to my life to keep in order.* He would leave the keeping things in order to the other poor slobs. The guys who still think they can keep everything together, control things, survive, barely living so they barely fall.

Michael began to think of the mountains. He had stared into the blackness there and awoken from it. He breathed gently, feeling pain in his chest from a fresh coughing spell as he made another decision:

not to stay for the coming conversation. Michael had a pretty good idea where that conversation was going to take him and he just did not want to travel that road. He rose and left the doctor's office.

When he walked out of the medical center, a warm breeze caressed his neck. The late-afternoon sun reflecting off the silvery glass of the building directly across from the doctor's office created scattered shards of red, yellow, and orange light that punctuated the sullen and lazy shadows at Michael's feet. He paused and stood watching the light as his mood, too, changed from bright day to fading dusk while he grasped at some sense of understanding.

There was an ever-present, always wanting of living; that had been his only certainty. But now, the fear of a present darkness, of a present nothingness, of a present emptiness growing within him was almost intolerable. He had had a subconscious strategy up until now: Let me run faster, let me live brighter, let me find... true love, he smiled, surprised at his own surfacing thoughts. The idea of slowing had been intolerable, unthinkable, lest some darkness would overtake him; as long as he was running faster, expanding, he could experience himself as feeling alive But now he knew the time had come to slow: he must decrease, he would have to face a truth, his truth, the truth.

Michael began to walk again, one step at a time, stopping just inside the edge of the sharp, angled shadow of the glass edifice. He paused once again to feel the gently moving wind, thinking about a newspaper article he had read days earlier. It had said that just over a century ago, a nondescript patent civil servant was on his way home, traveling in a street car, when he wondered to himself, "What would the city's clock tower look like if observed from a streetcar racing away from the tower at the speed of light?" A question appeared into the man's thoughts unbidden, the seed of brilliance born of a simple question. The clock, the man postulated, would appear stopped, because light could not catch up to the street car, but his own watch would tick normally. "A storm broke loose in my mind," Albert Einstein later remembered. He produced five papers in 1905, and the world was changed.

What do I know? Michael asked himself. *What do I know is true?*

The Doctor says I am dying. Death, the most feared element of life, is just something that I cannot comprehend. Since that day of falling steel and shattering glass in New York, death has been on my mind, sitting close to my thoughts, and I witness death around us constantly. I often wonder if it was always so close, so often showing its face. Perhaps I just never noticed, breathing, looking outward and upward from youthful eyes. Which was the proper vision: then or now?

I used to wonder why everything appears to begin and end. So I searched for and contemplated those things that do not have a beginning...or an end. But somewhere in my past, I strayed from this line of thinking.

Michael thought about riding his motorcycle, pushing the speed and the leans until his heart beat hard, and the energy of fear rose within him. He had learned to control the fear; he learned to feed on it, he told himself, and felt as though he were facing death. Now, he understood that he had been doing the opposite: It was now clear to Michael that he rode hard, fast, dangerous to feel more alive so he did not have to face what he could not comprehend. He had believed he was facing death by taking dangerous rides, feeling adrenalin and the rush as he brushed death, but from every one of those experiences, Michael came back. In fact, the point was to come back and not actually die. There it was, a veil falling: He was not experiencing and facing death, he had been avoiding it entirely.

Michael began to walk again, in slow, sedate steps as though he were sleep-walking. His mind kept moving, and so did his body; while he was thinking, his body moved him to his car, took the keys out of his pocket, opened the door, sat him in the car, and pulled the door shut, awakening him to the suddenly quiet vacuum inside the car. A memory flashed to him in the stillness. He was shuddering in the thick darkness of smoke and ash. He could hear the reaper hissing, wheezing to him gently. He stood beneath a stone arch, in sudden momentary silence, as the dense, black, hot air began to drift and lighten. He slowly descended the stone step toward the soft sound when, appearing from the gray fog, was a twisted steel beam embedded into the invisible sidewalk just feet below his sight.

The beam glowed softly, crackling a quiet song in the moment between cognition of events just before and the events to follow. He shuddered and found himself back in the car outside the medical center.

Since that day in 2001, Michael had been losing himself, thinking himself special—special because of trauma, because of events, because of his experiences. His memories were like a drug, altering his awareness of the present, focusing his attention on a series of self-created personal recordings from his past. This one was loud, and when he was still, like now, recordings like this were loud enough for him to hear in his conscious mind. He was aware of how they clouded and manipulated the experience he was having at this very moment. He was recreating fear so he would have something to feel. But he was beginning to realize that in truth there had never been anything to fear, ever. He was tired of re-creating those fear thoughts that triggered emotion so he could feel something, anything. Enough was enough, he decided.

So what is true? The gift of transformation was wrapped in the fragile bubble of a question; the answer was within the question itself, like a fortune cookie. Just then, he thought of the words above the entrance to Curly's Bar: "Hoka hey." He remembered the note Doc had given to him. He pulled out his wallet, opened it, and found tucked into it a folded piece of white paper with a name and phone number written on it.

Michael felt he had taken the wrong road somewhere in his past. He began tracing back in his mind, back to that point, looking for that fork. In his search for meaning, he was still looking for something, not seeing that the most important thing for him was to find out what the most important thing was. (A laughable situation if seen more clearly, but Michael was just beginning to suspect he was on some sort of mental treadmill.)

All he could really see at this moment was that something had touched his own fire. He was trying to find out who he was, how he moved, how he brushed his teeth—not just thoughts and concepts. He was looking for his source, the beginning, but also the impending ending: He was searching for God, even if by another name.

Michael called it the search for truth, like it was an acquisition, and the more he searched, the more he realized everybody seemed to know something but him. He thought liberation was to be gained by attaining some missing knowledge but he kept discovering that everything he "knew" was his conditioning, his own thoughts. He just could not get around it.

He picked up the phone and dialed the number.

PART 1:
The Consequence

"To begin with, for you to be here now trillions of drifting atoms had somehow to assemble in an intricate and intriguingly obliging manner to create you. It's an arrangement so specialized and particular that it has never been tried before and will only exist this once. For the next many years (we hope) these tiny particles will uncomplainingly engage in all the billions of deft, cooperative efforts necessary to keep you intact and let you experience the supremely agreeable but generally underappreciated state know as existence.

Why atoms take this trouble is a bit of a puzzle. Being you is not gratifying experience at the atomic level. For all their devoted attention, your atoms don't actually care about you—indeed, don't even know that you are there. They don't even know they are there. They are mindless particles, after all, and not even themselves alive. (It is a slight arresting notion that if you were to pick yourself apart with tweezers one atom at a time, you would produce a mound of fine atomic dust, none of which had ever been alive but all of which had once been you.) Yet somehow for the period of your existence they will answer to a single overarching impulse: to keep you, you.

The bad news is that atoms are fickle and their time of devotion is fleeting—fleeting indeed. Even a long life adds up to only about 650,000 hours. And when that modest milestone flashes past, or at some other point thereabouts, for reasons unknown your atoms will shut you down, silently disassemble, and go off to be other things. And that's it for you."

– Bill Bryson

Risking It All

Early Summer 2001

The doorbell rang, and Michael slid in his socked feet from the small bedroom-turned-home office, down the narrow hall, and across the wood floor to answer the door. He had been waiting impatiently for a package from his boss: the Emblem Corporation bid for electrical supplies. Emblem Corp. was the single largest property manager in the country with headquarters in midtown Manhattan, an unlikely place for a Southerner like Michael to succeed.

Michael's employer, Universal Spectrum Corporation, had dominated every market they were in—and they were in every major market of the world—but they had not been able to crack the New York City market. Emblem was one of a handful of large corporations that owned and operated the large skyscrapers of Manhattan's behemoth skyline, a skyline so impressive that it called for new words like cityscape to describe it. These large corporations were run by the same families who had landed at Roosevelt Island only a few generations earlier. Many of the current CEOs' grandfathers had started their rise to social and economic prominence by sweeping the busy streets lined in two- and three-story brick buildings, cleaning up after the horses and donkeys that provided the power and transportation of the growing city.

Universal Spectrum had been part of that amazing growth, supplying power and ingenuity not only to New York but to the entire nation, inspiring through invention an atmosphere of opportunity for anyone who wanted it and was not afraid to sweat their way to success. The birth of this multinational conglomerate corporation was a quintessential American success story. At the young country's Centennial Exposition in Philadelphia in 1876, the founder of Universal Spectrum Corp., Richard Middleton, a scientist/inventor, introduced the latest technologies and ushered in a new era of what he called harnessing imagination.

Close to the end of the nineteenth century, Richard Middleton brought together several of his business interests under the newly growing concept of a one-roof entity called a corporation. And in 1896, Richard Middleton's newly formed corporation became one of the original twelve companies of the newly formed Dow Jones industrials. Several pioneering young companies figured out a way to harness electricity, and coupled with the invention of the light bulb, growth in the new industry was assured.

By the 1960s Universal Spectrum had become one of the early big companies to drive consumerism and change American society. Always moving, making acquisitions with a seemingly unquenchable hunger for growth, the corporation had become part of daily life in America. Its growth, though, was almost imperceptible to the average person, because for people like Michael, Universal Spectrum had always been there. So many, controlled by so few, with limited liability and as a separate legal entity, freed the corporation from nearly all human considerations. Universal Spectrum had become a formidable organization that employed thousands and no individual was aware of anything more than their small part, never understanding fully how their role contributed to an unseen prime objective. It seemed that no one ever questioned it.

Michael was no different: He was proud to say he worked for Universal Spectrum. His first job offer at the manufacturing facility had come in 1995, and at the time, it seemed like a godsend. He was young and in love, and his poetry and songs were not paying any bills. A steady job made him much more attractive in many ways, especially to potential in-laws. On the surface, he did not seem like the normal recruit for such a prestigious corporation. Universal Spectrum advertised itself as being full of Ivy Leaguers but the truth was that the company was run by second-tier college grads who had averaged Bs and worked their way through school. That was the company's "secret formula" and Michael fit the mold perfectly.

In Michael's middle-class family, work and school existed simultaneously, and those wanting a better life and a better neighborhood were willing to work to get it. Being raised in that environment, Michael never considered any other possibility, and once given the chance, he thrived, moving to a new position with growing responsibilities every year. He was recognized by the corporation as a moneymaker from the start. With what seemed to be unending energy and a natural love of what was referred to as "the hunt," plus no small measure of intelligence, Michael moved up the corporate ladder at an accelerated pace.

Michael's latest boss—a young, brash manager who was as arrogant as he was talented—spotted Michael and pulled him onto his business development team, sending him to every training course he could find, grooming him for action at a higher level. Michael ate it up, even the long hours of travel to cities all over the United States.

When Michael's boss finally thought he was ready, he sent him to New York to break into the property management world. There had been pressure from above not to use a Southern man. A prestigious post like Manhattan was usually held for the educated elite; after all, the families who controlled Manhattan also controlled large sums of money and politics. But after much back-and-forth, Michael's assignment was approved, and unbeknownst to the managers at Universal Spectrum, Michael had more in common with the wealthy elite of New York than they would ever have imagined. Many of the families that owned much of Manhattan had immigrant fathers or grandfathers, hard-working people, who worked their way up, and they had a healthy respect for anyone doing the same.

Michael rolled up his sleeves to work hard, and he was a no-nonsense, "look you in the eye and do what he said he would do" kind of guy. He was hungry for success, he was almost handsome, and he looked the part of successful New York businessman in a suit and wing-tipped shoes. All these things looked right on the surface, but Michael Tantalus also had an advantage that no one at Universal Spectrum knew about: a history in Manhattan and "friends."

There was a summer long in Michael's past when he had been working as a bartender on the west side of Manhattan—the area called Hell's Kitchen—and he had gained an intimate knowledge of how Manhattan worked. He knew who mattered and who didn't, and it was no secret on the streets whose hands needed to be greased and who needed to be avoided. He knew the important details about who was in charge of which borough if you wanted things to go smoothly (or go at all). Yes, Michael Tantalus was perfectly suited for his next job.

So when Michael opened his Charlotte, North Carolina, door to the postman, he was expecting an exceptional presentation designed to win the first major electrical supply contract for Universal Spectrum in Manhattan in nearly 40 years. His boss had taken on the responsibility for putting together a "killer bid", and Michael was to deliver it in twelve perfectly packaged copies by noon the next day.

Michael opened the door and the light from outside shone on the dark wood floor, forming a crooked rectangle the color of the outside sky. Momentarily blinded by the bright sun, he could only see the silhouette of the deliveryman, who thrust a thin envelope toward Michael.

"Where's the rest?"

"This is all."

"Are you sure? Can you look?"

"This is all," the deliveryman said in a matter-of-fact manner as he turned to hop hurriedly into his truck, gone in an instant. Michael ripped into the cardboard envelope and pulled out a few pages paper-clipped together. There was a terse message from his boss written on a small, yellow sticky note on top: "Make the twelve copies and deliver." Michael reached for something to throw; finding nothing, threw the three pages of his boss's thinly constructed bid for the Emblem Corp. project. They floated lightly in the air, meandering back and forth until gently finding the floor.

Disgusted and almost shaking with anger, Michael pulled out his cell phone to call his boss. As the phone rang, he tried his best to clear the rage from his mind.

"Hello?"

"Dan," the word came out hard and terse.

"Yes, Michael?" came the slow, measured reply.

"A FedEx arrived, but I think there must be more."

"How many pages do you have?"

"Three."

"That's it: Make the copies and make sure the bid arrives on time."

"Dan."

Still the word came out too harsh, so Michael let out air he was holding and changed his tone.

"Dan, this doesn't address any of their concerns. I know we can do better." The honest words brought out the same in his boss.

"Michael, two large bids came in at the same time. You did a great job getting us this far, and it is a great start for you in New York but, quite frankly, we only had time to do one. We've never even come close to winning an Emblem bid and no one wanted to commit the resources for another lost bid. And besides, we just don't have the right political connections to win it. Sorry." The last word did not come out apologetically but as the end of the conversation.

"Thanks, Dan, for being straight with me," Michael said, doing his best to make the reply sound sincere, but it did not matter to Dan, as he had already hung up. In one movement, Michael folded his phone and launched it into the plaster wall across the room, shattering the phone and releasing his anger. He walked across the room, rummaged through the pieces, then picked them up and carried them into his office, where he put them in a drawer. The desk phone rang.

"Hello?" he answered cautiously.

"Hey, honey," came his wife's pleasant voice.

"Hey," came Michael's deflated reply.

"What's wrong?"

"Dan sent the bid: It's shitty, we have no chance of winning, and I worked months just to get us on the list. Even worse, it has my name on it! I barely have time to get it delivered and it sucks. My name in Manhattan will suck... they will laugh at how crappy this is; they will know we gave up."

Michael stopped ranting, as he was getting angry again. His wife Deborah could feel his darkening mood.

"What would the bid look like if you had done it?"

"Very different."

"Why don't you do the bid yourself?"

"I have no authority, no time, and it's due in Midtown by noon tomorrow, no exceptions."

"What time would you have to fly out in the morning to make a noon deadline?" Michael's silence told Deborah she had him hooked, and although she couldn't see it over the phone line, his eyes began to dart back and forth like he was having REM sleep. Deborah knew her husband and she knew he was money when under the gun of pressure.

She continued, "You get going on the bid, I'll check flights for you, and stop by the grocery store for some coffee. Get ready for an all-nighter like the time you crammed a full semester of differential equations in one night of studying. I seem to remember you aced that exam."

"Highest grade at the university," he smiled then added with humility, "Thanks, Hon."

Little more than an hour later, Michael's wife opened the door to their small house carrying a large bag of groceries, light snacks that go well with coffee, a bag of unground coffee beans, and a bottle of wine for herself. She knew she would find Michael happily immersed in his work when she arrived. She paused on the way to the kitchen at the end of the hall that led to the bedrooms and home office. She could hear him on the phone.

"That's good ... that's great ... got the email and the link. Thanks again, I'll be in touch soon," Michael's manic voice broadcast his pleasure. She could hear the sounds of him humming to himself, the shuffling of papers, and a busy printer. She continued to the kitchen to set down the bag. After a minute, she ground the coffee beans loudly; the coffee was soon brewing so she walked down the hall to the door of the office.

Michael was in his own world, deep in creative mode. It was rare to take such creative license with a major bid, and he figured if he was going to take a risk with his job he should go all the way. He had been very busy since Deborah had sent him on his mission, researching his own company and learning that his own company's capabilities were more extensive than even he had known. He had been on the phone with the West Coast energy arm of Universal Spectrum and then with the European financial arm. One website after another led to one phone call after another; everyone was eager to help on a bid for Emblem Corp., as many had much to gain.

Presentations, lists of capabilities and technologies, and access to transportation systems, capital, and more—their presentations came by email rapid fire and Michael skillfully wove them all into a beautiful and impressive bid. He was pretty sure he was not promising anything that Universal Spectrum could not deliver on, but much of his information came verbally from fellow associates that he barely knew or not at all. But he wrote down the things they said they could do, taking quite a few liberties and trusting his instincts.

Deborah watched him, but he was so engrossed in his work that he had not noticed her. She looked at the stacks of paper he was moving from place to place on the floor in an unseen grid, keeping his finger on a stack while he looked around the others as though he were playing chess, holding play until he was sure that he had moved the piece to the most advantageous location. She left the doorway to retrieve fresh coffee, pouring before it was finished brewing. She walked carefully through the minefield of reports and presentations scattered about the floor and set the coffee down near Michael.

"Thanks, hon," he said, never looking up.

"You are booked on the 6 A.M. flight."

"Excellent," he said, still not looking up, "La Guardia?"

"Yes," she answered, walking back down the hall.

Michael was now getting all the information into one document, as he wrote, re-wrote, edited, and manipulated text, pictures, charts, and graphs.

"Hey, I'm going to need you to be my editor," he shouted down the hall.

"I figured … I am going to have a cup of coffee first so let me know when you are ready."

"Can I have some coffee?" he yelled to the kitchen.

"It is, 'May I have some coffee,' and it's next to you by the phone," she shouted back, correcting his grammar. His eyes searched his desk swiftly, and spotting the coffee, he answered quietly, "Oh, thank you."

"You're welcome," she shouted, knowing what he had said without hearing him.

"May I," he mimicked her while typing. Then he paused, looked over what he had been typing, stared at the screen for a few moments, then picked up a pencil, which he put into his mouth like a bit in a horse's mouth. It was a habit from days of scratching notes before computers: The world had changed but he got comfort from the taste of wood and sound of slight crunching as he bit down on the pencil. Since childhood this habit had helped him think, soothing his doubts.

Michael pulled out a large drawer in his desk. The files were neatly hanging perpendicular in the drawer, all labeled in order alphabetically, divided by colored tabs. The order in this drawer gave Michael comfort, and the feeling that everything was in order and controlled enabled him to keep moving toward his dream of success. He thumbed through until he reached the "Es," finding Emblem.

He compared his notes one at a time with the presentation on his computer, scratching notes on a clean notepad to make sure he covered everything, satisfied every need, and answered every question. He was lost in his own confidence and creative endeavor with no sense of time until his wife yelled from down the hall.

"Its three A.M. Better wrap it up to leave in time for the print shop to make your copies." He did not answer; he simply moved to the next task. Every element was now on or in the presentation for the bid, he moved a few more graphs and charts from the Internet to his presentation, making bold black boxes to hold and highlight certain concepts and titles, changing text, labels, fonts, colors, and styles. All of the pertinent information was in the written text, so now he went to work on the aesthetics, moving things in to the right order, the right place to tell the story he wanted to tell, bolded words here and there designed to catch a quick passing glance, to pull in the critical reader, to say through words and symbols the things that Michael knew would resonate with the reviewers of the bid.

Michael finally leaned back in his chair, stretched the aching back muscles that had been hunched too long. He knew that the bid presentation was good but he also knew he was way out of line, out of compliance with every process check designed to prevent men and women like Michael from doing just what he was doing right this minute. He leaned back further in his chair and let his head hang over the back. With bare feet flat on the floor, he began to swivel from side to side, thinking about what he was doing. He knew he could get into some trouble, and that did not bother him, but he also knew that his boss had put his neck on the line to get Michael into this job and he didn't want to blindside Dan or get him in trouble.

He decided to fax a copy of the new bid to his boss and his boss's boss at the same time, explaining that he had "added a few things" to the bid before submitting, things that he had forgotten to tell his boss. He did not feel he was crossing any lines, and he knew that the deadline prevented him from going through proper channels. This should get his boss off the hook in case the changes backfired.

Truth was, Michael was taking a gamble but a gamble that he felt was worth the risk. He printed the final copy.

He threw on his favorite old sneakers, worn and dirty, and pulled a sweatshirt over his head. He grabbed the final print and headed for the 24-hour copy store. He felt good on the drive; the empty streets were inviting, so the drive to the store was twice as fast as normal. The man in the store ignored him at first but Michael engaged him, let him in on the coup: "I am off to storm Manhattan, need your help, how would you like to make an extra $100?" Michael smiled. The man in the store did not; that is, until Michael held up the $100 dollar bill, always more impressive than five twenties, saying, "Uncle Benjamin could be all yours."

"What do you need?" came the droll response.

"This has got to be a winner... need your help to pick out the paper stock, the cover, everything," Michael was holding up the bid presentation. The man walked over to the counter, looked at the presentation, then pushed his glasses farther up his nose.

"Let's see, what weight paper, and what kind of cover?"

"Not sure: What do you think? I need it to look sharp, professional." Michael knew that if the man made his own choice on the binders, he would make sure they looked good. "I have to go back to the house, shower, pack, and be back here by 5:00 A.M. to make my plane. I am not going to have any time for corrections or changes. I know I don't know you, but I have to count on you."

The man did not look up at Michael, but he sighed as Michael slid the bill across the counter. "I took this job to get away from pressure."

"I am really sorry. Someone left me in a bind and I am trying to make it work." Michael apologized as the man picked up the bid and the bill.

"Alright. 5 A.M.?" It was not really a question but a statement to let Michael know how much of an inconvenience this whole thing was.

"Great!" Michael called cheerfully, hurrying out the door. Funny, he thought to himself, sometimes our fate is in the hands of a hapless stranger, and sometimes they buy into what you are doing and sometimes they just do not care. Michael was betting on the former.

———·•·———

The drive back to the house was even quicker, and Michael knew that he had done well—he had a chance on this bid. He also knew that he had a secret. He wondered if it would matter in Manhattan. I am sure that is all long forgotten, he thought, but a small contraction of fear ran through him, I have friends in Manhattan but I have enemies too, better to let the past be past. He packed quickly. Though his mind and body were tired, the familiar routine would allow him to pack everything he needed and nothing more. After a quick shower, cool to help keep him alert, he wrapped a towel around his waist. Still wet, he picked through the closet, selecting his best white shirt, his most professional, neat charcoal suit, black belt, black wingtip dress shoes shined spotless and reflecting the light from the bedroom, long black dress socks, and his lucky red tie. He kissed his now-sleeping wife, then walked quietly out of his house and out of the restful neighborhood, headed to the always-busy streets of New York.

A quick stop at the all-night print shop on the way to the airport yielded a very proud all-night manager. He had read the bid while printing copies and binding it into the best paper and best shell. It told him something about how important it was and reading the lines he was drawn in.

"I made a few changes, thought a few things would look a little better. I centered a few of the other charts as well," he declared, proudly showing Michael the changes he had made.

"Very nice!" Michael confirmed, his smile saying everything that needed to be said. Michael knew that it was not the money that had made the man want to make the bid better: It was the sharing of his human condition, inviting the man to passionately participate in Michael's dream. It was a talent that Michael had. He always had instinctively known that there were no successes in a vacuum. What many considered luck or fortune was actually the ability to involve others, sometimes total strangers, in the endeavor's success.

It was not a manufactured technique for Michael, it was sincere and natural. But he was conscious of its effect on others.

Next, the two men packed the twelve copies neatly into a box. Even the unplanned details were coming together. When something is working, when you are moving towards some imagined success or prestige, all of the fearful and doubting thoughts sleep, and there is comfort in the movement. Michael carried the box to his car, got in, and rolled down his windows, letting the cool morning air pour over him as he drove to the airport. He swelled with the feeling of a job well done and a not-unpleasant, warm fatigue. He was not attached to the outcome of his effort, but he rested in the effort alone—it was pure and clean and it made his thoughts pure and clean. A slight smile came over him as the still-distant sunrise began ever so slightly to lighten the night sky.

It was still early enough that Michael was ahead of the regular commuter traffic, so parking, catching a shuttle, getting his ticket, and moving to his departing gate were simple without any of the exponential complications that can occur while traveling. Once he boarded the plane, Michael carried his box and briefcase to his seat—a window seat, as always. He put the box in the overhead and slid his briefcase under the seat.

The plane departed on time, and as it accelerated down the runway, there was a slight thrill. There was still a little of a young boy in him and the acceleration was fun so he smiled through his fatigue. The plane lifted and angled high into the sky and soon there was the steady, even roar of plane engines and rushing air over the sleek fuselage and long, outstretched aluminum wings. It was all a familiar and soothing lullaby for Michael.

"Coffee, sir?" the flight attendant asked.

"Yes, please," he responded and relaxed. The coffee appeared before him and he took in the warm smell. He did not drink; instead, he put the cup on the seatback tray and looked out the window at the clouds that sat seemingly motionless, stretching to somewhere near eternity. The sky was familiar and welcoming for Michael, it seemed like flight was effortless. He felt like he had years ago in his parents' station wagon, lying down in the back on the way home from a long trip, looking out the window at the clouds without a single care. The sky held him now as he let himself nod off, to rest for the already dawning day.

One last thought: Was everything in order? He confirmed to himself that it was and imagined that he was fully in control of everything, then drifted pleasantly into sleep, lulled by the reassuring hum of the moving airplane.

Michael's next sensation was the bump onto the runway at LaGuardia Airport. His eyes resisted opening, and at his first sight, he noticed that the coffee was gone and his seatback tray had been returned to its resting place. He sat up from a slouch and began to get his bearings; he straightened his shirt, buttoned the last button on the collar, and then shimmied the knot on his tie back into the collar. The tightness was uncomfortable at first, as it always was, but it helped signal that it was time to move to the next thing. He zipped his briefcase shut, stood, and retrieved the box of twelve carefully replicated bids all in the required format. He made a quick stop at the restroom near the arrival gate to neaten himself further, examining his eyes and deciding his face needed a little splash of water. Then he jumped into a controlled dash to the cab line.

"Midtown, take the Midtown Tunnel." It was a surgical statement, a sentence designed to efficiently let the cabbie know that Michael knew what he was doing and where he was going. It was also a not-so-subtle statement: no shenanigans. Phrases said just right were designed to eliminate any thought in the other person of taking advantage. New Yorkers knew them instinctively and most were not even aware of their effect. It was like a protective coating they wore to protect themselves and move trouble-free through a chaotic tangle of streets, cars, cabs, trucks, and pedestrians. Precise statements such as directions without asking questions and barely acknowledging the other person were really saying, "I am not a tourist, don't screw with me." Michael had absorbed the statements and the confident, intentionally distracted behaviors naturally and so thoroughly that, but for his Southern drawl, most would mistake him for a New Yorker.

The cab plunged downward, following many other yellow cars into the tunnel and below the river with only dim, dingy lights to fight the darkness. Michael's eyes quickly adjusted and there was only the sound of the moving vehicle. The sudden near-silence made the closeness of the cabbie, just in front of Michael, seem awkward. Michael reached across the silence.

"Where are you from?" he asked, breaking his own rule of distracted silence, and for just a moment, feeling vulnerable. The man looked at Michael in the rearview mirror, sized him up, then decided to answer.

"I am from India." He paused to judge Michael's reaction. "And it came as natural as talking to a long-lost friend; Michael connected with people naturally, and this was no different. "Where in India?" he asked, and the man began to talk about where he was from. Once the silence was broken, the man talked on and on, and Michael listened as they crossed town then headed south to Michael's destination.

The cab double-parked on the street in the shadow of a tall skyscraper, then Michael put three twenties over the cabdriver's shoulder and exited the yellow vehicle while the two men exchanged pleasantries.

"Blessings to you, my friend," the cabbie offered and Michael accepted with a nod. He turned and stepped between two cars and onto the sidewalk, and in a reflex action that was the second clue that he was not from the city, Michael looked up at the height of the broad steel tower, so tall that its sides appeared to come together at the top somewhere in the clouds above.

He moved in a quick, serpentine manner through streams of people on the busy sidewalk, working his way to the door and into the lobby of Emblem Corporation's signature building.

Opulent Dealings

Summer 2001

Michael walked slowly once in the lobby, looking everywhere at the detail and opulence inside this showcase building. It was nearly noon and the lobby was busy with people walking in every direction, attending to their workday rituals, coming in and out of doorways all in a seemingly chaotic order. The floor was polished marble, so polished that Michael, could clearly see his face. Contemplating his own reflection on the floor, he judged his appearance: Some classic features, he thought, hearing his mother's voice in his head, but he added to himself, *Am I missing something?* He judged himself as he judged everything, but more so when it concerned himself; the judgments were things that he had heard others say were wrong with him. And he always believed the negative and mostly ignored the positive.

The doorways and arches of the stores lining the lobby were trimmed in gold, broken by large windows towering to the ceiling far above. Michael looked closely at his gold reflection in the broad trim around the elevator; he turned his head from side to side, then showed himself his teeth. He straightened his tie and looked disapprovingly at his suit, *I need a decent suit*, he berated himself. Gradually more and more people entered the lobby of the tall tower as lunch time neared; he watched them intently, looking at their ties, their shoes, judging in his mind who were staff and who were executives. The suits he was seeing were custom-made, he told himself, new looking with sharp angular ties, blaring bright red success and confidence. They walked different, taller, more important, and richer. They were the American aristocracy, he told himself.

The elevator doors opened, people began to board and Michael was swept by the group.

"Thirty-three, please," Michael asked, pinned against the wall away from the elevator buttons by the numerous people, a few others called out floors, 23, 17, 14. There came no answers but all the appropriate buttons were pushed: Everyone knew the routine, no one looked up, no one spoke once the elevator began its ascent. No one ever looked into the eyes of anyone else. Michael too was silent. The elevator stopped many times but Michael did not care, he was going to make his deadline, *And then I can sleep,* he thought. He watched the numbers across the top, and when the elevator halted at thirty-three, he stepped out and walked down the long hallway.

Michael walked in fatigue, physical fatigue from going without sleep, the rest that the body needed, and mental fatigue from going without dreaming, the electrical disbursement of a day's worth of accumulated bioelectric stress. For Michael, this actually was perfect, though he was not conscious of it: His own effort or planning at this point would have only gotten in the way of the events to come. The moment-by-moment, day-to-day decisions that Michael made to control situations were the decisions that separated him from his own infinite inner world. In other words, typically he was getting in his own way, but since he was fatigued, he was content to let his awareness go along for the ride and observe. Here, at this moment, his higher consciousness was able to take over because the part of his mind that thought it was in control was simply fatigued.

Michael was looking ahead now and could see where the hall bent and joined a larger main hall. Once around the bend he could see a large desk with a woman behind it monitoring people coming and going, a computer screen, and phone calls all with ease, moving from one to the other as though she were dancing.

"Good morning," Michael greeted the receptionist warmly, "I am here with a supply bid." The receptionist looked at him and quickly sized him up, thinking she now knew everything there was to know about Michael, then began to dial even before she lowered her glance.

"Mr. Braunstein, there is another bid here. Are we still accepting?" Her business like frankness in front of Michael was very normal for New York.

"Yes, still just shy of noon, have the courier put it down in the lobby and I will send someone to get it shortly," Michael could hear the muffled voice squeaking from the phone.

"Jonathan, it is not a courier, it is….," she put her hand over the receiver and motioned to Michael with her facial expression; he understood, smiled then capitulated.

"Michael," he whispered, "Michael Tantalus," and smiled at her once more. She silently motioned to him again, this time with her eyes.

"It is Mr. Michael Tantalus of…" He was in sync with her now, handing her a business card, "of Universal Spectrum," she finished the sentence and turned her head as she was listening to the voice on the phone. Michael could not hear what Jonathan said to her before she hung up the phone. But her expression was puzzling and she looked at Michael as if trying to see something that she had missed moments earlier.

Michael of course knew who Jonathan Braunstein was. Michael had never met him, but his name was on the bid, and everyone knew he was very important and critical to the decision-making process for who would win the bid. The receptionist turned to face Michael, this time she smiled at him, "Please have a seat, Mr. Tantalus, Mr. Braunstein would like to speak with you."

"Thank you," Michael replied.

He was at home in this small lobby, or any lobby, he knew the rules, he knew the game. He sat with crisp intent, but softened immediately into the exquisitely soft leather. It was the money effect, he thought to himself. Money could take an ordinary chair and turn it into art with adjectives like, luxurious, lavish, and affluent. *Yes,* he thought, *there was big money here.* Though he was adept at business dealings of all kinds, these were going to be opulent dealings and the stakes were going to be higher, like any sport that ends in playoffs. Where everything speeds up with more observers and those not prone to mistakes make simple ones like forgetting who they are and trying to act like or be something that they simply are not. Michael would not make this mistake, he would be just who he always was with the added condition of being tired when he meets Jonathan Braunstein.

Michael sat patiently for a few moments when a sharply dressed man walked in his direction. It was Jonathan Braunstein, not particularly tall, but handsome, and very well groomed. Giorgio Armani glasses, *tortoise shell*, Michael was noticing every little detail. Neatly cut hair, light and very curly, manicured nails, everything about him reminded Michael of the rich leather chair. As the man approached he extended a hand.

"Jonathan Braunstein," Michael stood and met his handshake in one smooth, but not too quick motion.

"Michael Tantalus."

"Yes, yes, you are Michael Tantalus," he said it with some emphasis as he looked Michael up and down, smiling, "Bring your bid and follow me, I want to show you something." Michael turned toward the receptionist: They were still communicating silently, Michael looked at his suitcase, she nodded and stood to wheel it behind her desk. He gave her a different smile as he followed Jonathan down the hall, she raised her head to look at Michael, with a blank expression on her face for just a moment as she was caught in his stare, then she smiled as she returned her eyes to her work. Michael followed the well-dressed man down a maze of halls and into a large corner office that was bright with sunshine from the overly large windows that offered a view straight up an avenue in one direction. The avenue was lined in what appeared to be endless tall spires on both sides of the street stacked tightly and neatly next to each other like tall, proud soldiers at attention waiting for an inspecting commander. Michael recognized that he was looking straight north up Lexington Avenue.

Jonathan turned to Michael and pointed to the adjoining wall to where the boxes, folders, pouches, and parcels were all stacked against it like large misshaped stones of a lost, ancient castle wall. Michael was stunned at the number and diversity of packaging. The bid seemed so specific and yet here was such variety in interpretation.

"Your bid, Mr. Tantalus, is the only hand-delivered one. Please put it on my desk and have a seat." Michael Tantalus was on-stage, how he walked, how he talked, how he looked, how he moved would all be judged, sized up, and would influence how he did, business-wise from here going forward. He knew it and was perfectly at ease, showing confidence but no sign of the arrogance that was so often associated with men and women from Universal Spectrum. The corporation recruited the brightest and the best, and too often, they knew it. "Why did you hand-deliver your company's bid?" Jonathan asked.

"I wanted to make sure it got here on time." Michael put very little energy in his reply but smiled just slightly while looking directly into Jonathan's eyes. Jonathan opened the box and pulled out one of the bids and put it on his desk between the two men.

"Every three years, Universal Spectrum mails in a halfhearted attempt at a bid, that frankly, I don't even waste my time reading and this year Universal sends me a man with a name that I have never heard before, and what is that accent? Would you happen to be from Texas? And Tantalus, not a very common name, it sounds Greek?" Jonathan Braunstein examined Michael closely for a moment longer then looked down and began to page through the bid while Michael answered his questions.

"Yes, the accent is Texan but I have not lived there in a long time. Most people never guess I am from Texas. I grew up in Houston, so the accent is urban Texan, if you can imagine such a thing. And Tantalus is Greek, but my family would say they are Texan." Michael smiled and Jonathan looked up, nodding his head.

"I heard a story once about a Texan with a Greek name," he said it a little bit under his breath then moved his attention to the bid, "Where did you get all your information? Your bid is insightful, you address some key issues that are, how would you say, peculiar to The City." "The City" was how New Yorkers referred to New York City because, in their minds, it was THE City, just as it was in the minds of many across the globe. Michael did not answer the question, which was not lost on Jonathan as he continued reading the bid, making notes, unseen to Michael. "Are you new to Universal Spectrum?" Jonathan was asking questions without looking up.

"No, I have been with Universal Spectrum for about five years now—I'm just new to New York," Michael paused then clarified, "Or rather, I am newly appointed to Universal Spectrum in New York, I spent some time in Hell's Kitchen back in the early eighties so I have an idea how things work here, in the city, that is," Jonathan took off his expensive spectacles one ear at time and stared at Michael as his mouth fell open slightly, then he asked Michael,

"Where?"

"50th between 9th and 10th avenues."

"In the early eighties?"

"Yea, it was a little rough back then," Michael said understatedly, but that was how it was said by New Yorkers.

"I am a little familiar with that neighborhood," Jonathan folded his arms and narrowed his gaze at Michael, then smiled, "Yes, a little rough, that neighborhood is near Times Square. I seem to remember Teamsters would not go to Times Square after dark back then. Yes, I would say a little rough," Jonathan repeated again and both men held to their serious tone, but both were completely amused.

"It's like frickin' Disney Land now," he added. "Where did you hang out?"

"Here and there. Irish pubs mostly—all those dumps near where Studio 54 used to be."

"I know the places, lots of character and lots of characters." Jonathan's comment made Michael smile. "I suppose that explains why you know Local 33 needs to be in the bid. Have you had lunch, Mr. Tantalus?" It was a rhetorical question.

"I am starved, and call me Michael, please," Michael had not yet realized that Jonathan knew who he was.

"Call me Jon." It was a subtle exchange, but in it, Jonathan Braunstein was telling Michael a lot of things. The two men continued casual talk as they walked down the hall to the elevator, coming out into the lobby and then out of the building and into a waiting limousine. Michael climbed into the back of the long black car like he had done it a thousand times; he slid his hand across the nice, clean, shiny seat and continued his conversation with Jonathan Braunstein. Hundreds of millions of dollars' worth of business for Universal Spectrum was now in play, Michael knew it, he was no longer feeling the effects of no sleep, he was no longer fatigued: He was exhilarated, and he was calm. He would not miss on this opportunity, he was conscious of his own confidence and it was comforting.

"So, tell me about your time in Hell's Kitchen," he turned to the driver before Michael could answer, "our usual, David." The driver looked at Jonathan in the rearview mirror and nodded. He was a very large man with a thick neck partially covered by a large beard that spilled down past his jaw, and he wore a suit.

"Nothing too exciting," Michael answered while looking out the window as they passed throngs of people hurrying in all directions, walking purposefully. Michael wondered what important things they were all moving so swiftly towards. "I worked at The Blarney Stone," he added while turning his curious eyes back towards Jonathan.

"Which one?" Jonathan asked.

"The one that used to be near Times Square." The answer made Jonathan smirk.

"You are not a Westie; what were you doing hanging around there?" Jonathan asked, looking at Michael without blinking.

"No, I am not a Westie. I guess I was 'Irish enough' to work there, and maybe I acted a little crazy a time or two... I think that's why they really let me work there," Michael replied and both men laughed.

"When was the last time you were there?" Jonathan asked the question this time while looking out the window."

"Couple of weeks ago."

Michael's answer made Jonathan look at Michael.

"Couple of weeks ago, hmmm? How well do you know the West Side?"

"Well enough to make the bid work for your buildings along the Henry Hudson," he said referring to the river.

"Is that so, Mr. Tantalus?" Jonathan asked, smiling, then added, "I think you may be buying lunch."

"I expect so, Mr. Braunstein—I mean Jon."

The questions stopped as Jonathan switched his attention to the driver, leaning forward to speak softly to the man. Michael did not try to hear what Jonathan was saying. After traveling south for some while, they began to cross zig-zagging streets and avenues until they were on a small side street. As the limousine pulled alongside what looked like a restaurant, Jonathan and the driver exchanged glances through the rearview mirror, a communication that Michael noticed but could not decipher, then both Michael and Jonathan got out of the long car. Michael searched over the tops of the large windows for the name of the restaurant but there was none. *Odd*, Michael thought to himself, *there is no signage at all.* Then the thought that he was dreaming crossed his mind but he assured himself that this was reality. No signage was odd for the world where Michael had come from, but here, this was the norm: a neighborhood place. Anyone who did not know this place did not need to be here so there was no need to advertise.

There was plenty more for Michael to learn. He knew that money has levels but this was a new one. When men have enough money and power, they can always find doors to places that most never know exist. The rules in these places are different, and you had better know the rules. Michael could sense this, and he found himself watching carefully, measuring his own movements.

The neighborhood was busy with life, people moving about, but not like where they had been earlier. A few streets away, people dressed in suits bumped quickly past each other with no one making eye contact or acknowledging one another in any way, they pushed their way through throngs of flesh brushing by other humans as though they were tall weeds in some unresponsive, unconscious jungle. But here, people looked at one another, called out to each other, some sweeping the streets, some standing in front of small stores while others sat in groups of two or three on stoops and stairs laughing, arguing, and talking. The buildings themselves were brown and brick mostly, with overly large windows of an old-looking ornate iron, Michael was taking it all in: The buildings were all four to six or seven stories tall, stacked next to each other with no space between.

The limousine did not elicit any unusual response from any of the people walking or sitting about. A long dark car belonged here, was a normal occurrence, making the whole scene all the more foreign to Michael, it was as though he were getting out of a plane in a different country.

"This way," Jonathan motioned to Michael, who was looking down the street at all the buildings, trying unsuccessfully to see where they ended. He snapped out of a slight trance and smiled as he followed Jonathan into the restaurant. Inside, it was considerably darker, and the two men stood just inside the doorway for just a moment to let their eyes adjust to the low level of light. A short, overweight man with a small white towel draped over his shoulder stood straight, looking haughty as he greeted the new guests.

"Mr. Braunstein, a pleasure," he said, bowing slightly then showed them to an old wooden table set underneath one of the large iron windows. The chairs were small and straight with worn red velvet on the backs and seats. The brick walls had been painted brown so many times that they looked plastic. Jonathan was familiar with the table, and the waiter knew Jonathan and where he was going to sit. This was one of those levels that Michael would learn about. Restaurants with no markers outside and tables inside that belonged to people and corporations and other associations. The waiters here did not bring menus, you walked in, sat, and talked about the fresh catch brought from the market, the South Side Seaport. The waiter exchanged pleasantries with Mr. Braunstein while Michael looked around the restaurant. Men in suits were gathered around the tables, drinking and smoking and quietly doing the business that mattered in Manhattan. The more Michael looked, the more he recognized people: He was pretty sure against the back wall were a couple of players for the Knicks. He continued to look around until he noticed the conversation at his table had stopped, he turned to see the waiter and Jonathan were looking at him,

"Wine, Mr. Tantalus?" the waiter asked. Whoa, Michael thought; the waiter knew his name,

"Sure, do you have a pinot noir?"

"Certainly," he answered as he bowed away from the table.

"Do you know where you are, Michael?" Jonathan asked, looking at the window.

"I think I am somewhere in SoHo."

"Yes, SoHo, but look across the street at the windows, look at this window..." Jonathan prompted, putting his hand on the iron, running his fingers over the curve of twisting leaves and vines that were exquisitely connecting imperfect glass with the brick edges of the window.

"After the Civil War," Jonathan said, taking pleasure in sharing this place, sharing his thoughts with Michael, "there was a surplus of scrap steel and iron. That surplus was cheap, and the architects and constructors of these buildings molded and forged out of the remnants of that war these big, beautiful, ornate window frames. And they soon found that these big, beautiful, ornate window frames became part of the structure of the buildings. Mankind could go higher than with just brick, and along with a few improvements to things like the elevator, well, Mr. Tantalus, you are sitting in the birth place of the skyscraper, the very structures that represent what this city, this country meant to generations of immigrants, looking for something bigger and better, something shinier." He was smiling big as his speech grew. He paused to drink, the ice tinkled in the short glass as he tipped it to his lips and emptied the liquid contents. It was taken away and replaced with a new one as he was setting it back down on the table. "Opportunity, Michael, they came for opportunity for a better life for their families, for themselves; right here in these few blocks, capitalism, a religion with an unwritten dogma, was fertile in the minds of people from everywhere who came here to express that inner desire, to express their ambition to better themselves, stepping out of class and cultural limitations and into opportunity, to climb higher and higher all the way to heaven," he paused and leaned back into his chair. "The veal here is magnificent," he transitioned from broad, booming proclamation to what would be good for lunch so quickly that Michael could only react to the latter.

"Sounds perfect," he responded then looked back at the windows and thought of what he would say next, but the windows and capitalistic opportunity conversation kept playing in his mind as he imagined all the people who wanted more coming here to America and marrying, having children whose genes were full of 'wanting more' DNA breeding a country of individualistic people who would forever want constantly more and more. The word individualism that echoed in Michael's mind, "Individualism," Michael said trying to sound intelligent.

"What?" asked Jonathan.

"The sense of individuality, people wanting more," Michael added.

"Yes, individuality," Jonathan echoed.

Then Michael remembered something he had read once: *It is this sense of individuality in us that causes our experience of pleasure and pain. This idea of who we are and what we should be, constantly measuring ourselves against some hidden score card, and we never quite can measure up, no matter how much effort or any amount of success. It is an evolutionary chip, a perpetual feeling of not enough.* Michael tried to think where or when he had read it but was brought out of his thoughts by the waiter asking, "Another glass of wine, Mr. Tantalus?"

"Please," he answered and, once again focused on the table, moved the conversation to the business for which he came and for which he was well prepared.

"Hey, look over there—not now, in a moment," Jonathan whispered, "That's Johnny Stones and some of his wise guys, you know, 'good fella's'?"

Michael nonchalantly turned his head briefly to look, then smiled.

"Yeah, I've heard of him. What's he doing here? Out of his territory, wouldn't you say?" This place was like a who's who of athletes, businessmen, and wise guys.

"Don't worry about it," Jonathan feigned an Italian accent, making both men laugh silently. "You ever see anything like this?"

"No," Michael smiled. Jonathan was enjoying watching Michael look around like a kid at a ballpark staring wide-eyed at all the sports stars, only these were sports stars and other celebrities, some famous, some infamous and it was the infamous ones that put an edge on the large room. Michael could feel the intensity of energy that was being exchanged in glances, orders, and business negotiations; he was sure that this was one of those places where things happened and now he was here trying to make something happen for himself.

The lunch arrived quickly. Ordering it had been a short negotiation between Jonathan and the overly warm waiter, it smelled delicious and tasted magnificent.

"Good?" Michael was not sure if it was a question or not. "Terrific—almost as good as Charlotte's Italian food." His sarcasm drew a smile from Jonathan. They settled down quickly to business: Jonathan pulled out the bid he had been making notes on and asked Michael questions, scratching more on the paper, turning pages quickly forward and backward.

"Michael, we are going to have make some changes. You did a good job of identifying the properties owned verses the properties that we just service, but there are some changes coming that you would not be privy to that I would like you know about and include in the bid… and I want to talk more about this upfit idea of yours. It's interesting and could generate some extra revenue for us: very smart."

Jonathan looked up at Michael at that last comment, closed the pages of the bid, and folded it.

"Nice job, Michael. You did your research: Servicing a large number of properties in Manhattan takes sophisticated logistics and…" He emphasized the word "and," then he paused briefly before adding, "connections."

Jonathan then said in a whisper but with a certain emphasis, "I think it's time you met the boss."

Michael had to make himself breathe: In a few words, Jonathan Braunstein had just said to him, "You are in the running for the bid, you have a chance to do business at the Emblem Corp, and it is time to meet the boss." Michael was cool and calm but he was completely speechless.

"Sounds good," was all he could manage to say. The day's events had completely taken over any fatigue from his lack of sleep and Michael was waiting for the bill to arrive so he could reach for it casually, smoothly, the way he always had, without even looking at the waiter. But lunch was concluding and the bill had not come, and looking around the restaurant, Michael noticed that no one was getting their bill, they simply finished their lunch and their business and exchanged more pleasantries as they moved toward the front door, like they were talking to relatives and taking for granted their meal, just as they would if they were leaving the table of their home. Michael was beginning to get the picture.

"I thought I was buying lunch," Michael said as he smiled at Jonathan.

"You will, Mr. Michael Tantalus, you will," Jonathan said as he smiled broadly then slapped Michael on the back.

Michael was more at home and comfortable in this situation than any other endeavor: He had been trained, or more accurately, conditioned for this situation since he was a child. His mother had orchestrated his involvement and participation with his father's business dealings. There had been many hosted dinners and parties by his parents with international business guests from Spain, Japan, China, France, Italy, and many others; this was as natural as breathing for Michael. The experiences as a child made for easy grace and composure at a table where careers were at stake, where wealth and failure lay in the balance of a spilled glass or awkward glance. He noticed the waiter cautiously approaching the table so Michael turned and greeted him warmly and by the name he had heard several others use.

"Tony," he said, his facial expression showing his deep satisfaction the meal, "marvelous, no words, thank you."

"My pleasure, my young friend," Tony said, speaking with his hands. Michael was carrying himself in such a confident, naturally friendly manner that it made people want to do business with him. It was an ability that few at Universal Spectrum understood about Michael; they just knew that business always seemed to increase, without ever identifying what it was exactly that he was doing, but it was this ability to generate business that got him past everything else. For Michael, it was just natural to make those around him feel confident in what he was saying and doing. So, while many of Michael's peers had found their refuge and their confidence in numbers and knowledge, Michael looked people in the eye, and without uttering a word, conveyed in his movements and his mannerisms that everything was going to be fine, and of course, it always was. That was the confidence Michael exuded.

The two men walked outside and were greeted by the loud, continuous noise of the city. They crossed the just-swept sidewalk and entered the waiting car. Jonathan was also comfortable in this setting and, like Michael, had come from somewhere different. Jonathan Braunstein had connections but he had worked his way to his wealth and therefore appreciated everything it had to offer. As the car wound its way through the chaotic traffic of cars, cabs, and pedestrians, the two men got to know each other. Though they had grown up in vastly differing parts of the country, both men were cut of the same cloth, similar in many ways, and they both recognized it. They continued to talk once they arrived at the building, chatting through the lobby, up the elevator and back to the same floor. Only this time, Jonathan walked Michael in the opposite direction from his office, down a quiet hall punctuated by evenly spaced paintings. In the divided spaces between paintings, vases sat on pedestals, small placards beside them telling what year, what dynasty, and what civilization had created these antiquities from Rome, Corinth, and Greece. Michael slowed to look at one of the vases on which tiny, intricate designs formed flowers and vines and images depicted long-forgotten daily routines and life scenes of royalty.

"That one that you are looking at is worth more than most people make in a lifetime," Jonathan said as he smiled and raised his eyebrows while moving Michael farther down the hall.

"This one?" Michael asked as he moved slowly toward the next vase, approaching it as though it were a new-born fawn that any quick movement would scare away. He read the neat letters beside it, "14th Century Ming Dynasty Vase." It was decorated in copper red scrolling and flowers and was well-preserved.

"Quite rare," Jonathan told him. Michael moved his attention to the paintings, each of comparable size with similar gold frames, all dark from another era but breathtaking nonetheless for Michael. They walked slowly and Jonathan smiled while watching Michael catch the vision of each painting as they passed down the hall.

At the end of the hall were two large wooden doors impenetrable as gates to an ancient medieval castle. And sitting just outside the doors was a security man dressed in a navy suit and wearing an ear piece talking to an unseen person, the doors opening, as if by magic as the two men progressed.

"Good afternoon, Mr. Braunstein," the man greeted as he bowed his head slightly.

"Afternoon, Thomas," he answered without looking at the security man. The doors opened to a world that Michael had only heard about. The room was expansive, the ceiling seemed somewhere in the clouds, and the carpet felt comforting through Michael's tight black leather shoes. He wanted to look around the room but his focus was entirely on the man sitting behind what appeared to be a desk under the windows to the universe, across a large expanse of the room talking on the phone.

"Benjamin Adler," Michael whispered to himself, his heart began to beat so he purposefully slowed his breathing to calm himself. Jonathan walked Michael across the room and motioned him to sit down.

"Talk to you soon," Jonathan whispered as he extended his hand. "Be yourself and impress him," the last comment was delivered as an order. Michael settled himself into a leather couch that swallowed him, then turned his attention back towards the man behind the desk. Benjamin Adler's gaze was directed straight at Michael and its intensity made him sit up tall although the impressive man's attention was on the person on the other end of the phone line,

"I do not care, I want them out of there immediately," the words were harsh, crisp, and final. Michael turned his attention away from the intensity of Benjamin Adler's stare and began to look around the room to gather information, looking for things to use to connect— family pictures, any college affiliation—and Michael found plenty. Pictures of Benjamin Adler with Mayor Giuliani, with former Mayor Koch, with the current governor, and a few of him standing next to Knicks players and Yankees, some current, some retired, all sitting on a shelf behind the desk. And on the other side of the phone towards the end of the desk, a picture of President Clinton shaking Benjamin's hand; there was writing on the photo, but Michael could not make it out from the skewed angle of the picture frame.

Michael sat quietly on the couch and tried to think of what he would say when Benjamin Adler hung up the phone; as he thought nothing came to mind so he just waited and looked out the windows behind the large persona before him. Behind Mr. Adler through the wall made of glass and a thin, shiny steel frame was what appeared to be all of Manhattan, busy but moving in utter silence so many floors below: None of the noise of the city from the machinery of dense human activity reached these heights or penetrated these windows.

From this point of view, every frame, everything moved slowly, quietly and in organized patterns verses the chaos and complexity that Michael had experienced moving in the streets below only moments earlier. He watched the time stretched movement below the way he watched ocean waves, acknowledging its simplicity, its beauty, and holding the feeling that there was more than he was seeing, something just beyond his senses calling him gently.

He broke his own wanderlust trance and looked down at the coffee table in front of the couch where he was sitting. Sitting facing the chair across from where Jonathan had him sit, presumably, he thought, where Benjamin Adler was going to sit, was his bid. Emblem Inc., was bold across the top with Universal Spectrum slightly smaller, and on the bottom, a subtle but effective change from every other bid that Universal put its name on, usually at the top, saying we are first, but the change by Michael was intentional and said something different. And Michael was careful not to put the word "partnership" anywhere, for it improperly implied a contract, words were everything in this arena. None of these changes went unnoticed by Jonathan and were pointed out by little symbols written on the cover. Michael reached down and thumbed through his own document and found it fat with sticky notes, red ink and a few hand written inserts.

Michael looked over at Benjamin and, motioned towards the bid; Benjamin Adler nodded and turned his head then his attention back to the phone. Michael methodically went through his own written bid and began to absorb every comment and red mark, in numerous different handwritings. It appeared that while he was at lunch with Jonathan a team of analysts had been thoroughly through the pages that Michael had spent the night creating; the close scrutiny sent a small amount of doubt, not about anything in particular, but in general. He forced himself to think of nothing, the way he did whenever he wanted to escape from voices in his head, unrecognized voices from his childhood, casual things said to him that he adopted as true and spent much of his life trying to prove wrong.

Benjamin Adler hung up the phone, and looking at Michael, remained motionless, as if pausing to file away the recent conversation before transitioning. He rose and walked towards Michael. Michael rose and met Benjamin's handshake. He extended his hand horizontally with his palm facing downward, a dominating gesture that said, I am in control. Michael extended his hand palm up but clasped hands firmly, taking a submissive position but showing strength and confidence.

"It is a pleasure, Mr. Adler," Michael offered with his voice pitched in a professional manner. They both sat and Benjamin Adler picked up the bid.

"First decent bid we have seen from Universal Spectrum," Benjamin smiled like the Cheshire cat. It was not intentional but natural, as his head was large and round, and his smile took the whole bottom of his jaw. "I am wondering if Universal has any idea who you are, but we know who you are. It did not take long to confirm. Who is your boss?"

"Dan McCulloch," Michael answered coolly but his pulse quickened and thoughts ran through him as he replayed Benjamin Adler's words in his mind, *we know who you are.*

"Don't know him…who is his boss?"

"James Caldwell."

Benjamin looked at Michael, lowered his head and his voice, and asked one more time. But all Michael could think was, *My God, do they know about Hell's Kitchen?*

"Who is his boss?"

"Peter Stanford."

Michael knew the questions would stop, because Peter Stanford was the CEO of Universal Spectrum. Benjamin Adler smiled, rose without saying anything, and walked to his desk to page his assistant.

"Christine, get Peter Stanford on the phone," he said, looking at Michael with his broad smile, slightly nodding his head.

"Yes, of course, Mr. Adler, I'll buzz you as soon as I have him," came the more-than-polite reply from the speakerphone.

"Michael, is there anything you want to tell me about this bid before Peter Stanford gets on the phone?"

"I may have made a few changes that my boss is not aware of...yet, and I am sure that Peter Stanford has no idea what is in the bid...yet."

Michael's voice dipped a little at his last comment, making Benjamin smile even more broadly, something that Michael thought should have been impossible.

"And by the looks of this," Michael held up the red inked bid from the coffee table, "I think we are going to make a few more changes."

This time Michael smiled broadly as the two men faced one another eye to eye. "I see the final number crossed out: How much lower do we have to go?"

The question was a slight mistake; it showed that Michael was still a little naive.

"Needs to be higher."

This time Benjamin Adler did not smile.

"Of course," Michael answered, this time with a steady, calm demeanor, which Benjamin noted; the two men were once again on the same page. Being able to read communication when there were no words forthcoming was a valuable attribute and necessary to do business here in the City. The two men understood each other; any other answer or question would have killed the deal. Michael knew how precarious his situation was and he remained calm. Benjamin kept looking at Michael, smiling.

"Michael, are you calling in a favor?" Benjamin asked him suddenly.

"I don't know what you mean, Mr. Adler," Michael replied, and he really did not. Benjamin Adler's smile broadened.

"Michael, do you know who I am?" Benjamin asked.

"Yes, sir, you run this place."

"That's not what I mean, Michael. Do you know anything about my family?"

"No sir, I should have been better prepared... I had no idea I would be meeting you," Michael was beginning to feel he was losing the deal. *Maybe I am in over my head*, he thought. But Benjamin Adler began to laugh.

"Michael, sometimes life shows itself as a beautiful and mysterious woman."

The phone buzzed, "I have Mr. Stanford on the line."

Michael was stunned. Benjamin looked at him as if to say, "Get ready," then pushed the button that brought the famous voice of Peter Stanford into the spacious office and the conversation.

"Peter!" Benjamin's voice boomed.

"Bennie, how are you?"

It was Peter's warm New England accent, but there was just enough of an edge to his voice that Michael immediately realized there was some tense history between these two men; they were intimately acquainted. *Of course they know each other*, Michael thought to himself, and knew that he would never know what had transpired between these two industry giants—he only hoped not to get crushed between these two bulls. He felt fully alive. The air was sweet and thick and the light in the room seemed to grow. Michael could detect minuscule details in the room as all of his senses increased their capacity. The two men exchanged pleasantries about family, travel, business, then Peter got to the point, "To what do I owe the honor of your call, Bennie?"

"Your man Michael Tantalus walked a Universal Spectrum bid into my office this morning. My staff tells me that this bid could not possibly have come from Universal, that it's first-rate and I should consider it, and they like your man Michael."

"Yes, good man, Michael Tantalus," Peter Stanford said very slowly. The words struck Michael like the smell of cotton candy. He wanted to laugh, because he was more than sure that before just now, Peter Stanford had never heard the name of Michael Tantalus. And suddenly in his mind, he could see dozens of people in the room with Peter, scrambling for information, sliding notes across his desk, and whispering what they were finding.

"Yes," Peter said, his voice a little weak, "I am looking at the bid as we speak."

Michael sat up and began to speak, but Benjamin motioned him to stop.

"Peter, throw that garbage in the trash. We are making a few changes—your man Michael here has all the notes for a counter. It's about time you sent me someone who doesn't have their head up their ass," Benjamin said, clearly enjoying this moment.

"Look forward to doing business with you, Bennie," Peter responded, the sound of a lion back in his voice. The two powerful men exchanged more pleasantries then Benjamin hung up the phone.

Benjamin Adler leaned back in his chair, entwined his fingers, and slid his clasped hands to the top of his head then slid them backwards to catch his falling head as he let out a bellowing laugh. Regaining his composure, he leaned forward to look at Michael.

"So, Mr. Michael Tantalus, tell me more about your time in Hell's Kitchen."

Michael wondered when Jonathan would have had time to talk to Benjamin but surmised that they had been doing their homework on him, finding out where he had come from and if he was for real.

"Well, I tended bar some, couple of different places, and was a desk clerk at the Plaza."

"I am more interested in any scars you may have acquired," Benjamin commented, folding his hands and watching Michael closely.

So they have done their homework, Michael thought, *I wonder just what they know.*

"Specifically, Mr. Tantalus, I would like to know about the bullet scar under that corporate white uniform you are wearing," Benjamin Adler said, stone-faced.

"Wrong place at the wrong time, I would say."

"Some might say that, Mr. Tantalus, or perhaps you were precisely in the right place at the right time," Benjamin Adler began laughing again.

"What was going on? Tell me more," he was asking as though he really did not know, but Michael could tell that he most likely knew everything—his was another test, but for what, Michael was not sure.

"I think that there was a little trouble between the Italians and the Irish," said Michael, hoping that answer would suffice but knowing it would not.

"Yes, Mr. Tantalus, tell me more."

Benjamin was goading him now.

"Something to do with the Javits Center, that's all I really know."

"Yes, the Javits Center, Michael, but the Italians and the Irish?"

Michael smiled, "Yeah, I guess it was a little trouble between the Irish and the Irish," Benjamin smiled and nodded. There was so much that Michael was not saying, and both men knew it.

"We are going to get along just fine, Michael, and call me Bennie. My grandfather came to this country through Ellis Island; he swept donkey shit in the streets of Manhattan not far from where you used to live. Funny, all these big corporations come to us with some Ivy League smartass, telling us how everything is going go when they haven't a clue about anything. The families, Michael, the families that own all these buildings are families like mine: They started as hard-working immigrant families who came here and worked their way to the top. We respect someone like you who will listen, knows how to keep his mouth shut, and will work hard to do what they say they will do. And your past will be helpful as well; it will open doors for you as it has already opened doors for you.

It is important to know how the streets work, but you will also need to know how we work, at this level. So, I am going to introduce you around tonight. Where are you staying?"

"The Time," it was a trendy hotel on the West Side near Times Square, just off Broadway. U2 had stayed there once and Michael liked thinking he was living like a rock star. It was what he imagined New York to be like—everything there felt different, and it made Michael feel special in a way he could not describe. There was a prestige, not the kind born of money but of an imagined level of innate "coolness" that he loved to immerse himself in. Just now, he felt the need to explain why he stayed there.

"I like to stay in the old neighborhood," he heard himself say almost by reflex.

"A car will pick you up at seven for dinner. See you then, Michael."

Michael immediately stood, knowing the meeting was over, and shook Bennie's hand. As he was walking out, Bennie said one more thing without looking up, already focusing on the next task: "Nicely done, Michael Tantalus. You just accomplished more in a day than most accomplish in years, so you'd better be ready."

When Michael paused to look back, he saw that Benjamin Adler's broad grin was back. Michael was not sure what the last compliment meant but it left him with a small, uneasy feeling in his stomach. Suddenly, he doubted himself. *Am I ready? Exactly what have I gotten myself into?* All the internal voices that are in everyone, the self-limiting beliefs we adopt as children, the unseen mechanisms driving behavior, keeping all of us from venturing outward. Michael could hear the whispers and typically was able to override them. Courage was what he usually felt, the ability to override all of the imagined scenarios of failure. He had never understood what "fear of success" meant, but he wondered if that was what he was feeling now. He walked out the big wooden doors and down the hall toward the elevator. He knew he had done well.

It occurred to him to turn his cell phone back on; he had turned it off so as not to be disturbed during his meeting.

It immediately began to buzz, two, three, four messages, then once again, five, six. He perused the missed calls list on his cell phone: his boss, his boss's boss, then some numbers he did not recognize from a New England area code.

He laughed just a bit, "Guess I've caused a stir."

Then he smiled, thinking about the phone call his boss, Dan, must have received. He began to listen to the voicemails, the first one from Dan.

"Michael, what the fuck is going on? Call me!" The rest of the calls were about the same, only they employed different expletives and colorful metaphors. It always amazed Michael how creative people could be when they were angry. After he retrieved his suitcase, he eased along the hall, down the elevator, and through a less-busy lobby to hail a cab to his hotel. His fatigue returned, but it was mixed marvelously with a feeling of accomplishment.

"Westside, The Time on 48th." The cabbie nodded put his suitcase in the trunk of the cab as Michael slide in the back door.

The cab stopped just a few short blocks away from Times Square in front of the Time Hotel. Michael stepped out onto the sidewalk and stretched pleasantly while fatigue wrapped around him like a warm blanket; he would rest soon, but he had a few things to do first.

Michael looked at his watch as he rode the elevator to the lobby; he wanted to check in quickly to be in a quiet place to make, what was to this point, the phone call of a career. Exotic accents met Michael at the check-in desk. The faces, the voices, the dark navy uniforms were all beautiful, or—better said—sexy.

"I am afraid I am in a hurry," he said to the desk clerk, settling his hands on the desk. He was met with a smile from an attractive young woman. People in suits and ties and staying in expensive hotels must be important or rich or both and should always be met with a smile. It all was plastic sincerity, but Michael liked it— no, loved it—it served some part of him that he was not even aware of or why. He just knew it made him feel more important, more substantial.

Sometimes he felt as if he were in a play, playing businessman, imagining all sorts of splendid business scenarios, and he often looked around at the people coming in and out of the lobby and wondered what they did, where they had come from, and where they were going. He was sure they were all far more important than he was. There was constant judging and comparing going on just below the surface, and right now, he was comparing quite well against the others walking about him.

The clerk looked up again, handing Michael his room key. She pointed her left hand toward the hallway, "Your room is to my left and your right. Is there anything else we can do for you, Mr. Tantalus?"

"No, thank you," Michael said, distracted. He was thinking of his call and did not want to wait for the porter so he walked to his suitcase, slid his briefcase onto the suitcase's extended handle, and pulled them both behind him down the long, dark hall. There were tiny televisions dotting the hall, providing small amounts of flickering light. He noticed the televisions but not what was being broadcast on them. He slid his key into the door, opened it, and stepped inside, dragging his suitcase, which was feeling heavier. The room was square and blue: blue walls, blue carpet, blue drapes, blue pillows, and a blue bedcover. He let go of his suitcase and stared at the bed, feeling its invitation. He sat for just a moment to gather himself and his eyes were drawn to the small glass box of blue jellybeans on the bedside table.

"Damn, it's already time for my call," he said aloud. He was not ready but he dared not be late.

"Michael Tantalus," the voice on the phone answered his call the way a parent would say the name of their impetuous child.

"Hello, sir."

Michael rolled his eyes at himself, thinking he sounded dense.

"No more..." Peter Stanford stretched out the next word in a New England accent with just the whisper of a speech impediment, "....improvisation! All documents must be cleared through my office, understood?"

"I understand, Mr. Stanford."

"Goddamn right, you understand. All right then…" his voice went from anger to reassuring in a blink, "Call me Petah, about damn time we got something going in New York. Tell me, how much do you know about Benjamin Adler?"

"A little…" Michael started to say more but was interrupted by Peter's laughter.

"I'll be Goddamned…" Peter chuckled.

"He is taking me to dinner tonight."

Michael's words ended Peter's laughter and Peter remarked, "Hope you have a strong constitution."

Michael could hear a muffled, unintelligible conversation between Peter and someone else in the room with him.

"Michael, there will be a fax on its way to you shortly on Benjamin Adler. Read it and destroy it before your dinner. And Michael?"

"Yes, Mr. Stanford?" Michael realized as he heard himself that he had asked to be called Peter. "…Peter," he added.

"Do not fuck this up. Good job."

Michael hung up the phone and began to laugh. He picked up the phone and called the front desk.

"Yes, Mr. Tantalus," answered a polite, prompt voice.

"I am about to get a fax…confidential. Will you put it in an envelope and have the porter slide it under my door? Oh, and please ring my room in one hour."

"Yes, Mr. Tantalus, fax and wakeup call in one hour."

"Thank you," Michael said, hanging up, sure the last part was missed. He looked at the clock and decided to set its alarm as a backup; he was not going to be late for this dinner. He pulled off his tie and lay back on the bed, letting himself drift to sleep in his clothes. He never felt rested after sleep but he lay still letting his body and mind recover the best they could to be ready for whatever the evening ahead would bring.

It was not very long before a soft swoosh announced the arrival of the fax under his door. The noise was slight but it was enough to awaken Michael from his fragile sleep. He sat up, rubbed his eyes, and retrieved what turned out to be a very thorough dossier on Benjamin Adler. Michael wanted to tell Peter Stanford that he already had done his homework on Benjamin Adler, but as he read through page after page, he realized just how little he knew about this very important man. He seemed to be connected to everyone, including a woman in a picture that piqued Michael's interest. It was a fax copy but clear enough to see she was beautiful: Her name was Audrey and she was Bennie's mistress, a former Penthouse Pet.

"Wow, look at all this," Michael whispered to himself, seeing lists of organizations, political affiliations, and some pages blacked out by broad black marker. It all amused Michael: *Secrets, so many secrets,* he thought. While Michael was reading, he noticed at the end of the glass-topped desk was a paper shredder. He grinned, surmising what kind of businessmen stayed here and what kind of business they were doing that required a shredder in every room. And then it occurred to him that <u>he</u> needed that shredder and he laughed aloud at himself. The chain of events had left Michael charged with energy. *I am making it,* he thought.

Becoming One of Them

Late Summer, 2001

Michael's experiences the summer he came into Manhattan grew in intensity and heat as the steamy season progressed. His flights to LaGuardia had increased from every two months to every month to every week; he was a regular commuter now. He had begun recognizing but never overtly acknowledging the dozen or so other regulars from Charlotte—men and women all dressed in suits, carrying briefcases, reading documents as they walked, never making eye contact or speaking to one another.

At the time, Michael had no idea that he was in the process of foregoing one set of standards and ethics and adopting another. Nonetheless, a subtle split developed within him over these summer months. As a small crack in a mountain fills with ice during winters, Michael's small compromises expanded and contracted, causing grand-scale shifts. Michael had always been stalwartly truthful, passionate about the need to stand for something, the ideals and concepts instilled by his parents

Michael never made a conscious decision to lie or compromise the values he held for any imagined gain. He was idealistic, and to this point he had lived his ideals and was sincere in his actions. Later, though, he looked back on that long-past summer of 2001 and thought of it as the year that he became a different person, lost his true self in ambition and success.

The feedback he received from Universal Spectrum came fast and often. Congratulatory letters from Peter Stanford, small cash bonuses, and public recognition by his superiors in front of his peers. People began to treat him differently, as though he had some unknown super-abilities that they all admired. They began to ask questions: He received phone calls at all hours from young business development associates saying that their boss had recommended they ask Michael what he would do on this account, that product, or such-and-such marketing campaign.

He was totally immersed and hooked, and who wouldn't be? He was experiencing himself as successful, as bright, as needed and appreciated. The positive feedback all fed his subconscious, the elephant of his evolutionarily developed biological machine. What the elephant wants, it so often gets; once charging, the sheer mass of the beast makes it nearly impossible to stop. And though it would not be what Michael *said* that was a lie, it was what he did not say that was his first lie. Once the lying began, it never ended.

That first dinner with Benjamin Adler had gone well and morphed into dinner after dinner: moving from cocktails to late-night raids on bars, parties, and happenings, with flashing lights, pounding music, and alcohol all mixing to create a world dedicated to base sensual satisfaction. From dinner to dinner, building to building, and one family introduction to another, Michael remained an observer. He was rolling and he thought he was keeping his business dealings and home life separate. However, this constant exposure was silently incubating the disease of decadence deep inside him. In just a short few months, his resistance to the temptation of this lifestyle was weakening, although he did not yet know it.

Michael began to love the city, where there was constant movement and noise, all of the chaotic restless sound merging into a soothing hum. He felt at home on the crowded streets and alleys crisscrossing the long, narrow island, masking in steel and cement the once rocky and lush land. He had become more accustomed to this pace here, too, sleeping better with the comforting hum pierced sporadically by sirens than he did in his quiet neighborhood in Charlotte where the gentle play of wind and trees was interrupted only by the occasional family dog barking. The smells that had once seemed pungent and only a small step above revolting—exhaust, heavy dust, and stale garbage—were now familiar and almost welcoming. In some strange way the city smelled powerful, just as he felt he was becoming, and the dull sweetness of flowers and shrubbery back home seemed weak and bland.

He left his hotel room early to catch the city in transition from businessmen and women to tourists; near Times Square, there were always people dressed oddly for these city sidewalks, carrying cameras and wearing shorts with socks pulled high. He realized it was all part of the city, and though they did not really belong far from Iowa, Indiana, or where ever they came from, they belonged: They were part and parcel of "The City" on any given day or night.

Michael walked out into the street to feel the people as they passed, to watch the setting sun glow in a brown haze, to breathe in the city's odors—and it felt marvelous. When the shiny black limousine pulled alongside him on the curb, he could see the neon signs of bars and restaurants reflected in the long automobile's beautiful curves and smooth doors. Michael was enraptured by the dreamy music of self-assurance, he thought that he had never seen anything so beautiful. *Success once in the body is like being in love: Everything is beautiful, everything is possible, and death and failure are mere dark shadows.*

The dark-windowed limo door opened from inside and Michael climbed into the car's near-silence.

"Good evening, Mr. Tantalus," the chauffeur greeted him while Benjamin Adler continued ranting into his cell phone, then nodding aggressively when he heard the response.

"Good evening," Michael replied to the large, thick-necked man sitting in the driver's seat.

"NO! Absolutely not," Benjamin Adler exclaimed, then changed his tone slightly, "Yes, yes, okay." He folded the phone closed, concluding his conversation abruptly. He turned toward Michael, saying, "I have to make a stop on the way to dinner," and watched for Michael's reaction.

"Not a problem," Michael said easily, relaxing back into the comfortable seat. Benjamin leaned forward and whispered something to the driver. Then he, too, settled back into the seat, sighed as if he had something on his mind then turned and began to make small talk with Michael, unusual for Benjamin Adler. They soon arrived out front of a tall, dark, ancient building. The doorman was waiting by the curb, opening the limousine door even before it had come to a complete stop, greeting Benjamin Adler.

Ignoring the doorman as they scooted out of the car, Bennie took Michael by the arm and began to talk to him quietly.

"Sometimes, Michael, business is not pretty, and sometimes it can get rough," Bennie was gesturing with the back of his hand then he stopped and turned to Michael, lowering his voice and looking him intently in the eyes to ask, "Are you with the FBI?"

"No, should I be?" Michael asked. Bennie's body began to shake a little before the sound of his chuckle surfaced.

"You had better not be," he laughed, then slapped Michael on the back. The dark mood and muffled discussions had Michael's thoughts racing: imagining large dark men in bad moods, he was not prepared for what was to come. The men rode a very small elevator up in silence. When the doors opened, Michael could hear music coming from a set of doors at the end of a long narrow hall. They walked across old, worn, and dirty tile down the dimly lit hall almost shoulder to shoulder until they reached the doors. A large man in a suit stood almost at attention with his hands folded in front of him.

"Good evening, Mr. Adler." The man's voice was very deep and his accent was decidedly not New York...perhaps Polish? Michael tried to place it in his mind but he just was not sure. The doors opened into a very large room, filling the small, dark hallway with light, laughter, and music. This had once been (or perhaps still was) a residence. The building was old and nondescript, and the elevator and hall were ordinary and small, giving no hint of such a glorious interior room. It featured the décor of an era at least 100 years past, with ornate carved chair legs, gold trim, ancient mirrors, and opulent paintings. And in the middle of this properness—*properness* being the only word Michael could summon in his mind—were many men wandering about in various states of undress, stumbling around among scattered women, most of whom were sharply dressed and closer matching the long, expensive hanging drapes than the crude, inebriated men. There were various seemingly unmatched couples scattered about, some were dancing, and some were engaged in loud intense conversations which were audible but not understandable. Benjamin Adler, as he did so often, took Michael by the arm and led him, this time toward a large kitchen counter that had been converted to a bar.

"Paul, this is Michael Tantalus, a special guest with me this evening. Would you be so kind as to take good care of him and make sure he gets whatever he wants?" Benjamin winked at the bartender. Then he turned to Michael, saying, "I have some business to attend to. It may take a little time, so please enjoy yourself," and he gave a grand sweep of his arm motioning to the entire grand suite. Then Bennie disappeared quickly. Michael wanted to ask the barkeep what strange event was going on in this beautiful place, but he had learned not to ask questions.

"What would you like?" the bartender asked as he put both hands on the bar and leaned towards Michael to hear him better through the noise of the party.

"Well, what do you have?" Michael looked at the man; he had a smile on his face that was closer to a smirk.

"Are we talking ladies or a drink?" The question caught Michael off guard, but he showed no outward sign of surprise. But in his mind he said to himself, *Of course, these ladies are hookers*, as he looked around a little. They seemed so well dressed and he supposed he was in a different world from those to which he was accustomed.

"I'll have a vodka tonic," he ordered, standing as relaxed as he could. Michael not only did not drink vodka tonics, he had never had one before tonight. It seemed to him a more appropriate drink for the situation he found himself. *A more appropriate drink*, Michael heard himself thinking, wanting to laugh aloud. *What could appropriateness possibly have to do with this party.* After taking his drink, he turned to his right where there were two large French doors opening onto a large balcony. Michael had just arrived, and he already felt the need for air.

He walked outside and the beauty of the New York skyline took his breath away. The stone and steel walls and guardrails of the balcony were exquisite—old and badly in need of refurbishing, the over-painted iron leaves of the rails gravely peeling. It was worn but romantic and Michael was stirred: Finding himself in such beauty was a glorious surprise, at once making him feel lonely and longing for something, something that was missing.

He turned away from the beautiful cityscape and headed back into the grand old suite. As he faced the room head-on, he was flanked by the huge, square, iron-gridded windows that reached from the wide wooden planks of the floor to the high, arched ceiling. At the opposite end of the broad room was an immense fireplace surrounded by dazzling mirrors. Heading toward a set of doors leading off the main room, Michael sipped his strange-tasting drink and wandered into the menagerie of odd couples, businessmen, and dignitaries. Most all of the men were deeply engrossed in their separate endeavors so no one gave Michael the slightest glance as he walked past.

He stood in the open doorway of one room and looked in; a naked man with flaccid genitals lounged in the bed with two women while a dozen or so drunken men stood around the bed. Some cheered, some jeered the man, whose sexual ability was diminished by the alcohol or the public attention or both, but who attempted to go about his business as though nothing was wrong. A shock ran through Michael; he had never seen anything like this in person, had in movie scenes. Experiencing it in person caused a spiritual discord: The scene playing out before him flew in the face of everything he was raised to embody, but too, he was enthralled. He told himself that he was different than any of these men, feeling morally superior, but he was in their world.

Michael continued through the maze as the rooms changed themes and scenes as quickly as changing channels on a television.

He turned into a brighter, more formal room, perhaps once a sitting room. The furniture here was dainty and delicate as though it were designed only to have the rarest of flowers sit upon it. Michael tensed as the furniture withstood a barrage of careless, drunk barbarians stumbling and staggering around the room, crashing carelessly into the furniture and one another. Further across this room, which once sheltered the whispers of the courting wealthy and elite, two women sat together on a white, high-backed loveseat. To Michael's surprise, one of them was looking directly at him with an expression that intrigued and confused him.

Something about this woman drew him like a wind calling him to look over a high cliff to a tumultuous sea. Her beauty seduced him instantly. She was wearing a formal yellow dress, long and sheer, that showed off her best attributes. Her shiny red hair was pinned up high with curly wisps trailing down her long, graceful neck. Michael began to walk towards the glorious beauty, who seemed to be protecting herself from the boisterous rabble. She was a flower of contrast, appealing to Michael with her appearance of innocence, sedate in chaos, and sober and somber in the midst of riotous intoxication.

As he made his way toward her, she locked her glance on Michael. He was different—something told her he did not belong here—and she could sense his discomfort with what was going on at this party. They were drawn to each other, instinctively seeing in one another a rare oasis in a desert of decadence. She held her head high and confident but there was apprehension in her eyes. Michael kept walking steadily towards her and before the first word was spoken, he fell under the spell of his own desire, and once under that spell, there would be no other world or existence. All resistance, regret, and guilt were for the moment suspended.

He paused just shy of her, looking at her as she continued to gaze at him. Her eyes were wide and a deep, crystal green. He couldn't believe how much he wanted her. He suddenly found himself in a place where men who wanted things took what they wanted without reproach. He searched for what *should* be wrong right now with this situation but he could not find grounding in anything. And in the growing heat of the present moment, he felt no barrier between his desire and her body. He could not believe she was a prostitute, she seemed so different; and then he realized he had nothing in his experience to compare to this situation. He stood motionless, still in thought but not emotion: There was no question that he wanted her and was going to take her, and his heart beat wildly. Burning in desire and burning in ambition, he nonetheless held firm to the chivalry of his idealistic youth.

"Hello," he finally said to her.

"Hello," her voice was strong. "You are a Southerner," she said with some surprise in her voice.

"No," he breathed out the word, almost chuckling to let go of some tension—some of it nervousness, some of it desire. "And you are from…" he paused, moved his fingers to his chin, and without realizing, flashed her a boyish grin, "Long Island?"

"Well, that was a brilliant deduction. So if you are not a Southerner, what are you?" came her smart reply, which though abrupt, was also charming.

"Texan." There was pride and emphasis with his answer.

"Are they not the same thing?"

"Noooo, not even close," he asserted. There was a gentle strength in his manner that she was not accustomed to. She tried to place what it was that was appealing about this stranger, attempting to put him in a category like she did all males in her life—she was used to keeping some space in a busy, dangerous city where men always wanted something, especially from an attractive woman. She knew the game and knew how to get things with what she had. Other than her looks and her large, full breasts, her mother had always told her, she did not have much. "Tits and a mug, that's what you got to work with, dear," she had told her more than once. And like so many things that adults say to children that are not true, this assessment had been the catalyst for spending too much of her life trying to prove that she was more—much more.

Although her mind kept telling her to put up her guard, she was smitten with this nearly handsome young Texan. "I am not sure how to say this and I know it is going to come out awkwardly but I don't know any way other than direct..." Michael began. He seemed so serious to her that she sat motionless for a moment. Her companion rose and left them alone.

"I'm Josephine Kelleher," she said as she rose and reached out her hand. Michael smiled, his serious tone lost in the realization that he had not even introduced himself. *I'm bumbling,* he thought to himself, *she must think I'm some kind of jerk.* "Everyone calls me Jo," she looked down at her own extended hand. Michael jerked like he was awaking abruptly from a trance.

"Michael, Michael Tantalus. It is a pleasure," and he took her hand, which had been suspended in the air far longer than she was accustomed. Her hand was warm and soft. As his heart began to beat again, he swallowed. Michael continued holding her hand, for far longer than Jo normally would have allowed. But she did not resist; her hand was lost in his and it was rough, not like the soft, manicured hands of any of the other city men. She looked at Michael's hand, which was dark, a little sun-worn, and strong. These hands were like her father's, his blue-collar friends', and her early boyfriends from her neighborhood. Yes, she thought to herself, hands hold no secrets.

Michael had always been able to read people; his mother and grandmother had had the same skill. Sensing subtle signs, twitches, gestures, and idiosyncrasies, he could take it all in and act accordingly, from men to women, from children to elderly, from a powerful CEO to the taxi driver that brought him into the city. In rare instances, like now, he wasn't capable of monitoring, categorizing, or judging any signs. Instead, Michael Tantalus found himself fully engaged in the eyes of another, a strangely familiar stranger. Jo was familiar to him as if he had known her in a previous life. Although he was not even sure he believed there was anything past this life, the thought of having already known this stranger was part of how he rationalized his attraction to her. For whatever reason, Michael and Jo were connecting at a primitive level—something deeper than human.

Jo's guard was down, she knew, but she saw nothing but sincerity in Michael. Usually, her instincts were dead on, but there was more going on here. Their eyes were locked and she could not even say what attracted her, but it was strong. The closest word she could find was peacefulness, which made no sense to her, because she also was sensing his restlessness. The noise and motion of the party were imperceptible to either at this moment: For now, two confused souls reached out to one another in wordless recognition.

"I want you," he blurted out inappropriately as he stood boldly like a man but then he blushed and bowed his head slightly like a nervous boy. He realized they were still holding hands so he let go in an attempt to return to a normal engagement. And in a sudden and impetuous act she grasped for his hand again and led him on a desperate search for a place where they could be alone. She pulled him as she might a lagging child, passing room after room, looking in and seeing each occupied, some by multiple couples. Like an animal looking to escape confinement, she kept moving, tugging on Michael as he tried to fathom the activity in each of the rooms they passed.

Finally, near the kitchen, she stopped in front of a door: It was a closet, but she pulled Michael in and shut the door, plunging them both into a dark, cramped void. They bumped awkwardly for a moment then they stood perfectly still until under the veil of darkness, modesty and propriety fell from them both. Jo stood on tiptoe and held Michael tightly, reaching her cheek high to meet his. He felt her with his entire body as they pressed themselves closer in the tight space. For what seemed like an eternity, they held each other, existing only in the feeling of that moment, thinking of nothing else. And in that moment, it felt as if they were floating in the darkness, clinging to the one person in all the world who was meant for them. In stark contrast to everything that was happening, it was as though divine guidance led them to this point and both could feel it.

Something emotional was torn loose, and Michael felt free. Jo unbuckled Michael's belt, and his dress pants fell to the closet floor. The two undressed one another as the temperature in the closet began to rise. The skills of discernment, which Michael held so precious—his ability to separate sanity from insanity, and the sane from the insane—were all now rolling away with the droplets of sweat beading on the soft curve of her skin. Jo turned her back to Michael, reached her long arms up into the darkness of the unseen walls of the tiny room to support herself, and arched her back. A thin sliver of light, angled through the narrow space between the door jamb and the old wooden door that it held, made the small streaks of sweat that ran down the crease of her spine glisten and highlighted her soft, muscular back. Michael gently ran his fingers down her dampened skin; she was as supple and pliable as water.

Michael entered her in what anyone would describe as a baseless act of the physical world, but that instant created a space ever so slightly between his heart and his weary soul. He was touching something deep, something too deep to fathom within himself, but he could sense it, and it came to his mind as questions: *What was in her eyes, eyes he was sure he recognized, had seen before and sure he would see again, eyes of a restless soul, like a mirror.* The two took their bodily comfort, soothing their own secret pains, as they tangled in near-darkness.

Michael quickly returned to his present situation, he had been lost in passion and his mind grasped to be back in control. He suddenly realized he was holding her and they were both once again motionless. Slowly, they released their desperate hold, and began to dress, bumping together in the small space. Once they were fully clothed, Michael fumbled around in his pocket and pulled out his wallet. Her skin, though more than warm, ran suddenly in goose bumps as she tucked her hair behind both ears, watching the shadows of Michael's movements. He pulled out all the bills and he counted them,

"One hundred bucks, it's all I have, I am not sure it's enough," and he handed her the money. She looked down at his hand, then back at his eyes; her stare was oddly blank, though their faces were still close enough to feel each other's breath.

"No, no it's fine," she said dully as she took the money.

Michael turned to open the closet door but the old crystal knob spun uselessly, not catching anything; there were no gears, no tumblers that would free them. Sweat was now running down Michael's forehead and the side of his face. In the sliver of light, he turned back to face Jo.

"The knob doesn't work, we're stuck," he sighed. But then suddenly, light exploded into the closet, making them both squint, blind in the brightness.

"There you are, Michael." Benjamin Adler spoke calmly as though there was nothing awkward, embarrassing, or the slightest bit unusual about the situation. Benjamin put his hand on Michael's shoulder, leading him off as Jo slinked away behind them; Michael looked over his shoulder and she was gone. With Benjamin in the lead, he met person after person—a name, a title, and then Benjamin whispering some detail or another about the man's significance. They slowly but steadily made their way toward the door, and as they were leaving, Michael looked over his shoulder once more searching for Jo. Finally, he spotted her across the room, but when she looked up, she did not acknowledge him, so he turned and left.

Michael didn't feel bad in any way nor would he have said that he felt pleasure in any sort of way. Yet he wasn't numb; he just felt a long way from home. He had begun to compartmentalize his life. Home, church, and family comprised a sort of postcard existence. And here in New York, where he visited characters and played a game called business, it was like going to the zoo, looking at the tigers through the glass but never actually getting into the cage where it was dangerous. But now, he realized, he had truly left home and he was in the cage among some exceedingly dangerous animals.

As the door of the apartment slammed behind him he heard someone lock the door, the music became muted, and he and Bennie walked in silence along the hall to take the elevator back down to the waiting limousine. They got into the long dark car.

When the car began to move, Benjamin leaned up toward the driver, laughing a little, "Our boy here just bagged Jo Kelleher!"

"Bullshit," the driver blurted, then added, "Sir." He craned his head back to look at Michael, then back to the road ahead, then back and forth once more: "No F'n way," he announced. They were both waiting for a response from Michael. He looked at both of them and then etched out a poorly thought-out explanation: "We were trying to find a place to talk." He looked out the window uncomfortably, continuing, "You know the music was so loud." Both Benjamin and the driver burst into laughter.

"Holy shit, you little shit," the driver yelled out while shaking his head, "You know how many guys have been trying to get into Braunsteins's Marketing Manager's pants?"

The comment confused Michael. "Marketing Manager?" he stretched out the words, "I thought she was a hook..." He never got the rest of the word out, though, because the two men had gone wild with laughter. Benjamin doubled over laughing so hard, his eyes began to tear up.

"Perfect, perfect," was all Bennie could get out as he struggled to regain his composure. Every time he looked at Michael he began to laugh again. Michael was in the "boys club" now: This was the point he became one of them and he began to live two divergent lives. He now had a foot firmly planted in each of two entirely different worlds and it disconnected from his own belief structure leaving Michael a little like a boat without a rudder.

After driving for a while, Michael tried again to get clarity, "You mean she isn't a..." and again the two men laughed uproariously. Michael put his hand on his forehead. He was squarely in now, but with a more subdued soul. For the rest of this trip to New York, the meetings went on and on, and person after person, Michael took it all in, remembering as much as he could. The bid meant almost nothing now, he was in and doing business, by cocktail and by handshake.

The flight to Charlotte had been uneventful but Michael dreaded going home. His wife knew him and he was sure she would know everything the minute she saw him. He steeled himself and parked the car, walked the long walk to his doorstep, put the key in the door, and entered. He walked into the den, where his wife sat on the couch next to one of her girlfriends.

"Hey, hon," she said, never looking up. "Don't forget to take out the garbage," she added. He did as she asked, taking comfort in moving the cans out to the curb, a life so strange from the one he had just left.

"I am pretty wiped out from the traveling, so I'm going to hit the sack." He casually tossed the words to her from the hallway that led to their bedroom, feeling like he was not quite in his body, as if he was watching himself. He had the strong urge to yell something at his wife to get things in the open, but instead he swallowed his thoughts and walked down the long, dark hall. In their bedroom, the covers and all but the fitted sheet were on the floor along with the pillows, and rather than neaten them, he lay on the bare bed. He had the sensation of being an exhausted fish on a hot wooden dock, with no fight left, unable to breathe. He let himself drift off to sleep, still wearing his shoes, lying motionless under a glaring incandescent light.

His wife slipped in later, turned on and muted the television, turned off the lights, covered Michael with the sheet from the floor, and carelessly threw the pillows onto the bed. She was purposely waking Michael, seeking sex; he woke enough to oblige and as they rolled, he put his head over her shoulder, never meeting her eyes and never kissing. Nothing in Michael was connected to anything else.

In the flickering lights of the television, he was dimly conscious of making a trade: doing for talking, tolerance for connection, and orgasm for love. And the sacrifice was subtle…was it his family, or his heart? While his body was engaged in satisfying his wife Deborah's physical needs, he had strange thoughts, thoughts of the movie *2001: A Space Odyssey*. It was now 2001, and it seemed to him that all the stars in the universe were moving further and further apart, like people. And no one seemed to look up to notice just how far apart they are drifting, as the universe expands and stars blaze their way to loneliness, hurrying into the darkness of the void.

So there it was, or at least there one was, a moment he could point to later when he was closing down, shutting the windows to his soul, looking but not locking eyes. Functioning only as pieces of himself, quick responses for excitement, to give and to take, enough for what he needed but always trading. He thought about his wife Deborah, then he thought about Jo, realizing they were both the same in one way: They wanted to be saved.

Suddenly, his wife's quickening breath halted as her entire body tensed. She collapsed onto Michael for only a moment then she rolled off and turned onto her side facing away from him. Michael turned to look at her back as she quickly drifted into sleep.

Michael was not sure he could even save himself and he thought about what he could do to reach out to his wife, but the moment came and went, and the process of shutting down minimized any pain or guilt. Michael knew there was a downside, *I feel like I'm free-falling* he thought. Then he began to consider the two words, free and falling, he thought them over and over to himself as he rolled onto his back while looking at the ceiling and waiting to fall asleep.

Michael began minimizing any mental discomfort he felt, in whatever form it came—whether guilt, or anger, or the feeling of failure, the feeling of letting people down or the sickening feeling of lying—and he found it was easy. But what Michael did not know was the consequence. On a scale of ten, where ten is extreme pleasure and one is intolerable pain, Michael's simple decision to consciously not experience anything below a three led to a narrowing of his experience. In drawing the line at three, he inadvertently limited his possibilities of experiencing pleasure in like measure, now limited to a seven, two above the neutral line of five. And in this narrowing band of experiencing sensation, Michael's universe likewise narrowed. He was inadvertently limiting experience and limiting possibility, living and experiencing a life less than his capabilities and less than his birthright.

Michael drifted off to sleep.

Spires to Heaven

Still Late Summer, 2001

"We shouldn't wish for so damn much," Michael said aloud from the back of the dark limousine.

"Pardon, sir?" the driver was always very polite with Michael, but never familiar or too friendly. He was different with Benjamin Adler, though. There was a devotion that appeared to Michael to go far beyond the normal employer-employee relationship. He wondered fleetingly if he would ever truly know the real story behind their relationship. And Michael had, of course, noticed that Benjamin Adler treated him differently as well. Others noticed it too, but no one ever said anything about it and Michael and Bennie never discussed it.

"Oh, nothing, I was just thinking out loud," Michael replied, looking out of the window, observing that he was approaching the tall gold building where Benjamin Adler worked. Michael's growing position with Benjamin and the collection of very important men that they were always around had changed his perception of himself. Feeling that he was of greater importance gave Michael a sense of solidness he'd never had before. Yet at the same time, knowledge of how high he had risen made him acutely aware of just how far he could fall. *It's fear of success, perhaps*, he thought silently to himself, *or maybe just plain old-fashioned anxiety*. He knew he was doubting something but he could not put his finger on what it was.

It was as if Michael had been bitten by a poisonous snake and the venom that cursed through him, that restricted his breathing, was obligation. As his stature grew, his obligations grew and at an exponential pace. Because Michael now had a close view of many "successful" men, he was able to observe that many of them had in one way or another gone mad, as though the poison of obligation had permeated their entire being. Michael himself was having mild nightmares, chasing down important papers and contracts blowing uncontrollably down busy avenues. He, like the men he was emulating, became accustomed to placating the growing discord within himself. He wanted the success these men had—the money and the power—but he did not want to be like these men. On the surface of his mind, the conscious thinking level, he reassured himself that he was different. But in his heart and deeper in his mind, he knew he was becoming more like them every day.

There were two main opiates that helped these over-achievers ignore their uneasiness about their ambitions. First was over-working—long hours, always away from home, helped them maintain the delusion that everything would be all right. The second opiate, indulgence, was far more powerful. The first indulgences were simple: exquisite dinners with expensive wine, scotch, and cigars. But over time, long business dinners became less and less about the business and more and more about sensual satisfaction. Dinners spilled into late-night drinking binges, and sometimes, drugs, but more often, women.

Most of the powerful men had second lives, second loves, and sometimes even second families living in the City in condos or high-rent properties, but always in complete and separate homes. Michael learned things about these men, things such as pills like Viagra were not used for impotence but rather for the gluttonous and lustful to far exceed the bounds of nature. When he paused to think about it, Michael supposed that the more powerful the men became, the more voracious were their appetites. They ate and partook of the City so ravenously that they never seemed to taste the bitterness or aftermath of consequence, always moving "forward" as they eagerly sought relief from any fear of possible retribution and any amount of anxiety to keep what they had attained.

Michael often wondered when these men ever slept. He always had the refuge of flying back to Charlotte, and sometimes, sleeping for an entire weekend, but many of these men rarely visited "home." His endurance during the work weekdays was one of the attributes that allowed him to climb the business scene so swiftly; Michael never seemed to be overtaken by alcohol and he never seemed to need sleep. *I am having the time of my life*, he told himself. The routine of long meetings, shaking hands, signing agreements, and driving all over town in the long, dark limousine to various dinners, parties, nightclubs, and condos—always deep into glittering Manhattan nights—*I am living the dream*, Michael thought to himself often as if he needed to convince himself.

The limousine slowed, and the door, as always, opened just as they arrived curbside. Standing in the open door was Benjamin Adler, smiling, holding in one hand a crystal carafe partially filled with a dark fluid and in the other hand two cocktail glasses. He was seated in an instant, taking ice from the small chest in the limousine, dropping it into the glasses from a higher than normal height, letting the exaggerated sound of the ice hitting the glass act as a signal that a celebration was about to begin. Bennie was in an excellent mood and he handed Michael the glasses so he could pour the drinks. The phone rang.

"We will be a little late; we have an errand to run. Yes, yes, we'll be there, you can be certain. Oh, and start without us," then he said something too quietly for Michael to hear; he was talking to Audrey, his mistress. Michael always knew when he was talking to her as his voice became softer, almost childlike. Smiling, Bennie sank back into the soft leather, closed the phone, and began to pontificate. "Michael, do you know why a farmer will sometimes find it necessary to burn his own barn?" He did not want an answer from Michael. Benjamin Adler looked as if he were in a trance, staring into the distance, talking to someone Michael could not see. "Sometimes, Michael, the rats get out of control and the only way to get them out of the barn is to burn the barn and start over." Bennie tipped the glass to his lips, sipping, prompting Michael to do the same without asking what he was drinking. It was smooth and cool with almost a sweet burn that was quickly followed by a slight surge of pleasure.

"Cognac?" Michael sipped again.

"Yes, you won't find this on any liquor store shelf."

Michael assumed Bennie was going to tell him what they were drinking, but instead, Benjamin Adler continued his speech. "Michael, we—the owners and property managers of these stately, steel TOWERS—" he emphasized the word (Michael had never heard Benjamin Adler refer to the skyscrapers as towers before.) "... have reports," he continued, looking finally at Michael, "that tell us when the rats are skimming too much."

He looked back into the unseen distance, but he was still smiling, "So Michael, because the rats have gotten out of control, we're going to burn the barn." Michael pursed his lips and wrinkled his forehead, unable to disguise his perplexity, then sipped the unnamed cognac while he waited for clarification from Benjamin. "The way we burn the barn, Michael, is we trade properties. We watch the numbers, and when the wise guy's fingers start to get too sticky; we buy and/ or sell our properties to each other. And of course, when a property is sold, the staff is dismissed because the new property managers will always want to bring in their own staff. The barn is purged and we start over," he folded his arms and looked at Michael with a smile that just kept getting larger and larger.

Michael noticed they were headed south down the West Side Highway and was beginning to realize what Bennie was telling him.

"Cheers," Michael returned the large grin and raised his glass. Bennie clinked his glass, and then his tone turned to the more serious Benjamin Adler business tone. Michael often had observed him change from one to the other in a blink and back again.

"The Silversteins have bought the lease rights to the World Trade Centers, so we, Emblem Corp., will be running and managing the most magnificent structures in the City, and you—Michael Tantalus of Universal Spectrum—will, among other things, be our electrical supplies provider."

Michael smiled. "I like the way that sounds."

"I thought you might. And I thought you might want to take a look at your new conquest." Michael smiled again even broader as he began to say something but Benjamin Adler continued talking so Michael listened. "A lot on Manhattan Isle has length and breadth, but does not stir imagination and inspire awe," he said, then looked again at Michael, lowering his head to whisper, "or make *profit*." He winked as he said it, so softly as though he were commenting on his soliloquy and did not want to interrupt himself. "Until, Michael…" he now raised his finger and voice for effect, growing animated "…until, Michael, there is a major assault on the third dimension. Height, Michael: height is the measure of value, the measure of money. It is a symbol of greatness, a monument to capitalism if you will. The Twin flames burst through the clouds and scrape the sky, they define the skyline, the cityscape of our Manhattan Isle, capitalism's heart."

Bennie took a breath and another drink, then continued his monologue. "Money is energy, money is the oxygenated blue blood of civilization, feeding it, allowing it to live and thrive. *Money doesn't make money until money moves*, and Michael, Wall Street is what moves the money for our entire country, for the entire world. Wall Street is the heart, pumping the blood, moving the money, the life energy to the body of the civilizations of the earth. And Michael, the Towers are no ordinary buildings; they are the twin chambers of the heart, stronger than any other before them. They symbolize the free market system, capitalism, materialism." Benjamin Adler relaxed, his impassioned sermon not nearly complete, and began a more sedate history lesson.

"George Fuller solved the problem of load-bearing capacities," Benjamin began, his demeanor changing. Michael saw a side of the powerful man that he had never seen before, noticing how physically small Bennie was; he could see him in a school room, wearing thick eye lenses, spouting facts, and running from the bullies when class was over. Odd, Michael thought, how power changes everything in a man: Now Bennie was the bully.

Bennie continued, "By inventing a structure of steel, a steel cage if you will, and Michael," he paused for effect, "the assault on the sky began, man reaching for the clouds, reaching for the gods," he paused again, taking in his own speech. *Like the Tower of Babel,* was the thought that crossed Michael's mind but he dared not say it out loud.

"Michael, the seeds of the World Trade Center were first planted after World War II. Our country built up a tremendous manufacturing base that helped win the war in two corridors of the world. Unlike the rest of the world, there was practically no damage to our manufacturing capability, and as our young soldiers returned home, our work force only grew. A few visionaries *knew* America needed to prepare for a new surge of economic growth. Everyone could see that the reconstruction of Europe would necessitate a huge increase in transatlantic trade. Men like the Rockefellers wanted to capture these opportunities, so they pushed the New York Legislature to form a World Trade Corporation to explore the potential for a trade center in Manhattan." Benjamin paused, looking at Michael to make sure he was listening. "Do you know who Daniel Burnham was?" he asked. Michael was not sure if he was really asking a question or being rhetorical.

"No, I don't," Michael knew how to play his part in their discussion. Benjamin Adler was relishing his tale of "The City" and of the roots of the towers. "Daniel Burnham was a turn-of-the-century architect who built the Flatiron Building," he continued.

"New York's first skyscraper," Michael responded, making Bennie smile.

"Yes, Michael, that's right." He patted Michael on the knee, took a deep breath, then continued, "Well, there was a man named Tobin, who worked for—or should I say, was running—the Port Authority after the war and he used to quote Burnham: 'Make no small plans, for they have no power to stir the blood.'" Bennie thrust his glass into the air, and Michael felt a small swell of pride.

"I suppose you know by now where we are headed?" Bennie asked.

"The Village?"

Michael did not usually joke with Bennie but Bennie smiled, responding: "It's Salsa Night at Windows of the World. Do you Salsa dance?"

"No, never tried… I am assuming you do?" asked Michael.

"Yes, and don't look so surprised, you should try it. Can you count to seven?"

"I have trouble counting to two when dancing the two-step," Michael quipped, enjoying his new status.

"Let's go see what's happening—que pasa, my man," Bennie was beginning to laugh at himself a bit, "Anyway, it should be interesting."

Their exchanges were becoming steadily more familiar; Michael was becoming increasingly part of Bennie's not-so-secret second life.

"The World Trade Center has definitely 'stirred the blood'," Bennie resumed pontificating about the Towers. "As controversial as they are tall. No matter how you feel about them, their impact on New York has been colossal in every imaginable way: architecturally, economically," he searched for another word but let the sentence fade into a brief silence. "The Twin Towers have become as global a symbol for New York as the Eiffel Tower has for France or the Pyramids have for Egypt."

Bennie began to chuckle with successful pride and took another drink. "What the hell does that even mean, global symbol?" Gesturing with his free hand, he said, "It is the world's largest office building, nothing more, nothing too fancy, just straight up. It is amazing to me that the Port Authority was able to overcome the bullshit of state, local, and federal politics. *That* is the true feat, not their height."

The two men rode silently for the last few traffic lights of their journey; Bennie was preoccupied with his cell phone, then leaned up to whisper instructions to the driver as they approached their stop. This was all routine by now for Michael: happenings, happy hours, and of course "events." This was one of Bennie's favorite words to describe what lay ahead of them most evenings that Michael was in New York: evenings of pushing boundaries followed by tedious early-morning business meetings. And now Michael was crossing a cultural boundary: Salsa Dancing at Windows of the World.

The music greeted them as the elevator doors opened high in the Twin Tower, and Benjamin Adler began to move his body in the rhythm, looked briefly at Michael, then charged ahead into the pulsing action of the bar. Michael followed a bit slower, tentatively moving into the action as large Latin bouncers on either side of the door eyed him suspiciously. He knew that if he had not been with Benjamin Adler, he would not have been allowed in the door. The beat of the music was enthralling and felt marvelous to Michael, but he began to feel out of place; he was one of very few Anglos, he had lost sight of Bennie, and he knew he was walking about awkwardly, an unusual state for him.

The hot, smoky room began to shrink with the movement and engagement between men, he could almost see their chins rise and their chests bulge as they passed each other; they seemed to Michael to move with bravado and rhythm he did not possess. There was dancing on the floor in syncopated, purposeful movement under wildly flashing lights, and mixed in the music was a roar of men and women trying to communicate, aided by their constantly moving bodies. There were rules here that Michael did not know so he moved cautiously. He walked towards one of the club's large namesake windows only to discover the windows were too steamy to see the view. He was suddenly aware that he needed clearer air and a more distant view. He left the club, pausing between the two door guards, looking first at one, then the other; neither smiled.

Michael took the long tourist escalator the remaining distance from the bar lobby to the roof. He was expecting to walk into the limited visibility of thick clouds and fog but was surprised to find that he emerged into a crisp headwind of air that followed the natural law of convection, heading down to center of the structure from the large high opening at the top of the building. Once outside on the roof, Michael found it was cool and quiet, both unusual sensations for a midsummer night in the city. The air was inviting and the noise of the metropolis below was muted both by the height of the building and the soft whistling of the wind. Michael took a deep, refreshing breath and then was struck with awe at the extensive spread of lights in every direction. There were brilliantly lit grids across the entire island that continued on the other sides of both the Henry Hudson and East rivers, stretching into New Jersey to the West and into Staten Island and Long Island to the East. And beyond the grids, long bright lines connected to even further clusters of light that faded into darkness at what looked like the edges of the earth. Countless moving headlights and taillights that were very small from this distance and appeared to be moving in slow silence.

Michael felt serene; he stood and faced north, then turned west, then south, and then east. In the far east, there was the darkness of the sea. He could not see, smell, or hear the ocean— his senses had boundaries and darkness was all he perceived— but he knew that it was there and he imagined its splendor. He looked upward where no stars were visible and the underside of the clouds glowed from the light of the city, except for two large round openings out into the universe, giving the strange illusion of infinity contained within a large skull.

His cell phone rang.

"Ready to go?"

"Yep," Michael answered, with as much enthusiasm as he could muster.

"Where are you?"

"On the roof… I needed some air."

"Meet me downstairs outside. Look for the car." It was an order, but Michael was ready to go, he had feared the dancing could go for hours. He surmised that Bennie had done whatever he had come to do. A connection made, a word spoken in the right ear, maybe something else; he stopped trying to imagine and headed down the escalator and two elevators that it took to reach the expansive, austere lobby. He walked outside to the warmer air, and though the downtown traffic of cars and people appeared to be light, there was more noise than up on the roof. They were headed to the much busier nightlife of Midtown and knew it would be far noisier there.

Everything appeared to be going great. Michael's career was skyrocketing. But the more time he spent in the fast moving business world, he began to long for or miss something else. He tried to pinpoint what he was feeling, it was a slight dissonance. He wanted the success but somewhere deep a part of himself was being neglected, *my spiritual life*. The thought surprised him and he was sure that the wrong words had come into his mind so he supplanted them with words that made more sense to the surface of his mind—*my love life*—and he smiled as he thought it, *Damn everything does lead to sex*. He made himself chuckle and the dissonant feeling subsided.

He stepped just outside the spinning doors where the broad, shiny steel of the building met the cement of the walkway and waited patiently for Bennie and the car. As he leaned against the Tower, he was jolted by the coldness of the steel through his shirt. He looked at the building and wondered how deep into the rock of the island the steel penetrated. The word *island* was a strange descriptive to him in this moment since there was no sign of dirt, grass, trees, or anything else that signified that there was living and fertile earth somewhere beneath his feet.

He looked upward, his eyes following the steel and glass of the seemingly eternal edifice. It was so substantial. Then suddenly, appearing in his mind seemingly out of nowhere were questions: *How long will this building stand? Four hundred years from now? One hundred years, ten years, one year, a month, a day? How will it fall? Will its demise be rust or a planned disassembly? Perhaps it will be a great national disaster, a calamity, maybe the destructive hand of man... How will the inevitable end come?*

Michael had the disconcerting impression in that moment, though he did not completely understand how or why, that these questions were coming from someplace other than his own mind, *Perhaps the universe is speaking to me directly.* *Universe speaking,* the phrase played again in his thoughts, spurring a memory of having used the phrase once before in the presence of an atheist. The words had sent her into a tirade. "You are one of those people," she accused him, "You undermine everything that logic and reason stand on, you slap the face of science, you send humanity back into the Dark Ages!" she was spewing impassioned fragments of phrases. He had the impression that he had stepped into an argument from her past. One, like many we all have, that played over and over in her mind, convincing her to maintain a stance and defend her position: satisfying her need to be right.

Michael did not feel that need. Whether or not the universe just spoke to him did not matter. *But there had to have been a beginning—a source—of everything,* he thought, and as Michael played the memory, he noticed his thoughts and began to follow them backwards, upstream, searching for their source, but the searching ended in oblivion, he could not sense the source of his thoughts. They seemed to simply appear out of nowhere. But as he kept his awareness at the gateway of his conscious thoughts, he noticed that he felt peaceful.

Michael again reached out to touch the cold, immovable object, the glass and steel edifice. And as he imagined its death, he felt as if he was touching some unperceived place, that was the source from where his thoughts emanated, like a link in a chain, between the manifest and the un-manifest. But since that place of silence within him had no substance and was not busy with thought or imagery, it remained for now to Michael, elusive. But he was aware that he felt a pleasantness and a stillness, and for a moment, he wanted to pursue this newfound discovery of a still place within himself, that though it appeared in his senses as nothing, was the author and source of all his thoughts. Then Bennie and the limousine pulled up alongside the curb.

"There you are. Get in, our girls are waiting. They are hungry and they want to go dancing," shouted Benjamin Adler, smiling and holding a fresh glass of cognac in one hand and a cigar in the other.

"Our girls?" Michael emphasized the "Our" curiously.

Veil of Sultry Shadows

Summer of 2001

They came in a side door of the restaurant, where they were welcomed by the pungent smell of hookah pipes. Soft light filtered through wispy clouds of smoke that twirled languidly in the breeze of the barely oscillating ceiling fans. Exotic music mixed with the steady murmur of countless people talking; the tables were placed so close to one another that Michael couldn't distinguish where one table stopped and another began. Bennie led them toward the back corner, weaving his way through men and women relaxing on floor cushions, legs extended as they leaned on pillows or someone next to them. Everyone seemed to be deeply preoccupied in conversation or eating, barely noticing as Bennie and Michael pushed their way through the crowd.

Across the room, clear and bright in spite of the reduced visibility, Michael could see Jo anxiously staring in his direction. Her head was tilted slightly to the side, her deep auburn hair loose, wild, and flowing. *She looks as beautiful as a model in a shiny fashion magazine*, Michael thought. *What is she doing here?* And suddenly, he had the sensation of a large, dark shadow passing over him, the same sensation a small rabbit would have as the shadow of a large hawk passed over.

"Hey, honey," Jo greeted him. The words sounded strange as Jo stood to take him by the hand, leaning in for an awkward kiss that signified a far longer relationship than a closet tryst. Michael was still and silent, unsure of what to do next, but the sparkling of light on Jo's dark red hair was a pleasant distraction. She kept moving, taking him by the arm with her free hand, smiling all the while into his eyes, mesmerizing him as she led him away from the table. She turned back to the table where Bennie and the others were now seated and said, "Will you excuse us for a moment?"

"Young love," said a nearby woman, sighing a bit as she watched them exit through the side entrance.

As soon as they were out the door and out of sight, Jo spun Michael violently toward her, thrusting her face into his. The welcoming smile was long gone and she yelled in a harsh whisper: "What the hell did you tell Bennie?"

"I told him we were just talking," he whispered back.

"You idiot! You should have told him you were banging my brains out! He would have thought you were lying like every other dog!" Jo turned away from Michael and let out a long stream of air, then turned once again to face him. She stood tall, fully reclaiming her composure. "Okay, here is the deal," she declared, looking evenly and coolly into his eyes, "First of all, that will NEVER happen again. Secondly, I do not want to TALK about it, and third, as far as everyone at that table knows, we are lovers—madly in love with one another, made for each other—but helplessly locked into loveless marriages that we are committed to, GOT IT?" Her stare burned into him.

"May I ask a question?"

"NO!"

"Okay, yeah, I think I got it."

"I don't know what Bennie sees in you. I have been working this job for four years..." Jo was getting worked up, venting and not communicating in complete sentences. Michael was pretty sure she was talking to him, but she half appeared to be talking to herself, "Top of F'n Fordham's Business School, grades, extracurriculars, and references out my ass, 12-hour days, bustin' my F'n ass, and never a word, never anything from management, then, then, who knows what the F I was thinking, and, and," she was motioning her hand at Michael and wrinkling her face, "Suddenly, everyone thinks you and I are some kind of frickin' Romeo and Juliet, then Benjamin F'n Alder calls me to his office to ask me my opinion on our marketing campaign and budget. Suddenly he wants to know what I think."

Jo stopped talking and gesticulating wildly to take a deep breath. When she looked at Michael, he was grinning at her charmingly.

"Oh, no, that won't work with me. Stop it right now... stop smiling," she glared at him while pointing her finger. Michael did his best to stop smiling, but slowly but surely a smile began glowing on Jo's face until it showed fully on her beautiful lips. "Okay, now you just look gay or something," she said, and they both laughed.

"Hey, nothing wrong with being gay," he finally was able to get in a word.

"There is if you are going to be MY Romeo." She stopped smiling, "You're not gay are you? I mean, that's okay and all?"

He began to laugh, "No, I am not gay."

"Don't screw this up for me." This time when she said it, it was more a request than a command.

He smiled and looked at her, a dynamo turned vulnerable in the space between syllables of a single word. "Of course not, how could I screw it up for my Sweet Juliet?" He knew he had said it too sweetly, too sincerely, so he tried to move quickly to humor: "Romeo and Juliet? Can we not use a different couple as our model? Don't they die in the end?"

"Very funny, and just shut up, would you?" She sounded relieved.

"'Did my heart love till now? Forswear it, sight! For I ne'er saw true beauty till this night,'" the words flowed from Michael with ease and without the strain of finding words from some deep memory. She was stunned, motionless for just a moment, and then recovered herself.

"'O Romeo, Romeo! Wherefore art thou Romeo? Deny thy father and refuse thy name. Or if thou wilt not, be but sworn my love and I'll no longer be a Capulet,'" she said the lines melodramatically, exaggerating her arm movements. Now Michael was astonished.

"What? You think you are the only person around here who took a college poetry class and can spout a little Shakespeare? That romantic trap crap doesn't work with me." Jo finished her short tirade and temporarily looked away from Michael, hiding from him an uncontrollable reaction as she closed her eyes, pursed her lips, and let a little stream of air that carried with it a small and barely audible ecstatic moan. She turned back and quickly changed the subject.

"Oh, and there is another thing: A hundred bucks?! You think you can have me, Josephine Kelleher, for a hundred bucks?! What are you, some kind of moron?"

"Well, I never, you know, never, well—actually, I am a moron," Michael agreed. She pulled out the one hundred dollars and showed it to him.

"I think it is so nice the way you give money to charity," she said with exaggerated sarcasm.

She grabbed his hand and began pulling him the length of the alley until they reached the main avenue, and once around the corner, turned her head from side to side surveying the length of the sidewalk in both directions until she spied a homeless woman lying curled almost fetal against the building adjacent to the restaurant. As they approached, Jo still dragging Michael, they could see the woman was sleeping, wearing at least three coats even though the night was still warm, and she was dirty. Jo crouched beside the woman and surveyed her up and down: She was elderly and had many small, seemingly worthless trinkets tied in bundles to various strings and loops attached to her many coats and sweaters. Jo found an open pocket and inserted the bills, inspected the woman once more, then raised her palm toward Michael.

"And I don't want to talk about that either," she said emphatically. Michael was not sure which "that" she meant but decided it would not be wise to probe.

Jo stood a little too quickly and closer to Michael than she intended; finding her face so close to his she kissed him softly, then slapped him. His face jerked to the side and he began to recoil in anger, but then smiled, the sensation of her kiss lingering.

Smiling again, bright and open and full of confidence, Jo asked, "Okay, ready for show time?"

"Ready as I will ever be," he eked out in a whisper, partly to Jo, but mostly to himself. They walked back to the side entrance of the hookah lounge in silence, not looking at each other. But just as they reached the door, Jo paused to wrap her arms around Michael's arm, looking up at him with seemingly complete vulnerability. He gave her as reassuring a smile as he could muster, then they entered the smoky lounge in lockstep.

Benjamin Adler, Jonathan Braunstein, and their smartly dressed companions all were sitting at a table in the far corner of the spacious but crowded restaurant. Bennie sat between the two beautiful women, leaning against two large red pillows in the corner. The low table stood upon an elevated dais; Bennie, Jon, and the two women all sat comfortably on large floor cushions. It was obvious that the maître d' was more than aware of Benjamin Adler's importance, as he ushered in and out various waiters and waitresses as well as the tuxedoed sommelier toting the required fresh bottle of wine. Bennie looked up to watch the approaching couple, his wide smile appearing ready to burst into laughter at any minute. He was obviously pleased at the pairing of Jo and Michael but Michael was searching his own thoughts to understand why.

Jo was on her game, perfectly playing the part of a coy girlfriend. The new twist to Michael's relationship with Bennie and Jon was that now, in their eyes, he was one of them—rather, just like them—with a mostly unseen 'real' family somewhere in the shadows of their thoughts. Here in New York, their families showed up only as pictures on a desk, certainly not in a fast-paced, enticing place like this. In this realm, the subtlest body language of looks, the eyes raised or lowered, all had a heightened sense of importance. The money that these men moved was enormous, so everything it touched seemed so significant that any behavior that might normally be questioned was rationalized or ignored.

Business had been good that summer, and as the business grew, these wildly successful men likewise grew so much that they were living multiple lives: multiple relationships, barely sleeping, going from event to event like it was a race to do as much as possible. None of them ever really considered slowing down enough to take anything in, to reflect or to question; they just lived with the constant forward movement.

But as Michael listened to the conversation around the table, he thought about his awkward new pretend relationship with Jo. Suddenly, he realized that he had been pretending all along—everything was false—he was pretending to be one of the boys, pretending to be friends with them, pretending he loved this life. As these sudden thoughts crystallized in his mind, he realized that he was feeling very small and very lonely.

His thoughts were drifting in and out as he halfheartedly kept track of the table conversation, when suddenly, he recalled standing on the top of the World Trade Center. He grabbed on to the thought—the peace of looking out into darkness, feeling and smelling the breeze—bringing that feeling into the restaurant. He sensed everyone and everything around him and he felt himself as an individual but also could sense himself as one with and part of the ebbing and flowing of the sounds of the hookah pipes, of the exotic music, and of the raucous bursts of many conversations. He closed his eyes briefly, and from his peaceful place, the collective noise seemed like a forgotten language, and he listened intently, trying to discern its meaning.

When he opened his eyes, he beheld the lovely Josephine Kelleher, who was laughing, reacting to the conversation that moved about the table like a playful game of catch and toss. Michael observed her reactions, but he was hearing the blended sound of the entire scene, not comprehending details of anything that she or his other tablemates were saying. She glanced quickly at Michael but something about his eyes pulled her away from the light, meaningless conversation. As she slowly turned to face him, her smile faded but then it returned: this time for him, and this time sincere. She blushed and looked down, then around the table at the others, turning to speak to the woman beside her. Looking back at Michael, she saw that his eyes were steadfastly on her, and she paused for just a moment, returning the intensity of his gaze. She silently mouthed to him, "Stop," but then she smiled again, quickly turning her head back to conversation at the table, flipping her hair unconsciously.

Michael returned his focus to the people seated around the table. Bennie winked, shooting him a knowing glance so Michael returned the smile. Then, Bennie turned his attention back to Audrey, who was telling a funny story; as everyone laughed heartily, Benjamin put his arm around her. *She is beautiful*, Michael thought. Michael remembered that she was a former Penthouse Pet—Bennie had even shown him pictures of her—but in person she wasn't at all what he had expected. She was smart and savvy, powerful in her own right. In fact, looking at Bennie and Audrey now, watching them interact, Michael thought that they made a good pair. He wondered how she tolerated their arrangement and what she got out of it other than a condo on the East Side. Maybe she genuinely loved Bennie—who knew? Regardless, she clung to him as though she knew her job.

The woman with Jon was attractive, no doubt, but in a manufactured sort of way: obvious, large fake breasts, hair bleached so pale it was almost white, heavy makeup, and eyebrows waxed and penciled into an unnatural shape. She wore an overly tight dress that barely allowed her to sit so she fidgeted constantly with her hemline, trying to stay covered while seated on a floor cushion. She was in this for the fun and she said so over and over, introducing herself as Tabitha Hill, but Michael wondered if that was her real name. Jonathan was in it for the sex and he said so in front of Benjamin and Michael, over and over. He never mentioned her name except when relating one of his by now infamous all-night sexcapade stories. Jon only seemed to use Tabitha as his playmate when out with Bennie; he did talk about his wife and kids when he was at lunch alone with Michael. Michael had the distinct feeling that the wild stories and lavishly sexy playmate Tabitha were only for appearances in front of Bennie. When away from Bennie, Jon seemed different.

Audrey had been seeing Bennie for more than two years now, *So maybe she does really love him*, Michael thought to himself. She was approaching middle age, perhaps 10 years younger than Bennie. When she laughed, she would tip her head backwards and open her mouth with a slight pause before any sound came out. There was something very attractive about her beyond her looks, and Michael wondered what her story was. Could she possibly be happy as a mistress? In every social situation that Michael had attended where Audrey was present, he had noticed that she was always fully in charge. The other women—in tonight's case, Tabitha and Jo—seemed to know this, and always followed her lead. *There must be volumes about this unwritten social order with countless rules and guidelines*, Michael was thinking. There was clearly a pecking order where she was queen.

Just then, Audrey picked up her purse, an unspoken signal to the other two women. "Pardon me, gentlemen," she said as she stood, gracefully and with all the etiquette propriety of a diplomat's wife, and the other two women followed her lead. Michael folded his arms and watched the three women weave through the tables, chairs, and floor cushions while deftly dodging the quickly moving wait staff. He watched until they slowly faded out of his sight into the heavy smoke that hung about the large room like a dark fog.

Michael returned his attention to Bennie and Jon; Bennie was waving his hand to a passing waiter, and while Michael could not hear what he was saying, he found out soon enough when a young woman came to the table with a large hookah pipe, tobacco, and hot coals. Michael watched intently because he had never seen a hookah pipe before but he did not want to look too unworldly in his present company.

"Hookah," Jon yelled over the noise to Michael who nodded his head. "It comes from India, I think," Jon added, still looking at Michael.

"*So many things come from India*," Michael thought to himself. "*So many gods*," and he remembered an Indian phrase he had once heard, "*It's all Atman*": In other words, "It's all God." As the thought floated around in his mind, he tried to tie some significance to it... the word *God* evoked so much inside of him, so now he searched for some deep meaning in these present events. But after a moment's longer thought, he realized he could find nothing special or divine about smoking hookah. It was simply another place where the divine did not exist. Like everything about his life now in Manhattan, this felt like watching a movie, observing these events and experiencing them as separate from his "real life."

"Ever smoke a hookah pipe?" Jon's question brought Michael out of his thoughts.

"No, I never have," he answered while shaking his head no.

"Want to give it a try?" Jon asked.

"Sure," Michael answered confidently. He wanted to appear game for anything. He looked at the pipe: at its head was a bowl, *Ceramic or maybe marble*, Michael was thinking as he examined the apparatus sitting before him. He watched the woman in a dark, tight, low-cut top bend over as she put tobacco into the bowl. She paused and looked sensually at Michael. *Most likely part of the show*, he thought. Bennie was watching Michael stare at the woman, and it made him smile. Next, she added a perforated foil screen, then with metal tongs, carefully placed several hot coals on top of the screen just above the tobacco. She caressed the stem, tracing her fingers lightly over several wooden grommets and down to the large glass water jar. Then, cradling a long, slender flexible tube in her other hand, she brought the apparatus over to Michael. He was not expecting to be first, but he readied himself, signaling to the woman with his eyes that he did not know what to do. In response, she smiled slightly as she moved seductively with the music toward Michael. At the end of the hose was a wooden mouthpiece which she gently placed on his lips, leaning her more-than-ample breast into his face as she whispered into his ear, "Draw in the smoke, firm and steady, but not too hard."

He obeyed, and to his surprise, the coals on the top brightened to red. As he inhaled, Michael watched the smoke move through the hookah like a child watches a toy train. He was mesmerized and totally unprepared as the smoke passed into his lungs; he pulled the hose away from his mouth, suppressing the growing urge to cough. Bennie and Jon watched, chuckling a bit as Michael's face turned beet red and he finally exhaled the smoke.

Handing the hose over to Jon, Michael relaxed and his eyes began to wander around the large room. The aged building was contrasted purposefully by the newer, architecturally balanced lines and angles of faux beams and the overly bright colors of modern art prints and paintings on all the walls. Long, blood-red curtains ran from near the top of the high, industrial ceiling to the wooden floors. The clash of old and new gave the grand room the feel of a movie set, as though everyone was an actor playing in a well-rehearsed production. The waiters and waitresses wore elegant costumes and moved purposefully within the manufactured opulence; everything was calculated to heighten and delight all the senses.

These vivid sights, combined with the sounds of exotic music and the odor of pungent hookah smoke, made for an intoxicating ambiance that left Michael feeling a little high. The seductive mood was further enhanced by the subdued light of wall sconces and scattered flickering candles. Michael thought of Jo.

"Gentlemen, I need to use the facilities," he announced, waiting for a response. Bennie and Jon were locked deep into a conversation. Neither looked up, but Bennie waved his hand towards Michael like a king giving his consent. Michael rose and began to push his way through the crowd, brushing the back of a tall man in a suit, then standing briefly chest-to-chest with a busty woman in a red dress; her eyes locked with Michael's and she smiled invitingly as she held her martini glass high into the smoky air above. He turned away, politely pushing one more time through the throng, and finally he was free.

The broad wooden steps that led down to the restrooms were steep and flickering light from candles below made its way up the stairs. Michael descended the shadowed staircase slowly and carefully, and as he approached the bottom, he saw Jo, Audrey, and Tabitha lined up on a long bench facing the bathroom doors. Jo was transfixed, mesmerized by something but she broke free from her apparent spell briefly to motion Michael to sit next to her. Michael sat silently, trying to determine what so enthralled the three women.

"What are we doing?" Michael whispered, only to be hushed by Audrey putting her finger to her lips. He followed their gaze to the smoky glass of the bathroom doors, which were lined up across the length of the opposing wall. Behind the glass danced anonymous figures, all engaged in typical activities—one woman washing her hands, another brushing her hair, a man standing using the bathroom—dancing veils of moving shadows. As Michael looked closer, he realized that all three of the women were focused on a single door.

"Sir," the sudden appearance of the waiter startled Michael, making him realize that he too had slid into a subtle trance. The waiter was holding a tray with a single martini. Michael had not ordered the drink, but he took it without asking what it was.

"Thank you," he whispered, then turned his attention to the same smoky glass door that held the three women's attention. Just beyond the glass, a ballet of shadows, two people's movements, beautiful and mesmerizing.

Michael looked over at Jo, who was biting her lower lip. When she felt his eyes on her, she gave him a warm smile, putting her hand on his leg then turned her attention back to the couple behind the glass door. Jo felt warm as Michael put his arm on the seat back behind her, stroking her back with his fingertips gently, almost unconsciously, as he too was drawn in by the scene behind the glass: a man above and behind a thinner figure, a woman. Jo began to stroke the inside of Michael's thigh, sending sexual energy sparking on a long fuse that moved up his spine and across the top of his skull, raising every small hair with its power.

The waiter returned with champagne for the three ladies, each of whom took one of the tall, thin glasses while keeping a keen focus on the dance before them. The shadow-woman behind the glass turned to put her arms up around the neck of the tall shadow-man, stretching up to kiss him as he leaned over her to meet her mouth with his. One of the women on the bench released a small, slight moan but Michael did not even wonder which one; they were all as one in this moment. The shadowy woman arched backwards, her hair swinging into the shadows, and it was difficult to tell where flesh stopped and shadow began. The man held her now with one arm, his hand at the small of her back, and their hips and legs appeared to merge. The couple began to turn, their hips instigating thrusts, and the woman let go of the man's neck, arching further backward like a dark swan. The man held tight to the small of her back with one arm, and his free hand danced down her chin, her neck, her chest, and her stomach, all the while keeping a pelvic rhythm to some deep, unheard music that controlled the sexual dancers and the voyeurs all the same. Then the bodies behind frosted glass moved as one from the sink, to the wall, to the floor.

Jo pressed closer to Michael, gripping his thigh tightly. Goosebumps ran wild on his body, and heat seemed to rise from Jo's skin. Her breath was shallow but quick, her body reacting as if she were in the shadow dance. And as the couple's motions intensified, their moans began to emanate through the glass door, audible over the music in the small lobby. The sound made one of the women sit back; it was like a small tremor before the coming quake.

The four voyeurs held their collective breath, the end seemed imminent. A small bead of perspiration formed on Jo's brow and she moved her hand slowly up Michael's thigh. He leaned in to smell her hair, the fragrance of rain flooding his senses. He was instantly and completely overtaken with desire. She continued to caress his leg but she never turned her gaze from the translucent visage before them.

Michael breathed deeply, holding the air in for a moment, then letting it out slowly. He gently ran his fingertips down the small of her back and then softly slid his hand under her shirt, over the back of her bra, and then out of the collar up into her hair. He gently but strongly gripped a handful of Jo's glorious hair and his heart began to pound. He felt it when Jo swallowed. The love-making in the bathroom pitched again, and again, and again.

Then, with no warning, the shadow-woman screamed. She was falling, and as she fell, she grasped awkwardly for a secure hold; finding none, she landed hard on the tile floor, kicking open the bathroom door as she went down, exposing the scene behind the smoky veil. The woman scrambled and slid on the wet floor until she was on her hands and knees, motionless for a moment on all fours. She looked up at Michael and the three women, a mere four feet away. Her eyes were swollen almost shut, her dark makeup ran in black streams down her cheeks and she scowled pathetically at her spectators, who were all caught somewhere in the midst of shock, embarrassment, and disgust.

The woman began to scramble about the floor drunkenly for scattered pieces of clothing that had been strewn about, as the pungent odors of spilled wine, stale beer, and urine wafted out of the bathroom. The man behind her stood nearly naked—his trousers on one leg—and began to laugh, watching the woman struggle. The woman initiated an attempt to stand, first pulling up onto the toilet, then the sink, and as she turned, Michael could see wet toilet paper matted in her hair. Jo turned away, repulsed.

"Oh, Gawd," Tabitha gasped as the small group recovered from their shock. The man pulled the door closed and the spell was fully broken. Something deeper within Michael shattered too. And as with so many events, the only conscious thought immediately available to Michael was that there had been some impact within him, some consequence of what he had just seen. The significance of the evening would remain elusive to Michael for now, but it would begin to affect his psyche going forward, it would change the way he viewed his own relationships and the way he viewed other things that he believed. When looking at things going forward, he would want to open the door to see what was going on inside.

"I feel sick to my stomach," Jo said to Michael in a half-mocking tone, putting her hand on her abdomen. They all rose quickly from the bench, laughing nervously as they started up the stairs.

"That little vision could ruin a wet dream," Michael spoke nervously, trying to cover his uneasiness about what they had seen.

"I was close to orgasm but now I am not sure I'll ever have another orgasm again," Tabitha added and they all laughed.

As they reached the top of the stairs, Audrey paused, turned to Jo, and whispered to her while discreetly handing her a set of keys: "I called your husband and told him we were working late on a contract...and you would be staying with me at the company condo tonight. He said he understood and that it was no problem. Why don't you give him a call in a little while."

Jo was stunned, but just nodded her head and took the keys, not wanting to give away her surprise. She turned to look at Michael; he was still coming up the stairs behind her, laughing with Tabitha. She gave him a look telling him to wait, and he did as the other two women headed back to the table to join Bennie and Jon.

"They left me keys to a condo... they think we are staying together," she told him, her face blank.

"Yes, of course they do. No sweat, we can leave together, and then I'll head up to my hotel in Midtown." His answer caused a relieved expression to emerge on her face.

"One stipulation though," he added, tilting his head.

"What stipulation?" she asked, slowly looking into his eyes.

"You have to tell them I was great."

"What? Is that all you can think about?"

"Deal, or no deal?"

He folded his arms in mock defiance, and she smiled.

"Okay, I'll tell them that Catherine the Great herself would be pleased."

They both smiled broadly and broke into gentle laughter. They turned and followed Audrey and Tabitha back to the table.

Michael joked as he always did when things were tense. The sexual energy that had seemed so strong, so important, so overpowering, was gone in an instant. Love and sex moved in separate directions. Michael felt something for the woman behind the glass but he did not know what it was. Empathy? *No. Do I feel sorry for her? Maybe.* He realized it was more the loss of something inside, an image or concept of how everything fit together.

Love and sex were two different things: like the distinction between his work in New York and his home life, this was another schism. His mind pushed to keep things the way he believed they "should" be; he kept telling himself that the things he felt in his heart were in no way connected to the scene he left down the stairs. Nonetheless, how he felt moments before the door was kicked open, watching the sexual shadows... and then how he felt after, watching the woman struggle, drunk on the wet floor, seemed irreconcilable. Yet they were connected. What was playing in his mind, what he saw hazily through the smoky glass was special and beautiful, but the reality struck him as ugly and disgusting.

Fanning the Flames

Summer of 2001

Michael and Jo reached the table to find Bennie and Jon ordering food and wine for everyone. Michael looked inquiringly at Jo, who had pressed her hands into her pockets, but he could not read what was in her mind.

"Do you want to leave?" he whispered.

"Yes, I want to go." Jo answered a little too quickly, and a little too loudly, but Bennie smiled.

"Young love," Bennie announced to the rest of the table, as if to make excuses for Michael and Jo. Then he returned his attention to the couple. "See you tomorrow," he said, smiling his knowing smile. *Maybe he does know more than the rest of them,* Michael thought. *Maybe he can see things that even Jo and I can't see.*

After exchanging more pleasantries in farewell, the couple made their way arm in arm toward the door through the now-thinning crowd. As they navigated their way across the restaurant, Michael continued to reconcile the heat he felt with the disgust and dismay after he and the others had witnessed the shadowy bathroom coupling. When the veil of sexual illusion fell away, a door opened somewhere inside of Michael, a place where there are no words, primal and instinctual, but real nonetheless. And to see that the realness of the bathroom encounter was mostly constructed in his mind was a shock. Things were not as they appeared.

Something that had seemed real, something that he saw and heard with his senses. Something that had elicited a reaction from his body, had engaged his mind and his emotion and had real energy. *I could feel their love for one another and how much they cared for one another,* he thought. But then the door was kicked open and the illusion was revealed. Michael was experiencing a narrative in his mind of his own creation, he took something that was base and meaningless and created a story of deep love and beauty. And it was all in his thoughts.

But as Michael thought about what he had just witnessed, another veil fell away, only this one was not just of love and sexual illusion, it was instead a veil of surety of what was true and what was real. *How many things do I believe are true, based on my observations, are vulnerable to a door being kicked open?* The realization that some of his beliefs could be wrong did not make Michael feel less, but in a way he could not understand, made him feel larger, just less concrete. He felt less sure of things but more open to the experience of what lay ahead.

Michael and Jo were moving slowly up the alley, back to the main street to catch a cab, when Jo looked up at Michael. She was not smiling when she asked, "Do you mind walking? The condo is just across town to the East Side and I think I'd rather walk." She stared into his eyes, still no emotion showing on her face.

"Yeah, sure, I'd like to walk; I can catch a cab from there back to Midtown." They walked to the corner of the building, turning eastward. The air was warm, and as they faced into the night breeze, Jo took Michael's arm. She held firmly as if seeking security as her blouse danced wildly in wind. They meandered together, stopping now and again to look into the windows of the various shops along the avenue, slowly making their way across the island.

Suddenly, Jo let go of Michael's arm and hopped like a schoolgirl to a store window that fascinated her. Large glass boxes on both sides of the entrance featured jewelry, pipes of all sizes and shapes, and cameras laid out seemingly haphazardly, but with the larger things staked further back making them look like trees climbing up a hillside. Countless shiny things, from Indian trinkets to Japanese electronics, were arranged in no apparent order other than size behind the nearly invisible glass.

"Let's buy each other a gift!" she exclaimed as she turned excitedly to Michael.

"Okay," he nodded, trying to match her enthusiasm.

"Ten-dollar limit and we are on our own…let's surprise each other, and no peeking at what the other buys!"

"Agreed," Michael said emphatically, then asked, "Does the $10 include tax?" Her look told him the answer: *Don't be ridiculous*. Michael found a place in the shop where there were many interesting charms; some looked very old. The first thing he picked up was a silver leaf, and when he examined it, he found a small white price tag tied to a string: $23. He looked over his shoulder at Jo, who was smiling, enjoying herself. He thought for a moment more, knuckle to his chin as if the weight of thinking required extra support, considering buying the leaf. But somehow, playing by the rules was important so he put down the silver leaf and continued to skim through the scattered charms. Three small hearts—all different but striking—caught his attention. They were made of metal, silver, he thought, but old, handcrafted for sure because the surface of each was rough and aged.

He picked up the first and on a small rectangle of white paper nearly as large as the heart stuck to the bottom, he found the price: $3. The next heart he picked up was rounder and fatter, but still only $3. The third was bigger yet and its price tag said $4. *Perfect*, he thought.

Michael headed toward the register just as Jo found a small gift that she was more than pleased with, so much so that she rushed to the register to get in front of Michael. She clasped the little gift in her closed hand and held it unconsciously over her heart.

"No peeking," she reminded as she turned to look over her shoulder at him.

"Not a chance," he smiled. "It's you who's likely to peek," he teased.

"What makes you think you know me?"

"Tell me I'm wrong…I bet you always looked for your Christmas presents." Her pouty smile told him he was right.

"Well, aren't you the know-it-all, Mr. Smarty Pants," she laughed.

As Jo paid, keeping herself between Michael and the gift, he pretended to look over her shoulder. She put the gift straight into her pocket and turned to give him the disapproving look of a Catholic school nun. Then she moved behind him, turning her back to let him pay without her seeing his gift. She bumped him firmly from behind, making him smile.

"Hurry up," she said impatiently as he finished paying the man behind the register.

"Alright, now do we exchange?"

"Nope," came her short answer.

"Okay, then when?"

"When I say and not until the time is right." She was smiling and pursed her lips and tilted her head in a manner that told him she was in charge of this project.

"So when will that be?" Michael asked.

"I'll let you know," she answered as she turned and headed out of the shop. He followed her out and matched her pace; she was smiling and walking with a lighter step now. They passed under a streetlight that illuminated her hair as it moved, sparkling in the wind. Michael stopped to watch her as she kept walking. Noticing that he was no longer next to her, Jo stopped a few feet away and turned to look at him. She followed his gaze, looking down the street to see what had caught his attention.

"What do you see? Can you see the river from here?"

"Right now, you're as far as I can see," he said, meeting her eyes. She stopped smiling, looked down, then walked resolutely toward him to take him by the hand. She solemnly looked up into his eyes with an unreadable expression. They began to walk again, slowly drawing nearer to one another.

"Famous Ray's Pizza, The Original!" Michael read the sign with even more enthusiasm than Jo had shown at the charm shop. "I have always wondered where the original was, and here it is!" He turned away from the glare of the neon sign toward Jo.

"We have to eat here!" he cried.

"Here?" she asked incredulously. "Are you sure?" She dragged out the last word—"sure"—as if to convince him otherwise.

"Yes! I mean, it's Famous Ray's." He paused for effect, then added, "The Original?" He extended his hands convincingly. Jo looked at him for a moment, hesitating.

"Oh, all right," she breathed out, shaking her head and smiling. They went in, got in line, and each picked out and paid for a slice, then looked for a table. They were all high and had no chairs; this was a standing-only pizza parlor. There was little ambiance with little charm, and unfortunately, the taste of the pizza matched the décor.

"Is it time yet to exchange gifts?" Michael asked.

"No," came Jo's curt answer.

"This pizza is awesome!"

"Noooo," she replied vigorously. "This is poorly flavored cardboard. I actually think that cardboard with my mother's sauce on it would be much better." Michael did not look convinced, so she added, "Are you from Texas or something?"

"Well, yes, actually," he answered, smiling. "'Something,' anyway." They finished up the pizza quickly and continued walking down the avenue. The night was pleasant and the streetlights filtered through the leaves of the few scattered trees. They strolled easily across the sidewalk: cement blocks that met one another awkwardly, seeming to pitch on the constantly moving earth as if each had decided where to move and choosing the most comfortable place to sit. They walked into the gentle breeze all the way to the water's edge where lights stretched up the entire length of the river as far as the eye could see. Just before them, a bridge was dressed in lights—long drooping rows raced up the centuries-old stone towers that shouldered the daily weight of commuters, cars, trucks, and pedestrians.

Jo, who seemed to glow in the city lights, pulled her hands into the sleeves of her sweater and crossed her arms.

"Now," she said.

"You go first," Michael replied. She reached into her pocket and pulled out a flat, metal lotus, It was intricate, dainty, and beautiful in design but a little dull with age.

"I think it must be from an earring. It stuck in my mind…who bought it, what it meant to them, and how was it lost. It looks old, very old." She handed it to him. He took it and looked at it closely, holding it up to the streetlight above them, rubbed it between his thumb and forefinger then he pretended to test it with his teeth. He made her smile.

"A lotus," Jo said in a deep, gravelly tone as Michael looked deeply into her eyes. Then, she turned her head a bit and spoke to try to break the spell that was coming over her: "So…what'd you get me?"

"Close your eyes," Michael commanded, staring intently until she obeyed. "Put out your hand," he said.

"If it's anything moving, I am going to scream."

"It is not alive," he said, trying not to laugh.

Jo slowly put out her hand and Michael dropped the three small hearts into her palm, then closed her hand around them. She slowly opened her eyes and her hand, touching the hearts gently with the forefinger of her other hand. As she picked up one after the other, she felt her own heart opening in a way she had never experienced.

"They are beautiful," she said quietly as she moved them with her finger in her palm. "Three hearts: what do they mean?"

"What makes you think they mean anything?"

She raised her brow at him: "I've watched you. You are one of those people. You're one of those 'everything has meaning' guys."

"Is that so? Who's the smarty pants now?"

Jo was smiling at him and he returned the smile as he answered: "Three hearts, each representing one of the three kinds of love."

"Keep talking," she urged, looking into his eyes again. Michael began to walk slowly around her in a circle, hands in his pockets. He looked up, then paused, kicking his shoe against the pavement, as if the motion would help him speak.

"Well, I am not sure about the order, but let's start with Eros: erotic love."

"You mean true love?" She asked.

"No, I am not sure that Eros is true love. I mean, it sure is the love that makes people do crazy things, you know, attack-Troy-to-get-Helen kind of love."

"Are you sure you have your facts right?" she teased him.

"Do you want to know what they mean or not?" he mock scolded. She pretended to pout.

Michael continued, "This kind of love is romantic but it's based in how the other person makes you feel. So, not true love." Jo gave him a skeptical look.

"Next is, um…" he looked up again as if the answers were in the distant stars. "…Philos love," he grinned at her, proud he could remember.

"And what does 'Philos' mean?" she asked, smiling.

"You know, don't you?"

"Yes. Philos love is the love between friends," she said. "Continue."

"The third little heart represents Agape: unconditional or God's love."

"So which is true love?" she asked seriously, her smile gone again.

"All of them together."

"They're beautiful. I love them," she whispered as she put them in her pocket. "You make love sound so simple," she observed as they began walking together along the river again in no particular direction. "Besides," she continued as they walked, "Love is a dangerous word."

"How so?" he asked as he turned to her, his hands still in his pockets.

"Well, there are so many things attached to the word. Everyone has history, or some thoughts about what it is. Everyone talks about finding their true love, they look so hard that they find someone that fits all their ideals, then they project on that person some concept, only finding supporting examples of things they do, then nature pours on the endorphins and you are intoxicated, unable to see anything or anyone else."

"Sounds like you are talking about someone in particular," Michael replied, startling Jo a bit. She looked down at the sidewalk, then out at the river, then stopped walking. Facing Michael and brushing back her windblown hair, she explained: "I guess I loved my husband. I mean, he seemed like the right choice. Our families were connected, I knew he'd be a great father, a good provider, and he is very good to me. It seemed like it at the time," she was searching for words, for thoughts that she could not find to describe things she was feeling, something that was not yet clear to her.

"The mind is always the last to know things," she said. Then they began to walk again in thoughtful silence. Jo knew there were things that she was feeling that she dared not say out loud. "Sometimes the body and the heart feel things that they shouldn't."

"What kind of things?" Michael asked, sincerely unaware where she was going with her words.

She began again, "If I had known when I was younger that a person could feel things—powerful things—but that what everyone else wanted and saw as perfect might not necessarily be the right thing."

Suddenly Michael knew what Jo was trying to say, but he remained quiet.

Jo went on: "Powerful feelings make you feel out of control. I don't like feeling out of control. And I cannot live in two worlds at the same time," she looked at him, hoping he knew what she was saying.

"I think I understand what you are saying," he said slowly. In his mind he thought she was telling him in a nice way that they would never be together.

"What do you think about love?" Jo abruptly changed the subject and Michael went along with it.

"Well," he said, rubbing his chin theatrically, lightening the mood of their conversation. "You know I am a bit of an expert amateur philosopher—I mean, I had two semesters in college."

"Just answer the question, smart guy," Jo retorted, happy for the easier tone their conversation was taking.

"Love, I think, is not something we find by searching for it. You know the Rumi description of the fish in the ocean, swimming and swimming searching for water."

"Fish, in the ocean?" her tone was sarcastic, and she was about to laugh. "I talk about romantic love and it makes you think about fish?"

Michael smiled as he replied, "I think we are already immersed in love...we cannot avoid it. We sometimes think we are missing it, so we search for it...and it is in searching that we begin to imagine that we don't have it. We search, find someone, imagine we feel true love, then when that person has failed us, we think that love has failed us. Such love is blind, it is merely infatuation. This kind of love is bound to fail. We feel addicted to the other person, when all we were really addicted to was ourselves. We wanted the other person to give us something and when we didn't get what we wanted, we pouted or ran away or sometimes, worse."

"Then what is 'true love'?"

"True love is what is made of God, not the religion stuff or the relationship stuff."

"I mean with another person…what does true love with another person look like?"

"Oh, that. Well, when we find another person who makes us feel love no matter what is returned. If you love someone when they don't love you back, or are mad at you or something, and you just love them, you feel love, you have love, you want the best for that person even if they want someone else, that is true love," Michael concluded, pleased with his answer.

"That is the biggest piece of sentimental crap I've ever heard," Jo answered.

"Do you want to come up to the condo?" she asked, suddenly. There was a momentary pause during which neither of them moved nor spoke. The question caught Michael by surprise but he was trying to pretend that it hadn't.

"…to listen to some music, maybe grab a bottle of wine at the corner store on the way," she was on the move again, walking towards the condo. "Hey, Audrey told me these condos have gas logs. Will you light the fire for me?" she added the request awkwardly.

"A fire in the summer?" he asked her.

"And why not?"

"One summer fire coming up."

His answer pleased her.

"Oh, and yes," he added, "I would like to come up to listen to some music. That would be nice."

"Why do so many powerful men and the women who work for them have affairs?" Jo asked.

Her direct approach to everything should have been no surprise to Michael by now, but it was, keeping him a little unsettled in a way that he decided he liked. Michael took a deep breath and made a serious attempt at answering the question.

"Well, I think for the woman, she gets all the things she wants in a relationship: trust, in the know, full disclosure, it probably feels more like a relationship than anything she gets from anyone else."

"What about the man?"

"Well, for most men, the woman only needs to be attractive... and interested." They both laughed as he added the last part.

They approached the small, overstocked corner store and walked in, squeezing in among the shelves that ran from floor to ceiling. The busy store was suffocating to Michael, who had been raised in open spaces so unlike these big-city streets, and he felt uneasy as he followed Jo too closely down the narrow aisles. She was efficient, snatching a bottle of wine, good cheese, red grapes, and a long, slender baguette wrapped in brown paper. After Jo paid, they walked in companionable silence to the condo, making their way up the long broad stone steps into a large vestibule, then up the stairs to the condo door.

Michael held the groceries while Jo fumbled with the key. She looked into his eyes as she turned the key, thinking that this moment should be awkward but it felt amazingly comfortable to her. She opened the door with a little effort and they both peered in, a little astonished at the lavish room before them. Everything inside was modern, elegant, and new.

"Is there is a whole side of our business that I never knew existed?" Jo quipped, breaking the silence. They both entered the condo, moved naturally now: Michael to the fireplace and Jo to the small kitchen that opened to the cozy den. Michael found a lighter and a key for the gas logs, opened the flue, and lit the fire.

"Nice logs...these are the expensive ones," he spoke aloud but mostly to himself. Then he stood up to examine a small stereo on a tall, thin table against the wall, locating the power button and tuning it until he found a soft romantic rock song. Meanwhile, Jo cut the bread and cheese and rinsed the grapes. Michael opened the wine and found two glasses. When they converged on the leather couch facing the fire, it was as though they had done this together a thousand times. Everything felt right, nothing felt awkward. They sat comfortably together and stared into the fire.

"I'm married," she broke the silence.

"Yeah, I know. Me too," he answered her.

"Kids?"

"Two," he replied. These were questions about things that they both felt that they should have known by now; it was as if their relationship was merely continuing from some earlier point and they were filling in all the gaps.

"I have a girl," she said, knowing all the questions before they were asked.

"What age?" he asked.

"Four," she answered, "And yours?"

"I have a girl and a boy, four and two."

"What the hell are you doing fooling around?" she asked, moving away from him just a bit, but noticeably.

"Hey, it takes two to tango!" was Michael's instantaneous response, but as the question sunk in, he asked, "Are we fooling around?"

Jo smiled just a little looking into his eyes and he noticed what it did to him, penetrating to some place that rendered him powerless. He wondered if she knew. He leaned closer and kissed her as softly and as lovingly as he was able. She did not return his kiss nor did she resist. As he slowly withdrew, she was looking intently into his eyes, first one, then the other, back and forth, not smiling, but absorbed.

"I don't want to have an affair." She spoke more honestly than anyone Michael had ever known.

"I know. Me neither. No one ever wins and it is bad for everyone."

"Hold me." It came out like a demand so Jo said it again differently: "Will you just hold me?"

Michael was looking directly into her eyes now and he had the slight sensation of falling, but he could not sense in what direction...

just falling. He leaned back and held her, an act that seemed somehow more intimate than anything else. He could sense it: It was closer to love than anything else. Closer than kissing, closer than sex, closer than making love he was sure, but he also was sure that he did not know why.

Unfortunately, he was sure that by holding her now—and being held by her—there was going to be pain ahead. One way or another, no matter how things played out, someone was going to get hurt. Michael thought he could face fists, crashing in his car, or dodge bullets, but the thought of how hard two reckless lovers hit when they crash was more than he wanted to think about. So he decided not to think, and he stayed in her arms discovering that he liked to be held; even more, he realized he had longed to be held, something he had not allowed himself to acknowledge before this moment. He did not allow a single thought beyond this cozy and warm little room.

Looking into Jo's open and endless eyes in this moment, Michael knew that she could see it too. He felt an urge to run—from a possible relationship, from her— not because he judged that what they were doing was wrong and not because he feared retribution, nor an angry husband nor a punitive wife. He wanted to run because he feared for his own heart. And though his heart began to pound, he stayed.

"I want you." He said it differently than he said it that first time. "I don't want to own you. And I am not saying that I will want you 10 years from now or even one year from now. I am not asking you to leave your husband and I am not offering to leave my wife. I think that this must be—has to be—some crazy, temporary thing that will fade—has to fade. But right now, I want you and I am more than content to just lie here and hold you."

He was not even sure what he was saying so he just stopped talking.

"I know," she said, "all the more reasons I love you." Jo stopped speaking abruptly, then stammered, "I mean, drawn to you." But the word was already said. "I mean love you like... like I would love a dear friend. Ah, fu..." she sighed heavily. And now Jo stopped talking, feeling uncomfortable, wondering how she had let the word slip out, then quietly acknowledging to herself that she had meant to say it. *But how could I possibly love him?* she thought to herself.

"I want you to stay." Again she made a demand but she re-phrased it as a question: "Will you stay just to hold me all night? I don't want to have sex but I want you to stay."

"Of course," Michael said, then put his arm around her and pulled her closer. The strength of his arm and his pull felt substantial to Jo: It felt real and it made her feel desired, wanted, needed in her now-crazy world. Michael leaned back deeper on the couch and she leaned on him. He lay still now, his breath easing and steadying. She lay her ear on his chest and rested, listening to the air entering and leaving his lungs. Then, leaning on him gently, she pulled a blanket off the back of the couch and spread it over them.

Settling in and snuggling into him again, everything felt pleasant—the fire, the warmth of each other's bodies, and the music. Jo twisted beneath the blanket and under her clothing, then her hand appeared from under the blanket, dropping her bra to the floor. Michael began to get more comfortable too as he squirmed to unbuckle his belt, then his pants, kicking them out from under the blanket. They both began to giggle.

"I feel like a teenager on my parents' couch," he laughed.

Then they were both still again, watching the hissing fire, listening to the song on the radio: Neil Young was singing about searching for a heart of gold. Their thoughts moved about softly with the melody of the song, and the vibration that touched them was theirs, a collective vibration in that moment, stronger than anything they could imagine, memories from before being here or thoughts of how things would be after they leave. Jo grasped Michael's arm with both her hands, her eyes beginning to well a bit, and she was not sure why. They breathed together, both feeling expanded in some way.

"This feels right," Jo said, letting the words out for herself to hear. "But this could not possibly last, this feeling."

"What are you feeling, Jo?"

They were whispering to one another.

She paused for a moment, caressing his bare arm and staring into the fire.

"Right now, I feel I would give everything to stay here, stay just like this. It would destroy my life and hurt everyone around me. But all I can think about right now in your arms is how I am going to keep myself together once you are gone."

"Let's not think about anything. Let's just stay in this moment: It does feel right. It feels…..I just can't put a word on it. This feels…"

"Like home," she finished his thought for him.

"Yes, it feels like home," he said, louder, no longer whispering.

"Yes, it feels like home," she echoed then nestled deeper into Michael and closed her eyes to sleep. Again, Michael had the sensation of falling, and while normally he would have tensed to brace for an impact, this time he didn't tense nor brace himself. He did not resist but let himself free-fall. He straightened up a bit, and Jo opened her eyes to look into his. She pulled tighter.

Not having sex was not keeping them from intensifying their feeling towards each other but just the opposite. With no relief from the building energy, their hearts drew closer. Neither could sleep but both closed their eyes and pretended to drift off.

This is better, Michael thought to himself, *less complicated*. Making love only acts as a catalyst to so many constellations of cause and effect within the mind, constellations of "if this, then that," guilt, baggage, negative thoughts. *Yes*, Michael thought, *lying here is just fine, warm by the fire but not in the flames of passion and deceit.*

At just that moment, Jo leaned up and kissed him deeply. She rolled into him, tangled her legs with his, and put her arm around him. She unbuttoned her shirt, then lifted his white undershirt, pressing her ample, supple breasts against his bare chest. His mouth was near hers and he felt himself breathing in her breath. He ran his hand up into her hair and grasped a handful. They caressed each other; he moved his foot under hers, gently rubbing the arch of her foot.

Jo was letting herself fall into Michael and the feeling was overwhelming. She spoke to cut the tension: "I can't believe you lit a fire in the summer."

"You asked me to."

"Do you always do everything people tell you to do?"

"Yes," he said, mock-seriously, rolling back a little. "Everything!"

Jo was smiling playfully now.

"Lick my nose," she commanded. He leaned over and licked her nose. "Eew." She wiped her now-wet nose, then started laughing. "That was gross."

"You shouldn't have asked me to lick your nose," Michael grinned. Jo was looking into his eyes, and her smile once again left her. Her skin flushed as her body reacted to his, and she had never felt like this before.

"I just don't understand how I can feel like this. This is crazy. I barely know you."

"Zzzzz," he feigned snoring and sleeping. She pretended to pick his nose and put a pretend booger in his mouth, making him snap awake. "Okay, that was uncalled for!" he exclaimed, tickling her until she laughed aloud. They lay still for a moment, both smiling. She ran two fingers across a round scar on his chest, then to a linear scar just below that was about three inches long.

"Is this a bullet scar?" she asked softly. He did not answer. "They say you are a killer," she went on, words just falling out of her mouth.

"Who says?" His mood instantly changed to serious.

"Sorry, baby, I don't mean anything by it. I know what kind of a person you are, and you're no killer. I am sorry I brought it up. I just want to know everything about you."

"I am not a killer. I am a survivor and there is a difference," he said as though he was speaking to himself but he knew that killing a man was no easy thing to get by, and he occasionally tortured himself with thoughts of not deserving happiness or deserving entrance into any imagined heaven. After pausing for a moment he took a breath to continue but she put her fingers to his lips, "Shh, baby, shh."

Michael stopped as Jo lay back into him and he relaxed again.

"I do love you," she said. "It should be strange saying that to you but it doesn't feel that way."

"I love you too," he responded simply. Then they held each other tightly, tangled naturally and comfortably together, fitting next to one another as though they had been sleeping together for lifetimes.

"I am sorry I asked about it. I won't ever ask again, it doesn't matter. I know you and I am holding you. That's all that matters."

"It's okay, baby, I'll tell you whatever you want to know. I'll tell you everything."

"I want to know everything. I want to have you completely." So he began to tell her, it was the first time he told anyone.

Hell's Kitchen

Fall of 1982

It was getting late and the streams of office workers wearing suits and overcoats had dwindled. Now, the people of the night, dressed mostly in black and leather, were awakening to fill the clubs and bars of Westside Manhattan. A young Michael Tantalus, who had been walking for miles, sat down, choosing a place without knowing why. He was not tired but he was ready to meet someone, to connect with these people he watched walk by: There were more people than he had ever seen in one place.

He was fresh in the city, and he stood out in the way he walked, the way he dressed, and most noticeably, the way he talked. His hair was long, thick, and wavy, lightened by long hours in the bright Texas sun. His skin was deeply tanned and his lean body was muscled into a physique born of the long and heavy labor of growing up on a ranch. He had grown up performing the kind of labor that made a young man grow up fast, hard, and handsome; work that also wore men out, leaving them withered before old age. His hands were rough, as was he. On the ranch, though, he had never considered his life one of labor. He loved the bright, open prairie, the southern end of the plains on the Texas panhandle.

Michael's upbringing had made him strong and confident and it showed in the way he walked. And in a city where most looked down at their feet, went about their business quickly and without eye contact, his open and inviting manner was more than noticeable.

In fact, he was avoided by most New Yorkers, who held the ingrained belief that anyone looking to engage could be nothing but trouble.

He wore blue jeans so faded they were almost white but they didn't have a single tear. A wide Indian belt with symbols formed out of small colored beads roped through the belt loops, and of course, he wore cowboy boots: brown, well-worn, and very comfortable. His eyes were bright because the city excited him. There was neither fear nor trepidation in him as he walked in the wilderness of glass and steel, greeting anyone willing to meet his eye.

"Howdy," he smiled at an old woman with silver, wispy hair as she passed slowly, carrying a brown bag of groceries. She looked up and smiled back, giving him all the encouragement he needed to be even more enthusiastic in his salutations as people walked by him on the busy sidewalk.

The night air was cooling but many of the bars still left their doors and windows open to the summer. Rough-hewn wooden tables and unsteady chairs spilled onto the sidewalk outside of the bar where Michael chose to sit under the dappled shadows made by the neon light of a large sign shining through a tree. Michael had been walking since earlier in the day when the streets had been busy. But now, as night overcame the dusk, the noise moved from the pavement outside into the bars, loud with jukeboxes, bands, and people trying to shout over the music but not really wanting to talk. From where he sat, he could see the corner where hookers and johns danced around one another, sizing up their opportunities and haggling their worth.

Eventually, the bartender noticed him and walked over to the table. "What can I get for you?" he asked. The question only partially pulled Michael's attention away from the movement of the women walking down the street wearing very short shorts and higher heeled shoes than he had ever seen.

"Tequila. No salt, no lemon. And a beer," Michael gave his order without ever looking away from the corner. Then he asked, "What exactly is going on down at the corner?" The waiter turned to look at the prostitutes waving at the slowly passing cars. Michael's naïveté dawned on the bartender, and a large, kind smile came across his face as he asked, "Where is home, friend?"

"I live just around the corner a few blocks away above the Blarney Stone, that's where I work," Michael was still looking at the corner watching the curious behavior of the women and the passing men. The bartender smiled, tossed a towel over his shoulder, and asked what he wanted to know.

"Where did you grow up?" he asked.

"Seronia, Texas, a little south of Amarillo. I'm afraid it's not much of town."

"Well, my friend, that nonsense going on up at the corner? Well, that's just the city being the city. We're closing up the sidewalk so why don't you come in and sit at the bar?" Michael nodded and rose to walk into the barroom. Just inside, Michael paused to survey the room, spotting an open stool about three quarters of the way down the long, narrow bar. He walked slowly, feeling the energy in the crowded tavern. As he sat down, the bartender met him with the tequila and the beer, setting it in front of him.

"There you go, buddy. Can I get you anything else?"

"Nope, I think I'm good. Thank you," Michael smiled as the bartender walked away. He tipped up the shot glass and let the tequila pour down his throat. There was a sting and then an almost immediate warming. "Ahhhh," he let out the sound naturally, unaware of anyone around him. He began to pick the label off of the beer bottle in front of him for lack of anything else to do.

"They say that sexually frustrated people pick the labels off their beer," the woman next to Michael said to him. He immediately stopped, turning slowly towards the woman, first with his eyes then the rest of his head.

"I'm kidding," she said, but didn't smile.

"Whew. I was pretty worried there for a minute." Michael flashed her as big a smile as he could without laughing.

"Let me guess, that is not a Westside Irish accent, is it?"

"Not unless you mean the west side of Texas?"

"Let me guess again... I'm really good at this, a psychic almost. Let me see, you are from TEXAS?!" the woman teased.

"Lucky guess. Hey, you know how to figure out for sure if someone is from Texas?"

"Okay, I'll bite, how does a person figure out for sure that someone is from Texas?" She was as sarcastic as she could be.

"You don't have to figure it out: They'll tell you within five minutes of meeting you."

"I am Arella," she smiled genuinely, offering her name with a slight nod of her head.

"Michael. Michael Tantalus." He extended his hand then started to retract it, thinking to himself that it is rude to extend your hand first to a woman. It did not matter to Arella as she grasped his retreating hand firmly.

"It is nice to meet you, Michael. What brings you to our lovely city?"

Michael noticed that Arella was shaking just a little—she was nervous—and her eyes wandered about the barroom as she engaged in light conversation with Michael.

"Are you expecting someone?" Michael asked her.

She smiled in recognition that she was talking to Michael but looking elsewhere, then said, "Yes, my boyfriend."

"Should I be worried?" Michael's mocking concern was lost on her.

"Oh, no, he is not that kind of a man," she answered seriously, almost glowing. It was obvious to Michael that she was in love with this man.

At just that moment, he appeared in the door, pausing for just a moment to search for Arella, then made his way to her. They greeted with a quick and nervous kiss as if on a clandestine tryst. The man had dark, curly hair, a slightly large nose, and an olive complexion. The couple's appearance clashed in some way but Michael was not sure how. Ethnicity maybe, but Michael wasn't sure. He looked at the two, trying to use his upbringing as a reference point. But in Texas, there were just Texans, Native Americans, and Mexicans. They were more alike than different; differences are lost in a harsh, arid land where everyone gathers on Sundays to pray, mostly for rain.

The jukebox quit suddenly in the middle of a song. The silence exposed the soft murmuring of conversations across the bar room and they wound down to silence. Michael turned to see three men standing in the doorway. Arella was staring determinedly in the other direction as if hoping not to be noticed by the men. Michael suddenly noticed that all three of the men were holding guns.

"Everyone stand up, and slowly. Make sure your hands are where I can see them!" the man commanded, waving his gun blatantly to make sure everyone could see it. The gun was a large, shiny revolver: an arrogant display of a firearm. Not a gun that was carried as a concealed weapon but a gun that was carried for other men to fear. The lead man walked unwaveringly into the bar and his two dangerous, laughing men followed, taking prearranged posts. The largest man stood guard by the door; he had unplugged the jukebox. Now, he bent down and plugged it back in.

"This concerns nobody here except two people. Most of you in here know who I am and you know what I am capable of doing. I want you all palms down on the bar and nobody moves. Nobody has to get hurt." He was now waving the gun.

Michael's eyes were fixed on the large revolver, a six shooter. He had grown up around guns and around men who wielded them, so he knew about guns. He knew this gun was large caliber with lots of firepower; while one shot most likely could kill a man, it was not very accurate.

Michael's ancestors had been good with guns. Knowing guns and being efficient at killing meant survival. It meant that their families could live, so the knowledge of guns, shooting, and killing had been passed along the line. Killing for meat for the family to eat meant hunting was essential. But it was often essential to kill men, too—those who threatened the ranch or livestock in a vast untamed West Texas desert, where the only laws were your family and your gun. It had been kill to live, kill to survive in the not-so-distant past of the wild and lawless open lands called "Indian lands" until the mid-1800s.

The skills that enabled these men to survive were passed down, and as the need to protect oneself and family waned with the growing presence of law enforcement, these groups of men were called to the military. They fought for their country; there were Texas war heroes from every war: Texas Independence against Mexico, the Civil War, WWI, WWII, Korea, and Vietnam. The men of Michael's family had lived with death, and as the men of Michael's family came home from war, he had learned that you could tell by their eyes who had killed and who had not. So as Michael stood, with strangers so far from home, he was able to size up the situation. These men—all three—were killers, there was no doubt in his mind.

Along with everyone else there, Michael put his palms on the bar. He was surprised by the amount of information that was coming through his hands, as if his senses were heightened so he could sense the smallest textures and vibrations. His heart began to pound and his mind cleared. Tears began to run down Arella's face and the man to Michael's right began to whimper, "They're going to kill us. They're going to kill us all."

The lead man clubbed Arella's boyfriend in his back with the butt of his gun, knocking the air out of him. As he slouched, trying to regain his breath, the lead man slung him by one arm into the tables and chairs against the wall. Michael, frozen, could feel the grain of the wood on the bar. The sudden violence drew a gasp from the small crowd but Michael remained silent and motionless. Then, the lead man walked slowly to Arella, put the gun against the back of her head, and pulled the trigger.

The blast momentarily blinded and deafened Michael and the horror left him in shock. He waited for the next move, expecting it to be his death but the man put his gun down on the bar a short distance away from Michael and moved toward the man who was now cowering and crying, crouched against the wall.

Arella's blood had splattered across Michael and was beginning to drip down his jaw. His ears still were ringing loudly but his sight and thoughts slowly returned to him. Arella was dead: a bullet in its un-judging execution of its circumstance had pierced her mind and all that was Arella was now on its way to dust.

Arella is no longer here. Arella is gone. Arella is dead. Michael played the thoughts over and over, trying to find his bearings. Then his thoughts began to race. *Arella is dead. Everything will die. All living things, all things will wear away. Eventually, even the sun will extinguish, the sun will die... all the stars, everything, all matter is on the path towards total dissipation into nothing.*

"Stop. Stop," he whispered to himself, trying to halt his own obsessive thinking. *Our time here on earth is a blink in the life and eventual death of the entire universe.* Somehow, this last thought was more fearsome than the murder of Arella that he had just witnessed and more terrifying than the thought of his own death. A murder resulting in the tragedy of a few less breaths, Arella's premature demise meant little in the larger scheme of planets, suns, and space.

But in Michael's body, a fever was rising. He took short breaths, trying to gain some sense of self-control and still his mind was telling him to remain calm. He could even hear his father's voice in his head saying the words he had heard so many times before, *"Remain calm."* As though the words could soothe and quiet his body.

But a woman he had just met had died. The sudden violence, the blast of the gun, and the splattering of her blood all together began to fester within him like a sore exposed to every kind of uncleanliness. "Blatant disregard of...," Michael never finished his sentence and no one in the bar was listening to him anyway.

Rationality proved unable to convince his body to accept what his conscious mind was saying was the right thing to do, to accept its rational conclusion but it was a subjective and limited truth. Ultimate truth was served in Michael's genetics and his conditioning and his instincts. The beast within Michael, like an unbridled elephant of his subconscious, threw the chattering monkey of his conscious control aside and took over the situation.

Three men, one shot gone, five bullets, five shots left....perhaps. He was calmly and methodically taking inventory of the situation. And he allowed just a bit of doubt to linger. The man at the end of the bar had a gun that Michael was unfamiliar with, some type of machine gun, an Uzi perhaps, he was not sure. But no matter, because in Michael's calculations, he represented the most immediate threat: He would be Michael's first target, definitely. *The man in the corner, he would be next. If he's a dead-eyed shot, then I'm dead.* Michael processed the thought as coolly as if he were reading through a recipe before he began cooking. *If the man is slow to react or anything less than an expert shot from, oh, I would guess 25 or so feet, then I have a chance.* Michael was thinking to himself. *Let's see, that brings me to the asshole beating Arella's boyfriend—if he has another gun hidden somewhere, his boot maybe, then I'm dead, but he's wearing loafers.* This observation made Michael laugh a little.

"They're going to kill us all," the man next to him predicted again, crying openly now, still keeping his hands on the bar. Michael looked again at the three intruders as though they were the only men in the bar.

"Don't be stupid, they are not going to kill us," the bartender whispered to Michael. He looked up across the bar into the bartender's eyes. Unblinking, the bartender shook his head no— a movement so slight, so subtle that no one but Michael could see. "Not worth it," he mouthed so that Michael could read his lips. At that precise moment, another drop of Arella's blood dripped off of Michael's face onto the bar. Both men stared at the crimson drop. Then Michael looked down at Arella's slumped, motionless body. His ears were still ringing. He looked up from Arella's blood-matted hair, and once again, looked at the gun on the bar just seven or eight feet away.

Three steps, five bullets, three men. Three steps, five bullets, three men.

His heart pounded as his mind made the words into a mantra. The now-raging elephant of his subconscious took over his heart, his soul, tapped into his genes and his warrior, ancestral past...the wealth of coding and conditioning that knew well just what to do next. His ears rang loudly as adrenalin pumped into his bloodstream, elevating his pulse and breathing, but he felt calm and focused. He was observing, watching himself from some high place where there was no fear, no doubt.

The monkey of his mind—reason—tried to speak but could not be heard over the conditioning. The moving elephant could not be stopped. The vibrations from the rock-and-roll blaring from the jukebox were barely audible to him, but they moved from the speakers to the floor, through the air, and into Michael, and he moved to the building beat. His rage grew, whether from the murder of Arella or the deep-seated drive to survive, to live, it did not matter: Michael was about to go into motion, and once moving, there would be no stopping him.

Three steps, five bullets, three men. He was no longer weighing the odds but beginning his attack. His thinking mind was pushed aside and his stomach took the reins while his heart whispered encouragement. He looked down the bar to the spot where the arrogant killer had left his gun after wiping Arella's blood off of it, fearing the action of no man. Perhaps he had never been challenged in his entire life, but that was about to change.

Streaks of Arella's blood were still visible on the gun and the bunched cloth the killer had used to wipe his gun was run in red. Michael looked back at the gun. *Yes,* he thought, *it's a large-caliber revolver.* This gun was to intimidate, hardly concealable, and it was meant to intimidate other men. Michael looked at the three men again. *Yes, they are all killers.*

And coming from a long line of men who had killed out of necessity—whether in war or protecting their lands in lawless times—Michael had known that men who had killed were different somehow. And now for just a moment, Michael thought about how they had been different from other men. He sensed that these were men who "had blood on their hands," as his aunt would have said. They all carried some wound that kept them at a distance; Even when in physical proximity, there was always space between them and the ones they loved—wives, mothers, sisters, daughters, sons, grandmothers, nieces, and nephews. They carried a certain quietness, but not a stillness or peacefulness. It was as though things that needed to be emptied from them were instead being carried on the inside.

Michael knew these men had been men of God, God-fearing, and all of them knew the story of Moses, shouted by preachers in dark suits standing at the pulpit with clenched fists. Moses led his people for 40 years through the desert, but because he had killed, he could not go to the Promised Land. And a man who had killed feared God and knew the story. *Well, to that man,* Michael was thinking, *surely there was nothing in life that could penetrate deeper. There was nothing more to lose and nothing more to fear when you are damned, but still walking the earth.* Michael had observed these men; some tried to make up for their transgressions, but walked without fear and did as they pleased, while others crawled into a bottle. The one thing they shared was that they weren't held captive by the limitations felt by others, by men who had not killed. And all these thoughts passed through Michael in a fraction of a moment. He looked at the gun, feeling the heaviness of "blood on his hands" before he even began.

Three steps, five bullets, three men, and the safety is off, the gun is ready to fire. Michael lifted his palm off the bar and stood, stepping over the fallen woman, and he was making his play. No one noticed nor reacted until Michael's second step. But then the killer wheeled away from his assault on Arella's boyfriend. Still holding a tight fist he began to scream at Michael but Michael heard nothing as he took the third step. Time slowed as everything in his body and mind sped up, adrenalin surged into his blood like gasoline and his heart pounded like a piston in a rapidly advancing machine. He felt completely serene, moving his hand to the gun on the counter as explosions of wood splinters moved down the bar inevitably toward him. He picked up the gun steadily, almost calmly, while bullets whizzed through the air all around him coming from the gun of the man standing at the jukebox. Michael looked up into explosions of barrel fire, but he remained focused on his task. As simply as if he were in the woods near his childhood home, he raised the gun, steadied as he aimed, breathed out, and gently squeezed the trigger. And with one shot, the bullet found its target, piercing skin and shattering the bone just off-center of the man's forehead. He immediately went limp and fell backward into the jukebox, then slid and fell forward in a lifeless heap.

Michael kept moving with the gun still raised, bottles on the shelves behind him shattering and exploding one after another. The man in the corner fired his gun angrily. Michael raised his gun at the second shooter, while the killer stood screaming, pulling the trigger too quickly, less steadily and less sure. The two men exchanged fire at a mere nine paces, and the bar filled with loud pops and strings of smoke. Michael kept squeezing, losing count of his shots and where the bullets were going until the second man fell forward, discharging his handgun once more on the floor. Silence, smoke, and stillness overpowered except for the still-blaring jukebox against the far wall. Now the final killer was moving. Michael spun in his direction as he approached, causing him to freeze.

"You are out of shots, and now I am going to kill you!" the man shouted at Michael. Then, he crouched down and lifted his pant leg, exposing a switchblade. Michael kept the gun pointed at him, but in truth, he had no idea if he had any shots left. He tried to count in his head; and while he was able to replay the sounds of the gunfire, he was unable to separate his shots from the others in his mind. The killer began to laugh as he pulled out the knife and rose slowly, extending the blade with a single click. The man stopped laughing then lunged at Michael just as Michael fired. The last bullet from the shiny gun found the man's skull and he collapsed on top of Arella's body.

Michael stepped over the man in a trance-like state. No one else in the bar moved. He walked to the first man, calmly bent over and picked up the machine gun. He looked at it for a moment, felt its still-hot barrel, then shot the rest of its bullets into the jukebox until it was silent. He dropped the gun and turned back toward the bar and the still-motionless other people, all stunned. As he began to come back to his senses, he began to shake. His breath was labored and he could feel a gurgle in his lungs. He sensed burning in his side and then heard a drip; he looked down to see a deep red splatter on his right boot. As he looked up and met the bartender's eyes, he felt himself fall backwards into the now-shattered jukebox as if in slow motion.

The bar slowly grew with movement. The cowering man never stood but crawled to his lover's body, pushing the killer's corpse off of her. He threw himself onto her cooling, bloody body and wept loudly. The bartender made a rapid phone call, and as he hung up, made his way to the jukebox just in time to catch Michael as he fell. Michael could hear sirens but his senses were fading as people rushed into the bar. He struggled to keep his eyes open as his sight darkened; he could still hear voices and feel the confusion of people all about him.

"There's a doctor waiting," the bartender was shouting orders. "Let's get everyone out of here!" More men came in the doors and quickly removed Arella, her lover, and Michael. The bartender announced, "I'm going with the kid," and that was the last thing Michael heard as he slipped into unconsciousness.

The bartender helped two other men put Michael in the back seat of a car, got in the back seat with him, and pulled off Michael's shirt, saying, "In the chest, he's hit in the chest."

"Doc wants to know where else?" The question came from a man in the front seat talking on a cell phone. The bartender looked over Michael quickly.

"I think that's it...miracle if you ask me, bullets where flying everywhere."

"Doc wants to know how much he's bleeding," the man in the front seat asked.

"God-damned lot, he's bleeding all over the place." The man in the front seat relayed the information back to the doctor on the phone.

"Doc needs to know what his blood type is."

"Hell if I know. Tell doc he's out, unconscious."

"Doc says keep talking to him, don't let him go out, and if he can't talk to you, see if he has a driver's license. The Doc says sometimes blood type is listed on it." The bartender began to fumble through Michael's pockets nervously.

"Hey buddy, stay with me, can you hear me?" he asked.

"Hey, what, what, where?" The words came out of Michael in moist, incomprehensible whispers. The bartender found Michael's wallet and pulled it out, holding it to the window of the swiftly moving car to get enough light to read.

"Type O positive. The license says he is type O positive." The bartender kept reading, "His name is Michael Tantalus, from Texas. Jesus H. Christ, he's a kid, not even eighteen years old and takes down a hit squad!"

"Holy shit, what was he packing?" asked the man from the front seat.

"Nothing, he used Poundstone's gun." The two men in the front seat looked back at the slumped and again unconscious Michael.

"You are telling me a kid took down Poundstone and two of his goons with their own gun?!"

"I know, frickin' unbelievable. Get this car to the doctor, we ain't no way letting this kid kick off!" The men turned back around and pulled down a narrow alley and to a back door of a tall brick building. They hurried Michael out of the car, into the building, and to the doctor, the movement bringing Michael back to some sense of consciousness.

The bartender began to talk, reassuring Michael. "Hey, we are at the Doc's place; he's going to fix you up, no worries. But we gotta get you out of the city for a while, maybe a long time. But you pull through and you got it made in this city. Man, do you got it made. You have any idea whose ass you saved tonight? It's big and everybody's going to know, you are going to be a frickin legend." But all the talk was lost on Michael. The bartender began talking to the doctor, but all Michael heard was whispers as he fell back into unconsciousness. He would never remember being here or having this conversation.

Michael fell into a dream.

Michael, aged five, lay on his back in soft green Saint Augustine grass next to his Grandfather, looking into an endless blue sky interrupted only by a few large puffy white clouds passing slowly by. Michael was holding a balloon and now as when he was a child, he had little or no thoughts. And as the child, he scanned the blue: There was nothing but the blue in his mind, no thoughts, no judgments, nothing but the joy of the moment.

He let the balloon free and watched as it rose and rose and became smaller and smaller into the sky that seemed like everything. A warm spring breeze caressed him, comforted him, even loved him as he lay watching the balloon with no thoughts, no judgments, and no fears. He was the balloon, he was the grass, and he was the sky. The balloon's rising stretched to the limits of his senses, to the edge of his sight, then it crossed into nothing, and at that point he felt divine.

"Michael, can you hear me?" the doctor's voice came into Michael's thoughts, bringing him back to the small room off a back alley in the meat-packing district, close to the Henry Hudson River. "Michael, if you can hear me, squeeze my hand." Michael responded to the distant voice, now sensing his hand being held by another hand, and he squeezed it. He tried to open his eyes, but the light was foggy and his head ached. "Very good, Michael." The doctor was doing something but Michael could not tell what. "You are going to make it, Michael. You have had quite a trauma but you don't need to do anything now but rest and heal. We have to move you, and I am going to give you a sedative, so rest Michael, Michael Tantalus."

The doctor said his name with some amount of respect but Michael could sense nothing. His thoughts began to come to him, jumbled: First, remembering how sick he had felt next to the jukebox looking down at the bloody body of the first man he had shot, then suddenly thinking of spring with its fireworks of mother nature, of life, and the blossoms and beauty. Now as he thought of the glorious green of the awakening forest that serpentine the valleys of his childhood farm, lining and following the creeks that ran through the land. The bright growth of spring seemed to give a definition to death, birth and death always married, a pair, one could not be without the other. He felt so far from right, and he searched his own mind for thoughts of how things should be and how they should not be. And he thought now of the balloon, how it had existed, rose into the sky, and then dissolved beyond the limitations of his perception. And then he slid effortlessly back into unconsciousness...

"I can't see it anymore, Grandpa! I can't see the balloon. Is it still there?"

"Ah, my young grandson, questions such as this one, it is the type of question that should be asked and answered," Grandpa started to chuckle just a bit, then continued, "We cannot know for sure that the balloon is there since we can no longer perceive it. But I believe that it is still there. There are many things that we cannot perceive or sense, Michael, that are indeed still there. You see, our senses are limited to some degree, this we know and accept, but so too are our minds. And this we do not so readily accept; in fact, most of the time most of us defend our limited minds as though our very existence depended on it." Then, Grandpa began to chuckle again. He was thinking of a distant memory or a situation long past and his attention drifted.

"Our minds are limited, Grandpa?" Michael's question brought his grandfather back to the subject at hand.

"Well, yes, Michael. You see, to sense things is one matter, but to interpret sensations and construct an event takes a mind program. And if you do not have a mind program for a certain experience? Well, then likely, you will not be able to have that experience. These biological mind/body machines we exist within were built and designed for this one realm here," the older man paused and looked over at his grandson. Michael was still looking up to the sky.

"Grandpa, that cloud looks like a puppy," the boy said, then began to giggle. Grandpa looked at the boy and was filled with joy. He lay back down into the cool grass and looked into the deep blue sky dotted with large pure white puffs of clouds.

"Why, yes it does! And look at that one: It looks like a bull!

Assorted Dealings

Morning, September 10, 2001

Sleepwalking, everyone is sleepwalking, Michael thought suddenly as he walked off the plane into the terminal of New York's LaGuardia airport. He had just flown in on the 6 a.m. flight out of Charlotte Douglas as he did every Monday. He meandered through a throng of people to the cab line outside, following all of the sleepy commuters, most of whom were wearing dark, warm, protective coats and dragging behind suitcases on wheels.

Paying no attention to the weather or anyone else around him, Michael was soon through the line and in a cab. The taxi bumped over old, broken concrete out of the airport and into Manhattan via the MidTown Tunnel, moving quickly in the cab lane past the other cars. Though he was nearly asleep, Michael's body knew the routine; he was on autopilot, barely noticing the traffic or anything else he passed. Michael, just like the other thousands who came into the city every day—day after day—was a walking to-do list, living in his thoughts, moving from task to task, barely noticing anyone else and rarely making contact. For a stranger to speak to someone would likely trigger built-in alarms and defense mechanisms.

There was one difference today: Michael was going to the hotel first, not straight to a meeting. The cab crossed town to the West Side and deposited Michael at the Time Hotel, his home away from home. *Something's different,* he thought as he passed Goldie—he didn't know her real name, but everyone called her Goldie—on the sidewalk.

"Good morning Goldie," he spoke cheerfully to the elderly homeless woman. And this small break from routine, saying hello to Goldie, brought him off autopilot and he began to notice things. Goldie looked up and smiled. She was dirty, covered in a dust that existed only in big cities like New York. Michael thought about giving her a dollar but when he opened his wallet all he saw were twenties, and not wanting to give so much, he walked on past her as she made incoherent sounds, "Mum mum mum mum, mum mum mum." Her sounds had the rhythm of words and sentences, but they were unintelligible.

Michael had heard the doormen call the old woman Goldie, but he had never asked why, merely accepting the name and keeping mostly to his own business. He behaved differently here than his home city of Charlotte. It was as though he adopted the local ways, almost acting as a "New Yorker" as soon as he landed at LaGuardia.

Once he entered the hotel, Michael knew what was different: It was this lower level entry lobby. He had walked into what appeared to be a giant glass box, with water pouring down on top of the glass ceiling and cascading down the glass sides. From all angles, colored lights showed through the moving water, creating a beautiful and mesmerizing illusion. Invisible speakers piped in mysterious music featuring a mixture of modern sounds and a solitary, nomadic flute. The water and the music made Michael feel he was in a trance. Once his eyes adjusted from the brighter outside light, he spotted the elevator which was on the far wall and had mirrored glass doors that made it almost invisible in the subdued, moving light. He pressed the button, moving inside when the doors opened, then ascended to the main lobby.

"Good morning, Mr. Tantalus," the desk clerk greeted him enthusiastically. Michael moved methodically across the lobby from the elevator to the front desk, his body executing the routine he had developed over the summer. Without being asked, he put his hand onto the mood pad sitting between him and the young, overly attentive desk clerk. He lifted his hand, leaving a blue impression of his palm and fingers. The desk clerk looked at the blue imprint, then smiled and tilted her head before speaking.

"Looks like you will be staying in a blue room this trip, Mr. Tantalus!" She seemed very excited about the result: Michael wondered if there was something in this that he was missing, for it seemed he should have felt more excited by the color of his room than he was. In what appeared to be one motion, Michael handed the attractive woman his credit card and traded his signature for a room key.

He walked down the long hall that was lined on both sides every foot or so by small, one-inch-by-two-inch televisions in neat, even rows. Michael suppressed the urge to count the little televisions but his mind tried to estimate instead so with a little effort he suppressed this urge as well. There was a pleasant odor, fabricated but sweet and lemony, and its effect was invigorating, adding to the manufactured environment an intentional illusion of fresh and clean, boxed within an old and dirty building exterior. Michael was early, and passing the maid pushing a cart down the hall. "Buenos dias," he greeted her.

So much stimulation and all aimed at the mind and the bodily desires, he thought as he dropped his suitcase on the bed and put his computer bag on the desk. He dialed into a conference call on his cell phone, then pushed the mute button and the button to put the phone in speaker mode. He then lay the phone carefully on the upper right-hand corner of the dark wood desk. Michael looked at the phone, and feeling it was not quite right, turned it slightly to bring it into alignment with the edge of the desk. He then picked up the hotel phone and dialed room service while listening to a droning voice calling out numbers from the perfectly placed cell phone.

"Good morning, Mr. Tantalus," the gentleman on the phone for room service greeted Michael as if he knew him, but most likely reading his name from a list.

"Coffee, cream, two eggs over easy, toast, white and dry, thank you."

He hung up the telephone without waiting for a reply. The voice on the conference call seemed small as it came from the cell phone, still perfectly placed on the desk. He thought about Jo, knowing he would see her soon; he reached into his pocket and pulled out the metal lotus that she had given to him. He smiled to himself, then stopped his mind before it could question the way his world had divided into two lives.

Movement always served to distract his mind so he rose and opened the curtains. It let in only the small amount of light that was able to find its way down the tall corridor formed by towers of brick, steel, and glass on all sides. He was opening the curtains out of habit only, as he rarely looked out the window these days. The movement was a shell of a habit formed when he was young, when he had wanted to see things, but now he didn't look… he had things to do.

Michael unzipped his computer bag, pulled out his computer, and placed it in the middle of the desk, equidistant from all the edges with all angles aligned, keeping the aesthetic symmetry that pleased him. He plugged in the power cords, first the computer, then the cell phone, always in the same order. Then the hotel's network cord, and he began to connect to his company's main system as the computer navigated all the security firewalls for him.

"Mike, you agree?" Hearing his name brought him back to the teleconference. He looked at the cell phone and had no idea what the question was.

"Yes, yes I do," he answered decisively, emphatically. He listened to the call for a moment to see if there was anything important being discussed, and after a small amount of time, decided that there was not. It was his opinion that these calls rarely discussed anything critical or even helpful. There seemed to be an endless number of calls set by people trying their best to justify their jobs and feed their endlessly hungry egos. *If not for the business being done on the streets by the sharks,* Michael thought, *there would be nothing for any of these remoras to feed on, and yet they act like they were the hunters themselves.* They were the self-appointed controllers and Michael loathed them, for in his estimation they added nothing, and the larger the corporation the more of them there were. They were the people who felt the need to control the out-of-control sales people without whom none of the controllers would have a job. They felt the need to limit the very activity that made their jobs possible. It was the same in everything, a few people made things happen then everyone else feeds off of their activity. *Why can't there be more men like Benjamin Adler?* He thought, but he doubted he really meant that. He thought briefly of his late grandfather. *There was nothing about this business world that Grandpa would have understood…or respected.*

Once again Michael sought to divert his own attention. He looked at the computer which was busy downloading emails. He picked at the breakfast, eating far less than he ordered, then took *The Wall Street Journal* from his computer bag and opened it across the computer keyboard, scanning the front page as he monitored the computer screen, searching both for anything important. He thus divided his conscious thought between the paper, the computer, and the teleconference. He felt fine when he was doing this work—even good—not realizing that it was like taking a pill to mask the pain of a migraine, avoiding the underlying discomfort. It was nearly always there, the signal that something was not right, but rather than investigate or even allow himself to acknowledge the signal, Michael just made himself busier.

Soon, the conference call was over and Michael was on the move again. He grabbed his briefcase and cell phone and hurried out the door and down the hall. He looked at each of the miniature televisions on the walls as he passed. They were all on the same channel and, though tiny, they bounced flashing lights on the walls, ceiling, and floor of the corridor as if signaling some unknown emergency.

"Good morning, Mr. Tantalus," another maid greeted him as she wiped down the shiny mirrored doors and walls of the elevator. Michael stepped in and looked straight ahead into the mirror, seeing only himself and everything that was not quite right. He straightened his tie and at the same time lifted his chin. Once satisfied, he dipped his chin and looked at himself on each side. There was a tuft of hair pointing the wrong way, and he neatly redirected it.

He never answered the maid because he never even heard her. The elevator doors closed then opened moments later, and Michael walked quickly through the multifaceted lobby infused with artificial colors, smells, and sounds. He walked straight out into the roar of cars and people, stepping into an ocean of movement and sound. He passed Goldie who was now sitting on the dirty sidewalk, her back leaning against the hotel wall. She was hugging her knees to her chest, her head down; she and the building seemed to be the only things that were not moving. Michael's success had effected many changes, many of which he did not even notice. He didn't register the fact that every door was now opened for him, from inside the hotel all the way into the waiting limousine. He no longer acknowledged or even noticed the hands moving ahead of him opening this door or that one. From the building to the car, there were eyes that followed his every movement and made his way easier. No one looked at Goldie.

"Good morning, Mike!" The greeting came from a new co-worker assigned to Michael to "assist" him, on the logic that his remarkable success surely would necessitate assistance. *More like a spy*, Michael thought to himself, *and why does he call me Mike? I never told him to call me Mike.* Michael liked to be called Michael, but he was more irritated that someone would automatically shorten the name, as if they were longtime friends. And he was more than annoyed to have what he considered a tail. His success had been greeted back at headquarters with some amount of jealousy and he was sure that his antagonists were spreading skepticism concerning "how" he was winning so many bids.

Whether or not his new assistant, Thomas O'Reilly, was a spy or not was not what mattered to Michael. He liked to move about without having to worry about anyone else. He was dubbed a "lone wolf" by his peers, another way to detract from what they saw as his overachievement. His success made others look bad and the word was how they tagged you as not being a team player. It was all a bunch of bureaucratic bullshit, was what Michael was thinking as he returned Thomas's greeting.

Michael's irritation showed in his curt response: "Morning." He did not even look at Thomas as he settled into the seat. Thomas pressed his fingers together nervously. He was not a tall man but he was powerfully built, a trait not lost on Michael. As he sized Thomas up, Michael reviewed the impressive internal bio on him in his mind, *A Marine, tank commander in the first Gulf War, three years out and into business, a West Point grad.* It was hard not to be impressed, and though Michael mistrusted why he was there, and disliked having a tail, period, he admitted to himself that he liked Thomas. He was a little nervous and trying too hard to get on Michael's good side, but apart from work, he seemed like a regular guy. Michael reminded himself not to trust anyone. Then he thought of Jo again and it made him smile.

"Hey, I am really glad to be here, just to watch how you do what you do," Thomas said, feeling the need to fill the silence in the cab as they rode to their appointment. "He really gives them hell! He never blinks…no fear," Thomas was now describing Michael to the driver, but really he was talking to Michael. It was true that Michael never blinked. He didn't have to: He knew how these meeting were going to go before he got there. That was the piece his company never grasped in New York, the negotiation is done long before everyone sits at the table. When Michael's boss or one of his company's attorneys came to one of these meetings, they observed Michael, who never squirmed, never blinked, and had a confidence they did not understand. Of course, it was all Bennie, telling Michael which way to swerve, whom to talk to, what to bid. Maybe this was what made upper management nervous, but not nervous enough to put obstacles in his way. So Michael had developed a reputation as fearless.

Michael began to think about what Thomas was saying. *It is all aimed at feeding my ego.* Flattery was a very good strategy for most but not for Michael, who hated it. *It's true,* he thought further, *I'm not afraid of anything but it has nothing to do with the reasons they suppose.* It was deeper for Michael, and when his mind touched on these thoughts he could feel the burning of his bullet scar. He noticed the connection but the physical sensation brought him out of his thoughts and back into the car.

"So, are we going to see Spartacus tonight?" Michael's question caught Thomas off guard, and he smiled, then began to laugh.

"Who told you about Spartacus?"

"I never reveal my sources," Michael answered brazenly.

"If we get this deal, then you may see Spartacus tonight," the exchange transformed Thomas from a brown-nosing, nervous salesman into the confident warrior that was just inside him. Noticing the change, Michael was pleased. *If he is not a spy*, Michael thought to himself, *then this guy's got some potential.*

"Thomas," Michael turned to look him in the eyes, "We are going to get this deal."

"I have never seen anyone in a business setting with so much courage," Thomas was once again talking to the driver but still wanted to flatter Michael. *Courage*, Michael thought wryly to himself, *drinking shots of tequila with Spartacus, raging into the night with Manhattan's elite, saying whatever I want to anyone. And yes, some people seem to know, facing bullets. I can see how people would see all of that as courageous, even fearless.* But Michael knew the truth inside of himself. He could hear all the little voices in his head and he was semi-conscious that everything he had ever done—and now did— was in response to fear.

Yes, Michael knew the truth of how he felt about things but he was afraid to say them out loud. Afraid it would change things, even if he was not happy with the way things were now. Standing tall, talking straight, and telling his wife that he was certain that she no longer loved him, that would be courage. Admitting that he most likely had his pronouns mixed up was more than he could admit to himself. Scared of what that would mean, what would happen after that.

He thought about it while Thomas talked to the driver and the buildings blurred by the cab windows as they moved through the city. He wanted to tell his wife that he wasn't sure what love was anymore. He wanted to tell her about Jo, he wanted to tell her that often, he just felt scared and lonely and wasn't sure about anything he was doing. But that would take true courage—courage he knew he did not have—and as he moved closer to being honest with himself, closer to his own heart, he did what he always did. He stopped the questions, stopped himself before he had to do something.

"Thomas, let's review those numbers for the presentation."

Of course, they got the deal. Michael appeared to Thomas to be cool and relaxed, almost bored. By now, Michael <u>was</u> bored. Ownership families typically approached Michael to tell him what deals he would get and how to structure his company's bids properly. Michael usually brought Thomas in afterwards, so the deals seemed to flow so naturally and effortlessly that they appeared as genius to Thomas. This deal was no different, so to Michael, the outcome was a given—this meeting was simply a necessary step to the end result. Thomas had sat as still as he could through the entire meeting, but adrenaline filled his bloodstream.

The car was waiting by the curb as they walked out of the building. The meeting had gone long, and Michael wondered how the drivers were always able to find the perfect parking spot when there was never a place to park on the street.

"Are we going to celebrate?" Thomas asked such an honest question, with genuine excitement in every word. Michael looked at him, realizing that it was not long ago that he had felt the rush of these negotiations himself, and it made him smile as if he were watching a child.

"Yes, of course, we're going to celebrate!" Michael answered like an enthusiastic grandfather encouraging his grandson on a new adventure. He leaned forward to speak to the driver, "Drop us at Times Square."

"Very nice!" Thomas was truly excited. The car moved quickly for short bursts, then waited in tangled traffic until the light turned and all the cars rushed to the next light. When they had crossed far enough across town, Michael let the driver know they were ready to get out.

"This is fine, we can walk from here. Thank you."

"Eight a.m. in front of the Time Hotel tomorrow morning?" the driver asked as he pulled the limousine to the curb.

"Yes, thank you," Thomas answered. Then the two men stepped out of the car into the dark shadows of a side street just off Times Square.

"Look at all that!" Thomas exclaimed as they turned the corner and found themselves immersed in a sea of people flowing through streets exploding with movement and light.

"An oasis of lights, a virtual eye candy land, like Disney Land," Michael said, gesturing grandly with his hands. The streets and sidewalks were completely packed; the walkways looked like meadows of wheat blowing in the wind, only the wheat stalks were masses of moving, swaying people. And the brilliant, flashing colors of the seemingly infinite lights formed a kaleidoscope of incandescent bulbs and neon tubes. "And yet less than half a mile in any direction you can find pushers and hookers lingering in the shadows," Michael added. His eyes were widely focused and he appeared to be talking to everyone, his tone almost gloomy.

Thomas was three years out of the Marines; he had proven himself in the first Gulf War. Michael and Thomas were not far apart in age but Michael often treated him as much younger even though the difference was purely business experience. Thomas typically was quite confident but something about this city and the business here made him unsure of himself. He watched Michael keenly, amazed by his ability to move through things as though he already knew the outcome. He thought again that at the negotiations today, Michael had seemed almost bored. It is his greatest strength, Thomas told himself.

He tried to picture himself running the show, wondering if he could ever be as strong, as sure of himself, as Michael was. Michael saw how impressed Thomas was with him and had mixed emotions. He looked at Thomas, whose own background was impressive—he was the "real deal" in Michael's estimation—a soldier who was brave, honest, and all the other words he had learned in the Boy Scouts. And as Thomas followed him admiringly now, all Michael could think was that everything Thomas was seeing was a façade, a bluff. However, it was a façade so strongly built that Michael was beginning to believe it himself; in fact, he *wanted* to believe it. His business success bolstered the feeling many people have before a great fall: invincibility.

But Michael was lucky because there was a burning in his side where a bullet had entered his body. It manifested itself only on occasion, and at odd times so Michael was always caught by surprise at the sudden pain. It was a none-too-subtle reminder of his mortality, and though the stories of his prowess years earlier in Hell's Kitchen grew, instead of feeding his persona, they kept him humble. He knew he had been scared in that bar and he had only moved to survive. The only time he had ever talked of it since was with Jo; it had felt good to tell her. In spite of that, he was every once in a while looking over his shoulder and it was starting to wear a little on him, recently growing into a slight fatigue. He had just a slight feeling that something was going to happen even though his trouble had been so long ago. But still he wondered if anyone recognized him, *I need to be aware of what is going on around me, just in case.*

By now, though, the summer was over, and the feeling had not left him. But it was a small thought in his head and Michael dismissed it. Intuition was still to Michael nothing more than an over-active imagination.

Michael and Thomas walked side by side on the busy sidewalk, but each man was engrossed within his own thoughts. They came to a halt once deep within the mass of moving people and flashing lights and surveyed the entire square standing back to back.

"How many lights in just the big one," Thomas said, pointing to a large sign quickly broadcasting letters and words. "It's mesmerizing!" he added as he looked around at everything moving. The movement was what caught his attention—anything still was overlooked. He watched people and cars, but mostly he focused on the words moving across large billboards. Even some of the billboards themselves were moving. In the great roar of Times Square, there was a barrage of sensual suggestion: buy this, try that, do this. Every message promised something but all perpetuated the idea that something is wrong with each of us, at least something on the surface. You're too fat, too colorless, dressed too plainly.

If you buy this cologne, you'll smell like the man on this poster and you will have the love of your life; wear these jeans and you will be young and sophisticated, desirable. Michael became subtly aware that he was observing a sea of marketing messages carefully crafted to touch people's insecurities, touch their fear, touch where they are vulnerable...then paint them a way out.

For his part, Michael was concentrating on a life-sized ad for a sports car which was lit from behind, making the car stand out: black, shiny, sleek, almost alive. Its curves looked dangerous and fast, and of course, there was a beautiful woman caressing the car with one hand while she looked seductively outward, desiring whoever owned the car. Michael wanted the car, and deep within his subconscious, the elephant of his desire moved and he heard just below the surface of conscious thought, Drive this car and you will be...loved.

The deception was so close to his insecurities, Michael was just beginning to sense it but chose not to see. Every search had been a dead end for him. Every search for love ended in the same place. He just could not see what was wrong yet. He wanted things, and he did not even know why.

Michael began to move again, Thomas following close behind, both men still in their own thoughts. Michael felt strong, invigorated by his success across the business table. He was basking in the glory of a modern-day gladiator, an illusion perpetuated by all the props around him, including his admiring new associate Thomas O'Reilly. But growing was Michael's internal discord, it was like he was acting in a play and was growing weary of his part, and again there came a subtle feeling that the play was moving towards some climax. And as he had done before, he shook off the feeling.

Michael thought of Jo: She made him feel strong as well. He had taken on a lover, and in this world, it was okay—more than okay, it was expected. He never even thought to call his wife or sit down with her to tell her that he was unhappy and lonely, that he felt something was missing. There was something he wanted and needed that was missing, but he could not put his finger on it to identify where the uneasiness was coming from. He could not have this conversation with his wife because he could not think it: *These are weak thoughts*, he told himself, *And I, as I keep proving, am strong.* But he did have these thoughts and ignoring only made them grow in ways that he could not have predicted.

"Let's get a drink and talk about our meeting in the morning." Michael smiled as he slapped Thomas on the back and steered him into a small pub.

"So much for celebrating," Thomas said, looking a little sullen.

"This *is* celebrating," Michael laughed a little. "I have to make a call. Why don't you go in and get us a table. I'll be there in five minutes." Thomas complied and headed into the bar. Michael watched him go in then pulled his phone out of his pocket to call Jo.

"Hey, you," she answered sweetly.

"Hey, how are you?" The words barely meant anything, just hearing the loving voice was all he needed—all anyone ever needed—moving him into a place of deep pleasure.

"Big day tomorrow!" Jo said.

"Yep, I'm meeting with the distributors early to let them know how everything's going to go, I am sending the rest of the team to the Towers to start things with the maintenance crew. Then the rest of us will head to South Tower for lunch to introduce everyone. Big deal, this one!" Bennie had introduced Michael to the Silversteins, major property owners in Manhattan. Michael began doing business with them and now they had just bought the lease rights to the World Trade Centers. Tomorrow's meeting in one of the Towers had been set up weeks ago and everyone was excited. Michael, like always, had attended to every detail, so he knew that everything would go smoothly.

"I have a gap between my morning meeting and lunch—why don't you catch a train and come have coffee with me?"

"Michael, I would love to see you, why don't we get together tomorrow night?"

"Can't. I have to get to Chicago. Come on, I really want to see you," he pled, knowing he didn't have to do too much convincing.

"Oh, okay," she said in mock irritation. "Where do you want to meet?"

"There is a coffee shop downstairs in the South Tower. I'll meet you there. Got to run now, though." He was smiling and wanted to say more, but he hung up the phone and moved into the bar.

"I look forward to it... Bye." Jo lingered on the line, wanting to say more, too. There was so much feeling, and so much they needed to talk about but she did not know how to broach the subject. Instead, she turned to paper to write out her thoughts.

PART 2:
The Fall

Yes they tumbled out
and yes, we could see ahead
the short distance of their remaining lives,
hurtling
in the grasp of… gravity
and the laws of the universe.
In horror we stood transfixed
As witnesses
of what lay ahead for those
that we judged as the
pitifully falling.
And yet, as our view, we hold ourselves
and our own lives as different,
yet truly,
we are just as pitiful.
We light a cigarette, we drive a car,
we don't exercise or we do exercise,
we wear a safety belt and we quit smoking,
And all the while,
We hurtle towards our end,
caught in the grasp of gravity
ne'r to bend a single law of the Cosmos.
No, we nor our circumstance are any different,

…we are all falling just the same.

A Beautiful Day

Morning, September 11, 2001

A fresh, hopeful morning greeted Michael Tantalus as he walked from the hotel. The sun had not yet lit the pavement directly but even the thin, dark, and dirty alleyways were filled with the lovely light. Michael walked a few steps into the crispness of the morning that was the first sign of fall; the summer was over. Michael stood still for a moment as he suddenly remembered the dream he had that night. He dreamed there was a coming tidal wave and it drew away the water from the beach and into the ocean just before destructively crashing back onto the land. Then in the dream there was a coming wave of evil that was drawing away even the subtlest of dark energy away from the city, leaving it sparkling in light. The fragments of the dream quickly faded and Michael stepped towards the car.

Michael was so struck with the beauty of the dawning day that he coaxed Thomas out of his seat in the already-waiting limousine.

"Good morning, Thomas!" Michael's mood was light and friendly.

"Good morning to you, sir!" Thomas was glad and surprised by his cheerful mood.

"Let's walk," Michael declared. "There is a diner on 8th Avenue, and I feel like having breakfast."

"Sounds great," Thomas said as he got out, then turned back to tell the limo driver, who just nodded, having already heard the change of plans.

"I know the place and will be waiting outside," the driver called to Thomas as the door shut. Smiling, Michael started walking down the sidewalk toward the diner. Even breathing felt easier than normal. He always had felt that you should be able to anticipate what's coming, but sometimes there is no way to know.

"Are you married, Thomas?" Michael asked, strolling easily along.

"Yes, sir," Thomas replied, more than a little surprised by the question.

"Any kids?"

"No, sir."

Thomas is several years out of the Marines and he still answers questions as though he is a soldier, Michael thought to himself. *I suppose he always will be.* Michael did not think it was odd that he didn't already know the answers to these questions. Normally, he would have known many things about Thomas by now but Michael's life was now far from normal. Feeling friendly, Michael continued the small talk before moving on to details about the coming morning meeting. First, he ran through the names of the distribution management who would be delivering light bulbs, ballasts, and other electrical supplies

"I, I mean you and I, Thomas, will run the meeting at the distribution hub. We'll make sure everyone is ready and know what is expected of them. I'm sending Joe Frank and his crew to the South Tower. Joe is a good man, experienced, knows the players and knows what to do; he'll get everything ready with the maintenance crew for the World Trade Centers," Thomas nodded as Michael recited the details, knowing everything in his mind and not needing to refer to any notes.

Then they talked about the lunch scheduled for later, when they would introduce all the suppliers and distributors to the facility management team for the property managers, the Silversteins.

The conversation spilled over into breakfast: eggs, toast, and coffee. The meal was pleasant and even the waitress was in an exceptional mood.

"Good mornin', gents," she grinned while pouring their coffee.

"Good morning, ma'am," Thomas greeted her formally.

"Good morning." Michael flashed a smile and flirted a bit with the much-older waitress and she smiled back in appreciation.

The breakfast had not been planned so they had to hurry a little, leaving cash on the table and waving to their waitress as they moved quickly out the door and into the car. They were running a little late but the traffic was good so the driver made his way swiftly down 8th Avenue headed downtown. Michael looked out the window at all the broken concrete and dirty streets. There seemed to be many people milling around and Michael wondered what they were all doing. *Do they live nearby?* he wondered, imagining lives of meager existence. Soon, though, the old and dirty streets gave birth to large, gleaming glass and steel skyscrapers.

Once downtown, the car made a few twists and turns; the streets were now very busy. They passed Chambers and Ventnor Streets and arrived at their destination, a small, ancient two-story brick building that was tucked around a corner very close to the South Tower of the World Trade Centers. Michael and Thomas, wearing their business uniforms of dark suits with bright-red ties, stepped out of the limousine and into the red and brown building. It was typical of the support businesses camped near the enormous structures housing the important corporate commerce centers that affected financial markets around the globe.

Leaving the action of the streets, they walked up a flight of stairs into a conference room. It was more sedate and quieter there, but the action was intense around a thick, rectangular wood table. The deals had already been hashed out, mostly over scotch and cigars, so other than Michael, none of the dealmakers were here. However, these were the men who would make the deal work—the Teamsters, local politicians, electricians, the distributors, and others—and the room was thick with mustaches and accents. Most of these men had worked their way up; they were good, hard-working men, and Michael respected them. Even the politicians in the room were blue collar, working for their neighborhoods, insuring the survival of the locals. Everyone was shaking hands firmly, looking one another in the eyes, intent in their manner, strong and confident about their part in the deal.

Supplying the World Trade Centers meant money for everyone in the room, so there was a cheerful undercurrent to the mood. Eventually, Michael stood up at the end of the table and everyone took the signal and began to sit down. Michael had made money for every man in the room, and they respected him for that, but not only that; whenever he spoke he had their total attention. These men did not normally respect a tie but rumors had gone out and there were always whispers when Michael was present. But no one ever asked Michael about the stories and it allowed him to be effective across the necessary groups, something that Bennie had noticed.

"Welcome. Thank you for coming." Michael looked around the table, ensuring he made eye contact with each man at the table. Then, suddenly, there was a loud boom from outside and the floor shuddered. The men in the room barely took notice, there was only the briefest pause. New Yorkers take pride in being unflappable, and similar noises were not uncommon. *Dynamite from a construction dig? A large pallet falling from a truck?* Michael's mind tried to identify the noise quickly but he decided to continue speaking. He instinctively looked at his watch, seeing that it was about 8:45 a.m. He did not want to be late to see Jo; acknowledging that thought made him smile, then he took back control of the meeting.

"Everyone knows why we are here, so let's get down to…" The door opened and small man with dark hair interrupted the meeting.

"The World Trade Center is on fire," he announced, not appearing to be overly distressed, and exited as suddenly as he had entered. Now there was a small commotion in the room and loud whispering and murmuring began.

"Everyone," Michael was able to recapture their attention easily. "Let's get through this quickly—I want to make sure that everyone knows their part."

The same small man opened the door again with an update: "It was a plane that crashed into the North Tower!"

This time the man was much more excited and he clarified, "A commercial jet."

The businessmen began asking him questions and Michael lost control of the meeting entirely. He thought to himself, *That can't be right, there is no flight pattern that ever takes a commercial plane over the city. He must be mistaken.*

"Let's see what's going on," one man suggested, and they all began to make their way out the door and down the stairs. Michael gestured approval but most of the men had already risen from the table, their attention elsewhere, asking questions of each other, and nervously bumping into one another as if disoriented.

Michael and Thomas made their way down the stairs, too, the last to leave the conference room. Several of the men had already gathered around a radio at the bottom of the stairs and they stood as if mesmerized, in disbelief as a voice came out of the small silver box. The voice had lost its professional tone, sounding almost panicked as it described smoke billowing out, thick and black, from the tall steel building. "There are people pouring out of the North Tower," the voice said.

Michael was no longer focused on continuing the meeting and walked past the men standing around the radio to go outside into the crystalline beautiful morning, unaware at first that Thomas was not far behind him. All the cars and trucks had stopped in the streets. Michael walked across the sidewalk, busy with confused pedestrians, to a large white truck that was parked, still in the street, but with its engine turned off. It was one of the delivery trucks from his distributor. The driver, a large, bearded black man with a round face, was sitting sideways in the seat, his feet in large boots hanging out of the open door. He recognized Michael from one of the earlier meetings.

"Yo, boss, looks like our first delivery is going to be late," he yelled to Michael across the crowd of people and he motioned towards the gridlocked cars ahead of the truck. Michael looked at the man; he recognized him as well, and he had chosen him to make the first delivery. Michael liked his work ethic and his pride in his own service. He could see that the man was disappointed with the situation but the man also knew that something more important was going on. The truck's radio was turned on, loudly narrating all that was playing out a mere block away. Bwop, bwop, bwop, emergency vehicles were blasting their horns, trying to make their way to the towers, fighting through the evacuating traffic, the confused and the spectators making their way only inches at a time. Policemen were blowing whistles and frantically waving their arms trying to get cars and trucks to move this way or that.

Michael and Thomas walked through the throng directly to the truck to talk to the driver and come up with an alternate plan but instead they began to listen to the radio with him. As they listened, they looked into each other's eyes, suddenly feeling linked as brothers. A few minutes later they were joined by a fourth, smallish man with heavy eyebrows who had been riding a delivery bike; he also worked for the distributor, and seeing Michael, stopped for guidance. He laid his bike down, walked over, and began to listen to the radio. There was no need to ask what to do; the four men looked at one another in astonishment and shock as they listened to the radio: Michael and Thomas in their fine suits and silk ties, the driver wearing bright white coveralls, and the other man dressed in a dirty blue deliveryman's uniform. The four were now bound together and they all felt it; when moments ago their different clothes meant so much, in this moment they were all simply men. They stared at the radio: It never occurred to any of the them to look up, nor did they understand just how precarious was their location.

Michael could see the clock on the radio, 9:01 a.m. He stared at the lights, but nothing was registering rationally. He had simply wandered away from his meeting and now stood with three other men, bonded with them in some way he did not understand. Their faces were etched into Michael's mind; he could see every wrinkle, every crease across their skin. He was seeing these men more deeply and clearly than any faces he had ever seen before. Without knowing it, he was seeing these two divine machines in their last moments of being intact.

Many times over the ensuing years, Michael would think back to this moment. There was nothing but horror in this immediate experience, but later, he realized it had been a gift of divine circumstance to be at such a place, at such a moment. It had caused a clearing, an awakening, allowing the scales to fall from his eyes. It was as if Michael were falling, just emerging from the womb with eyes blinking and stunned, but understanding just a little—such colors, such clarity. He looked away from the two men. A large shadow crossed over Michael, then he heard a loud, fiery explosion.

Awakening from the Fall

Afternoon, September 11, 2001

Later. Much later. Michael and Thomas, caked in ash, began to walk northward, not looking back over their shoulders. Everywhere, people were milling about, some shouting, some pointing, and some just sitting down where they were, crying. The day was warming rapidly and Michael's clothes felt heavy, as if he had just climbed out of water fully clothed.

"My feet are burning," Michael said calmly to Thomas. Thomas just nodded, saying nothing.

"Mind if I stop to get some shoes, something better for hiking?" Michael asked.

Thomas nodded again, still silent.

Michael slowed his pace, scanning signs over the storefronts as they walked past. Soon, he spotted a sign.

"Shoes!" he exclaimed, almost sounding elated. He turned back toward Thomas who manufactured a smile and nodded. Michael went into the store while Thomas posted himself just outside the door. The shop was bright and the staff cordial.

"How are you, sir," a young woman greeted him.

"I am looking for a pair of shoes, something better for walking."

"What size are your feet? I am afraid we don't have much left," she motioned to the shelves on the wall. Michael had not noticed as he walked in but the shelves were nearly empty, yet another oddity in a very abnormal day.

"I wear elevens," he answered as he scanned the lit white glass shelves.

"I may have something," she said to Michael as she disappeared into the back of the store, "Please, have a seat."

Michael sat down and he could see Thomas outside greeting people with a nod as they passed. The store clerk returned with two boxes of shoes.

"These are very nice—stylish, too," she said, pulling one of the shoes out of the box. Michael put it on his foot and inspected it; it was shiny brown leather with soft soles and looked very handsome.

"This one fits. What else do you have?" Michael asked her as she began opening the other box.

"Black tennis shoes, not fancy," she said, handing a shoe to him. It was not very attractive but as he held the sneaker up to examine it closer, it was light in his hand. He bent over and put the shoe on his other foot, then stood to walk toward a small mirror on the floor where he lifted his trousers just enough to see the shoes fully.

"I'll take the sneakers," he said as he smiled, "And I'll wear them out."

"The credit card machines are down. We don't normally take a check, but today we will, or cash, or if you want to write out an I.O.U..."

"Oh, okay." Michael was a little surprised. *So much information in one sentence. So many things taken for granted are discovered on a day like this. People can be gracious when needed*, he thought to himself. He stood motionless for a moment and the woman smiled at him. It was a sincere smile but one that he would not have received only a day earlier. Things were different now.

On this terrible day, New York's normal rules no longer applied. There was trust, eye contact, compassion. Michael wanted to stay with the woman a little longer, aware that there was something here for him to realize. At some level, though, he knew it was something he could not touch with his conscious thoughts. So he moved along.

Michael gathered his work shoes and put them into the box that had previously held the tennis shoes, then he walked to the door to a stoic Thomas. Both men looked down at Michael's new shoes at the same time, and as they looked up, Thomas smiled and nodded, still silent. They turned and headed north, up the West Side highway, in the direction of their hotel. As they crossed the street, a woman came straight up to Michael.

"Hello?" She seemed to be making a timid request.

"Yes?" Michael said as he looked into the woman's eyes.

"I was wondering, wondering what I should do?"

"What do you mean?" Michael answered her in sincerity.

"Well, I left work, but I am wondering if I should go back?"

"I don't think today you have to go back to work. I think maybe you should go home." Michael was as reassuring as he could be, but he looked at Thomas for support. Thomas turned to the woman and nodded his agreement.

"But the subways aren't running and there are no buses or cabs," the woman said, bewildered, disarming Michael so he stared at her for a brief moment.

"Where do you live?" he asked.

"In China Town, I live in China Town."

"Well that's roughly... oh, I don't know for sure... two miles, I think? I think you should walk home."

"Walk home to China Town?"

"Yes, I think you should walk home."

"Oh," she answered as if a weight had been removed from her chest, "Thank you, I will walk home." She stood a little straighter and nodded emphatically as she began walking. Michael and Thomas watched her walk away then continued their trek toward their hotel.

An urge to cough came suddenly to Michael; he gasped air inward then coughed violently, bending over in a spasm.

"Damn smoke!" he was able to wheeze out the words as he recovered, putting his hands on his knees. Thomas instinctively patted Michael firmly on the back, prompting Michael to give him a hard stare. Michael stood, cleared his throat, and they continued walking. Moments later, as they passed two youths on the sidewalk, one of the boys spoke to Michael, asking, "What's going to happen?"

"What do you mean?" Michael asked the young boy.

"What's going to happen to us?" There was a sense of desperation in his young voice. "Are more planes coming?"

"There is a federal building on the way home and we think that the terrorists might be attacking federal buildings," the other young man spoke up, worriedly. He was a near mirror image of the first young man. *Not twins, but most assuredly brothers*, Michael thought to himself. Michael stroked his chin between his forefinger and thumb as he looked at the two young boys, then he looked at Thomas for a moment. Thomas was still silent.

"Well, maybe you boys could walk a few blocks around the federal building, just to be sure," he decided. The two boys looked greatly reassured, and after thanking him sincerely, were on their way.

Several more times, Michael and Thomas were stopped by people asking them what to do, where to go. It was as if the event of the day had woken people from some trance—their autopilots had been disengaged and they just were not sure they remembered how to fly. Most just needed a little reminder, a little encouragement to move forward with their day. It was a very odd phenomenon, and when he thought about it, Michael was sure that it meant something, pointed to some significance of human experience, but he could not quite pull it into focus. He assumed he was too close to the action.

Suddenly, it hit Michael. *What should I be doing?* he thought to himself. In an instinctive move, one that had never let him down; he reached into his pocket and pulled out a small, folded piece of lined paper. He unfolded the paper, releasing small bits of debris that somehow had found their way into his pocket and into the folds of the paper. And as the small bits of whatever was in his pocket fell to the ground, it made him pause and wonder, *Had they been a desk? A wall? Part of a building? Part of a person....*

Michael stopped his mind from going any further and focused on the paper. He was amazed to realize that he could see its grain— just one of many minute details that had escaped him previously. On the paper were inked lines, each sitting just below a hand-written task. This list guided Michael through each and every day; as he completed a task, he put a checkmark in a small box he had drawn beside the item on his list. Expenses, Letter to Silverstein Maintenance Staff, Thank You Notes, Call the Boss, Send Pricing to Distribution, Make a New List. He scanned the list from the top to the bottom then again from the bottom to the top.

It was just a list he carried in his pocket, checking boxes as he moved through his day, an important little tool to make him effective, but as he looked at the list now, it seemed meaningless. Nothing on the list seemed to make sense to him, when just hours before, he would have simply pulled out his list to see the entire day ahead or measure just how well he was doing at any given moment. Little notes that ran his life and had seemed important only a few hours ago. But now, it was just paper with ink scratching, but nothing of importance. It signified nothing of love, nothing of life, nothing of truth, nothing of how he should be living his life, nothing to remind him of what was at the end of his road, of every road, but now he knew. He stared at the note then balled it in his hand and tossed it to the curb; it was useless to him now.

He stared at the crumpled paper in the street and thought of how close he had come to his last breath, and then he coughed again. As he hacked loudly and hard, he imagined coughing out bits of furniture and glass. Yes, now he knew, he had been wasting precious time and precious breath on the mundane and meaningless. And as he stared at the paper, he made a promise to himself that he would never again be a walking "to do" list. He would find out how to live.

He looked up at Thomas, who was still quiet, and motioned for them to walk. They continued walking northward into an easy breeze and the wind gently brushed dust and ashes off their gray-covered suits, blowing it back in the direction from which they had come. As Michael put distance between himself and his crumpled list, he was only dimly aware that another veil had fallen from his consciousness. The raw shock of this new world was overwhelming, and there was no time for reflection. He thought of the list, this time seeing it in his head, focusing on the line, "Letter to Silverstein Staff." In his mind, instead of checking the small box, he drew a line through the entire sentence, wondering if the Silversteins staff were alive. Suddenly, his thoughts rushed, considering all those who were in the buildings. He began to try to calculate the human toll. *More than 100 floors, two buildings...let's see, how many people on each floor? How many hardworking, intelligent, well-meaning people just perished?* His working mind kept at it for a moment longer until he coughed again. The violent explosions of air from his lungs so occupied his body that they caused him let go of his thoughts.

By the time they reached Midtown, the normally busy streets had all but emptied. Streets that had always seemed so narrow and congested now felt wide and expansive. All along the walk, person after person made eye contact, some saying hello, all very unusual for New York City. Michael and Thomas slowly made their way uptown until they finally reached 48th Street, where they turned across town toward their hotel.

Michael spoke: "I want to take a shower, make some phone calls, check email, maybe take a nap." The word *nap* sounded strange to him as he said it. He paused for a moment, then continued, "Want to meet later for dinner, say around six?"

"Sounds good." These were the first words Thomas had spoken since earlier in the morning. They approached the entrance to the hotel, where immediately noticeable was the lack of doormen. Their absence, like that of the missing World Trade Center buildings, was disorienting. Michael had stood still earlier that day, trying to get his bearings, trying to figure out a way to walk away from the ruins, and as he had looked up, there was a huge gap in the sky.

The sky itself was blue and beautiful but there was no building where there had been one: nothing. The large, shadowy structure—which Michael had perceived as boxy, sterile, and almost ugly—was gone. There was only blue sky and the tower's absence left Michael almost paralyzed, momentarily disoriented. *How could something he seldom noticed in his conscious mind have been so important in his orientation?*

The homeless woman Goldie was there by the hotel door, as usual, but now she was walking about and talking. It was strange to Michael, who had only ever seen her sitting or lying in the street, and had never heard her make any sound other than gibberish. She was speaking clearly to passersby, and Michael heard her reference her gold mine. She looked neat and clean, Michael was amazed to realize, and he stopped directly in front of her to address her.

"Goldie, you look…" he paused for a moment as he looked into her blue and gray eyes, "You look terrific."

"Thank you," she said then added, "You look like hell!" making Michael smile.

"What's this about your gold mine?" he asked, making a connection with her name, expecting a story. But instead, she lifted her skirt and pointed downward, where Michael saw not a stitch of clothing. "This here is my gold mine!" she pointed out with pride.

Michael turned to Thomas and said, "Now I have seen two horrible things today," and both men burst into laughter.

"If you can laugh on a day like today," Goldie told the two men, "Then you are going to be okay." Then she laughed with Michael and Thomas. Michael would see Goldie again after this day, but he would never again see her lucid.

The two men continued to the building, where Michael opened the door. The lack of doormen was disconcerting and they both walked quietly through the lower lobby to the elevator. They stepped into the lift and pushed their floors; Michael's room was off the main lobby just one floor up, while Thomas's room was several floors further up. As the elevator stopped one floor up, Michael stepped into the empty lobby.

"Six o'clock downstairs?" Thomas confirmed as the doors were closing. Michael wheeled around to face Thomas and replied, "Yes, six o'clock. See you then."

Michael was able to get out the words just before the mirrored doors of the elevator closed, leaving him utterly and completely alone. His own distorted image reflected from the closed chrome elevator doors in the dim light of the lobby. He saw that the image staring back at him was still covered in ash except for wrinkled cracks formed by sweat and moving skin. He looked ghostlike. Slowly, he turned to face the dark entry into the hotel's main lobby. He moved like a machine, taking slight notice of the blinking emergency lights and the odd, artificially lit lobby; only a few accent lights were on in the foyer. It seemed that everyone had left and someone had felt the need to turn out the lights as they departed.

Like the streets outside devoid of cars, the lobby appeared larger without people. It was quiet and deserted but he paused in front of the concierge desk. It seemed more than bare, empty with no warm voice to greet him, to remind him how important he was. He turned to the far wall where a chest-high sheet of marble normally separated the guests from the desk clerks, and this post was deserted, too. Michael began to turn slowly, his head and body moving together, 360 degrees, observing that the entire entrance was bereft of any living thing that he could see.

His mind filled the void as he thought, *It's like the Rapture has occurred and I am one of the unlucky souls left behind.* He put his hand over his mouth as if to keep himself from uttering any words that would affect this spell or dream. *Or perhaps I am one of the few taken and I am in some sub-realm.* Michael's thoughts seemed loud in the silence of the vacant lobby and they made him uncomfortable. He unconsciously grasped his left shoulder with his right hand, then brought his left hand up to his right shoulder, hugging himself tightly. If the movement was an unconscious attempt to reassure himself, the gesture failed.

Michael turned away from the lobby toward the hallway leading to his room. He paused once more at the edge of the lobby where the hallway expanded into a trendy cocktail lounge. The strange, dim light washed across sharp-angled wooden chairs and open-backed, flat couches. In the near-darkness, cocktail tables looked like floating ovals between the chairs and couches. Each table held unlit lamps made of stacked square blocks with wildly shaped lampshades; on one table was a square ashtray with a cigarette still burning in it. Michael watched the smoke rising in tiny serpentine streams upward through streaks of light, disappearing into the upper darkness of the room empty of living beings.

Michael began his journey down the dark corridor to his room, exhaustion suddenly taking over. He had a sensation that was unfamiliar to him and he searched his thoughts to name it; the only word that came to him was vulnerability. This thought and every other thought was pushed out now by his one desire: to get into his hotel room and shut the door behind him. Even this lonely corridor screamed silently about all that he had just experienced and witnessed. On the many tiny television screens that lined the hallway like the lights on an airport runway, miniature airplanes crashed into the miniature World Trade Towers, over and over, the entire walk to his door. It was like a trauma from the past playing in the periphery of his mind, affecting every step forward.

Once at his door, Michael paused, feeling strangely unsure of what to do next. He patted himself down, looking for his room key, small puffs of ash floating into the faint light given off by the small televisions. His arms and hands began to move more frantically, searching dust- and ash-filled pockets in an increasingly awkward and haphazard manner. He stopped himself, took a deep breath, then began searching again for his key in a purposeful manner, but his hands and his fingers seemed to float, not completely attached to his wrists and arms. The search for his room key now became a focused effort. While his body used to obey his mind, unconsciously compliant, now there appeared a gap between his mind's volition and his body's response—everything felt forced as he had to make a conscious effort to bridge the unseen disconnect somewhere between the two.

With hands in both pockets, the room key suddenly appeared in one of his hands and Michael let out a sigh of something like relief. He opened the door and moved inside his room in one quick motion. The sound of the door shutting behind him was shockingly loud; he had never registered the sound consciously before. This time, it was remarkable for the silence that came after. Once again, Michael felt the need to take inventory of his wellbeing. He started with his body, and though dusty, he seemed fine. Then his mind: there had been a shock to his system, or at least what he thought should be a traumatic event, but somehow he felt okay. There was tightness across his forehead and he knew he did not feel right but he could not locate any pain. He started to replay the day's events but decided against it.

Then it hit him, as his body drew in air and coughed—easy at first, then harder and more violently, as his whole body drew hard for air. He coughed out more than he ever had before, then another hard cough followed, and as he drew his clenched fist to cover his mouth, he noticed his hand. The hand's movement had begun before he realized he was going to cover his mouth; again, there was a disconnect between his mind and his body. Michael's next cough took him completely and he convulsed, nearly vomiting as his body tried to extricate whatever was inside him.

Finally, he was able to stand and there was the relief, however brief, of being in the hotel room behind the closed door. He looked at his hands, seeing for the first time that his fingers and knuckles were bleeding in some places and scabbed over in others. His hands were such a mess, and looking at them in the dim light of the room, he wondered how he could have missed it. As he saw them properly now, they began to ache. The skin was missing from the tips of his fingers and every knuckle. His nails were cracked, broken, and bleeding. He realized that he was shaking a little and tried to control it. He walked to the bedside table to turn on the small chrome lamp to better examine his hands. He clicked on the light and noticed that the bed had not been made. The sheets had formed into a spiral shape as he turned in his sleep and they remained in the same pattern as when he'd left the bed hours earlier. They were like a beautiful sculpture in white folds of orderly chaos, the signs of a peaceful, deep sleep—the kind of sleep he would not find again for a very long time.

The curtains were drawn and the room was dark but for the light of one small, trendy lamp and the dim glow from the bathroom light, which he had left on. Michael moved toward the bathroom, feeling that his body was moving of its own accord while he watched. In the bathroom mirror, Michael watched his own image emerge like an apparition from the darkness of the bedroom. The bathroom was adorned in chrome with nothing but a white rug and white towels, clad wall to wall and nearly floor to ceiling in mirrors. Michael paused beneath the lone illuminated spotlight directly above him and looked from side to side, his gray image appearing to extend into infinity, repeating again and again in the parallel mirrors. He looked at himself for a long moment as if had never seen this shell he was living in before. He was almost unrecognizable to himself.

Michael looked closer at his face. The ash had begun to fall unevenly from his cheeks and forehead, creating strange shapes and shadows on his skin. *Jesus, I look old*, he thought to himself. His face reflected the day's trauma the way a shoreline is reshaped by a violent storm in a single day. He slowly began to take off his suit jacket, holding it for a moment, then shaking it just a bit to watch the clouds of dust fall into the air, dancing slowly in the mirrored beams of light. The sight gave him the urge to cough but he suppressed the rising feeling and decided to undress slowly as to not disturb the ash. He turned to walk toward the closet to hang up his suit jacket, but stopped himself, remembering it was covered in ash. He stood motionless, waiting for the ever-present, decisive voice in his head to tell him what to do next but the voice was not there. So he stood in the bathroom, holding the jacket away from his body. When no suggestion came to him, he put his jacket into the small, oval-shaped chrome garbage can next to the commode.

Then, abandoning the thought of undressing slowly, he began to strip his clothes off faster and faster, frantically pulling at them, popping a button loose from his shirt in his careless shedding. He crammed article after article of clothing into the trash, forcing the last few pieces into the small oval can. Michael suddenly caught his naked reflection in the mirror and turned to stare at his image, feeling as though it was a strange apparition. Ash was on his wrists and his hands; it covered his neck and his face and was matted into his thick, disheveled hair. But his arms, chest, and legs were bare, so stark white it looked like he had been painted in places. It was not clear which was painted, the white-washed middle or the pale-gray extremities. He looked at the clothes overflowing the small garbage can and he did not feel far enough removed from them, so he walked the can out of the bathroom, across the small bedroom, and opened the door to the hall to place it just outside of his room, much as he had a room service tray many times before.

Finding himself standing one foot into the hall naked, Michael felt overwhelmingly exposed even though there was no one there to notice. He quickly shut the door, then strode purposefully to the shower and turned the knob, releasing the water. He was cold, and could smell the water as it fell to the tile, wafting a small breeze across his naked body. It made him think of the blast of wind that had thrown people through the air as the debris of the building rushed to the ground. He stood locked in the thought until steam emerged from the water. He put his hand under the spray, and its soothing warmth melted him as he stepped into the shower to give his body relief.

The showerhead was broad and hung from the ceiling, dropping water like gentle rain. As the ash began to rinse from his hair and his face, he became aware of a metallic taste in his mouth. He leaned his head backward and into the water as if he were being baptized, hoping to emerge from the water purified and changed. But the skin on his cheeks felt raw and rough, as though the ash was not coming off. Michael leaned forward and opened his eyes to see gray swirls on the shower floor, circling his feet before disappearing down the drain. He washed his hair, but it still felt gritty, so he washed it again. He stared at nothing and lingered, listening to the water as the steam enshrouded him, completely covering the glass door and walls of the shower with fog.

He watched the water, hypnotized by its falling, and after some time, his thoughts began to flow with the water. He watched it hit the shower floor, circle, then run down the drain to an unseen place. Then his mind took over from there, imagining where it went.

He stood looking into the empty darkness of the drain, watching the water continue to pour into a seeming void, and he was aware of an empty place in his gut.

He consciously reversed the direction of his thoughts and followed the water upward to the shower head, and now he began to wonder where the water came from, how it came to be warm, and how grateful he was to have it roll over his skin. The water came from an unseen place and then left or returned to an unseen place. Everything else was imagined. *Like a person's life, like the moments of my daily life.* All he ever had was right here, right now, everything else was imagined. It felt as if some great realization was about to come to him when a practical thought entered his mind: *I wonder what time it is?* He had simply lost all track of time.

He turned off the water, stepped out of the shower, and began to towel dry. Then he wrapped himself in his towel and walked over to sink into the bed. He was exhausted but did not think that he could fall asleep. Realizing that he had to make some telephone calls, he looked at his cell phone, punched in numbers, and hit the send button. The word *congestion* flashed across the small screen. Then he saw all the missed calls. And then a shock. The area code of 631 appeared over and over. It was a number that he knew and it sent him into momentary confusion.

"It can't be!" he yelled it in a whisper. He tried to call it back, then the word *congestion* again flashed across the phone. His breaths increased and there was tightness in his stomach. *It can't be, it's not her, I am never calling that number again.* But it was a call that he knew he could not ignore forever. And for now, he was trying to re-gather his strength and his thoughts. Every time things began to settle there came another blow. He powered down the cell phone and tossed it into a nearby chair, where it landed softly, safely. He watched it as it bounced on the cushion.

He picked up the remote control for the television and turned it on. He could not bear the sound, so he mashed the mute button. In silence, he watched the planes coming into the buildings, over and over, on every channel. He lay back on the still-messy bed where the disordered and restless sheets lay tangled about him. He thrashed about, trying to find some comfort. Failing, he tried to still himself and closed his eyes, falling instantly into a dream.

Some time later, Michael bolted upright in his bed, breathing hard from images of a dream still in his head. It took him a few minutes to shake himself out of the vision and back at the Time Hotel; he was alone, very alone. He climbed out of the bed and went into the bathroom where he saw that light from the overhead bulb glistened on the perspiration covering his body. He decided to go for a walk but first he rinsed his body again in the shower. He washed his hair once more and it had a texture that felt strange.

As Michael left the bathroom, he saw that his body had left a rust colored outline on the bed. The bed was wet and smelled of sulfur. Michael dressed quickly, then left the Time Hotel and walked two blocks eastward until he reached Times Square. As he turned the corner of the building into the square he stopped for a moment to look at all the busy lights. They still sold, cajoled, and flashed all the things—watches, cars, fashions—that promised a better life, a better person, and more. But the shock that hit Michael was that there was no one there. The streets had been teeming with people the night before, so thick that there was hardly room to move. Now the streets were empty. The lights and signs flashed and dazzled for almost no one. There was an odd wind blowing paper about the empty streets and it gave Michael a chill so he flipped up the collar of his blazer to cover his neck. The wind was the only noise, even more strange.

He leaned against the cold glass of a tall building. He scanned the square for movement, and across the connection of streets, he finally saw two women running in spike heels, wearing short skirts that exposed nearly the entire length of their legs. One of the women was tall, while the other short and a little pudgy, wearing an overly tight top. Michael smiled a crooked smile then said to himself, "Some things never break."

Then the time flashed brightly across a large digital clock, *I am late to meet Thomas*, so he turned and hurried back to the hotel.

Dinner in Hell's Kitchen

Evening, September 11, 2001

Thomas was waiting outside the Time Hotel standing on the sidewalk with his hands in his jacket pockets.

"Hey Thomas," Michael greeted trying to sound upbeat. The two men stood together on the walkway, not talking, the silence, while not long, was awkward.

"You doing okay, Michael?" Thomas asked while looking into his eyes; it was a sincere question. The question was like a stab to Michael. He had been somewhat successful in trying not to think about what had happened earlier in the day but the question seemed to take Michael right to Jo. He had not allowed his thoughts to go there, he had concentrated on putting one foot in front of the other. And now the vision of seeing the number on his phone flashed through his mind and it hit him in the gut. Michael stood motionless, he could feel the skin on his forehead so tight he thought his skin would split.

"I'm fine," he was finally able to get out, and while the word came out much more abruptly than he intended, it was successful in warding off any more questions. Thomas did not know exactly what had stopped Michael in his tracks, but he knew not to push for more information right now. Michael felt wrecked but he was still on his feet. "Let's have a drink before dinner," he added to soften his curt response.

"Sounds good, I could really use a beer," Thomas said. And the two men walked quietly towards Eighth Avenue. Michael was not sure why but he chose to go to… Hell's Kitchen. They came across a place Michael had never been and they went in.

At the first table in the bar, an older man dressed neatly in an unwrinkled dark suit and blood-red tie sat, heavy in stature and heaving in self-importance. His companion was an extravagant-looking, provocatively-dressed much-younger woman. They were drinking cosmopolitans, the combination of liquors glowing in the glasses while their new secret glowed on their guilty, pleasured faces.

Michael surveyed the bar for a moment longer, but he tried not to stand in the door long enough to be noticed. Spotting a stool in a near-empty section of the bar, he sat followed closely by Thomas. Michael found himself in a near empty place, physically and emotionally. Attempting to fill the void in his mind, he began to wonder about the pair seated near the door. As the man coddled his drink, he was looking down, unconsciously clinking his wedding ring on the thick glass container. He made little eye contact with the slender young woman who was dressed in a long, black dress that clung desperately to her tiny waist, making her desirable to nearly every man who walked past.

She used men, either consciously or unconsciously, Michael was sure of it. It did not matter, a tryst with her was most likely full of energy and lots of great sex, with highs not possible with most women. But most likely, any relationship with this beautiful, seductive woman would end in disaster and unimaginable lows. While these idle thoughts wound through his head, Michael found himself eye to eye with her. He gazed too long and she leered at him as if silently saying, "Mind your own business."

Michael immediately turned away, peering around the long, thin barroom, searching for something else to occupy his thoughts. He tried to look out the windows of the bar, but they were opaque with dust, age, and old event advertisements that had been taped on and left hanging long after their dates had passed. Michael looked past Thomas, he did not want to make eye contact, he did not want to encourage Thomas to ask more questions. Then he looked out the door which was propped open to the night.

The streets had always seemed so small because they usually were so crowded, but tonight they felt spacious with more than enough room for whatever needed to pass this way. Any other night, this street would be overrun in yellow cabs, but tonight the street held three young men, stumbling and laughing amicably. They all wore dirty, faded jeans, worn in the knees, and almost-matching dark sweatshirts, with their sleeves pushed up to their elbows. The three men all had thick muscles and thick accents. *Local Irish*, Michael thought to himself, *maybe Westies*. They carried on with one another, laughing loudly, and they sang and danced a little together.

The bartender approached Michael and Thomas, "What 'chou want?" the man asked as he rubbed a glass dry with a towel, never looking up.

"Evening, doctor," Michael said in a friendly tone.

"Drink?" the barman barked; he had been working at the bar since early in the morning shift. Then he let out a sigh and put the towel down on the bar, folded it, moved it once more as if it was not quite in the right place, then he set a glass down in front of Michael. He put both hands on the bar and leaned towards Michael, asking him with great patience, "What can I get you, friend?"

New York was different. Michael could see it plainly everywhere. He wondered how temporary this all was, or if there would be some permanent change. He knew for sure that he was changed but he wondered if his own state was temporary or permanent within himself. Little did he know, the change within him was small today but it would continue to grow until one day it would be all he could see. The truth may be barely perceptible, but once inside a man, it will grow until it is all that is left.

Just then, the three young men outside broke into raucous laughter that reverberated inside the tunnel-like bar. It clearly rattled the older man in a suit and he shifted his chair abruptly, throwing a disdainful look at the men outside, then huffing loudly to announce to everyone in the bar how annoyed he was with the young men in the street.

"Martini," Michael requested finally, turning his head toward the barman but keeping his eyes focused on the young men outside.

Then, "Beefeater, straight up, olives but not dirty," he added as he made eye contact.

"And how about you?" the barman asked Thomas who still had his hands in his pockets.

"I'll have a Guinness, please," he nodded as he said it.

"Coming right up," the bartender said, picking up the towel and slinging it over his shoulder. In a moment, the martini glass landed abruptly in front of Michael, spilling a little of the gin. Michael picked up the drink and held the cone of the glass in his hand, feeling its chill. Michael had begun drinking martinis while doing business in New York. He just started one night; it seemed to say something about the kind of man he had become, it matched who he thought he was now.

But as he sipped at this moment, the bite of the gin was overwhelming. He smelled it and sipped it again, but something felt different. He was repulsed, his body rejecting the drink in a reflex reaction. He looked at the glass curiously: There was something beautiful about its shape and the drink was desirable but his body wanted nothing to do with it (or what it would lead to). On the outside, Michael was still and quiet, but inside he was rattling and full of noise. He wanted the calm, the sedation that comes from alcohol, but something inside him was rejecting the distilled spirit. So he decided to try something else. He looked at the beer mug in front of Thomas.

"Hey, doctor," Michael called to the barman, "I think I want a Guinness."

"Something wrong with the martini?"

"No, I think there is something wrong with me," Michael replied and all three men chuckled a bit. The shallow laughter led Michael into a cough but he regained his breath and added, "I think I am just not in the mood."

"No worries, friend, beer on the way," the bartender said as he put a glass under the tap and let the beer spill into it about halfway, then flipped the tap closed and walked down the bar to attend to other patrons. Michael watched the foam in the glass settle; it had never been strange to him before how a light-colored foam settled into a dark liquid. Then Michael looked above the tap at shelf after shelf of bottles on the wall. *So many bottles, so many different shapes, and so many colors...so many ways to consume the medicine,* he thought to himself, *sedatives for all tastes.* His thoughts were broken when the barman returned to the tap, filling the last bit of the beer glass, letting the foam settle to about a quarter of an inch across the top. He placed the glass in front of Michael while talking to someone further down the bar.

"Cheers," Michael said to Thomas as he took his first sip of the beer.

"Cheers, " said Thomas as he drank down about half the beer. Then he stood and pulled off his jacket. Thomas was wearing jeans and a t-shirt that was tight enough to show just how muscular he was. Michael had never seen Thomas like this; of course, he had read "military background" on his resume, but Thomas now seemed to exude soldier warrior with his upright stance and short-cropped hair. *Three years out of the Marines,* Michael thought. Thomas looked formidable as he sat back down next to Michael. But even as he sat, his chest was out and his chin was up high. He flashed a broad, casual smile, almost a grin, wide across his face, with no hint of the horror earlier in the day. Nor did he remain silent as he had on the walk from the hellish rubble back to their hotel after the buildings fell. Thomas surveyed the glasses in front of Michael.

"Who here has a drinking problem?" Thomas asked humorously as he pointed to the collection of drinks sitting in front of Michael. The question and change of demeanor made Michael smile and he turned to look at his beer, martini, and glass of water.

"Would you believe me if I said that it is not as bad as it looks?"

"Of course, I believe everything you tell me, but then again, it is always just as bad as it looks and sometimes worse," and he flashed his big smile again. Thomas appeared different to Michael now; he had read "soldier" on paper, but now he saw it for what it was.

Just as the fireman were different to Michael now: They had almost been invisible, but now he saw them for what they were, what they did, and what may lie ahead for some. They had run past Michael, bumping past him on their way to death, they ran fast and they ran hard, sure in themselves, sure in their final moments, knowing what was coming, Michael thought he had never seen anything so beautiful in his life, tragic as it was beautiful.

"Yeah, no use in denial," he smiled back at Thomas, then asked, "How are you doing?" Michael asked the question instinctively and after he asked, wished he hadn't. Thomas tensed his face as if he was trying to decide how to answer. Despite his more jovial mood, tension showed on his face. Michael looked at him, still seeing things more clearly than normal. As he looked into Thomas's face, he saw a big, square jaw and a round, flat nose—a bulldog, ready to battle anyone or anything. His hair was still wet, and Thomas noticed Michael looking at it.

"I must have washed my hair three times…can't seem to get that crap out."

"Yeah, I think I washed mine four times," Michael gave Thomas a smile. Simple, mindless conversation gave both men the reprieve they needed from their harrowing day. Michael thought about how Thomas had walked the two or so miles earlier in the day from the rubble to Midtown in silence. And now, he was more talkative than usual. But now was not usual. The blessing of a shock is that it gets us out of our grooves. Where if we look, we can see beyond our normal walk, and if we desire, we can choose to walk a different path. Michael was at that place now and to suddenly find himself in a pathless land left him hesitant about every step. Motion in any direction could yield a different life.

The barman brought two beers and set them down in front of Michael and Thomas.

"These are on the house, gents." Michael and Thomas both nodded their appreciation but neither man said anything. There was no need for further words, there was rather some unspoken recognition of everything, and every human interaction now gave the opportunity for something deeper, something that everyone, nearly everyone, recognized but could not verbalize even if it was their desire. As Thomas drank the rest of his first beer and began to drink the second, he tried to think of something to say, he was grasping for normalcy, something that would remain elusive for him and Michael for quite some time, but especially while in the besieged city.

"Hey, should we go over our schedule? What about tomorrow's meetings? And do you think we can fly out of here tomorrow?"

"No," was Michael's only answer. Tension returned to his forehead. For some reason, thinking about tomorrow brought Michael back to what had just happened and thinking about what to do next was paralyzing. Michael turned his head and his body to look back at the couple near the door, first at the outsized man and then at the sultry woman. He wondered if they had any idea how obvious they were. They must know, he answered himself then decided that they must not care and turned his attention back to Thomas. Michael was not able to stay focused on Thomas, though. Instead, he was sensing tension—tension about to burst—and at that moment, the sound of loud laughter burst from the street and spilled into the bar.

Instantly, the heavy man stood, causing his chair to tip. It seemed that the three young men had crossed some unseen, unspoken boundary for a day like today, a day of disaster. As evening's darkness fell on the city, it seemed clear to everyone in the bar that it was time to sit quietly to assuage the guilt of being alive, most assuredly not an evening for drunken rowdiness or laughter. The man stomped his feet in righteousness, like a bull about to charge—and charge he did, out the door and into the fray of the three drunk young men.

"SHUT UP! Shut up, shut up, shut up. Show some decency, some respect for the dead. This is not a night for laughter! Go back to your families, appreciate them, be glad you have them, and love them!"

The man balled his fists and raised them as he yelled but he stopped abruptly as one of the young bulls rushed him. The younger, more muscular man slammed him hard against the stone and brick wall. Michael and Thomas leapt to their feet and moved swiftly to the sidewalk outside as the older man's companion gasped and made a noise that was close to a scream but closer to a whine. The young man jammed his forearm across the older man's windpipe, cutting off his air. As his face turned red, everyone froze.

Suddenly, the young man pushed his face into the heavy man's face. Then, he began to shake and tears streamed down his cheeks, falling onto his broad chest. He pointed his finger at the suited man's nose and began speaking in an Irish brogue.

"Today I lost me brother and I lost me Daddy, in the same God-damned day, and by God, I am respecting them just exactly as they would have wanted."

Then he released the heavier man, and as he retracted his forearm, he stood straight, suddenly seeming to notice all of the onlookers, then turned to lean his head back and let out a howl of a laugh aimed at the sky. He thrust his arm upward and yelled, "I know ye bastards are up there laughing at me: well, back at you, you lousy bastards, I love ye both!" the last word revealing his lamentation.

The heavy man slid to the cement and sat there with his head bowed for a few moments longer. He was caught in the confusion of right and wrong, of honor and dishonor; he had only chastised someone else for the very reason he felt guilt within his own heart. Such was the night—souls and hearts laid open and bare in heartache and loss, coping in any way that seemed to comfort.

"Let's get out of here," Michael said to Thomas, and he walked back into the bar to put down a twenty. Thomas followed him and added to the cash, nodding to the barman on the way out. Moving gave both the men relief from the tension of the scene at the bar but it would not help the night; moving could not conceivably help the night.

As they walked, Michael first thought to pull his cell phone out of his pocket and call home. He pushed the numbers and touched Send but the call did not go through. However, more voicemails showed, so he supposed he would have to go back to the hotel to call from a land line to retrieve the messages. He saw the number come up again. A chill ran through his body, he stared at the number, he just could not believe it was on his phone. He tried to think what to do but he just could not think of anything. He decided to find something to eat first and deal with the calls later. He just was not ready to take any of those calls, but their weight was substantial.

They were walking south down Eighth Avenue and Michael noticed that his feet felt funny as if they were rounded on the bottom. He walked like he was a little drunk. *But I've only had a few sips of beer,* he thought to himself.

"Thomas," Michael said his name a little too loud, correcting the volume of his voice before asking, "Are you hungry?"

"Yes, I think I am. Do you think we'll find anything open?"

"Of course, it's New York, The City," Michael said reflexively before he realized how ridiculous the statement sounded. Not talking, they walked for a while on the nearly empty streets as the night air quickly cooled. The silence was broken periodically by an emergency vehicle racing, sirens blaring—some headed downtown, some headed north. Several were covered completely in ash except where the windshield wipers had cleared the glass for visibility.

Thomas stopped suddenly and looked up into the black sky above them. There was the whine and then screech of a fighter jet as it came closer then streaked by high overhead and out of their sight. The city had been locked down: No one was coming in and no one was going out.

They passed a pub, open to the street with tables and chairs spilling into the walkway.

"How about this place?" Michael asked as he turned toward Thomas.

"Sure, looks crowded but at least it's open," Thomas answered. While they stood looking for a place to sit, a sturdy waitress approached them on the sidewalk.

"You'll have to sit outside at a table with others, cash only—the credit cards aren't working, the service most likely will be poor, the staff has been here since early this morning, we are all tired and won't put up with any shit—but everyone who is hungry eats, no terrorist assholes can shut us down." The tirade might have continued, but she paused to take a breath.

Grinning, Michael turned back to the waitress and said, "Sounds good, best offer we've had tonight. We're hungry."

"Good, what you want to drink?"

"What do you have?" Thomas's question was met with a 'you got to be kidding me' look so he quickly answered, "Beer—whatever you got." The waitress then turned to Michael, who nodded. "Sounds good to me."

He smiled but the gesture was not returned. She walked them to a table just outside the bar near a television where there were already five young men seated. When Michael and Thomas sat at the end, none of the men turned to look at them, their attention was on the television as President Bush, who had not been heard from all day, was about to address the nation.

"God, I hate Bush," said the tall young man seated next to Michael. The waitress was still standing next to them and heard the young man's remark. She turned toward Michael and Thomas, tilted her head, and spoke directly to Michael in a quiet tone: "We're a little tight, please be patient." She looked at the other men, then back to Michael, adding, "Everyone eats."

She looked back at the young man, who continued his tirade against President Bush. "Who wants to hear from him right now? No one wants to hear from him, he's just trying to cash in politically on this tragedy!" The young man paused for a moment then mumbled something to his friends. Michael realized that his and Thomas's timing had been perfect. The President was about to speak and they were seated within close proximity of a television. Michael looked around the crowded bar, noticing that people were positioning themselves so they could see one of the many televisions fastened in various places above the bar and on several of the walls.

"Jesus Christ, Bush is an asshole," the man next to Michael

carried on. Michael felt numb from the day and the evening so far, and he didn't want any trouble. He was pretty sure that was what the waitress had been telling him: to be patient with others. The President appeared on the television, but the young man kept talking and Michael's patience waned, because he genuinely wanted to hear what the President was going to say.

"God, I hate that man," the young man said, even louder. Michael's irritation toward the young man grew, so he played the words of the weary but determined waitress through his mind once more, *patience please, everyone eats.* Michael looked about the bar where nearly everyone was quiet and still, fixated on the President's speech. *It was the most important speech I have ever heard a president give,* he thought to himself. Michael looked out across the bar again. Some people were sitting and some were standing, but nearly all had voluntarily hushed, watching a frightened and shocked president.

Now the young man turned and directed his comments to Michael. "What a complete idiot, I cannot bear to watch him."

"Hey," Michael dragged out the word as he caught the young man's eyes. "Maybe today is a day that we should all support our president, whether or not we like him. I want to hear what he has to say, so do you mind keeping your comments to yourself?"

The young man leaned toward Michael menacingly, exhaled loudly, then belted out, "I am going to keep talking, so what are you going to do about it!"

The sudden confrontation drew the attention of the other four men at the table and they all glared at Michael, clearly supporting the young man who was with them. At just the moment Michael opened his mouth to reply, Thomas leaned forward with fire coming from his eyes and spoke to the young man in a slow, calm, but threatening tone: "I don't know what he is going to do about it, but I'll tell you what I'm going to do about it. I'm going to come across this table and grab you by your scrawny little neck and rip off your puny little head and shit down your throat. That's what I'm going to do about it."

For a moment, no one moved. Then the other four men distanced themselves from their comrade by averting their attention to other places in the bar, leaving the man alone, caught in Thomas's steely glare. The man looked down as a dog bowing to the alpha and said, "Hey, I...I didn't mean anything. I...I guess I am just freaked out, like everyone. How about I buy you a beer—both of you."

He smiled nervously, looking from Thomas back to Michael. It seemed for a moment that Thomas was not through, and he began to stand and lean across the table. But then he felt a firm grasp on his forearm, so he looked down at the hand and found that it was connected to Michael. As Thomas's eyes met Michael's, it broke his anger and soothed him just enough to relax, and he leaned back, then slowly slid down back into his chair. The hair was still standing on the back of Thomas's neck and a small amount of perspiration ran down his temple. He took in a breath, realizing he was grateful Michael had interceded. Then he let the breath out slowly and let a smile come to his face, it was a manufactured smile but it helped him. Then he turned his attention to the bright box hanging near the ceiling of a dark corner, where on the screen was President Bush. His hands were folded, wrinkles crossed his forehead, and each word he spoke seemed labored:

> *"Good evening. Today, our fellow citizens, our way of life, our very freedom came under attack in a series of deliberate and deadly terrorist acts.*
>
> *The victims were in airplanes or in their offices— secretaries, businessmen and women, military and federal workers. Moms and dads. Friends and neighbors.*
>
> *Thousands of lives were suddenly ended by evil, despicable acts of terror.*
>
> *The pictures of airplanes flying into buildings, fires burning, huge structures collapsing, have filled us with disbelief, terrible sadness and a quiet, unyielding anger.*
>
> *These acts of mass murder were intended to frighten our nation into chaos and retreat. But they have failed. Our country is strong. A great people have been moved to defend a great nation.*

Terrorist attacks can shake the foundations of our biggest buildings, but they cannot touch the foundation of America. These acts shatter steel, but they cannot dent the steel of American resolve.

America was targeted for attack because we're the brightest beacon for freedom and opportunity in the world. And no one will keep that light from shining.

Today, our nation saw evil, the very worst of human nature, and we responded with the best of America, with the daring of our rescue workers, with the caring of strangers and neighbors who came to give blood and help in any way they could.

Immediately following the first attack, I implemented our government's emergency response plans. Our military is powerful, and it's prepared. Our emergency teams are working in New York City and Washington, D.C. to help with local rescue efforts.

Our first priority is to get help to those who have been injured and to take every precaution to protect our citizens at home and around the world from further attacks.

The functions of our government continue without interruption. Federal agencies in Washington which had to be evacuated today are reopening for essential personnel tonight and will be open for business tomorrow.

Our financial institutions remain strong, and the American economy will be open for business as well.

The search is underway for those who are behind these evil acts. I've directed the full resources of our intelligence and law enforcement communities to find those responsible and bring them to justice. We will make no distinction between the terrorists who committed these acts and those who harbor them.

I appreciate so very much the members of Congress who have joined me in strongly condemning these attacks. And on behalf of the American people, I thank the many world leaders who have called to offer their condolences and assistance.

America and our friends and allies join with all those who want peace and security in the world and we stand together to win the war against terrorism.

Tonight I ask for your prayers for all those who grieve, for the children whose worlds have been shattered, for all whose sense of safety and security has been threatened. And I pray they will be comforted by a power greater than any of us spoken through the ages in Psalm 23:

"Even though I walk through the valley of the shadow of death, I fear no evil, for You are with me."

This is a day when all Americans from every walk of life unite in our resolve for justice and peace. America has stood down enemies before, and we will do so this time.

None of us will ever forget this day, yet we go forward to defend freedom and all that is good and just in our world.

Thank you. Good night and God bless America."

The speech ended and the bartender turned off the volume of the televisions. Everyone's attention returned to their own tables and conversations. Michael kept staring at the television, wanting more, wanting better answers. He was already forgetting the speech. He tried to recall what he had heard. One thought seemed to keep rolling in Michael's mind, "Evil attacked our freedom." That just did not make sense to Michael. It was despicable, yes—that implied innocent loss of life—it was tragic, no matter who you were. "The search is underway for those responsible," was a statement that Michael did not doubt; nor did he doubt that, "We will not distinguish between the terrorist and those who harbor them," because he was pretty sure that there would be plenty of innocent blood shed in the name of justice.

The ironic thing, he thought, *is that the President said they were attacking our freedom, and our country's response itself would be very likely to reduce our freedoms. Every day, whether through fear of evil, or fear for food, or fear for taking care of ourselves, or fear of safety, every day we are getting closer and closer to all being on the reservation of the great father.* Michael wanted the speech to have been more like the waitress's. He would have liked it if the president had stood up and said, "Please be patient with one another, and everyone eats."

Michael turned away from the television and said to the young man next to him, "A beer would be fine." The young man had a blank look on his face until he remembered his earlier offer, then he nodded. Michael thought about the moment earlier in the day when Thomas had grabbed him as he was running: The ground shook and they held onto each other as the sound of smashing glass and steel was all about them, and in that moment, they were like two small children, shaking, hoping not to die. He looked at Thomas and could plainly see that this morning and this evening, he had been a true soldier, operating with cool precision and efficiency in the midst of chaos. But, too, Michael observed that Thomas was on the verge of coming apart. The thought made Michael wonder about his own mental state and the words of a Willie Nelson song came to mind: "After taking several readings, I am surprised to find my mind still fairly sound." It made him smile. "Funny what comes out of our mind at the damndest times," he thought out loud, but no one heard.

Michael busied himself further with his thoughts, subconsciously staying in his left brain to avoid the dangers of the emotions in his right-side gray matter. He watched the crowd, noticing small clumps of people, small groups within the larger group, but then he watched all the people together in the bar as one entity. Then he imagined people in all the other bars and apartments across Manhattan, his mind continued to expand to include those in New Jersey, then across to Pennsylvania, then Ohio, then he stopped and came back to this bar. Something was different, something was remarkable about what he was watching and it took Michael a few moments to see what it was: New Yorkers were being good to New Yorkers, polite, giving. Strangers were looking into the eyes of strangers and smiling in an understanding way.

How could a terrorist attack ever succeed? People were not withdrawing in fear or changing their thinking. Right now, it was not even important who had done this horrendous act. Everyone was pulling together, petty differences were lost, New York and New Yorkers, America and Americans were closer, cooperating in the

most unusual and spectacular fashion. Thoughts of the individual did
not vanish but were voluntarily superseded by what was perceived as
the need of the whole. It was spontaneous and brought out the best
in nearly everyone, and anyone who acted differently was quickly
corrected. There was a collective decision to pull in ranks.

There would be a reaction of fear, but not to recoil or change
some policy; these attacks would make America more dangerous.
There would definitely be retaliation against the perpetrators and
those who harbor the terrorists. Michael could see plain as day that
there would soon be the occupation of foreign lands, and many
responsible for this day would die. The world was just not as big as
it used to be and there was very little way to hide after such a bold
attack. There would be large amounts of spilled blood of innocents.
It was inevitable. The line dividing friend from foe was an imaginary
one, and the thought of finding evil in a single skin color or a single
religion or a single geography just was not plausible. But on the
strength of fear, for the desire for justice to show others that this was
not acceptable, a line would be drawn, and those on the other side
would feel the fury of the collective blood line of warriors from all
over the rest of the world. Always, we fight ourselves, and the fights
between brothers seem to be the most brutal.

Then Michael imagined the motives of a terrorist group.
Surely they wanted America to fall. And one day America will fall,
he thought, *all civilizations do, but not at the hands of an attack. Attacks
only strengthen countries like America. All one would have to do to destroy
America is to leave it alone for long enough and let the Great Father, the
American government, draw more and more people onto the reservation, and
once enough of its people give up their own thoughts and ways of life, the
system will collapse of its own accord.*

Just at that moment, the waitress bumped past Michael, jarring
him out of his spinning thoughts. She stepped off the curb into the
dirty and nearly empty street. She walked diagonally towards the
firehouse across the avenue, where in a steady but exhausted march
toward her was a fireman wearing no helmet or jacket. His hair
was matted with sweat and ash against his forehead. His boots were
heavy as he walked, and his overalls were pulled off his shoulders to

expose a tee shirt, dark with perspiration. His facial expression was grim as they met in the middle of the street.

Michael was close enough to hear as the fireman labored to say the names of those lost during the day. Each name came at the waitress like a dagger, one after another in slow-motion thrusts into her heart. Her mouth fell open and her head tilted back as her hand covered her mouth to muffle the sounds she was making. She began to shake and fell into the tired but sure arms of the fireman, who held her firmly as she quaked with emotion, and they cried together. Now Michael noticed how small she really was; her bold talk and strength had made her seem larger, stronger than her stature.

Michael watched the scene, and tears streamed down his cheeks. He wept as quietly as he could, and while no one seemed to notice, the dam controlling his emotions crumbled then broke. He turned away to make sure no one would see him like this, weeping for the waitress, weeping for the fireman, weeping for the lost men, and weeping for what was within him and what was coming out and for what he had experienced that morning.

Michael rose and walked towards the waitress. The waitress quickly regained herself and reached her arms up high to put them around the neck of the fireman and hugged him with assurance, letting him know that she was going to be okay. She turned, straightened her clothes, and wiped her eyes. As she approached, Michael spoke to her: "Hey, I am really not that hungry and I was thinking that maybe…," but she stopped him mid-sentence.

"Everyone eats, nothing stops because of those bastards," she said, her steel blue eyes glassy. Michael watched her as she moved past him, then let out long-held sigh as she disappeared into the bar. *I have never seen a more beautiful woman*, he thought to himself. She seemed different to him now than she had only moments early. Michael moved back to his seat; he had become unhinged, only now he knew it.

The waitress walked back to their table trailing a young woman.

"This is Alina. She wants to eat and your table has the last seat."

"Oh, there's plenty of room and we would be honored for your company," Thomas answered immediately and began adjusting the chairs and the drinks on the table to accommodate the young woman.

"Thank you," she said, and her accent was heavy—Polish, Michael suspected. "This is so disturbing," she added. "My friends and I are here to see New York and are headed to Chicago next, but now I do not know when we can fly." She seated herself next to Thomas and the two of them continued talking, but Michael's attention wandered. He began thinking about a book he had read a long time ago: Dante's *Inferno*. He remembered that in the story, Dante saw even the fires of hell as a manifestation of God's love.

As thoughts played through his mind, he watched them pass with the sensation that he was not thinking at all, but merely watching his own thoughts pass by. It was as if he had no connection to them at all, and the experience left him tranquil. He leaned back in the old wooden chair and it let out a loud creak. A cool breeze blew across his neck and southward down the avenue, carrying thoughts and the smoke from the burning piles of rubble out to sea and into the darkness.

"The problem with Hell is that the fires don't consume you," Michael whispered aloud. And he could not help but think of Jo and began to shiver.

"Sorry, I missed that. What did you say?" Thomas turned from the young Polish woman as he asked the question, and they both looked expectantly at Michael.

"Oh, nothing. Sorry, I was thinking out loud," he responded.

Alina and Thomas quickly resumed their conversation. *That was a Joseph Campbell quote... and Dante? I am remembering my college literature*, Michael thought to himself, then shrugged, *Strange.*

"If terrorists can strike America, then there is no place that is safe," Alina said, bringing Michael temporarily into the conversation.

"I want blood," Thomas said, adding, "I am thinking about reenlisting."

Michael faced the breeze, watching crumpled bits of paper

blowing down the pavement. They danced and bounced about beautifully, ignorant of the day's terrors. Michael thought back to the President's speech. *He had quoted Psalms and rightly so,* Michael thought to himself. He did his best to remember the quote but could only recall the first line, so he whispered it to the passing bits of bouncing trash: "Yeah, though I walk through the valley of death, I shall fear no evil."

Michael was not sure if he was remembering words exactly, but in his estimation, the President had picked the perfect verse, though very likely for a different reason than why Michael thought it was appropriate. Michael's thoughts left Psalm 23 and began to uncoil like a compressed spring, *Right, do not fear evil, don't even resist it. If we are to reach God, or reach a place of good, it will not be by attacking the darkness, but by enhancing the light.* His mind continued with questions about what he had witnessed earlier that day. *So many lack the ability to discern the difference between truth and what is ultimately good, and falsehood and what commits atrocities such as crashing a plane full of men, women, and children into an office building of innocent dads, moms, husbands, and wives. And by retaliating, the cycle will only be perpetuated. No one's beliefs or concepts, false as they may be, will change or be altered.* He wanted to know what was true, in all the destruction, what was really true, what would break the cycle, what would heal?

He remembered the dream and Michael imagined all the angels above and the devils below, and all those entangled in struggle between the two opposites, and then he asked himself a question: *Can there really be a threat to God?*

The Next Morning

September 12, 2001

The morning after the catastrophe. Just one day before, Michael had walked from his hotel room with an idea of what to expect and surety that his own effort would allow him to meet any goal he set. Just 24 hours earlier, he had no awareness of his feet touching the floor when he walked; he merely moved about, thinking of the things he had to do.

This morning, Michael thrashed about in the bed, not really sleeping and having no idea of the time. He heard a noise at his hotel room door and rolled out of bed to investigate. Each foot felt new sensations and each step was different. The walk to the door, a mere three yards, felt like an expanse. Michael opened the door to emptiness, but on the floor was *The New York Times.* On the front page were the towers, and the flames. He picked it up and read snatches of the headline article.

U.S. Attacked: Highjacked Jets Destroy Twin Towers and Hit Pentagon in Day of Terror

It kept getting worse.

The horror arrived in episodic bursts of chilling disbelief, signified first by trembling floors, sharp eruptions, cracked windows. There was the actual unfathomable realization of a gaping, flaming hole in first one of the tall towers, and then the same thing all over again in its twin. There was the merciless sight of bodies helplessly tumbling out, some of them in flames.

Finally, the mighty towers themselves were reduced to nothing. Dense plumes of smoke raced through the downtown avenues, coursing between the buildings, shaped like tornadoes on their sides.

John Cerqueira, 22, and Mike Ben Fanter, 36, were working on the eighty-first floor of 1 World Trade Center when they felt the collision. "People were freaking out," said Mr. Fanter, a sales manager. "I tried to get them in the center of the office. About 40 people. I led them to the hall down the steps."

He continued: "We stopped on the sixty-eighth floor. I could hear people screaming. There was a woman in a wheelchair. John and I carried her down from the sixty-eighth floor to the fifth floor, where we got out. We started to see people jumping from the top of the World Trade Center."

A person falls head first after jumping from the north tower of the World Trade Center. It was a horrific sight that was repeated in the moments after the planes struck the towers.

Some Trade Center workers blessed their luck for being late for work. Kathleen Dendy, 50, had gotten her hair cut and so never got to her office at her usual 8:30. She worked on the ninety-ninth floor. Rajesh Trivedi, 40, a computer programmer, normally reported at 7 but he had to drop his son off at school and so didn't get in. He worked on the eightieth floor.

Lines five, eight deep developed at pay phones, but many of the phones didn't work. Most of the downtown businesses were closed. People borrowed cell phones but the heavy phone traffic made communicating hard if not impossible. Countless people spent hours not knowing where a wife, a husband, or a child was.

For hours people lingered, uncertain where to go or what to do in a no longer plausible world.

"It's eerie," said Monet Harris, 22, a transit worker. "You always look for those two buildings. **You always know where you are when you see those two buildings. And now they're gone.**"

Michael folded the newspaper and tossed it to the floor. He was overcome by an odd feeling. As he read the article, noises and smells played across his senses. He tried to assess what he was feeling, but nothing came to him. Not knowing what else do, he ordered breakfast, then read *The Times* more thoroughly for the accounts of the day. He was careful about reading the details, searching for some piece of information that just wasn't there. Although he did not know what he was hoping to read, he was left unsatisfied.

He turned on the television and watched replays of the disaster, feeling little or no connection to his own experiences the previous morning. He satisfied himself that he was fine, that he'd faced nothing he couldn't withstand. A knock at the door seemed to come from another world, and it took Michael more than a moment to realize that someone was there. He looked through the peephole at a room service bellman. His head was down; Michael wanted to see his face, but after a too-long pause, he opened the door. The man pushed a small cart into the room and began to lay everything out across a stiff, white tablecloth. The sun found its way down the building and into the window, alighting on the silverware and a small, silver cup of cream. The reflected sparkles danced across the rolling table and the smell of eggs, toast, and coffee began to soothe Michael. He tipped the man who nodded in silence as he left, closing the door behind him.

Michael looked at the eggs, cooked over-easy with dark flakes of pepper sprinkled across them. He picked up his fork and carefully ate the white away from the edges of the yolk, not wanting to spill the warm, yellow fluid held by its thin, unseen membrane. He had better luck eating the toast, applying copious amounts of butter and jelly. The cool orange juice quieted his annoyed throat, an irritation that he was unaware of until he had relief. He smelled the coffee but did not drink it; his stomach refused.

The hotel telephone rang. He stared at it as if he did not know what was causing the noise, but suddenly, he lunged to pick up the receiver. On the other end was a lonely, worried voice, weak in its inquiry.

"I am Amanda Frank," the woman's voice said, pausing. Michael said nothing. "I am Joe Frank's wife," she elaborated. The name hit Michael like a train. His stomach fell and his heart raced. In an instant, everything came back to him. "Hello," was all he could muster.

"I understand my husband was in a meeting with you yesterday morning?" Again, Amanda Frank paused. Michael did not breathe. Her next words came fast, deteriorating into a whine and then into sobbing: "I have not heard from Joe, and I am worried." She gasped to catch her breath, trying for a moment to regain her composure, but the next words came out as only sounds mixed with sobbing.

And so began Michael's gruesome job of making telephone calls and having difficult conversations.

He connected to the Internet and began downloading emails. He was late to the task of accounting for the men in the meeting. When were they last seen? Which way were they headed? What were the last words they spoke? Michael had no idea why he had been so slow to engage. And now, to frantic and most likely widowed wives, the last words husbands had spoken were extremely important. They sought to understand the inflection and feelings behind those words. What were they thinking? What were they doing? Were they scared?

The details that came to Michael surprised him.

"Amanda, Joe was thinking of his family, said that he wanted to get home and make sure his family was okay. I believe he headed up Broadway... he left a short time before the buildings fell. I have not seen nor talked to him since. Have you checked the hospitals?" Again, the sobs. The calls lingered far too long, but Michael kept his tone concerned, hopeful, and businesslike, even though he had no hope for these men. He felt sick to his stomach. He kept asking questions: Who have you talked to? Where have you called? On and on he gently guided strangers, the missing men's loved ones, giving them direction to anywhere there might be hope.

Michael worked for hours on the telephone, on email, connecting every way he could think of to try to account for the men. He returned all the calls he received except for one. Then he began to delete the voicemails; again, all but one. A knock came at the door, and Michael bolted up to answer. It was the maid, who had not come the day before, but Michael didn't want to be disturbed.

"Could you come back later?" he asked. She nodded, then handed him some clean towels and pushed on. Michael began to dress quickly; suddenly, he needed movement to relieve his tension.

Mostly, life hits you like little jabs to the gut, and men like Michael are taught to keep their arms up to protect their heads and to tighten their stomachs and take the blows. Sometimes, though, life throws haymakers: hard punches that they don't see coming, punches so hard that they lose all their air and recoil in an attempt to recover.

A lucky few find the arms of a soothing lover or some task, any task, important or unimportant, but something to keep the mind and body engaged and busy, anything is good enough for the task.

More often, though, these men tense so hard that they are still on their feet, but they're not able to breathe or talk. They don't feel able to lower their arms, to let down their guard, and they're locked within themselves. With no solace in stillness, they move in the other direction, into motion, into adrenalin, and too often, into a bottle.

The Afternoon After

Afternoon, September 12, 2001

Michael met Thomas in the upper lobby. They began walking before they knew where they were going, the immensity of their recent experience eliminating any chance of small talk. So rather than say meaningless things, they were quiet, looking awkwardly about as they boarded the elevator and descended into the lower lobby.

"We have to do something to help," Thomas blurted out, changing the subject from small, unimportant things to what was really on his mind.

"Like what?" Michael knew exactly what he was talking about. The elevator doors opened and they walked into the dark lobby where the waterfall, the lamps, and the music were all turned off. Michael did not notice it right away, he noticed that something was different, but he wasn't aware of what had changed.

"Let's go give blood. I saw something in the news last night… they may need blood for all the survivors."

"Hopeful thinking," Michael said to himself, quietly enough that Thomas did not hear. The doorman was back at his post, standing tall and smiling. Thomas spoke to him.

"Hey, do you know where we can donate blood?"

"The New York Blood Center is up on 67th Street," the doorman answered in a heavy New York accent.

"Thank you," Thomas answered, then he looked at Michael.

"Yes, that sounds like something we should do," he said as he nodded. Michael turned to the doorman, asking, "Cabs running yet?"

"No, not yet, but I'll see if I can find someone to run you guys uptown." He was eager to help.

"No, no worries, we can walk it...besides, I feel like walking." Michael said it as if he were talking to himself.

"Anything else I can do for you, Mr. Tantalus?" the doorman asked. His tone was different; everything seemed different. Michael put his forefinger to his lips then turned back toward the doorman, "Do you think you could find a rental car? The company travel agent says that there are no rental cars anywhere on Manhattan. Airports are closed; I need to find a way to get home."

He used the word "need", and it was the right word. Only finding home would not be as easy as finding a car and driving back to North Carolina.

"Sure thing, Mr. Tantalus, I'll see what I can find."

"Call me Michael," he said, making eye contact with the doorman, who nodded and smiled. Michael turned and headed out the door to the street.

He paused just outside of the dark lobby in the unusually open and inviting street, stopped in his tracks by a definite, solid feeling that something was different—and not "just" that the Towers had been attacked. Searching with his senses for that something, mistakenly looking for something that had been added. Not identifying what was different, Michael caught up to Thomas, who hadn't immediately noticed that Michael paused.

"Everything okay?" Thomas asked.

"Yes, yes, everything is fine," Michael replied, but he continued searching, perplexed by the strength of his feeling of difference and his inability to identify what had changed.

As he and Thomas made their way to the blood donation center, it suddenly occurred to him that what was different today was not something newly added, but rather, something that had been there all along, flowing underneath everything else that normally occupied his senses. He felt clearly it was something that held everything else: silence, silence on the inside and silence on the outside. There was no constant roar of traffic, no honking horns, no thumping of passersby walking coldly and swiftly on their way to some appointment.

For a moment that morning, Michael was complete, wanting nothing, needing nothing. Strangely, he felt content; upon that realization, he stopped walking and looked up at the sky. Thomas paused too, looking at Michael, then looking about, searching for what held Michael's attention. Seeing nothing there, he asked, "What, Michael? What are you seeing?"

"Nothing, Thomas, absolutely nothing, and that's what's so strange."

They resumed walking, heading north toward 67th Street. They walked into what was only a slight breeze, and the sky above was cloudless and blue.

"Hey, smell that?" Thomas's words made Michael stop for just a moment.

"Yeah, smoke? Slight smell, but definitely smoke." Michael turned right and started walking faster down 48th Street with Thomas at his heels until he reached Broadway. He turned the corner of the glass building, and looking south down the wide thoroughfare, he could see the smoke rising from the still-burning buildings downtown. Thomas and Michael stood in silence a few minutes watching the rising smoke, then without saying a word, they turned to head toward the blood donation center.

Michael put his hands in his pockets and looked into shop windows as they passed; some stores were open, but many were closed. As they approached the blood center, the noise of crowds slowly grew. And when they reached a cross street and turned west onto 67th, they could see where the noise was coming from: thousands of people waiting in line to give blood. A chill ran down Michael's neck, realizing that everyone wanted to help, everyone wanted to do something in the face of the crisis.

There was a gathering positive energy in the face of evil that made people look at one another, smile at one another, and think about what they could do to help each other. Some human capacity had lain dormant until the need was great enough. And the need was great now. This was a wound to the international symbol of capitalism, a place that for most symbolized freedom and opportunity, but for a few symbolized something that needed to be attacked. And the attack, while directed at America, was aimed at something other than America as a country.

There was a woman shouting, addressing the crowd: "We are at capacity. We have more blood than we need or can store unless you are AB or AB negative. Thank you, everyone, for coming out." She continued to walk along the line, repeating her shouted status report. Many people stayed in line, talking with one another about the events of the previous day. Michael turned his head to see the end of the line, which was still lengthening, despite the woman's words.

"O positive," Thomas said as he looked at Michael.

"Me, too," was Michael's quick reply.

They stood looking at each other, not knowing what to do.

"There has to be something we can do," said Thomas.

"Let's walk in and take a look around," Michael said and motioned towards the blood center. Inside, near the entrance to the brown brick building, there were gurneys side by side, packed in closely in neat rows. They were all occupied by all kinds of people; the staff, volunteers, and donors were barely distinguishable from one another. It was busy and chaotic, but everyone was patient and polite and smiled at one another.

Michael walked about the room watching, witnessing a side of New Yorkers he was sure he had never seen before. What he was seeing now flew in the face of his conception of New Yorkers as a collective. As individuals, New Yorkers were often charming and bright once they knew you, but as a collective people on the sidewalks every day, they appeared busy and self-absorbed and, frequently, downright rude. But the scene unfolding before

Michael was a city of decent people wanting to do whatever they could to help. Michael surmised that what he was seeing now was the "true" New York; most likely, he was seeing how "true" New Yorkers had always behaved to one another, but reserved from strangers. Today, though, even a concept like "strangers" was blurred; people were all in this together, finding commonality in shared tragedy.

"I'm ready to go," Thomas said looking at Michael.

"Yeah, me too," Michael replied. They quietly turned and walked out of the building. Many more people were coming into the building and the line to give blood was still lengthening. The same woman who had been walking the line earlier was still yelling to those standing, but people lingered anyway, feeling some small sense of satisfaction knowing they were willing to do something, however small. The information that they were not needed did not seem to matter.

Michael and Thomas stepped off the crowded sidewalk and into the street to pass by the throngs of people standing and milling about. Walking in the road was a feat not normally possible, but now the unusually wide stretch of pavement was devoid of cars. It felt so strange that Michael and Thomas walked as close to the curb as they could. Normalcy and rules were suspended and no one minded; they finally ventured diagonally across the road, walking leisurely with no particular destination.

"Thomas," Michael began, "What do you think about dreams?"

It was an odd question coming from Michael, and Thomas asked, "What do you mean?"

Michael took a deep breath before he began, weighing just what he should and should not say, but after a brief pause, he decided to dive in to explain what was on his mind.

"Yesterday, after we got back to the hotel, I took a shower, then lay on the bed. I fell asleep... at least, I *think* I fell asleep, I don't remember actually falling asleep. What I mean is, I know I fell asleep because I had this dream. An especially vivid dream..."

Michael paused to look at Thomas, who was looking at Michael, transfixed, not because of what Michael was saying but because of the way he was saying it.

"Anyway, I was lying there, and I sensed that someone was in the room. I bolted straight up, I tell you, it startled the crap out of me. And standing at the foot of the bed is this little old man, not four feet high, looking like some ragged old gnome. He had these piercing blue eyes with a shit-eating grin like he knows me."

Right at that moment, a fighter jet screeched across the sky. Michael and Thomas looked up. The jet was far ahead of its sound, and both men stood silent watching until it was gone from their sight. Michael looked at Thomas and Thomas looked back at him, neither saying anything, just looking at one another until the jet's sound faded, easing back into silence.

Michael began again, "So this little man starts talking and I can barely make out what he is saying… he is speaking with some kind of thick Gaelic accent. So I bolt up in bed, and when I do, I see this immense sword beside the bed on the floor."

Michael made a grand sweeping motion with his hand to emphasize the size of the sword.

"This large shiny, polished steel was gleaming with light, so bright I had to squint. And I realized that there was more light coming from the sword than was in the room."

Michael stopped walking again and looked down, thinking about the dream and what to say next.

"Then, this strange little man says to me, 'Pick up the sword, and you will remember,' and I am thinking to myself, remember what?" Michael paused again, then put his hand out, replaying the dream. "And so I did, I reached down to pick up this mammoth sword, and at first, it was so unbelievably dense and heavy that I could barely lift it, but the longer I held its handle in my hand the lighter it got, or so I was thinking at the time. But then, it suddenly dawned upon me that the sword wasn't getting lighter, I was getting stronger and bigger. Within moments I had these huge hands, and as I lift up the sword, I am looking at these powerful forearms and massive white biceps. My skin had turned to a brilliant white. I grasped the sword with two hands and lifted it up, even with my eyes, and I could see all these engraved symbols all over the base of the sword. The longer I looked at them, I began to be able to distinguish their meaning, and I began saying what was on the sword in deep, vibrating tones that reverberated light everywhere. And then I knew who I was." Michael said this with finality, as if he were through telling the dream.

They walked for a bit, then Thomas asked, "Well, who were you?"

"I was none other than Michael the Archangel," he said matter-of-factly. "And this little man was The Sword Keeper. You see, he explained to me that when a warrior first attempts to walk a spiritual life, he has to lay down his sword and the Sword Keeper hangs on to it in case he needs it. I was dreaming that being an angel was reality and that my life now was the dream. I had been dreaming that I was Michael Tantalus the businessman."

Michael had never defined himself in this way before, and saying it out loud made his life suddenly seem very unimportant. "And then, this little man directed his penetrating blue eyes right at me and says to me, 'You are needed today.' He said it in a whisper, but the words ran up my spine like a sudden chill, and powerful wings unfolded from my back like they had always been there. I flew out the hotel window and high into the sky." Now Michael was making wide sweeping motions with his arms as if he truly were flying upward.

"And as I flew up above the clouds there were more archangels waiting for me. I don't recall any words, but I was hearing sounds, feeling vibrations, and I was in communication with the other angels as we circled into a tight formation and then headed down the island toward where the towers had been. Then we came in to this, this…" Michael was searching for the right word, "…sub-realm like thunder, like sonic booms, we entered this realm one after another."

Michael balled his right hand into a fist and thrust it into his flattened left hand, making loud popping sounds, "Boom, boom, boom! One right after the other with each of us sending a shock wave that reverberated throughout this place, whatever—or wherever—it was."

Michael paused once more, swallowed, then continued. "And Thomas, the place where we were was a tear in the universe where heaven, hell, and earth were all pouring into one another." Michael looked up and motioned a hand heavenward, "And up above, I could see the sky extend into heaven. It was like a massive cone of angels as far as I could see. And down below," Michael looked downward, his hands following his gaze, "there was darkness and more fires of hell. And out of this darkness, beasts of all kinds, like nothing I have ever seen or imagined, were coming out of hell and into this realm."

Again Michael paused; to Thomas, it was as though he were reliving the dream. "Floating in between the angels and the hell beasts were all the people killed in the towers and the planes and… and people walking below," Michael stopped as a tear slid out of his eye. Thomas did not move, they were both suddenly immersed in the moment. Neither knew what to do nor say, so they said nothing. Eventually, they started walking again, and neither one looked at the other. But after a bit, Michael continued describing the dream, only now, his voice was quieter and he was much less animated.

"In between were all these people, floating, spinning in a large spiral, like the stars in a galaxy, but very slowly, and mixed in with the people was some debris, but nothing I could recognize. It looked like a small, slow-moving hurricane revolving upon an unseen eye. And what was happening, Thomas, was that these slimy, hideous beasts were throwing chains that would wrap around the people there." Michael made motions with his hands and arms, demonstrating how the chains would wrap around the people.

"And then they would drag them down into the darkness and into the fires. And my job, and those around me," Michael said making sweeping motions with an unseen sword, "was to cut the chains between the people and the beasts, freeing them to float up into the angels, into heaven."

Michael paused, looking down at the cement. He took a deep breath, then continued.

"Thomas, this dream was so vivid—strangely, more vivid than the reality of walking right now. I flew across this woman, and she is as clear in my mind now as if she were right here before us: She was wearing a red tweed dress, with a golden brooch pinned to her lapel. She was standing over her own crushed body and she was pulling and tearing at her dress."

Michael pulled on his shirt, showing what the woman was doing. "She was lamenting, sobbing loudly, so I circled around her," he said, making a circling motion with his hand, "and I whispered to her, 'Look up. Look up, you are fine. Just look up!' Then the woman in spirit began tugging on her dead, physical body with both hands, making these strange, frantic squeals, so I kept speaking to her, 'Listen, just listen to the singing! All is well, and you are fine. If you listen to the angels, you will be fine."

Again, Michael paused while he and Thomas took purposeful steps.

"Then, just moments later, I came to a man who was ensnared by several of the beasts and he was screaming, 'Allah, Allah, Allah!' I think he was one of the hijackers. And it was strange, Thomas: As I circled him to cut the chains and free him from the beasts, I don't remember hearing a voice, but I knew that I was to let him go, I was not to cut his chains, and I watched the beasts drag him away. All the while, he was screaming, and I cried, watching a soul being dragged into the darkness. The battle raged, sometimes between the angels and beasts directly."

Michael went quiet. He put his hands in his pockets, feeling odd, awkward after sharing such a dream. Michael became aware of himself as Thomas's boss; he was not speaking the way a manager should. But the feeling quickly faded and Michael was left only with a strong feeling of vulnerability.

"Then what happened?" Thomas asked.

"Well, I woke up in the bed," Michael answered, smiling. "For a minute, I thought I had wet the bed, but then I realized that most of the moisture was around my head, neck, shoulders, and back. I was completely drenched in sweat, and the really odd thing was that when I woke up, I could smell sulfur. I realized that it was me... I am guessing that my skin and body had some strange reaction to the ash."

"But the ash was only on our heads and hands," Thomas sounded perplexed.

"You're right. It was just a strange day all the way around."

"Wow," Thomas said quietly, then turned to Michael, "You dream like that all the time?"

"No, never... Well, I mean, I dream sometimes, but never like that! I have never dreamed I was an angel." Both men walked in silence as they made their way to their hotel, but after a block or so, Michael started talking again.

"After I woke up, I felt like I needed to go for a walk, so I decided to head over to Times Square. It was already dark and the Square was completely empty except for newspaper blowing all around and down the street as fast as a cab."

"Empty?" Thomas questioned, "No people at all?" He sounded surprised. Michael chuckled, then replied, "Well, no one except a couple of hookers running like they were lost, one behind the other. But the strange thing was that they waited for the walk signal to cross the street. There were no cars, no people, but the hookers were waiting for the street signal to let them know it's okay to cross the street... Strange, I tell you. It was then that I realized that my dream had seemed more real than real life. It still does a little bit."

Michael and Thomas stopped at the entrance to the Time Hotel, not knowing what to do or say next. The smell of the smoke blew across them, suddenly strong, and while their expressions registered the bitterness in the air, neither felt the need to mention it or its source.

"I know what you mean," Thomas finally broke the silence, "Nothing feels real."

"I think I'll go upstairs and do a little work," Michael said, nodding toward the entrance.

"I think I want to walk more. Meet later for dinner?" Thomas asked.

"Sure, just buzz my phone," said Michael. As he began to turn toward the door, Thomas extended his hand; Michael instinctively reached out to grasp it, and as he did, the fresh scabs on his fingers and knuckles smarted and he winced. Thomas quickly released his hand and said, "Man, I'm sorry." Then, he looked down at Michael's hands, and without looking up, he said almost in a whisper, "I am really sorry."

Driving Home
September 14, 2001

The doorman stood just inside the doorway, swaying proudly like a child presenting a report card of "As" to an adoring parent. He was proud of his resourcefulness; just outside the door sat a white rental car, a Mustang. While all the travel agents said there were no cars to be found on the entire island of Manhattan, this young doorman knew whom to ask and what palm to grease. He was accustomed to doing favors for important men. And of course, he knew who Michael Tantalus was, who he did business with, and he was most certainly an important man. But that was not why the young doorman did a favor for Michael Tantalus. He knew that Michael was looking for a way home, and the doorman wanted to help, just to help—New York was different now, and he was different, focused on showing genuine care and compassion for others.

Michael and Thomas said goodbye to each other in the upper lobby, aware that they had shared more together in the last few days than most people do in a lifetime. They made eye contact and simply shook hands, as there were no adequate words and they realized they probably would never see each other again. Thomas was headed back to his room; he was going to wait another day to see if the airports would open. Michael had packed up when he received a message from the doorman telling him that he had found a rental car and the George Washington Bridge was open.

Michael watched the shiny metal elevator doors close. And though trimmed and supported by steel, all the walls of the elevator and its surrounding walls were made of glass. Michael shuffled silently away from the door to the glass elevator wall, and pressing his hands and forehead against the invisible wall like a young child, he stood mesmerized at the inner workings of what appeared to be a well-choreographed dance of cables, pulleys, cogs, and a rising and falling glass box.

Though the elevator's inner workings had always been visible, and Michael had ridden it many times, he had never watched the mechanical play of glass and steel. He had come and gone, ascended and descended without ever taking a moment to consider what moved him, what held him, or how solid was the thing he stood upon. The experience he had endured three days earlier opened his eyes and his ears to everything; in fact, every sense was alive in some new way. It was as though he had just been born, or born again. This rebirth, though miraculous and beautiful, was fraught with pain, and he was cold, overwhelmed, confused. There was an emptiness as if he were hungry for something, but hungry for what, he had no idea.

He felt a cough coming, but he cleared his throat and suppressed it, trying to avoid convulsing in a deep cough. He looked at his phone where one more undeleted message waited for him. He thought about deleting it—he had listened to it already—but he still did not feel strong enough to deal with it. The doors to the elevator opened, he stepped in, and he felt every cable, watched as the pulleys moved and the glass box descended into the once-again pleasant lower lobby. There was a growing feeling of panic within him, trying to escape. He put the phone back in his pocket as the doors to the elevator opened.

Turning from the glass at the sound of the doorman's voice, Michael stepped out of the elevator. He paused and listened to the deep resonance of recorded gongs sounding intermittently within the echoing, gently pulsing music of the lower lobby; every so often, he could hear birds and chimes. And essential to the symphony of sounds was falling water—he looked up at the glass ceiling, which was catching a waterfall from above and diverting water down the four brightly colored glass walls that made this amazing room.

He turned slowly with his mouth slightly open taking in the total environment, spellbound. When he finally faced the doorman, his eyes found a smile that warmed him, and he smiled broadly back at the doorman.

Michael nodded and crossed this astonishing room slowly, approaching the doorman with his hand outstretched. Their hands met firmly and they locked eyes. Michael could see every feature of the doorman's face clearly; he was recently shaven but with visible thick dark whiskers pushing through the skin, he had a large nose, and his face was dominated by thick, dark eyebrows. Michael and this man had grown up far apart, essentially in different worlds, and most of their lives ran in different circles. However, in this moment there was a clear and unspoken connection between the two men.

"What do you think, Captain?" the doorman asked as he motioned toward the bright white Mustang convertible.

"Not bad, mate!" the two men were spontaneously talking like pirates, and they both chuckled.

"This all you have?" the doorman asked as he reached for the small bag.

"Yep," Michael answered as he looked at his bag. "It's a long journey, better travel light," he added with a smile. Up until that moment, Michael had traveled lightly—compact and strategic; it was the way he moved, the way he walked, and the way he talked. He lived and kept everything in tight, neat boxes, only the necessities. But as Michael prepared to leave New York, he now carried with him and within him more than just the dust of the fallen buildings.

The Mustang accentuated Michael's feeling that he was moving in a dream world. But he was conflicted: Part of him wanted to get in the car and drive away as quickly as he could, but another part of him felt as if he should stay. The emotion that came to him was guilt and it came suddenly and without warning, cutting into his gut before his mind had enough time to ward off the feeling. Out of habit, he took inventory of all the reasons he should stay and compared them against the reasons he should run. He felt deeply that he should stay, but not one thought appeared on his imaginary list of reasons to stay. And when he considered reasons he should leave, none of them were safety or return to family. Rather, what occurred to him, what really motivated him to leave, was that the sun was bright and the streets were clear of traffic, clear of noise, no blaring horns, no constant roar, and the roads were inviting and nearly peaceful. It was clearly a good day for a drive.

It just did not seem like New York to him, he thought as he moved toward the car. It was different without the crowds, without the tight, tense drivers pushing and stressing to move inches at a time. Despite the heaviness of tragedy, there was an ease about the streets, making everything feel wide and spacious.

"Take the Westside Highway to the GW...it's the only way off the island," said the doorman as he opened the car door.

"See you in about a month," Michael said as he climbed into his white-wheeled symbol of freedom (or escape). He put his hands on the steering wheel and sat silently for a moment, taking in the fresh smell of a new car. He looked at the odometer which showed 40 miles, his age, and he smiled, again feeling as though he were dreaming. He looked ahead down the street, seeing that it was lined with tall facades like a glorious maze awaiting his exploration.

"I need to stay," he said softly to himself. Then his cell phone rang. It was his wife. They had barely spoken. Michael had called her from the hotel the day everything happened. He had reached a friend at their house, the friend said she would tell Deborah that he was okay. They had communicated briefly, but had spoken as if nothing out of the ordinary had happened. Perhaps she did not know how to ask Michael if he was okay. *How would she know anything? I can't expect her to know anything?* Michael stopped thinking and answered the phone.

"Hello."

"Hey, honey, when will you be home?" his wife's voice broke his dreamy daze. "Will you be home for dinner?"

"I am not sure, I am just about to leave..."

"Okay," she interrupted Michael, not getting the answer she wanted. "I guess we'll see you when we see you," she added, then hung up. Michael put down the phone; it was just the way they talked to each other now, or rather, *didn't* talk to each other now. Michael expected something different, wanted something different. *Okay, things are different for me, but I guess nothing is different for me.*

Michael started the car and the deep-throated rumbling of the engine gave him a jolt of pleasure. He began to laugh as he put the car into drive, but then a pang of guilt ran through him. Pushing on westward toward the West Side Highway, he rapidly reached the Henry Hudson River. As he turned north, he realized he had never made the drive to the river so quickly and he was suddenly conscious what a short distance it was from his hotel to the river.

Michael heard conflicting voices in his mind, and he was able to look deeper within himself, further than was usual. One strong thought was to stay and fight some imaginary battle, to stay and combat forces in some dreamed world between good and evil, where Heaven and Hell, angels and demons, were pitched against one another, struggling. The conflicting thought was not his wife's voice to come home, not really—this was just the form in which his anxiety came to him. The conflicting thought was actually his own ideas of "shoulds," the things he was "supposed" to do, the unspoken sense of responsibility in what he viewed as reality. *But is it reality?* he wondered now. *Or is it some skeleton of earlier imprinting, conditioning passed from his father and his father's father and so on?* Was this tradition of "should" passed on as tried and true wisdom or was it the "sins of the fathers"—some negative constellation of beliefs and half-truths. He considered further while driving. *Probably some mix of both*, he answered his own question. It was a gentle realization, and he promised himself to endeavor to examine his own thoughts and beliefs to figure out what was true.

Then out of the blue, an odd question appeared in his mind: *Are you happy?* It was a simple thought, one that most people asked themselves from time to time, but one that Michael had not taken the time to consider. He was beginning to realize that he had been on autopilot for quite some time, and by many measures, it had been working for him. He awoke every morning and began the rituals, first bathing, then coffee and the newspaper, then a review of his coming day, what appointments did he have, what items were on his list of things to accomplish during the day. Every day a race, with a measured amount of success; with each small victory came a checkmark in a tiny box beside each item completed. Of course, he added to the list every day, so there was no end to the empty boxes, more and more appeared every day, pushing him as he raced forward to an imagined finish line. Only occasionally did he glance at a growing bank account, having accepted without questioning that this was the marker, the standard of his success, the proof of his method, a method that was passed to him from his father. It said, work hard, keep a stiff upper lip, and always keep things rolling, good things will happen. And until now, mostly they had.

Jesus, he thought, how long have I been sleepwalking?

It took a disaster for him to ask himself the simple question, "Am I happy?" But of course, that led to more questions. This first small question was like a wedge into his chest exposing his heart, forcing its way in toward his soul, opening up a small gap through which came more questions: *Do you have joy? Would you give your life to be where you are now, to live the way you are now?* The answer to his last question was that he already had. Then came a question that stopped all the other questions in their tracks: *Do you have love?* He peered into himself, and just as he had pressed his face against the glass of the elevator seeing all the strange and beautiful workings inside the magically rising and falling box, driven by pulleys, cogs, cables, and belts all mechanically dancing together, he was able to see the inner workings of his mind, thoughts both seen and unseen. He was beginning to watch his thoughts, and he discovered just below the surface of his mind, just below the normally conscious thinking level, was a judge, a voice that was constantly telling Michael the things that were wrong with his individual life. *What is that voice?* He asked himself.

Continuing his drive across the city, Michael began to think of the terrorist attacks. A fragment of something he had heard or read popped into his head, something that said all avoidable suffering was rooted in ignorance, the ignorance of confusing what was not real for what was Real. He ruminated on the thought—yes, he was sure that he read it, because he remembered that the second Real had been capitalized. He was seeing things he normally did not notice.

"What is not real and what is Real?" he asked in a whisper, alone in the car. He felt that all his thoughts were like clouds flowing across the blue sky, or like dancers twirling across a stage, visions of past and present, of things Real and things not real, all mixed together, so inseparable that Michael stopped trying to sort things out in his mind. The thoughts continued but Michael stopped clinging to them, stopped judging them; he just let them come, then fade, as he drove north along a cement barrier to his right and the river to his left. He watched the river which was wide, flowing and mesmerizing, "So much water," he said quietly and wondered where it all came from. But he knew where it was going, all rivers flow to the same place.

The barrier on his right was covered in graffiti. Michael had passed this way many times having never even noticed it. He looked at it now, closely imaging all the things that the symbols communicated: signs of being, declarations of imagined territories, exclamations of hate, exclamations of love, all mixed together, painted over each other, again and again, mixed with various languages and symbols, some clear to many, some known only to a few, but collectively forming a beautiful kaleidoscope of vivid shapes and colors over broken brick and cement facades that seemed to grow out of the refuse of tire fragments, lost and rusted mufflers, and trash.

Michael had never seen beauty in decay and the realization was exhilarating. He took several deep breaths while the car was pulled from side to side by the uneven pavement of the road, catching in grooves cut along the cement for some unknown purpose. Michael's imagination took him to the dwellings beyond the graffiti-covered walls. The buildings appeared to be in decay, and he imagined a starving, decaying people abiding within the walls, locked in a ghetto of lost dreams. The sudden emotion of tearing up caught him off guard and he steeled himself to resist the impulse to cry.

Something caught Michael's attention—a long line of red coming toward him on the opposite side of the road, traveling south into Manhattan. Slowly and steadily the line approached until Michael could make out fire engines and ambulances, a solid stream as far as he could see, and they were all blasting their horns. Immediately, Michael's hand shot out to lay on the Mustang's horn, and goose bumps ran up his back, his neck, and into his hair across the top of his head. Cars full of people beside, ahead, and behind Michael all started to honk their horns, many eagerly rolling down their windows and waving enthusiastically at the emergency caravan.

The firemen entered the city like heroic liberators. Michael continued to honk excitedly, forgetting about the slums, forgetting about anything else, and his emotions swelled. Just the evening before, Michael had condemned overzealous nationalism as the result of misplaced heart that could lead to all sorts of evil. But now was different: he felt as though he himself had been part of a war, and thanks be to God, the troops had arrived, the cavalry was here. The fire engines and ambulances were covered in American flags, small little flags on the corners of the front and rear fenders, some larger flying from antennas, bowing and waving gloriously in the wind. These freedom-fighters were certainly just what this battered city needed. Truck after truck, they kept coming and coming, seemingly without end. Michael had never seen so many fire engines in one place.

He began to feel warm inside and swelled with pride. He had become aware in recent hours that he was proud to be an American and had a strong feeling of "us" against an unknown but very real "them." Michael rolled down all the windows of the car, and this time, when tears came, he did not fight them. Warm floods of emotion washed over him again and again, feeling like victory. Everything in that moment made sense to Michael: He was ready to go to war, to protect everything he believed he was or believed in, even though in this moment, none of the things he believed in were in his thoughts. He was ready to die to protect those things, whatever they were, and nothing seemed odd to Michael about feeling this way. It felt good, right.

In the white Mustang, Michael reached the George Washington Bridge where the road gave way to a large ramp that circled and climbed up high to the long suspension of steel and cement extending over the wide river. His eyes followed the long line of buildings – from medium-sized brick towers to tall glass skyscrapers – that lined the river for miles. But at the end of the island, Michael saw the smoke still rising from the remains of the fallen twin towers, along with other nearby and surrounding facades that still burned, billowing dark, solemn spheres of smoke that drifted away sadly.

Michael resisted the thought that was returning to him from yesterday, but it came anyway as he watched the continuous red line of emergency vehicles pouring into Manhattan. Just as he had when he watched endless numbers of blood donors' arms attached to endless tubes forming red lines, filling bag after bag with blood, now he thought, *For whom? Who needed all this blood? Who needed all these fire engines? Who needed these ambulances?*

This much had been clear to him on the morning of September 11: Stand here and you are alive, but stand there — a mere few feet away — and you are dead.

Michael's sense of national pride deflated and his mood slid downward from somber to sullen. As the bands of smoke on the horizon faded, all that had been clear to Michael only moments before dissolved into thin air. He stopped looking at Manhattan and down the river, focusing his gaze firmly onto the road in front of him. Chasing pavement and leaving things behind had always worked for Michael, and he craved the hypnotic and soothing effect of driving, so he pushed his foot onto the accelerator and moved on, making a conscious effort to not look back.

Once across the Henry Hudson River, Michael made the turn south so the city was now over his left shoulder in his periphery. He couldn't help himself: He looked at the city from across the river. He watched the smoke rise and dissipate while the sun fought to rise above the city. He passed the Statue of Liberty and she looked different to him. Her arm which once had stretched out as a beacon, a guide for all those lost and weary, now seemed to be reaching desperately and uselessly for lost loved ones. It appeared to Michael that Liberty herself was gazing horrified at the smoke, weeping over the ruins and the deceased.

As the whole scene passed to his rearview mirror, Michael felt that there was something bigger here for him to see – something larger than the awful scenes that ached to play themselves across his mind. A spot of blood, a sound, a smell, a burnt arm, fragments of things sensed, of things seen, successfully broke through into his consciousness, but Michael instantly and quickly buried them, forcing himself to think of meaningless things... green sign up ahead, speed limit sign over there, sensation of road under the car wheels. Yes, Michael thought, there was something more than just terrorists, more than just victims, and as he sorted through it, his vivid angel dream came back to him but he decided it was just a dream, nothing more.

Michael began to search for some music on the radio to distract himself, and as the first station came into tune, he raised the volume. The sound of a familiar, comforting rock-and-roll ballad eased into his ears.

"God, not that crap," he yelled out, even though it was precisely the type of music he usually listened to. He turned the knobs quickly, surfing for just the right sound, the right kind of distraction. He did not know what he was looking for so he tried all the usual—country, news (just more of what he was trying not to think about), sports, oldies, classical, but nothing sat right with him until he found a heavy metal rock station. While he rarely if ever listened to heavy metal, pounding music was just what resonated with Michael. He found that it was the only music he could tolerate, so he turned the volume as loud as it would go and sat back further in the seat. He could feel the wind blowing through his hair as he escaped from the city, trying his best to stop thinking.

"God, I am tired of driving already," Michael said aloud. He watched the lines in the middle of the highway pass by quickly one after another, but he felt as if he was getting nowhere. There was a pressure within him and it started with the feeling that he was going to cough. The feeling was deep down and he tightened himself to resist it. He gripped the steering wheel with both hands keeping himself and the car well within the lines that stretched ahead, unbroken on one side but dashed in the middle of the road, inviting him to change lanes when necessary. He was dimly conscious of not wanting choices right now. Choice required thinking, and any thought was like the cough deep down; if ever it started to rise, there would be no stopping until he was convulsing out of control. He felt that if what was inside him were to come out he would break.

He found that it helped to drive fast and with the hard, pounding music on the radio he was able to keep his thoughts deep down. He looked at his phone, which still showed one message. He decided to turn it off, and even then its presence was still too much, so he tossed it into the back seat and turned up the radio even louder.

The relentless pounding of the music resonated with the noise in Michael's head, and his inside awareness and outside experience became mirrors of each other. The hard beat pulsed through his entire body, and he moved his head to the clear beat of the drums while keeping his foot steady on the accelerator. As he began to put some distance between himself and the smoldering city, he began to feel like he was escaping – escaping from what he had become, escaping from a besieged city, but more than anything else, escaping from feelings of guilt.

The genie is back in the bottle, he told himself, taking a deep breath, but in that precise moment, he had a realization. He knew the way from New York to North Carolina, and there were several ways he could have driven, but he was in such a hurry to leave what was behind him, he didn't give a single thought to what lay ahead. Thus, instead of choosing a route he had let the route choose him, so now he was driving into Washington, D.C., and the highway that chose Michael took him right alongside the Pentagon. The genie was never back in the bottle. He slowed, registering the smoke that was rolling along low on the horizon, stretching across another scene of disaster.

Michael now knew just how raw he was. Everything within him was not buried but open to whoever might happen to look at him, and he hoped that no one would. For the first time ever that he could remember, he lost complete control of his thoughts and emotions. He thought about stopping. Absentmindedly, he turned the radio knob and found a local station which was announcing that there was to be a candlelight vigil near the Pentagon tonight. He considered it; it was a respectful thing to do. But slowly and with some amount of regret he kept driving. He felt that if he stopped, everything would spill out of him, and now a cough came, suddenly before he could control it, and he convulsed with it, holding tightly onto the steering wheel. Finally, the cough ebbed, his eyes watered, and his stomach itched. He turned the radio dial again until he found another metal rock station. He did not recognize any of the songs and barely understood any of the lyrics, but it didn't matter – the acid melodies and frantic beats were all he could stand and it was far better than silence.

Michael had pushed on as far as he could, he did not have the energy to go any further. Passing the smoking Pentagon had exhausted him and he decided to find a hotel. Michael suddenly realized he was praying.

"God forgive me," the prayer in his mind came to his lips, "Please, please, God, forgive me."

He did not have any specific thing in mind but, in general, for many things, he was fervently repenting. "Why the hell am I praying?" he was now talking to himself out loud. *Must be some conditioned response from my youth*, he thought, *my parents had me in church every Sunday*, "My misspent youth," he joked with himself and began to laugh. "I better get a room," he said as he slowed, taking the next off ramp. The exit rose a bit from the highway, and as he came to a stoplight he could see an economy motel nestled alongside the interstate. It was small, one story and maybe a dozen rooms long, all with matching doors and windows. There was no vegetation or anything decorative at all, and the only thing that stood out at all was a small neon sign blinking the word, vacancy. Michael eased the Mustang up to the office, got out of the car, and approached the desk clerk. He was thin and very young, holding a paperback book open to the middle but his attention was on a small portable television sitting on the front counter; there was a news station on, but the volume was turned off.

"Can I get a room?"

"Fill this out, and I need a credit card," the young man spoke as he pushed a sheet of paper for Michael to fill out, never looking away from the television. He took the credit card in silence and ran it through a machine that made an imprint, then pushed it back to Michael. After taking the paper and making a few notes, he slid Michael a key, still saying nothing.

"Thank you," Michael said as he turned to exit the office. He wanted to say more but he was feeling awkward. He wanted to tell this stranger about what he had been through the past few days – he felt the compunction to talk, but it just was not the right situation, this was not the right person to talk to. He realized that he would have the need to talk again, but the right situation would never present itself, he would never run across the right person to tell what he had seen and what he had done, because that person did not exist.

He moved the car to park in front of his assigned room, number 10. And as he unlocked the door, he noticed that he was between rooms nine and 11. The numbers would from now on catch his eye. He did not think it possible that he was being confronted by the numbers more now than he was before; it was just that the numbers nine and 11 now had meaning to him, so he noticed them. He wondered how many things he saw every day and did not notice—countless, he was sure.

The instant he opened the door, he noticed the artificial smell of what he thought was vinyl. Noticing stilled his thoughts. He stepped inside and reached to pull the off-white plastic curtains shut. He shut the door and found himself in the dark. He heard a truck roar down the highway. The sound should have comforted him, because sound meant another person, but tonight the sound made him see how alone he was. His hand brushed the wall next to the door until he found the switch that turned on a light in the small, rectangular room. He turned to face the beds – twins covered in bland beige spreads that neatly wrapped the mattresses. The room was completely sterile with no color other than white, off-white, and various shades of beige, and the room was nearly empty. After a few moments of silence, the room was again filled with the sound of an 18-wheeler roaring down the highway past the motel.

Michael stripped to his underwear, climbed into one of the beds, and pulled the covers to his chin. He was uncomfortable and restless.

"Why the hell did I not keep going?" Michael broke the silence with his own voice and it echoed off the empty walls. The fluorescent light in the bathroom was on and buzzing. The sound of the passing traffic was loud in the room. The passing cars and trucks sounded like gentle shushing, each addressing a rising and tempestuous thought, as though an unseen mother was soothing him to sleep. He felt empty and lost. He was not in the city, where perhaps his dream had been real, where he was needed, where he could make a difference. And he was not at home where he had duties, he was just in some in-between state, he was nowhere.

He lay in the bed and looked at the clock, and the shining red numbers were nine and 11.

"God bless!" he shouted at the clock and looked about as though someone was arranging props for some unseen entity's amusement. For hours he lay trying to sleep, finally succumbing after feverishly thrashing about in the tangled sheets and nylon blanket.

A House, But Not Home

September 15, 2001

It was early, but Michael finally decided to get up after thrashing about and barely sleeping. He could still hear the trucks on the highway and it was as if they were taunting him in some way. He showered in a tight bathroom in a plain white fiberglass shower and tub combination. It was a stark contrast from the morning before where sharp angles of polished chrome and clean glass met marble all illuminated in indirect and imaginative light, where large thick towels and a plush robe hung from large hooks on the wall. Here, in this small place, the water felt different. There was one towel and one washcloth, so thin that they folded almost flat. The lone light was a small exposed fluorescent tube perhaps twelve inches long, and the ballast within the fixture buzzed obnoxiously. Even the toilet paper was rougher. No shampoo and one small piece of odd-smelling soap wrapped in beige wax paper, with no writing.

Michael decided not to shave; he quickly dressed then headed for the car. He was focused on going home to see his family. As he sat in the car, the sun peeked over the horizon. Bright clear light flooded into the new rental car and it engulfed Michael with temporary optimism. And just outside of Michael's motel room was a small flower bed that he had not noticed the night before. Growing from the dark soil were several miniature rose bushes, vivid in the crisp morning light. The flowers were all in various stages of flowering: There were long green stems, there were small buds, there were freshly broken buds, and there were dead receding buds surrounding fresh deep red blossoms. Michael stared at the flowers, he had never noticed the buds in such detail, and as he looked at them, he had a realization.

"The bud must die to give birth to the flower," he said it aloud. "Damn, turns out I'm a freaking philosopher," he laughed and shook his head, but the thought stayed with him. He looked beyond the flower bed across the parking lot and behind the motel and could see dew sparkling across a small expanse of grass that ran alongside a dark slow moving river. It made him remember a time as a young boy when he had swum in a river that looked much the same. He remembered that after getting out and drying in the sun, he could still feel a thin layer of silt across his fresh skin; it did not feel dirty, it was comforting to him. He thought of coming out of the ash, and the feeling on the skin was much the same, he thought that he could still feel the ash on his skin now, but different from the river silt of his childhood because he now he felt dirty in a way that he could not describe.

He put the car in reverse and slowly backed away from the motel, and as he began to drive toward the nearby highway, he hesitated. *I need to get home to see my family*, he told himself again but he was unsure. Michael sat deeper in the soft leather seat of the car and pushed himself forward. He reached the highway as the sun was peeking over the trees, throwing light up into an open blue sky. He slowed the Mustang just enough to turn onto the entrance ramp to the interstate. He was on track to get home to North Carolina in time for dinner and the familiar interstate made him feel in control. It was an imagined feeling, a thin one that was about to break. The entrance ramp was bumpy with broken cement that had been patched carelessly. The right side of the road was lined with waist-high stone barriers, one right after the other, each ten feet in length and designed to keep the Mustang or any other car off the shoulder all the way to the main highway.

Michael thrust his foot onto the accelerator, the small white car leapt forward in near instant response, quickly matching the speed of the line of cars already on the highway. The on-ramp started low and below the main interstate, making it difficult for Michael to see the coming cars even as the on-ramp gained elevation. Michael was still gaining speed and, as he neared the top of the entrance ramp, quickly looked over his left shoulder to see what was coming. He could see the long line of cars but he could also see a break, enough room for him to merge. Michael signaled and began to move onto the highway: he had no choice because the cement abutment along the shoulder had ended his lane. Right at that point, the coming car behind sped up and closed the gap, leaving Michael nowhere to go. The last thing Michael saw and heard was a large man behind the steering wheel of the car blaring the horn. Michael was sure the man was sneering at him as he passed.

Then everything sped up, adrenalin surged into Michael's bloodstream. His body moved instinctually, his foot jammed onto the brakes as the accelerating car on the highway drove him towards the cement wall. The Mustang's tail came around the right side, and Michael's instincts first turned into the slide but then quickly the other way as the car careened towards the wall. As his body wrestled with the car and the laws of physics to avoid a crash, something in Michael watched, detached, only observing. And even though everything was happening within fractions of seconds, this observing component took it all in slowly and calmly. The tail of the Mustang now drove the car: Michael had avoided the wall but now was traveling backwards and blind across two lanes of the southbound highway and into a wide grassy median. Still spinning and with high velocity, the out-of-control car ramped into the air across two lanes of oncoming northbound traffic.

Michael could hear the squealing of rubber ripping against the hard pavement as cars braked and swerved, some as they tried to avoid the flying car. The Mustang came back onto all four tires and slid into the grass on the far side of the highway, Michael's hands were still grappling with the steering wheel as horns blared and scenery passed sideways across the front windshield. Michael slid to a stop just off the access road on the north side of the freeway. For a short moment, Michael and the car were perfectly motionless. He stared straight ahead with both hands embedded into the steering wheel, his body still vibrating from the large amount of adrenalin in his system and the aftershock of fear.

Then came the break. It was like a fragile ceiling of rock in Michael's skull fell into a deep cavern of molten rage sending lava and fire spewing from his body. The blank stare on his face creased into a scowl, and once again, his foot jammed onto the accelerator, only this time Michael was filled with rage. Strength exploded into his muscles as every fiber tensed in his body, terse across his face. The car lunged southward onto the northbound access road. The car accelerated faster and faster as the small red needle of the speedometer labored to keep up with the spinning wheels. Michael, in one grand swiping movement, crossed the narrow band of dead grass into the northbound traffic, then across the wide grass median, and bounced onto the southbound pavement of the highway. The cars on both sides of the freeway slowed and gave the errant Mustang a wide berth. The large, red, offending pickup truck appeared small in the distant horizon, but within moments, it was quickly growing as Michael's foot lay the pedal against the car floor and pushed harder with his leg, trying to go faster. He was pushing the Mustang to its limit, the pistons pumping harder and harder within the cylinders, small but powerful, countless explosions as sparks ignited compressed air and gas hastened the steel and glass vehicle closer and closer to the target of Michael's rage.

Michael announced his arrival to the two men by crumpling the front of the Mustang into the lowered tailgate of the offending red truck. The truck lunged violently and the sudden jolt sent the two men into a tirade that was lost upon Michael. He could not hear them nor their curses because of the accusations and hatred that were coming from his own mouth, mixed in the spit and slobber that were spewing with the words, like lava from a dark place within Michael.

Michael was no longer operating within his conscious control. His arm, without any discernible consent from his being, was thrusting a dangerously threatening finger again and again into the air in the direction of the two perpetrating strangers. He pulled his car alongside the truck. Both men inside the red vehicle were shouting but no discernible words reached Michael through the wind and his own fury. With wide sweeping motions of their arms, the two men motioned to Michael to pull over. He obliged them by pulling the Mustang slightly ahead and within inches of the truck, pushing both cars off the highway and into the graveled shoulder.

The man jammed on his brakes and the truck slid to a hurried stop. Michael slid the Mustang to a rest sideways just beyond it. The two young men jettisoned themselves from the truck, the passenger brandishing a large wrench. Michael furiously fumbled for the door lever, struggling to find it in the unfamiliar vehicle. He fell out of the car as he opened the passenger door but flew off the ground and ran in the direction of the two strangers.

The first man wearing overalls stopped and, standing wide, bent over and began laughing. Michael was in dress slacks with no tie and no jacket. He was angrily bringing a tall but slender frame towards a large square man of at least six feet six inches tall and a wide girth. The first man looked at the second man holding the wrench and they both began to laugh aloud, relieving them of their own tension.

"Hey little man, you better get back into that fancy little car and get out of here before we hurt ya bad," the man yelled at Michael in a deep threatening voice, but then began to laugh again.

Michael heard nothing. His skin shone bright red and his eyes were fully dilated. He threw his first punch while still in a dead run at the two men. The man, though surprised, was able to duck and recoil just enough to make Michael's fist miss his face, but Michael's following elbow found its mark; powered by rage and fueled by adrenaline, its force crushed the bridge of the man's nose. There was a crackling crunch and a large pop as the man's nose snapped. Tears blinded the struck man and blood began to pour into his mouth and throat, it was a devastating blow. The man instinctively turned away from Michael, covering his injured face with his hands. Michael furiously punched at the now falling man, landing the blows to the back of his head.

"Oh God, oh God," the large man was now on the ground crying out. The second man was stunned and stood motionless as though he was a spectator and not part of the scene unfolding before him. He gathered himself then yelled out like an animal as he raised the heavy wrench high into the air and attacked Michael. Michael was still punching at the fallen man as the three writhed in an odd violent dance. As he neared, the second man brought down the wrench, but Michael sensed the blow coming and turned while raising his left arm to block the blow, but only partially doing so. The wrench grazed the left side of Michael's head but caught enough of his ear to split its webbing. The still accelerating mass of the large wrench continued its path, careening off of Michael's arm and shoulder, headed towards the ground and carrying the second man into Michael. Arms and legs folded into each other as the two men committed to combat at an intimate range. Too close to punch, they grappled, scratched, and clawed at each other desperately to gain some advantage. They rolled over and over until Michael was able to gain the higher ground. He sat on top of the man, holding his throat with one hand while connecting two solid punches to the man's face with the other fist.

The man grasped the wrist of the hand on his throat trying to wrench it free while he covered his face with his other arm to ward off Michael's wild punches. Michael's furious fist slammed into the man's forehead, fracturing two small bones in Michael's clenched hand and knuckles. The pain was absent in the ferocity of the moment. The first man stood, holding his broken face with one hand and picking up the heavy wrench with the other. Still nearly blind in tears and blood, he raised the wrench and brought it down on Michael with all his force. His fist holding the wrench landed square and hard on Michael's back with enough force to drive the air out of his lungs. The pain made Michael arch backward and fall off of the man he had been punching. The large man threw the wrench into the weeds and gathered the other man on the ground. And together they headed back to the truck. Michael, still struggling to regain air, lunged at the men, grabbing one by the leg while the other kicked him in the ribs. As he recoiled, they got into the truck. As they were shutting the doors, Michael attacked again, only to be repelled by a rapidly raising window glass. He clawed at the glass, trying to get to the man inside. The truck roared to life, tires spinning and spewing gravel as it knocked Michael to the ground. Its tires squealed as they found the pavement.

Michael lay on his back; he turned his head to watch as the red truck disappeared into the horizon. He turned his head again to look into an empty blue sky. His chest was still heaving, gasping for air, but the kind and steady blue sky exorcised the deities of rage and darkness and soon he was hearing his own thoughts again. His breathing began to ease but he did not move. The thought that came into his teary and shaking body was, *"You are not right, man."*

Michael sat up and began taking inventory of his body and his injuries and, as pain came, so did judgment of his actions, of his thoughts, of how out of control he was. He had been in fights before but this was no drunken bar room fight over some perceived insult salted in beer and settled with one, two, or sometimes, three punches. Those fights had been more about relieving some kind of tension or even boredom; sometimes he and his friends went out looking for women or a fight or sometimes both. Those kinds of fights had been like two bucks locking horns, marking territory for the purpose of lust or retribution over spilt beer. Pushing, shoving, a punch or two, a shot of adrenalin with a mix of overactive hormones, and suddenly he would feel better, like a man.

But this was different, he lost himself to some dark place within his mind where rage ruled and it was messy. He did not feel better nor did he feel like a "man." All he felt was afraid. Afraid of what he had just learned was inside of him, afraid of losing control, afraid he would not be able to crawl out of the dark hole he found inside himself, but mostly afraid of what he might do. That's when it hit him, a cough from deep down surfaced so quickly that he was unable to suppress it, his body convulsed and he coughed violently, his body was trying to extricate an unseen toxin, a poison, an irritant. Something inside that the body deemed foreign, something that would cause damage, something that threatened the body from working as it should, something that inhibited health and happiness, and perhaps something that threatened Michael the entity from continued existence. The body was trying to get it out of his lungs, so as to repair damage. Michael's body was bent nearly double as the coughing spasms continued, making his nose run and his eyes water.

"Damn, I must have two tons of crap in my lungs," Michael thought, and though still breathing heavy from the fight, he was careful not to draw too much air in, lest he cough again. The poison that he was thinking about was merely physical materials: fiber dust, splinters of

edifices, and so forth. But then Michael thought again of the fight, and he knew that there were other poisons in him. Things seen, things heard, vibrations felt, words, thought, thought patterns, and beliefs. It was these things that had caused his chain reaction. These things irritated in his mind; these small unseen things that brought fear and anger might possibly bring disease if not extricated. But things in the mind and heart are not always easily extricated.

Michael was still shaking uncontrollably from the fight and from the coughing and he began to feel his injuries. He held his hands up to the sky to examine them, the scabs that had formed since Tuesday were all cracked, some of them missing entirely and he was bleeding from both hands. The two smaller knuckles of his right hand began to swell and pain began to throb from several different places; he could not locate any one place to address, so instead he lay back down in the gravel for a moment to gather himself. *I have got to get home*, he thought. He stood, walked back to the Mustang, opened the door easily with his left hand, and gingerly got into the car. He looked at himself in the mirror: blood had run down from his ear across the front of his shirt. *I'll stop at the next gas station, wash up and change my shirt before I get home*, he thought.

Michael drove the balance of the distance to the airport in Charlotte with no further incidence. It was as if the fight had let some amount of energy subside, but he felt it building again and pushed down the feelings that were trying to surface. Michael returned the rental car, explaining the dented front of the Mustang as an error of inattention. He had expected it to be a major hassle, but even here in Charlotte, far from the smoking piles of steel and rubble, people were at their best, offering to handle the issue for him.

"You were in New York?" the clerk at the rental counter asked.

"Yes, but not close to the action, thank goodness," Michael lied. He did not know why he lied; the answer just came out, and it was easier than the truth.

"I was at work when we heard," the clerk continued, but Michael interrupted.

"I am very tired."

"Yes, of course. Here's your receipt, Mr. Tantalus."

Michael walked to the shuttle bus, turning to look at the crumpled Mustang. He could not quite put his finger on what he was feeling, but he did not want to leave the Mustang behind. *Perhaps it is the road that I cannot leave*, he thought, then he forced himself to turn to get onto the shuttle. Soon, he was experiencing the familiarity of his own car. Familiar smells, familiar items—a shirt in the backseat, a coffee cup from his kitchen in the cup holder, one of his children's shoes. All of it should have comforted him, but instead he felt alien, a different person than the one who had left this car only days earlier.

The drive to his neighborhood took longer than he expected. It was dark, but the houses on his street were brightly lit and there was much activity. *What a lovely neighborhood I live in*, he thought, *everything is so beautiful and picturesque.* He rolled the car into the driveway but didn't push the button to open the garage door. He put the car in park and looked at his house from the outside. It was a large, two-story brick house and the outside lights were unlit—as though he was not expected. The blinds were open to the well-lit interior, though, and he could see his wife, children, and even his dog moving about inside the house.

You need to go inside. The thought appeared in Michael's head as a demand. *Should I knock? That's ridiculous, this is my house! I should just go in.* He turned the engine off and got out of the car, walking purposefully in the dark toward his front door. He put his key into the door and went in of the breeze of the dark night into the light of his house.

"Hey, honey," Deborah greeted him. "Glad you are home."

He was suddenly and unexpectedly paralyzed, standing speechless before his wife. He tried to speak, but nothing came out.

"Did you happen to roll the garbage to the street before you came in?" she asked.

"No," he responded, relieved to be speaking even if it was only a word, but the word came out of him like stale air. He could add no other words—there were no coherent thoughts, and he felt numb and exposed. Suddenly, he thought, *This mundane conversation is killing me.* He wanted to turn and leave, but he held his ground, oddly wishing his wife would slap him. He tried to say something to her; she was not looking at him as she adjusted the lamp on the entryway table. The grandfather clock against the wall ticked loudly.

"Well, be sure to take it out before you go to bed," she said, turning to head back toward the kitchen. He stood in the entryway alone, and he found that he was shaking. He wanted to blurt out everything.

"There is some dinner in the oven," she yelled from the other room. "Will you check your daughter's homework and make sure that your son is in bed?" These were more commands than requests, and the sound of her voice faded as she moved further into the house. She was still talking, but he couldn't hear what she was saying, so he dropped his bags and walked quickly to catch up with her. Finding her in the laundry room, he looked at her. She was mad at him—or so it appeared to him—but mad about what?

"What's wrong?" he asked her.

"Nothing," she said as she folded a t-shirt, "I am just busy...lots to do." Michael continued to watch her. *There is something disrespectful about how she treats me,* he told himself. *She has not always been disrespectful to me, but she has been for a long time: I wonder why I tolerate it.* Deborah looked up at him, forced a smile for just an instant, then pushed past him out of the laundry room and into the kitchen.

She's distant and cold. I need her and she's unavailable, Michael judged, then a pang of guilt gripped him. She knows. *She's smart—of course she knows. I could never hide anything from her.* His thoughts raged uncontrolled, and his body registered every thought like a physical blow. He could not go to her, but he did not deserve to go to her. He wanted to tell her things, but he was afraid that once he started to tell her things he wouldn't be able to stop, that he would tell her everything. There were so many things he wanted and needed to tell her...and so many things that he knew he should not tell her. As he approached her again, she stopped wiping the counter for a moment and looked at him, no expression on her face.

She smiled once more and moved, this time, to the den, stopping to pick up a pair of kids' shoes and scattered socks; he followed her back to the foyer of the house, where she put the shoes on the stairs before moving on to the dining room. She picked up a pile of papers and then began to straighten the chairs around the dining room table. Her hands were pushing the straight, high-back chairs into place as her head was already turning, focusing in on the next task. He watched her walk away, thinking she was unfamiliar to him. *Almost 20 years together and now I'm unable to say anything to her. This is my fault: I did this.*

She yelled something to their son, then came back toward Michael. He prepared himself for a confrontation, as she was coming swiftly right toward him, but then she passed by, huffing a small amount of air and giving him a slightly disdainful look. He realized he was expected to do something. Again, he wanted to say something to her, so he took a deep breath and turned to address her, but she was already gone, picking up pillows off the den floor, slapping them, then carefully placing them at the corners of the couch. He watched himself watch her for a moment longer, then she was off again to the laundry room.

Michael stood alone in the den, feeling that he did not recognize anything. He looked at the large picture of his family sitting on the mantle over the fireplace. "Who is she? How strange to feel like I don't know her," he whispered to himself, then he turned and headed out the front door. In the driveway, he looked at his car: It would be so easy to just get in and drive away. *You are being ridiculous,* he thought, then moved toward the garbage bin. There was a bit of comfort in the routine of rolling the bin down the driveway and placing it in exactly the same spot as always.

He stood looking at the bin for a moment in the dark, thinking about what an awful person he was. Having finally arrived home, he felt as if there was nothing here for him. New York seemed finished, but without his life there, there was apparently no life here, either, and he could not bear it. *There's obligation here, but nothing more,* he thought to himself. It felt as though, when he finally stopped driving, everything else began catching up with him everything he knew deep down but did not want to think about pressed in on him now in the lonely darkness of his driveway. Jo's teary face flashed across his mind. He stiffened to hold himself together. He wanted and needed to talk to Deborah. He wanted and needed to be held. But he could not put a word on what he was feeling and he did not know how to ask for help. The pressure inside of him was great, he felt like he was about to explode and he wanted to yell something. Then suddenly, he felt exhausted.

Michael walked back inside and stood at the bottom of the stairs that led up to his bedroom. Tension gripped his entire body. He felt as though he was at the center of a great vortex of life's events—standing in the eye of a hurricane where everything was momentarily calm, almost peaceful; he was certain he was only moments away from a wall of violent, rushing wind.

He considered turning around to find his wife, to take hold of her, to shake her out of her trance. Or perhaps he wanted to hold her, to be held by her, to weep with her. He could feel an energy expanding inside his chest, wanting to come out. He recognized the feeling from a memory of falling as a child, and getting up unable to breathe, unable to cry. Then, his mother reached out, picking him up and consoling him as air finally came to his body and he released waves of sobbing. He could feel that sensation now, but there were no arms to hold him, and he did not know how to let the feeling out of his chest.

And then Michael made a decision. Later, from time to time, he would wonder if he had gained discretion or had lacked courage in the moment that he turned and walked up the stairs into the darkness. It was the saddest moment of his life. *I have been so wrong*, he thought to himself, not thinking about how or why but just *wrong*. He took a step up. "I am just too tired," he whispered as he took another step. "It will all be fine in the morning," he said aloud, replying to the feelings in his stomach as he tried to console himself and convince his body that everything would be okay. The physical sensations were so strong he hurried up the steps, afraid of what he might do or say if he went back down the stairs.

He wanted to be mad at his wife. But he realized that he was not angry with her; she had done nothing wrong. The feeling in his chest welled up again, begging him to do something. He thought he might cry, then thought that he did not really know how. Pausing to look back down the stairs again, he saw light from the dining room pouring across the hall floor, and he could hear his family: soft noises of talking and moving, even the jingling of the dog's collar and tags.

Everything built to a crescendo, but Michael went blank. It was as if everything shut down. He did nothing and he said nothing. Michael was not conscious of deciding to do nothing, there was just no thought. His wife stayed busy downstairs as he wearily collapsed crosswise on the bed, stretching himself from corner to corner. He knew that Deborah would not be getting into the bed; she had not been consistently or even regularly in the bed for nearly 10 years. She was always having to soothe or give comfort to one of the two children, then she would fall asleep with the child in his or her bed. It had not bothered Michael before. He had always been content not to be disturbed, but now he was lonely.

He wondered if Deborah would come to him. If she did, he told himself that he would tell her things, even the things that might make her never come to him again. But if she did not come to him tonight? Well, then, that was a message from her. He pulled his body into a ball, hugging his legs with his arms. Then, he stretched out, rolled over in the bed, and pulled up the covers. He felt just the same as he had in the sterile hotel bed the night before. He sat up and punched the pillow attempting to make it more comfortable, but pain from his fist shot up his arm. He reached awkwardly with his left arm to turn on the bedside lamp, then he coddled his throbbing right hand, examining how swollen it was. *I should go get some ice*, he thought, then thought better of it. He did not want to go downstairs and face things.

How did I not see the state of my marriage? he wondered *What have I done?* He lay back down, trying to sleep. *How did this happen? How did I get to this point?* Thoughts ran through his mind until he heard his wife coming up the stairs. He feigned sleep. He had always said that he was fearless, but now he pretended he was asleep to avoid the storm of what he was afraid might be coming. His wife peered into the doorway, quietly walked in and turned off the lamp, then walked out, shutting the door as she left. He was alone again in the darkness.

As Michael's fatigued body began to settle into the bed, his mind drifted. He longed for touch and was struck by a memory of how soft the skin felt on Jo's abdomen. He turned onto his side and stretched his hand between the sheets, imagining the soft rise and fall of her breathing. Then her teary, bloody face flashed across his mind, and he could feel a half-million tons of debris rushing to the ground. His body recoiled at the memory and he sat up, taking deep breaths, trying desperately to push the memories away and settle himself.

He lay back down and looked around the dark room. There was just enough light filtering in through the blinds to reveal dark outlines of the furniture and paintings around his bedroom. It all felt like an alien landscape. Everything looked strange to him; although he recognized the shapes of the furniture, nothing seemed his, nothing belonged to him. Part of the reason he could not tell Deborah things was that, in a very real sense, he felt as if he did not know her. He reconsidered: Of course he knew her, and had known her for quite some time. But just now, she seemed foreign to him. He ran memories of their courtship through his mind. He had been a little wild and soul-searching even then. They had connected through song and poetry, but mostly through music. She was young and needed him back then, but now she was strong and self-sufficient—in many ways she did not need him. He respected her in many ways and he was sure that he loved her, but he wondered if she respected him in any way at all or if she loved or needed him. What did he give to her that was indispensable? Perhaps she just did not need him now. Life's circumstances demanded a soldier of the daily duties, and that simply took more out of him than he had to give.

Life with children, car payments, and a mortgage required holding the line in the trenches of the daily grind. Somewhere, he gave up searching for truth and finding what fed his soul and instead hardened himself against the constant onslaught of bills and "things that needed to be done," whether with a child or something around the seemingly always-deteriorating house. He held down soul-eating jobs, taking things from bosses and co-workers, biting his tongue or pretending to respect those he thought were ridiculous, all along making small compromises that buried his heart in the sediment of daily bullshit.

As he lay in the bed listening quietly, he could hear everyone come up the stairs one by one: the hopping of his son, the skipping of his daughter, and the tired, heavy steps of his wife. He could hear muffled "good nights" as each got into his or her bed, his wife climbing in with their daughter. Michael noticed the room growing lighter as the moon rose high enough to send blue light through the small slats of the shutters. When he was sure everyone was asleep, he got out of the bed and walked quietly down the wooden hallway, pausing at each doorway to look in at his son, his daughter, and his wife.

His wife lay on the bed facing the far side of the room. He walked around to face her. The blue light of the moon lit on her face. Michael sat cross-legged next to her. Even in the dim light, he was seeing things he had never seen before, noticing deep detail in her face. He could hear her soft, slow, and breathing. She was already asleep. She had always been able to fall asleep so easily, so swiftly. Michael remembered years of listening to her as she drifted off; he had learned to recognize over the years just precisely how close she was to sleep or how soundly she was sleeping.

The odd light and night shadows accentuated the crow's feet at the corners of her eyes. The creases around her mouth formed a terse frown on her face. He remembered her talking about her dreams— all the things she would accomplish in her life—when they were young and imagined themselves the age they were now. Then it had come upon her suddenly. "I want to have children," she blurted out to him one day. "Okay," was his simple answer, without thinking about what it meant or entailed.

Life, Michael learned, was always about compromises, it was like she bore nature in exchange for things she had planned in her mind; she was exhausted, she never rested, and she was continually distracted from her own dreams and own goals as the well-being of the children became her well-being. If one of them suffered, she suffered.

The children were like baby birds in a nest, constantly crying out, constantly needing. Yes, she was holding the line just like him, only she was holding the line tougher than he was and at greater sacrifice. He wondered if she was receiving any gratification within. If she was, it was hidden from him, as she seemed to Michael to be in a constant state of discontent. Where was her romantic soul, the one he had touched with his songs years before, the thing that, when they shared it, had seemed greater than anything? Where was all that? What was all that? Was it all just a trick by Mother Nature to assure the species' survival?

Was that same girl he longed for still there inside her somewhere, waiting to be drawn out? Was her soul locked away in a tall tower, waiting for a brave knight to slay the dragon and rescue her: Was she waiting for him? Where had he been? Even when in the house, where had he been? It seemed so ridiculous to him now, how had he gotten so off-track? Did he need merely to slay the dragon of quiet desperation against the daily grind? Did he need to gather himself with brave gallantry? Or no... should he quietly withdraw to his own soul? He had already failed her! And as he said it to himself, he contracted: He had failed her long ago, but only now, with the realization of his failure, did the pain surge into his heart.

Of course, there had been wounds over the years, some out loud and some silent and quietly endured. He had been bad, and as he looked at her in the moonlight, he could see on her aging, sleeping face the scars of his deceits and lies. Of course she knew: She had just swallowed hard, kept her head down, and kept holding the line. *Admirable*, he thought. They both just did their respective jobs and kept going; it was why they never talked anymore, he was sure. Most likely she already knew what had just occurred to him, and she was just as afraid as he was that, once they started talking, they would not be able to stop—and talking would lead to secrets revealed, secrets that would damage once said out loud.

She never bared her soul to him anymore. She had gone silent years ago, and he supposed that she had her secrets, as well. He knew the depth of feeling and thought within her, she was just shut down. And he had been as well, finding what he needed elsewhere. *God, it feels like living a cliché!*

But his trauma in New York had opened him, softened him, and his heart lay bare and exposed. He was frightened, truly frightened. Love, duty, obligation... everything was confused for Michael, and he tried desperately to find a place to stand. Even condemning and hating himself was a place to stand, but he could not even get to that point. He had the urge to nudge her, to shake her, even gently to wake her. He wanted desperately to talk to her even if she were to scream at him in hate. Again, he found himself wishing she would reach up and slap him.

He took in a breath and reached out his arm but stopped just short, letting her sleep. This woman with whom he was so familiar but barely knew was a stranger to him; as he sat in total honesty in his own wretchedness, he realized he could not wake her because she would wake to a man she did not know. He would be a stranger, too. To wake his sleeping wife and truly, deeply connect would require complete honesty, but that could be unbearably messy. Deepest pain always comes from those you love, whom you are closest to—you lie to them to keep from feeling that pain.

As he sat cross-legged looking at his wife, everything was inside out. He needed to talk to her to begin to heal, but as he looked, he began to withdraw. He stroked her hair gently with his swollen hand, and then he leaned forward to kiss her on the forehead. His secrets left him dreadfully lonely in his own house. *She has not slept with me in 10 years*, he had thought earlier, but he repeated it to himself again, here, now, sitting in the dark so close to her.

He leaned forward once more and kissed her again, this time, softly on the lips.

"Mmmm, stop." The sound she made and the one word were barely audible, but their impact was devastating. She frowned in her sleep and rolled over, simply the latest small rejection in a series of small rejections over the years. He felt a small pang of anger, but it was enough to move him past his own self-pity. He stood.

"I am leaving you. I have no choice—I have to go," he said in a soft whisper. Suddenly, he heard a voice in his head say, *She has already left you!* It took all the energy he had to walk back to his own bedroom.

Finding Speed and Home in Movement

October 2001

The leaves of the tree just across the street had begun to turn orange and red, late if still in New York but early for the Carolinas. Michael had not been back to New York; as a matter of fact, he had not even gone in to work. He dressed early each morning, took his brief case and computer, and headed out the door. He would drive all day. He had communicated very little with anyone other than listening in on a few conference calls here and there. He had always been busy, traveling somewhere, at the office or some function. And since Michael had kept his work life and home life apart, there was no one to put together that Michael had not been anywhere. His wife assumed he was throwing himself into work. She had not asked him about New York, she thought that Michael would tell her anything he needed to talk about. But he had been silent and Deborah had actually felt some measure of relief that he did not talk about it. She did not know just how close he was to the buildings when they fell. And so she assumed that he had not been much involved. Deborah had noticed a distance in him, she had felt it before, but it seemed more now. As always, she assumed that, whatever it was, it would soon pass.

Michael's boss Dan called the local Charlotte office and learned that Michael had not been in, that he was not returning phone calls or emails. Someone close to Thomas had learned that there had been some trauma from the day, and there was other talk and some rumors of things that might have happened. But mostly, everyone gave Michael space. Some of the men were still unaccounted for, and the big bosses were asking questions, mostly about the bids. What no one knew was that Michael was simply driving, hours at a time. A little further and further each day. As far as Knoxville one day. Four hours and he was on Interstate 40 headed west; he had pulled over for gas and considered whether or not to keep driving. *To the ocean, maybe,* he was thinking. But having driven only four hours west, he could turn around and head back to Charlotte and it would seem to his wife that he had just been to work. And each day for successive days, he drove a bit further, but each day he turned back, there was something building and growing in him. He stayed quiet, thought very little about his days in New York. He would wake up some mornings having dreamed of Jo, and as things dawned upon him, would push back all his thoughts and go for a drive.

Then one morning his wife asked, "Honey, will you go to the grocery store? The kids need milk for breakfast and there is a list on the kitchen counter."

"Sure," he said, then grabbed the list and walked outside and got into the car. Michael eased the car out of the driveway and into the road, slowly and with a certain amount of consideration; he drove to the end of the street, then turned out of his subdivision and onto a wider boulevard and a much faster road. It was a short drive to the grocery store and a quick errand for his appointed task of retrieving milk for breakfast. It was early and the parking lot to the grocery store was nearly empty. It was a large brick structure with a drugstore and coffee shop bordering its red expanse, and the three stores together were the centerpiece of a larger, picturesque strip of shops where even the trees were planted in neat rows. So many were in a single unnatural row, each the same size and shape as the next. The trees made Michael feel like nothing before him was real.

Michael was in and out in a flash and back in the car. As he turned the key, the revving engine gave him just a bit of pleasure. And for a moment he wanted to drive away. Instead, he turned back on to the boulevard towards his house, but as he approached his street he had the urge to keep moving. He turned back to look at his street as he passed as though he was surprised to have missed the turn. It made him giggle just a bit. The sunshine flashed at him between the trees as he passed the small gaps and creases of the branches just beginning to shed their leaves. He turned his head to the left and watched as the tall straight streetlight poles marched past, one after the other. Nearly a month had passed since New York, but Michael was still suffering from his wounds, which if he was not careful, exposed thoughts normally hidden below the static of daily living like running errands to get milk. And what he was looking at this particular morning was a layer of perpetual discontent, low in intensity, but always present. *Perhaps this is what drove me to Jo,* he thought to himself, *Stop, stop, stop it!* he rushed to contain his own thoughts. *Besides, that's just a rationalization.* He sensed that he was close to discovering something, so he carefully steered his own thoughts away from Jo and back to the feeling that he had discovered within himself. *What is this discontent? Why am I unhappy? Am I just longing for the days of no cares? Am I longing for the days of no responsibilities?* He looked out of the car window for a moment, resting his mind by simply looking at things without naming them or connecting them to any other thought. But then a realization came to him, *Am I stuck in the past? Missing the moment? Wanting everything to be like some other time or place? What bullshit!* Then he began to laugh.

He rolled down the windows then hit the button on the sunroof and watched as it gave way to blue sky. He immediately felt better. He reached a crossroad that headed south and out of the suburbs. He paused for a brief moment then turned onto the wider road. He pushed his foot on the gas then mashed the knob on his radio as music instantly mixed with the increasing wind. *I feel so good right now driving, but home feels so strange,* he thought. There was no home for Michael except in movement. The only thing that seemed willing to hold him, to console him, was the motion of driving. And so he pressed on down the road with no destination in mind. He kept moving and the faster he drove the better he felt. The faster he drove the less pain he felt and the more he felt alive.

Perhaps he was suppressing thoughts and refusing to let out feelings that needed to be expressed. Perhaps Michael's mind and body were like a shaken can of soda; he looked perfectly fine as long as nothing or no one popped his top. And of all the things that could have been a catalyst for Michael to break, that morning it was the combination of wind and a scattering of cars just ahead, cars that would only momentarily slow him, but it was enough tension that, when mixed with wind and music, it cracked his seal and popped his mind.

The festering energy burst out of Michael. First, it surfaced as a loud hollow scream, but then quickly traveled down his leg to his foot on the accelerator. The car lurched toward the rolling roadblock just ahead. Michael swerved sharply to avoid the cars, and instead of easing back to safety, pushed the car harder. He turned so sharply that the tires squealed as he crossed the double yellow lines. *Those damn lines are not going to tell me where to stay,* he began a monologue in his head. *Those lines won't keep this vehicle from hurtling dangerously towards others,* the thoughts kept coming, *and their rules, their double yellow lines meant to keep everyone in line and safe—well, those damn lines don't keep anyone safe!*

Michael's heart was pounding, and he let out another shrill cowboy scream of pleasure, "Yeeee-haaawwww!" The car shifted into passing gear, he surged past the slow moving cars and was headed up a hill.

"Those fucking yellow lines don't keep anyone safe!" he said loudly and with emphasis. Michael continued to accelerate, blind to what might be coming over the top of the hill, and the precariousness gave him a thrill followed by a surge of adrenaline. His pupils dilated and the air pressed in on him—it was hard for him to take a breath, but he pushed the speed, feeling his heart pounding in his chest and all numbness leaving him.

"God, I feel alive!" he shouted.

A car appeared over the hill directly in Michael's path, and it was dangerously close. Michael swerved hard back to the correct side of the road, and the oncoming car passed in a blur with its horn blaring hard and steady. He let out a laugh, then swerved hard left back across the yellow lines back into the wrong lane, pressing the gas pedal to the floor. He was passing the last car when it matched his acceleration, and Michael realized that he had picked up a young challenger. The driver was a dark-haired man who looked barely older than a boy, driving a small, black Honda that sat low, nearly to the ground, with a loud, clanking engine that was hoarse, as if it had been ridden hard and was missing a few parts.

Michael suddenly found himself in a drag race. He looked at the young man behind the wheel; he was staring hard at Michael from behind plastic, boyish-looking sunglasses. The two men locked eyes as they mashed their pedals nearly simultaneously and pushed their machines side by side down a two-lane highway. The two of them kept their eyes on one another, neither seeing the large diamond-shaped yellow sign with a big dark arrow warning of a sharp turn to the left just ahead. Michael was on the inside as they entered the turn, and neither Michael nor the other man relented.

The two cars hit the turn with too much speed and too much mass, so they both slid sideways into the hard turn. The Honda's back wheels slid off the pavement into soft dirt and gravel. Physics did the rest and the Honda went into a spin. Michael fought his car hard to keep from sliding into the out-of-control black car next to him, but he over-corrected so his car began sliding in the other direction. The Honda spun back onto the road, and once on the pavement, the tires grabbed hard and the small car flipped. To Michael, the small car appeared to float, and everything was beautiful, moving in slow motion.

Then there was a hard crash as the black car landed on its roof, its glass windows exploding, showering glass shards outward. Michael's car was still sliding, and he lost sight of the other car, but he still could hear the screeching of steel on cement. Michael worked the steering wheel into the slide of his car and hit the brakes. While his tires were squealing, he soon slid backwards to a gentle stop some 30 yards farther down the road than the Honda, which he now saw was on its top and front hood, its wheels still spinning and engine racing.

Michael ran to the upside-down car. He got on his knees and reached into the crunched driver's side window. He fumbled with his hand until he found the keys and ignition and turned off the car.

"Thank you!" the young man said.

"Are you okay?" Michael asked.

"Yes," he paused for a moment then said, "Yes, I'm okay. I'm okay!" his voice was shaky but grew in strength as he repeated himself.

"Good," Michael said, then he punched the young man in the face with his left hand. It was not a hard punch, and not with Michael's strong hand, but it made a smacking noise. Then Michael stood up and said loudly, "GOOD!" But it did not feel good to Michael, he could feel a dark mood overtaking his thoughts. He began to straighten himself when two small motorcycles raced through the turn threading the two cars without slowing down. Their engines were winding, and a chill ran up Michael's spine as his eyes followed them up the road and out of view. Just seeing them speed made him feel better. He knew in that moment the he needed to keep moving, to live, and the faster he would go, the more he would be living.

"Wow!" Michael announced. "That was awesome," he added as he stared in the direction the motorcycles had disappeared. "I have got to have a motorcycle!"

Going Back

November 11, 2001

Michael's boss had called under orders from the top. "How are you, Michael?" he had asked, adding, "We want you to take all the time you need."

What the hell does that mean? Time for what? Michael had thought. No one had asked him what had happened, or about his experiences, but everyone knew who was among the missing and presumed dead. Nearly two months had passed since Michael had been in New York, and he had communicated very little with corporate other than the mandatory calls, but mostly he listened and added nothing. Thomas had resigned over the telephone; no one wanted to know why, and no one wanted to talk to him. He and Michael had a brief conversation, and there was empathy in the long pauses between their words, even a feeling of brotherhood, but neither could get past the silence. They agreed to keep in touch.

What corporate really wanted to know was where they were on all the contracts. Dan, Michael's boss, had been calling Jonathan Braunstein, presumably on Michael's behalf. Jonathan never answered any of the calls nor did he return any. So at Dan's urging, Michael was back on a plane to New York.

"Ladies and gentlemen, I regret to inform you that our flight has orders from the *tower* to divert and land in Raleigh," the pilot's announcement was sudden and curt with no further explanation. Michael thought he had heard the pilot say the word *tower* funny.

No, I am sure I am imagining things.

"Oh no, not again," Michael heard the woman in the seat in front of him whisper to the man next to her. Michael's own thoughts wanted to jump but he kept himself in control. He pulled out his cell phone and turned it on, even though he knew he wasn't supposed to when they were still in flight. When it made a sound as it came on, Michael turned to see if anyone had noticed. The time displayed on the phone was 9:11 a.m.

"Shit," Michael said a little too loud, but no one seemed to notice. He took a deep breath, something he had stopped doing recently because it always made him cough, but it didn't this time. The breath touched raw parts of his lungs, though, making them burn just a little, and after a minute or two, the burn eased into an itch. Michael looked over the missed calls on his phone, scrolling down to the bottom, seeing the ones he had been trying to ignore, the ones that made it feel like something inside of him was falling. There were several new ones from one number but they had been decreasing in frequency; they made his phone heavy, and he decided that he needed to erase them. He began to erase them, but then he thought *What if I forget the number?* He put the phone down but then thought *Why do you need the number?* He looked up at the console of controls above his head, then turned the knob that let air blow across his forehead.

He looked about him, and in the seat pocket in front of him, found a paper napkin. In small, neat numerals, he wrote the phone number across the textured corner of the napkin. He was writing with a felt-tipped pen so the ink bled into the creases of the napkin as he wrote. He looked at the number, horrible and beautiful, then tore the number off the napkin. After folding it twice, he took out his wallet and searched until he found a suitable place to hide the napkin fragment from himself. He put the wallet back into his pocket and then erased the number from his phone. He settled back into the uncomfortable seat and shut his eyes until the plane jolted him as it landed 20 minutes later.

As he disembarked he looked at the flight attendants, who were smiling but tense. Michael walked off the plane and up the tunnel to the gate and he passed an airline employee, a woman consulting a piece of paper, giving directions to people who were wondering what to do next. Michael waited in the short line although he already knew what he was going to do. He had made the decision when the plane diverted to Raleigh. So he asked, "What's happened?" he asked, looking directly into the woman's eyes.

"There has been a plane crash," she said in a slow and serious tone. "But they do not suspect terrorism," she continued, answering his real question, "They suspect that it was *only* pilot error."

Only pilot error, Michael repeated in his mind; somehow, an *error* that killed people was comforting.

Michael had his luggage with him, and he did not wait for instructions from the airline. He simply walked off the airplane and headed to the car rental counter.

"Do you have any Mustangs?" Michael asked the woman behind the counter. Her head was down and she was finishing up paperwork from the previous renter. When Michael spoke, she raised her head quickly as if she was irritated. Perhaps she was, but she checked herself and forced a smile to Michael instead.

"Sorry, sir, the best I can offer you at this point would be a Taurus."

"That will be fine," Michael found himself trying to be cheerful. *Got to keep a stiff upper lip and all that...but why?* In truth, acting as if everything was okay did help. *It certainly helped those around the person keeping the stiff upper lip*, he thought.

Michael signed the contract for the car and took the keys. The woman behind the counter told Michael that it was a white Taurus, then gave him directions to the rental cars. He walked down a short corridor made of windows, the hallway overly warmed by the sun, and as he walked out the door, he was greeted by a cool breeze and a long line of identical white Ford Tauruses. After a bit of searching, comparing the license number on his key chain to the license plates on the cars, he found the right one and put his suitcase in the trunk and his computer bag in the front seat. He got in and checked his phone for messages. There were none, unusual for a work day.

The sky was clear and traffic was light; soon Michael was on the highway headed north to New York. It had not really even been a decision about whether or not to drive to New York or to go home. He merely rented a car and headed off to Manhattan for his meetings as though everything were normal. Acting as if everything were normal was a terrific coping method as long as there were no jolts. The pavement was smooth and Michael found quiet amidst the soft drone of the engine, the sound of rolling wheels on the road, and the wind blowing against the windshield. He drove 70 miles per hour and felt calm. He thought of his wife. She was attracted to him because he had always been able to remain calm in chaos and stress. He could even hear his father's words in his mind, *"Remain calm."*

The words were still powerful to Michael. Anytime he needed to, he just repeated his father's words and he could stabilize nearly any situation. It had worked for Michael in business, and as a father and husband. He could reproduce his father's strength, and when he said the words out loud, it reassured and calmed all those around. The key seemed to be delivering it as a command, and it had always worked as reassurance. But Michael felt different now. *Remain calm*, he repeated in his mind, but there was a nagging feeling that *something* was wrong.

"The only damned thing that's wrong is the grisly task ahead of me," he said out loud in the loneliness of the car, loud enough to stop other thoughts that wanted to come out. Benjamin Alder had called Michael and requested things that Michael's company could provide—things like refrigerated trucks, lighting, and other various effects to aid in the search-and-rescue mission that very quickly had become a search and recovery. The trucks were to preserve remains of people that they found. *Pieces of people*, Michael thought to himself. The thought stayed with him: he could not shake its sticky and pungent residue. One of his tasks was to visit the trucks and review remains to see if there was anyone or anything that he could identify. He had agreed when asked, but it was only now that he thought about what this task might entail. *She's not there*, he reassured himself then purposefully changed the subject of his thoughts.

I am sure my wife is wondering what is going on with me. The thought made him chuckle. As long as Michael could remember, sex had been something that his wife used to assert control. It was doled out or withheld as a means to reward or to punish, to incentivize certain actions or behaviors. The politics of it had almost killed it for Michael completely; it was always attached to something. Intimacy had become like an animal in a zoo, it still looked like the animal but something wild and beautiful was gone. Contact and activity void of passion. Then Michael wondered, *Incentive or punishment for what?* He answered his own question, *She sees sex as security.* He told himself that he was sure he was right. *I guess that's the price I pay for acting every day as if everything is okay.* But then Michael admitted to himself that everything usually was okay. Michael had always remained calm, no matter what; it was natural for him and not contrived, but by being calm, Michael had attracted in his life people who needed to feel that calmness. But now that Michael, the beacon of calmness, was facing his own world disturbed—his own soul tossed about restlessly—all the underlying insecurities of those around him became triggered and active. And that, he told himself, was why his wife was suddenly acting so needy. Then Michael's cell phone rang.

"Hello? Michael Tantalus."

"Hello, Michael, it's Jonathan."

"Hey, Jonathan, I'll be a little late. I'm driving to New York, but I should be at the hotel by evening."

"I take it you heard about the plane crash?" Jonathan did not wait for Michael to answer. "Don't hurry, I will send a car to pick you up in the morning."

"That's fine—what time?" Michael asked.

"Let's say nine A.M. sharp," Jonathan answered. There was tension in his voice but it was gentle.

"See you then," Michael answered, then hung up the phone. The conversation was strained, but there had been an unusual softness in Jonathan's voice and a certain sympathy in the way he spoke. Michael put the cell phone down on the seat next to him, looked at it for a moment, then turned on the car radio and sped up. Michael arrived at the hotel early in the evening when there was still some daylight. It had been nearly sixty days since Michael had been in the city, and he was only slightly surprised to find that the streets were once again busy with cars and the doormen were back at their posts. *New York is an amazing city*, Michael thought, *It's like a large holly bush, beautiful and always green, but prickly and nearly impossible to kill.*

Many people walked about, swift and focused, so Michael did not at first notice Goldie. But when he was close to the door, he saw her seated against the building holding her knees, her head buried in her arms. She was completely still and her dress was dirty and wrinkled. Michael was struck with empathy more than any other time he had seen her. She had seemed so lucid and alive the day he saw her when he was covered in ash. He immediately pulled out his wallet and counted out five $20 bills, folded them neatly, then bent over her and searched with his eyes until he spotted a pocket. He placed the money in a hip pocket, then used two fingers to push it in as deep into the pocket as he could.

"Good to see you again, Mr. Tantalus."

———— • • ————

The doorman's voice drew Michael out of his focus on Goldie. He stood and stared at her, wondering what he could do for her, but he was at a loss for what that might be. "Don't worry, Mr. Tantalus, we watch out for her," the doorman said as he put a hand on Michael's shoulder. Michael looked at the doorman, smiled just a little, then walked to the elevator. After checking in and ordering room service, he lay on the bed waiting for his food. He kept his shoes on and did not move, didn't turn on the television or his computer, but just lay there in the dark with his eyes open, hands clasped over his stomach. Room service knocked at the door, a man wheeled in a cart and uncovered the food, lifting metal covers and stacking them at the edge of the cart. Michael signed the bill, and after the man left, sat and looked at the food, but he did not eat. Instead, he put the covers back over the plates, thinking, *Perhaps I'll eat later.* Then Michael took off his clothes and got into the bed.

In the morning, the city was bright and the limousine was waiting at the curb outside the Time Hotel precisely at nine A.M. Jonathan was waiting outside the car, and he met Michael halfway across the sidewalk, greeting him with a hug. For a few minutes, the two men remained in an embrace while people walked past, some bumping them as they squeezed by on the overly crowded walkway. They both got into the car without speaking, and each man looked out of his respective window as they drove south down the Westside Highway.

"Do you want to hear about the funeral?" Jonathan offered.

"No," Michael's answer was short and more curt than he meant it to be. The limousine made a few turns, finally turning down Church Street, and the closer they came to "Ground Zero," the more the crowds increased. *Damned morbid people*, Michael thought to himself. Jonathan whispered a few words to the driver, who adjusted his route. Jonathan folded his arms, then turned toward Michael and let out a deep sigh. He reached out his hand and placed it on Michael's shoulder. The two men looked at each other as the car slowed to a stop. There were many people milling about the street but Michael soon discovered that it was in no way aimless, and these were not morbid viewers. Not waiting for the driver, Michael opened his car door, and the noise of all the people swallowed him. It was the noise of many mourning—some crying, some wailing, and some praying out loud—in many different languages and representing a number of different religions.

As Michael stepped out of the car, a woman put a picture in front of him.

"This is my son," the woman said, fighting back tears. Her voice was shaky but intense, "He works downtown but he did not come home from work Tuesday. He is such a good boy." The woman was polite but insistent that Michael make eye contact with her and look at the picture of her son. Michael acquiesced, first looking her in the eyes, finding that they were sad and exhausted. Then, Michael took the photo: it was of a handsome, young Asian male, from the shoulders up, wearing a gray suit with a red tie. Michael held the photo for just a moment, then handed it back to the woman.

"No, I am sorry, I have not seen him." Michael wanted to say more, but he had no idea what. The woman lowered her head and moved on. Michael watched her walk back to her post, a place where she could encounter as many people as possible walking past her. Then Michael turned back toward Jonathan, who was waiting patiently.

"They are everywhere," Jonathan said to him, "subways, bus stops, train stations... the same man stops me every morning in Penn Station to ask if I have seen his wife, and her picture is embedded in my mind..." Jonathan stopped in the middle of his sentence, starting to say more but letting the words fade as he began to shake his head. Jonathan seemed very different to Michael now; he talked differently and he walked differently.

The two men began to walk and turned onto Vessey Street, Jonathan walking a little way ahead of Michael. Michael tried to keep up, but he could not take his eyes off all the people walking about. A man handed Michael a Bible out of a large corrugated box as he passed. Michael looked at the small New Testament bound in soft leather, then put it into the inside pocket of his blazer. Jonathan had once again stopped to wait for Michael to catch up.

"Do you smell that?" Jonathan asked.

"Yes, yes I do," Michael answered, looking about and crinkling his nose. It was a pungent, smoky odor with a whisper of something sweet but at the same time a little foul. The smell was all about downtown and it was distinctive, like nothing Michael had ever smelled.

"Do you know what that smell is?" Jonathan leaned in to Michael, whispering.

"I don't know, I suppose it's everything. I smelled it last time too, and it has stayed with me," Michael answered as he looked around at the movement of all the people. There were lines and smooth patterns of people walking, shuffling—it was not the usual chaos of people rushing to work. These people were not hurrying, and it appeared as though everyone was moving together to some unheard slow, gloomy march.

"The word on the street," Jonathan began as he continued walking, "is that we are smelling the incinerated flesh of those trapped and burned." He stopped and turned toward Michael as he finished the sentence, waiting until Michael made eye contact. Michael gave no reaction other than nodding a recognition that he had received the information, but Michael wondered if it was true.

The two men reached a barrier that reminded Michael of the outside fence and backstop of a tennis court. It was a high, chain-link fence with some sort of dark fiber covering to block the public from viewing whatever was on the other side. On the outside of this temporary wall many people had placed flowers, pictures, notes, crosses, Stars of David, candles, and many other effects. The tall fence was nearly covered with bouquets, their stems threaded into the chain metal links. Some of the flowers were fresh and some were in various stages of decay. Michael put his hand over a small lump in his inside coat pocket, to make sure he remembered the rose he had bought at the corner store.

The pictures were mostly on paper, some covered in plastic wrap with the edges coming loose and flapping in the gentle wind. There were memorials and there were requests for information with phone numbers boldfaced and prominent with the hope of hearing anything. Some people walked around the perimeter of the barrier like it was the Wailing Wall. They knelt, they prayed, and they made their own offerings to the missing and the dead.

"The spilling of innocent blood tends to sanctify." Michael whispered the words, hearing himself utter them as if someone else was saying them, and with the words came the sudden realization that he was walking on sacred ground. A chill ran across his body, and the hair raised on the back of his neck. Jonathan was up ahead speaking to a guard at an opening in the barrier, and he motioned with his hand for Michael to come. He moved quickly to follow Jonathan through a narrow opening in the high barricade. The guard was dressed in a grey uniform and had his hat pulled down low, shading his eyes, but he was tall, and as Michael passed by him, he could see the man's eyes just under the bill of his cap: They had a steely look that made Michael wonder exactly what the man had seen.

"Michael," Jonathan's voice was terse, "I want to thank you for the trucks, and Bennie sends his appreciation as well."

"There are a few more on the way—I think eighteen in all."

"More than 10,000 remains have been recovered so far," Jonathan said like he was reading the daily sales report. His direct reporting made the conversation easier.

"Ten thousand people?" Michael had heard the number.

"No, 10,000 *remains*," Jonathan did not mean to be so curt, but his answer left both men in silence for a few moments.

"Oh," Michael finally said, feeling a little stupid.

"We are moving everything to a tent over on First Avenue, because it's closer to the medical examiner's office," Jonathan began talking in a logistical manner. "I am going to leave you to it," Jonathan put his hand on Michael's shoulder while looking at him, searching for the right thing to say. "Take your time, for…" Jonathan paused then looked down, "Michael, I am really… really very…" he searched for a word, but nothing came.

"Thanks, Jon. I'm okay. No need to say anything," Michael said, and meant it. Jonathan nodded.

"We can talk later, Michael, but Bennie and I—well, everyone— all of us are sticking pretty close to home these days." Michael wondered if "all of us" included the 'girls,' as Bennie referred to them.

"No worries, Jonathan, I am going take my time with this. Then I'll catch a cab back to the hotel… I've got a little paperwork I need to get to anyway. Tell Bennie I said hello."

"I will, and he said to send you his sympathy as well." Jonathan looked at the ground again, then back at Michael, "You know, this hit us all hard but for you, I can only imagine," then he paused again, and after a brief moment, gathered himself and said in a louder and clearer voice, "And Bennie said he wanted you to know, no worries about the contracts. Everything is business as usual— well, except for..." Jonathan stopped abruptly and leaned in to hug Michael again. Then, he straightened his suit and cleared his throat, giving Michael a smile as he turned to head for the gate. But then he stopped and turned back to Michael to finish his sentence. "I'll call you tomorrow. We do have to change the contracts a bit. Twenty buildings are gone, collapsed, burned, or condemned." Jonathan was back in business mode and it helped both men relax.

"Twenty," Michael said to himself as he watched Jonathan disappear behind the barrier. Then he quietly turned to confront the devastation.

Michael continued walking down Church Street toward Barclay. He was glad he was alone. The trucks could wait; there was something that he wanted to do first but he was not entirely sure what it was. Once he reached Barclay Street, he turned the corner and stopped at the bottom of the steps to St. Peter's Roman Catholic Church. He stood motionless, looking up at the doors. Somewhere in his body, he could hear and feel sirens wailing from all directions.

His heart began to pound—it felt as though his entire torso was beating, and his feet felt as hot as if he were walking through fire. He looked to his right, seeing that all of the windows of the large, flat edifice had been broken out, and dark shadowy bands of blackened brick streamed upward from each window. He looked back up at the church and tried to gather himself enough to move up the steps.

He knew this church. It stood less than half a block from the northeast corner of the World Trade Centers; he knew where the debris had fallen. On September 11, he had struggled as quickly as he could through, around, and over much of it, knowing it was all hopeless. He looked down the street now, and while it was clear of debris, dust and ash outlined every fissure in the cement of the street and the walkway in gray. Cracks that he had never noticed before, but now that they were filled with dust, they made a beautiful, disintegrating, fractal pattern.

Michael looked about him, seeing that there was no one around. He knew he was putting off the tough climb of a mere fifteen or so steps. Turning to look across the street he noticed pews, stacked haphazardly in the plaza, some with kneelers still attached. They appeared pitiful and sad; they still stood straight, but their material was all tattered, and although they had sat in the rain, they still looked dusty and ash-covered. Michael imagined that all those they had served over the years were most likely gone. The wooden seats were abandoned, doomed, left to succumb to the elements, sitting in the dirt under sparse, leafless trees. Michael wondered if they suffered, if they felt as if they had let everyone down, and he wondered if some of them wanted to throw themselves into the road into the path of an oncoming car, if only they could. Antiquated and lonely though they were, Michael was sure that the entire church suffered without them.

Michael took a deep breath and pressed forward up the steps, pausing again among the six grand Ionic pillars. He touched one of them, running his fingers across the smooth rounded stone, and it reminded him strangely of a young woman's soft curved leg. He immediately shook the thought from his mind, retracting his hand as though he had touched a hot stove. He looked upward, and the pillar that seemed so large and substantial became slender in the perspective of its height. It held the stone cross beam and roof beautifully and effortlessly, and at the top were volutes, large spiral scrolls that he imagined had important writings on them. But then he thought that the scrolls had to be blank—there could be no words as grand as this structure.

Michael then faced the large doorway. The wooden doors were propped open. Michael looked about once more, finding that he was still alone. He stepped across the threshold into the front foyer of the more than 100-year-old church, but then he paused, not sure he wanted to proceed, one foot in and one foot out, riding the fence. He had always heard to not ride the fence, and now he tried to think about what that meant, but standing on the fence was his only comfort right in this moment: He could not go backward and he feared moving forward, so he was momentarily frozen. He waited, sure that someone would notice him and ask what he was doing here...perhaps a person who would ask him to leave… perhaps, perhaps, perhaps. But no one was there, he again realized he was alone in his task, alone on a path not of his choosing, so he imagined. He could hear the noise of the city coming in the open door, but the noise came from only one direction and in the place he stood there was stillness. He stood completely motionless and did not let his mind wander to the times he had been in this spot two months earlier.

He stepped through the next set of doors into the heart of the church. He stood in the darkness, his eyes struggling to adjust from the brightness of the outside. There appeared to be no walls and no ceiling, as if he stood in space with infinity stretching in every direction. He could feel his heart beating and he became aware that he was shivering, though he was not cold. It was still and peaceful, and he thought that he would never move. That was when the punch came, disguised as one of his own thoughts: *Was she really here?*

Suddenly he could barely breathe; it felt as though he had awoken from a foggy dream to find himself in a cold and barren room. He remembered why he came and reached into the inside pocket of his navy blazer. He pulled out a single, short-stemmed red rose with barely any sign that it had once been a bud. He had found it at a corner store the night before, and even then it had been brown and a little wilted around the edges, but it had been the only one in the store. He had put it in water overnight hoping to revive it a little, but the grip of decay can be difficult to reverse. In the morning, he noted that it seemed worse and now it seemed even more wilted.

His eyes began to adjust to the darkness just a bit and he looked around the room. There was very little inside, and he felt the starkness in his heart. Inside the promising grandeur of this classic structure of proud pillars and shiny marble exterior was sad, damaged, dusty, dirty, and empty. He moved to the altar and placed the rose on one of the steps. It seemed to belong there, wilted and dying but innocent. *Yes*, he thought, *it belongs here, but I do not*. He stepped backward and could barely make out the rose, which seemed lost in the gloom.

"It is just not fair," he whispered, but the words sounded loud in the silence. He waited for a response, expecting to hear something from someone—anyone—even God should have replied. But there was no response. He felt weak. He wished for a priest, anyone to break the silence, but there was no one, so he withdrew, walking back through the doors into the open foyer, where the light hit him, causing a wave of emotion. His eyes and face contracted hard, and his body tried to cry, but he swallowed, beating the sensation into submission.

In the middle of the foyer was a white and yellow marble pedestal with a curved stone bowl at the top holding a small amount of water. "Holy water," Michael presumed. He moved closer and observed the bowl. Not Catholic, he was unsure what to do. He dipped the first two fingers of his right hand into the water and dabbed his forehead with it. And then, suddenly, before he could stop them, tears began to pour down his cheeks. With his still-wet fingers he reached down to the floor, which had been swept but the residue of ash remained. He swiped at the gray ash from the floor near the wall and made a cross on his forehead with it. He closed his eyes and clasped his hands in prayer but he could not think what to say, so he released his hands and opened his eyes. He pushed into his past for something and all that came was a passage from the Bible. He had learned a psalm as a child, and now after many years, part of it came to him and he used it as his prayer. *Psalm 51*, he thought, closing his eyes once again:

"Be gracious to me, O God, according to Thy loving kindness; According to the greatness of Thy compassion blot out my transgressions. Wash me thoroughly from my iniquity, And cleanse me from my sin."

He paused and opened his eyes, looking toward the altar and into the darkness inside the church, then continued, "For I know my transgressions, And my sin is ever before me."

After he said the words, he tried to feel them, but he could not. An image came to mind of standing in the smoke of a bar long ago with loud ringing in his ears from fresh gunfire, then an image of standing completely engulfed and lost in the dense smoke of the fallen buildings—these moments from his past tied themselves together. There was a moment of stillness before he moved, and when he moved he could see destruction in his mind of his own making, and it made both events and many others feel the same. He suddenly felt damned.

He thought of another Bible verse and he said it aloud as best as he could remember: "The sins of the fathers are born upon their children."

After he said the words, he looked up as if searching for God.

"I pray that that is not true, I pray for Jo's daughter, I don't even know her name. And I pray for my son and my daughter and everyone else's. How can we ever break the chain?"

He kept looking up expectantly, but there was nothing.

"Be damned, be damned," he said aloud as he looked outside; there can be no redemption for those who will not take it. And then he began to laugh, easily at first, then louder and louder, while at the same time tears fell out of his eyes.

Michael wiped the tears and stood a little straighter, surprisingly feeling stronger. He removed his jacket and put it over his arm, then he unbuttoned his top shirt button and loosened his tie. He rolled up his sleeves and slung his jacket over his shoulder. He stepped outside into the clear sun of a New York that was moving from fall to winter, but Michael was feeling warmer. He stepped down the stairs of the church and back into the street, finding strength in his self-perception of being damned. He began to think of what was ahead of him: *Ten thousand remains and the estimate of the dead and missing is three thousand.* He had the sensation of watching his own thoughts and as his moving mind began to do the math in his head he shouted out loud, "Stop it!"

He watched his mind moved as though it were separate from him, it was assessing, judging, *Ten thousand divided by three-thousand means...*

"Stop it!" he said aloud to himself once more, and then he turned up the street and headed for the trucks.

Resignation

November 13, 2001

Michael felt old and finished. He walked alone down an alley to Sixth Avenue, although taking a cut-through was not something he normally did in the city and especially not after the sun had set. His attire was also out of the ordinary for him. He was wearing polished black leather shoes, but nothing else about him said, "Professional businessman." He had on blue jeans, which were neat but unusual for a business meeting; he always brought them in case he wanted to roam the streets of Manhattan by himself after a day of work. He always had loved the feel of the city's energy at night, and he never wanted to look like "money" when alone on the streets. Today, he was wearing a button-down shirt that was very expensive but wrinkled with one shirt-tail hanging out. Over the shirt, he wore his navy blazer to ward off the cool night air, but he had pushed the sleeves up almost to his elbows. It was definitely not the usual attire he would wear to meet with an officer of the company.

The alley was narrow, allowing only enough room for the most necessary of facilities. It was formed by the back end of two large brick buildings, each more than seventy years old, and as Michael walked between them, he wondered how they had survived this long. *Aren't they past their utility? Shouldn't they have been replaced by more substantial steel?* Then he laughed at his own use of the word "substantial." Nothing felt substantial anymore. He walked past a rolling steel dumpster and saw that its top was open and a homeless man was standing on tiptoes rummaging in it; Michael wondered if he was looking for food or clothing for the increasingly cooler nights. Then, he passed two more men in the alley—one in a fetal position with a newspaper covering him, while the other was sitting up but swaying against the building, obviously drunk. Michael was not repulsed by the men, nor by the steam coming out of a vent mixing with the rancid smell of garbage. Michael rarely confronted a scene like this, and when he stopped to look back down the alley, he noticed that the man rooting around in the dumpster was gone. The smell that reeked in waves from the alley was unpleasant, but to Michael, today it was oddly comforting.

He crossed Sixth Avenue in the middle the street rather than walk to the corner for a traffic light. He dodged several cars, and a cabbie honked and yelled something unintelligible out the window. Michael walked directly into the NBC building, proceeding down a short hall at the rear of the lobby to an elevator. A guard wearing a long coat and matching cap stood in front of a short, velvet barrier draped in front of the door. Michael stopped directly in front of him and nodded in a familiar way. The man looked skeptically at Michael, then suddenly jumped to unlatch the velvet rope to let him through.

"Sorry, Mr. Tantalus, I did not recognize you," he said as he returned the rope barrier to its hook behind Michael.

"I barely recognize myself these days, Bill," Michael replied. The guard had always worn a name tag, but Michael realized he had never said his name before. Both men laughed as the guard pushed the button to open the elevator doors, and Michael stepped in.

The elevator rose slowly and steadily to the sixty-fifth floor, where the Rainbow Room was; The Rockefeller Plaza restaurant had long been a place to see and be seen. When the doors opened, Michael was greeted by the smell of cigar smoke. Reynolds Pierce's admin had called, saying Pierce wanted to meet with Michael, and the place—of course—was here, a home court advantage for Universal Spectrum. They owned the building and it was always where they took important clients. Who could resist the impressive, almost-historic space?

Michael looked into the round, spacious ballroom. There was a small orchestra set up underneath a long arch at the far end of the dance floor. And at the edges of the polished wooden dance floor were small round tables, each with long white tablecloths and softly glowing candles. Couples mostly hidden in the shadows were holding long-stemmed glasses containing every color of drink, some were smoking, and most all were looking wantonly into the eyes of the person across from them. It was as if the couples had all been chosen intentionally for their extravagant dress and promiscuous desire for one other. Above the floor was a shallow domed ceiling softly lit with deep, sensual colors, and a luminescing blue shown down, reflecting on any shiny surface.

Beyond the dance floor sat larger, darker tables where romance gave way to influence. Men in suits sat in more comfortable chairs to talk business. Tall windows revealed expansive views of Manhattan's thoroughfares below, and though the noise of traffic was muffled by the glass windows and the sheer height of the Rainbow Room, the lights of the city's endless streets and avenues below seemed amplified, accentuating Manhattan's dramatic cityscape, underscoring the self-importance of the businesspeople inside.

Michael knew what was likely in store for the evening. He had once met Reynolds Pierce at a company breakfast but he was sure he had not exchanged more than two sentences with the important man. Michael spotted Pierce beyond the orchestra, so he made his way back to the table where he was sitting.

"Michael!" the greeting was overly grand and too familiar for Michael's liking. Pierce was standing, holding a cigar in one hand and a glass of scotch in the other. He reached out, cigar still in hand and pulled Michael into a hug as if he were a long-lost friend.

"How are you, Michael?" he asked as he guided him to a seat at the table next to a floor-to-ceiling glass window that looked down on the tops of rows and rows of well-lit buildings. The streets stretched so far out that they seemed to meet in the distance. Already seated at the table were a handsome, middle-aged man in a pin-striped suit and two ladies, both younger than the man and both beautiful.

One wore her hair up and her red dress dipped low into her cleavage; the other wore black with pearls around her exposed neck.

"This is Michael," Reynolds announced to the table and everyone nodded but no one bothered with introductions. "Michael and I need to have a little chat," he continued, but again no one reacted; they simply returned to their drinks and their conversation as though Michael were not there. Michael didn't care. He was there to talk to Reynolds Pierce and he had no desire to force conversation with people who had no interest in talking to him. Reynolds guided him toward the end of the long bar behind the orchestra, where they sat and were immediately greeted by a bartender.

"Evening, Mr. Pierce, may I freshen your drink?"

"Yes, please, Mr. Adams," Pierce replied to the bartender, "And whatever my friend here is having." Pierce looked at Michael, his arm still around him. Michael could feel the pressure of Pierce's arm less on his shoulders now and more on his neck and felt as if he were being controlled.

"I'll have whatever Mr. Pierce is drinking," Michael said to the barman.

"Call me Reynolds," Pierce said, finally letting go of Michael.

"Of course, Reynolds," Michael said loudly, louder that he needed to be heard over the noise of the busy room. Reynolds Pierce was many levels above Michael's boss, Dan, but Michael was not sure how many. And when Dan had called to let Michael know he would be hearing from Reynolds Pierce's office, he could hear the obvious nervousness in Dan's voice.

"Be respectful," Dan had said to Michael; it was a strange request. Michael had never been disrespectful. It was always the way with men in large corporations, so firm, confident, and in control, demanding even to those that worked below them, but just the opposite when dealing with anyone above them. And the higher the corporate rank, the sillier men behaved, pouring on the compliments like schoolboys on their first dates; Michael had seen it many times.

Reynolds was older than Michael. *Maybe ten years*, he thought. Michael was sure that a call had gone out and Reynolds was the nearest officer to New York, most likely on a pleasure trip to the city, and he was asked to talk to Michael. If he disliked his task, he hid it well. Reynolds was fit for his age, and as he was a top executive, he was wearing the Universal Spectrum uniform: dark suit, white shirt, and a red tie. The only deviation from the standard was the cufflinks. Michael watched Reynolds talk to the bartender; this was always the way Michael learned quickly what he needed to know about someone. Reynolds was friendly and knew the bartender's name, but what Michael was watching for was in the more subtle body language. Reynolds reached his hand to shake with the bartender, a gesture meant to show that Reynolds was on the level, connecting, but his extended hand was palm down, forcing the bartender to extend his hand palm up in a submissive move. Reynolds needed reassurance that he was in charge. Michael now knew how their conversation was going to go.

Michael's drink arrived and he reached to sip it, feeling Reynolds looking him up and down, taking inventory. He no doubt had been briefed about Michael, but Michael was sure that Reynolds did not remember them meeting before. Michael was more than a little disheveled and his appearance most likely gave away more than he liked. No tie, shirt unbuttoned two buttons down said a lot without Michael uttering a word. Reynolds Pierce smiled at him, a good smile that came across as sincere, disarming Michael a little. *Maybe I am wrong about the man*, he thought.

"Michael," he began, "I am going to get right to the point. You have been doing great things in New York and we have noticed." He did not say who the "we" was. "We think that it is time for a promotion."

Reynolds looked at Michael to gauge his reaction. Like Michael, Reynolds had made a living reading people—most likely better than Michael—but right now, he had no way of knowing what Michael was thinking. Saying nothing, Michael sat listening carefully with an expressionless face. After a moment, Reynolds continued.

"We know you have had a shock and perhaps a little time off would be good…" Again, Reynolds paused for a reaction and saw nothing. Michael kept his eyes on Reynolds but reached to the bar for his scotch and sipped it, thinking to himself *What is this? It tastes good – I'm sure that if Reynolds Pierce is drinking it, then it is expensive.*

"This is good, really good," Michael said to him, making Reynolds smile.

"Indeed, Michael, indeed it is," Reynolds answered. Reynolds rubbed his knees then picked up his cigar and his scotch, quietly toasted Michael, then turned to look out the window.

"It's like sitting on top of the world—I never tire of it," Reynolds said, sounding sentimental. Michael followed his gaze, looking out at the endless lights and buildings.

"It's beautiful, Mr. Pierce," he said as he sipped his scotch, forgetting that he was supposed to call him Reynolds, but it didn't really matter. All that Michael could think was that he wanted out of the city; the last days had been unbearable. He had called Dan after he left the trucks; visiting the trucks was not the reason Michael resigned. He had decided to resign within a couple of weeks of being back in Charlotte. He had even found another job. The call with Dan was short: Dan asked Michael to wait in the city and told him he would call him back. The meeting with Reynolds Pierce was set up quickly. Michael had never even needed to leave the hotel. He slept. Neither Jonathan nor Bennie called. Nor did Michael call either of them. There was just nothing to say, or at least nothing that Michael wanted to say. He wanted to tell them he was sorry, but that really made no sense. *Perhaps*, Michael thought, *there is someone I should call.* But Michael knew he would never make that call; nothing good could come from it. It certainly would not make anyone feel better. Some wounds were better left covered to heal, if they could heal at all.

"I want to spend more time with my family, with my wife and kids," Michael finally said. It was a partial lie but Michael had heard it before and it always worked. Who could tell a man that he should not want to spend more time with his wife and kids? Reynolds let out a heavy sigh, but he kept his focus on the lights outside the window. He moved the cigar to his mouth to draw in some smoke, but he had held it so long without puffing that it had gone out.

"What will you do?" he asked as he turned to look at Michael.

"I made a few calls and have been offered a job with North American Trust."

"A bank? You are going to work for a bank?" Reynolds' smile returned as he reached into his coat pocket for a lighter to relight his cigar. "You would have me believe that you would leave all this," he motioned to the lighted city below them, "for a bank?"

He began to laugh. "You really had me going there," he said, and slapped Michael on the back. "No one in their right mind would leave all this to go to a bank!" This time, Reynolds held his arms out to gesture to everything around them and began to laugh again.

In their right mind, Michael repeated to himself, ironic use of words. Reynolds stood and Michael followed his lead back to the table where the others sat, still locked in conversation, leaning toward one another as though they were telling secrets.

"Will you join us for dinner?" Reynolds asked loudly and the others became quiet.

"Forgive me if I ask for a rain check?" Michael said, never intending to cash in. His reply caught Reynolds by surprise.

"Are you sure?"

"I am afraid so. I have other commitments. Please, next time," Michael replied.

"Of course," said Reynolds, "Let's talk tomorrow. I believe you will like what we have to offer you," he added confidently.

"I look forward to it," Michael said as he nodded to the others and excused himself. Michael planned on not answering the phone: He was done with Universal Spectrum and he was done with New York. The whole game felt finished, and he rushed to the elevator, feeling that he couldn't get down fast enough. Michael had already packed and checked out of the hotel, putting his suitcase and computer in the rental car. He looked at his watch, glad to see that it was still fairly early in the evening and he had time to get New York in his rearview mirror. Michael knew that as soon as he drove down the road and got some miles behind him that he would feel better. Driving was always a sufficient salve.

Telling Reynolds Pierce that he would talk to him in the morning was a small lie, just the same as saying that he wanted to spend more time with his wife and kids. Small lies, fragments of a conversation, the kind of lies the Michael told all the time for convenience and to make conversations easier. And it had never bothered him before, but it bothered him now. He thought about it for a moment. *Aw, hell. Lots of things bother me now.* It was a rationalization—another lie—this one to himself, and he knew it. Michael felt itchy and he squirmed on the elevator ride down. He felt a little better once outside and hurried to his car as though he was trying to outrun his thoughts. *I wonder how many lies I tell in a day. And why, why do I tell little lies? Well, no more*, he told himself. *I am tired of all the bullshit, even if it is my own damn bullshit!* Michael stood a little taller and walked a little faster.

He turned down the alley he had come through earlier. The foul garbage smell returned to his nose and he stopped to stare at the men there. They were all sleeping. *Or more likely passed out*, Michael thought. He looked at each man, seeing their faces, their clothes. He wondered why he had never looked closely before. But now he surveyed them intently. The clothes were mismatched, torn and dirty. *What were these men's stories?* He wondered. *Why are they here? What happened to them in their lives?* After a little consideration, Michael moved on.

He reached the parking deck and stood next to his car, looking down at his shoes. They were so neatly polished that they gave off a shiny reflection of the lights in the parking garage, and as Michael looked closer, he was sure that he could see himself. He took off his shoes and stood in the parking garage in his socks. He opened the trunk of the car and fumbled through his suitcase until he found his cowboy boots. They were bulky in the suitcase and he had never brought them on a business trip before. But he had had the foresight to bring them, and as he slipped them on, he immediately felt better. He looked at them, they were worn and the leather was scratched, it made him smile. He pulled off his blazer and stuffed it into his suitcase.

He climbed into his car, and drove out of the city. He drove in silence for a while, no radio and few thoughts. He felt exhausted. New York was over, it had become part of who he was, and now without the city and Universal Spectrum, he wondered who he was. He consciously stopped the pathway of his thoughts, and turned on the radio and accelerated, passing car after car. He drove for a few hours, and when he reached Washington, D.C., he decided he did not want to drive any farther. He called to reserve a hotel room, then called his wife.

"Hello?" she answered.

"I'm tired. I am not going to make it home tonight," he said more curtly than he intended.

"Fine," came the irritated reply, which of course meant that things were actually far from fine. Then she hung up without saying goodbye. Michael soon pulled off the highway and into his hotel. He checked into his room, threw down his bags, and flopped on the bed. *I need a drink*, he thought. So he got up, changed clothes, and walked down the street to a local blues bar.

The music was playing loudly and it immediately lifted his spirits. He sat down at the bar and tried to get comfortable on the wooden stool.

"What can I get you, buddy?" the barman asked. He was wearing torn jeans, a white t-shirt, and a black vest. An unlit cigarette was hanging out of his mouth, and he had another one tucked behind his ear.

"Shot of tequila and a beer," Michael replied.

"You got it, buddy." He put a shot glass in front of Michael. It was tall, narrow, and cylindrical. *Unusual*, Michael thought. The barman poured the tequila in front of Michael, then put a bottle of beer on the bar and opened it with one hand.

"Need any training wheels for the shot, buddy?" the barman asked. Michael smiled.

"No, I'm good," he replied, then picked up the glass and tipped it back. The tequila burned his throat a little but in a way that Michael liked. He handed the barman the empty glass. The barman took the glass with his left hand and extended his right.

"Anthony," he said to Michael.

"I'm Michael, good to meet you."

"Likewise, my friend. Let me know if you need anything," he said, smiling, and walked on to another customer.

Michael took a swig of his beer, set it down, then scooted off the stool, standing for a moment, surveying the bar. It had old wooden beams and a low ceiling. *Old place*, Michael thought, noticing that the wall behind him was brick and had small tables with rickety chairs pushed against it, *part of the charm*. Looking toward the back, Michael saw what he was looking for: a small sign that said "Restroom." The heavy heels of his cowboy boots clunked on the old, wooden plank floor as he walked down a narrow hall and to the door of the unisex bathroom. Michael opened the door, finding a single toilet with what looked to be a very old sink. After using the toilet, Michael washed his hands, and as he rubbed his hands together, the powerful smell of watermelons engulfed his senses. He rinsed his hands longer than normal, trying to get the smell of the hand soap off, but his efforts were futile. He dried his hands and returned to the bar.

Seated to the left of his stool were two women chatting with one another. Michael sat back on his stool, which was very close to the woman next to him, and he scooted it away just a bit. As he did so, the chair made a funny noise on the floor, causing both women to look at Michael. He flashed an awkward smile and nodded. The woman next to him was tall, maybe six feet. She was slender and athletic, had dark tanned skin and brown hair. She looked at Michael longer than was normal, but she never smiled. The woman next to her was petite and blonde. She gave a flirtatious smile that the taller woman seemed to disapprove of. Michael ignored the friendly smile, heeding the warning in the taller woman's glare. He reached for his beer, took a drink, and looked at one of the many televisions in the bar. The women returned to their conversation.

After a bit of time, the smaller woman stood and walked to the bathroom. Soon, she returned giggling and whispered to the taller woman. She held her hands out for the other woman to smell and they both began laughing. The taller woman stood and walked to the bathroom, quickly returning, smelling her own hands, and then offering them to the petite woman. Michael knew what they were talking about and as soon as they were both sitting back on their stools, he extended his finger towards the women. "Do you want to smell my finger?" he asked, flashing the smile of an eight-year-old boy.

"Not if it smells like watermelons!" said the taller woman, and all three laughed. "I never thought watermelons could smell so hideous."

"It's like a fruity chemistry experiment gone wrong," Michael added.

"I'll never eat watermelon again as long as I live," added the smaller woman.

"Michael Tantalus," Michael offered his hand to the taller woman.

"Linda Woodman," she said as she took his hand, finally smiling.

"Hello, I am Caroline," added the woman next to her, flashing another inviting smile.

"We know everyone that comes to this bar and we don't know you. Where are you from?" asked Caroline.

"I'm from Charlotte...well, I live in Charlotte," answered Michael.

"Nice to meet you. Why didn't you say hello when you sat down?" asked Caroline.

"You two did not look very friendly, so I figured either you were together or did not want to be bothered."

The young women looked at each other and laughed again.

"We get that a lot," said Linda. "We're best friends and we are together, but we are not 'together'," she used her fingers to make the quotation signs.

"Maybe we should try it," said Caroline, making Linda laugh nervously.

"Why didn't you guys say hello to me?" Michael turned Caroline's question back on them.

"Because you had that 'Rico Suave I want to get laid with two girls at once' look," Linda said, and they all laughed again.

"I've never had a threesome," Michael said.

"Well, it ain't happening tonight, so you might as well get that out of your head," Linda said.

"Damn... and I thought I was doing so well!" Michael said, making everyone chuckle.

"Let's do a shot," said Caroline.

"Okay, but we can't be drunk before the guys get here," said Linda.

"Guys?" asked Michael.

"Yes, we are double-dating tonight. I totally hate my date, but I am taking one for the team tonight," Linda picked up her beer and drank it down.

"Yes, but I would do the same for you, and Danny is so nice," said Caroline.

"No, he's not," said Linda, "He's a moose, a jerk moose." Then she turned to Michael. "You seem like a nice guy...better act like you don't know us when they get here. Caroline's beau is a huge muscle jerk, and he gets very territorial."

"No worries, I'll buy 'em a drink and they'll see I'm harmless," Michael said.

"Yeah, sure you are," Linda said as she looked Michael up and down, making him smile.

"Anthony," Caroline shouted down the bar to the bartender, "Round of fireballs!" she added. Anthony looked up and nodded.

"Make mine tequila," Michael shouted and Anthony nodded again. Soon, Anthony laid the shots out across the bar.

"Anthony!" Linda shouted over the music in the barroom, "You forgot the salt and the lemon!"

"He doesn't take salt or lemon, Linda," said Anthony, "He takes his tequila like a man!"

They all began to laugh, then they raised their shots up in the air toasting one another and shot the alcohol in one quick motion, Linda and Caroline slamming their empty glasses on the wooden bar before Michael did.

"Real man," Linda said, then laughed. All three were still laughing when two men walked in, making the girls quickly go quiet. It seemed to Michael that the two women did not like the two men; everything felt strange as they walked in, and the women were definitely uncomfortable. Michael was sure that he could break the tension, so he motioned with his hand for five drinks, then he pointed at his empty shot glass. Anthony nodded, then went to work getting the shots. One of the men stood next to Caroline, put his arm around her, and tried to kiss her. She resisted as her eyes met Michael's. It was an awkward moment and the man called Danny noticed. He was tall and thick, *Thick neck, thick body, thick everything*, Michael was thinking. And as Michael assessed Danny, he glared at Michael. Michael quickly turned away, making it one of those small moments when so much is miscommunicated. The man immediately thought Michael was acting guilty of something. And he quickly sized up Michael, *Small, scared and weasely*, he thought to himself. Linda noticed that Danny was focused on Michael.

"Danny, what's up?" Linda said, to break the glare.

"Who's the nerd?" Danny said, motioning his head towards Michael. The comment made Michael laugh, not helping the situation.

"He's just a guy at the bar," Caroline added, "Come on, Danny, relax. Let's have a good time tonight."

"Yeah, I'm just a guy at the nerd bar, I mean a nerd at the guy bar," said Michael, starting to laugh, which served to incense Danny even more. The second man was also large, but not as large as Danny, and he took his friend's lead, glaring at Michael but saying nothing, keeping his hands in his pockets.

"Well, don't be a smart guy... push on out of here, little man," Danny said as he stood up, as imposing as he could, as if to show Michael what was about to come down on him. The man had no way of knowing what was going on inside of Michael. Not even Michael knew what was going on inside of him. He was not angry, but he had no intention of being pushed around, and he felt no compunction to explain things—after all, he had not done anything wrong. Danny inserted himself between Linda and Michael, turning toward the women, pushing his broad back against Michael, nudging him off his stool. Michael stood, scooted his stool away, and sat back down, but Danny pushed farther and again knocked Michael off his stool.

"Danny, stop," Linda said to him.

"Stop being a jerk, Danny," Caroline added. The second man began to laugh and Danny joined in as he turned to Michael.

"Oh, I'm sorry little guy! I didn't even feel you there," he said, this time laughing riotously. Michael did not laugh, and something began to grow in him. His eyes fixed on the very large man.

"Look, I don't mean you any harm. I just don't like you and you are making everyone uncomfortable. Why don't you pay your bill and scoot, so I won't have to beat the shit out you. Deal?" Danny did not wait for an answer. Instead, he turned his attention back to the two women and his buddy. The buddy was smiling, but Caroline and Linda were shooting looks like flying glass.

"What?" Danny said, holding palms out innocently, "*I'm* the jerk? Come on, let's just relax and have some fun." Just then, the girls began to laugh, and Danny turned to see Michael smelling his finger. Missing the joke, Danny leaned into Michael and said, "Okay, funny guy. I am about to beat the shit out of you unless you leave right now," his face as close to Michael's head as possible.

"Here you go," Anthony said as he set down five shots of tequila, trying to ease the situation.

"Okay, I'll take the ass-beating, but can a man have his last drink?"

Michael's reply surprised everyone, but most of all Danny. The shots were supposed to be for everyone, but Michael began to shoot them one at a time. He raised the first one with his left hand and knocked it back quickly. Danny, at first stunned, was now heating up, and he began to roll up his sleeves.

"I am going to hit you harder than you have ever been hit, you little asshole,"

"That's Mr. Little Asshole to you," Michael said. Linda's eyes were glassy, and she was shaking her head "no" to Michael. Then Michael shot the second shot glass of tequila.

"Danny, you start any shit and I'm banning from this place forever," Anthony said.

"Shut up, Anthony, you're next on my list." Danny's face had turned red and small beads of sweat began to form on his forehead. It seemed as though the jukebox began to play louder and everything in the bar began to speed up. Fights, like so many things, were both exciting and dreadful, and everyone's pulse began to quicken. Michael put the second empty shot glass in his right hand while everyone was looking at Anthony, tightening his grip around the narrow glass. Then he picked up the third shot glass with his left hand.

"Is that for courage or for the pain that I am about to inflict on you?" Danny asked, laughing, still standing menacingly over Michael. Michael knocked back the third shot and as soon as the third tequila went down, he convulsed a little, as if the tequila was coming back up. Danny noticed the small spasm, and as Michael squeezed harder with his right fist around the slender glass in his palm, Danny laughed loud.

"The little guy is about to spew—he can't get down his shots," Danny shouted and looked toward the others, quickly turning his head from person to person in the bar as if to receive some confirmation of his superiority. Danny was the type of man who roams about bars like a shark evaluating everyone in terms of a potential lay or competition. He rightly saw Michael as competition, but it was different than Danny could have imagined. And while Danny was laughing, looking for attention from the crowd, he was not paying attention to the one person he should have.

And in that instant, Michael saw what he was waiting for. He had readied himself for his opening and he saw it. The large man's head was turned slightly and he was laughing, his jaw relaxed and open slightly. Michael zeroed in, *Bingo, there's the button*, he thought to himself, then in a blink he struck like a coiled rattlesnake. Michael's fist came up and across so fast that Danny never saw it coming, and with the added mass of the shot glass, Michael landed a blow right on his relaxed lower jaw, slamming it sideways. As the joints tore, Danny lost consciousness. He stood for a moment as his eyes rolled back and then he fell forward head first, slamming his face hard on the wooden floor. *Bonus shot*, Michael thought as he stood to deliver a second blow, but there was no need. The second man stood stunned for an instant then rushed Michael, whose only instinct was to duck. As he did, the second man's weight and momentum carried him over Michael. Michael stood abruptly, turning the man upside down in midair. And as the man's heavy girth and gravity conspired against him, he came down on the floor hard on his back, knocking the air out of him.

Linda stood, grabbed Michael by the wrist, and pulled him toward the door. He in turn grabbed Caroline's hand, pulling her onto her feet, and the three rushed to the door. Michael yelled to an open-mouthed Anthony as they were moving, "What do I owe?"

"Nothing, not a damn thing, these drinks are *definitely* on me!" Anthony yelled back, making a motion with his hands for them to leave quickly as the two on the floor were beginning to stir.

"Woo-hoo!" Anthony shouted, pumping his fist in the air. "Damn!" he added, "That was awesome!" Then he reached for one of the shots of tequila that Michael had left behind and drank it down.

The three ran out of the door hand in hand. Suddenly, Caroline pulled loose and ran back to the bar, moving as quickly as she could in tight jeans and high heels. She ran up to Danny, who had risen to all fours, and kicked him as hard as she could in the ribs. Then she ran back out of the bar to catch up with the others. Linda and Michael had moved into the doorway of the next bar down the street, and as Caroline passed, Michael reached out and took her arm, guiding her into the recessed doorway.

"What should we do?" asked Linda.

"I know what I'm going to do," said Caroline. "I'm having another drink!" She was smiling and looking at Michael.

"I'm in," said Michael, "How about this place?" He opened the door and headed in before he heard the girls answer.

"We know this place," said Caroline and followed Michael in. Linda was a little more leery, recognizing that they were barely two doors down from Danny and his buddy. She looked back up the street and saw the two men were outside talking, giving directions to three other men. Danny was bent over and holding his jaw.

"Just like a damn man," Linda whispered to herself, "Calling in reinforcements." The men turned toward her and she ducked back into the bar. She quickly lowered the blinds, then looked out through the window from the edge.

"Linda, what the hell are you doing?" a woman shouted from the bar, where Michael and Caroline had already seated themselves. Just at that moment, two men ran down the street past the bar, not giving it a glance.

"Three fireballs and three beers," said Caroline, again looking at Michael.

"No tequila?" Michael asked her.

"No tequila," answered Caroline while Linda locked the door and lowered the rest of the shades. A couple, the only others in the bar, turned to look at her, but then they turned back to each other to continue their conversation.

"What the fuck?" the bartender addressed Linda once again. Linda started to answer but she did not know what to say exactly, gesturing at Michael inarticulately.

"Well, he," she was pointing at Michael. "Wait, what was your name again?" she asked.

"For God's sake Linda, you are frickin' losing it," Caroline said. "His name is Michael Tickle Ass," then she covered her mouth and laughed so hard she almost fell off her stool.

"Close enough," Michael said as he picked up two of the shot glasses and handed one to Linda and the other to Caroline. Linda raised her shot glass in the air and Caroline and Michael followed; in unison they knocked back the fireballs. Then Linda sat down on a barstool.

"Well, Mr. Tickle Ass here knocked out Danny," Linda finally explained to the bartender. The bartender took a closer look at Michael, then stood back a little.

"Big Danny?" she asked.

"Yes, with one punch," Caroline answered, motioning with her tiny fist like she was delivering the blow.

"Are we talking Daniel Bonticonti?"

"That would be the one," Linda answered. The bartender looked at Michael again. He was half-sitting on the barstool; he was a little drunk and had a funny smile on his face.

"No fucking way," the bartender said as she began to refill the empty shot glasses, adding a new one for herself. She looked at Michael until he looked up at her.

"Amanda," she said, as she reached out her hand.

"Michael Tickle Ass," he said, "It is a pleasure to meet you." He started to offer her his right hand but then thought better of it and extended instead his left hand. She took it and shook it firmly, squeezing just enough to show that she was strong. Michael looked at her. She was wearing a black tank top and her exposed arms were covered in tattoos, so many that Michael could not make out any individual element in the low lighting. Her hair was long and black and her bangs were cut across her forehead; there was a ring in her lip and one in her eyebrow. She looked tough, but underneath she was pretty. Michael wondered why she felt the need to put on a rough exterior.

"Show me your other hand," she demanded. Michael acquiesced and handed her his right hand, palm up. "Oh my God, you're bleeding," she said as she gently took hold of Michael's hand. She held onto his hand with one hand and reached for a cloth napkin with the other. Then she looked at the hand and decided it needed washing. With Amanda still holding his hand above the bar he followed her to the end of the bar where there was a sink. She washed his hand with soap, and when she saw that it was swelling, she put some ice into the napkin and wrapped it around his hand.

"Did you really punch Danny?" she asked while securing the makeshift bandage.

"No one has washed my hand for me in a very long time," he said. She looked at him for a moment, then kept talking.

"Danny's a bully—everyone knows—why would you tangle with a guy like him? You got a death wish or something?"

"I didn't want to tango with him but I didn't think I had a choice," Michael answered. His answer made her smile.

"You always have a choice," she said with emphasis.

Linda and Caroline had started to dance together, and Linda stepped toward Michael, grabbing him by the back of his belt and pulling him to the middle of the floor. There was not a real dance floor, just chairs and tables scooted away from the middle of the barroom to create a makeshift space. The music on the jukebox changed again, and the girls began to dance with vigor. The couple that was in the bar when Michael and the two women came in decided that they wanted to leave. Amanda let them out and it was just the bartender and the small party still dancing. Amanda kept the drinks coming and several more rounds in, Michael threw his shot into the air, where the alcohol prismed into a thousand tiny droplets that looked like stars reflecting the light of the many neon bar lights and signs on the walls.

"That's so beautiful!" Caroline said, throwing her shot into the air, too, getting the alcohol on all of them. Then, she hugged Michael and kissed him long, holding on to him afterward. Linda reached over Caroline and put her hand firmly on the back of Michael's neck, and while Michael and Caroline hugged, she pulled Michael closer to her and kissed him deeply. The three of them hung on to each other in the middle of the floor, dancing slowly even though the music played faster and faster. For hours they drank and danced.

Finally, Amanda closed up the bar and drove them all to Michael's hotel. Michael, Caroline, and Linda stumbled into the lobby and stood by the elevator while he searched his pocket for his room key. A weary-eyed desk clerk watched them as they giggled, all holding on to each other. The smell of alcohol was heavy on all three of them, made stronger in the small space of the elevator. The elevator rose, and when it opened, all three of them had fallen silent. Linda and Caroline followed Michael to his room and he opened the door. There were two beds, and Caroline lay on one while Linda lay on the other.

"Rub my back," Linda said as she pulled off her shirt and lay face down. Michael kicked off his shoes while Caroline got up and moved to the bathroom. Michael sat on Linda and dug his thumbs into her muscular back. Michael worked his hands up her spine, and when he reached her bra, Linda reached back to unhook the strap and slid the bra off one arm at a time. Michael continued to rub her back. He could see the outline of her swimsuit: Where the straps would be, her skin was white, and where her back was exposed, she was dark tanned. The difference was striking and Michael could not stop looking at her skin. As he worked his thumbs back down her spine and into her pants, she reached down to unbutton her jeans. Michael sat up to help her slide them down her long, dark legs.

And then a hand reached under Michael to unfasten his pants. Caroline. Michael turned to see that she was completely nude. She lowered his zipper and slid his pants down his legs. He lifted first one leg, then the other, as Caroline pulled them off.

As she tossed them to the floor, his cell phone fell out of his pocket. Michael looked at it and Caroline picked it up and put it on the bedside table. Linda let out a soft moan and rolled over, pulling Michael down on top of her. He kissed her, and he could feel Caroline stroking his back.

The cell phone began to buzz on the bedside table. He reached for it out of habit. He was smiling and laughing a little, but then he saw the number. His body contracted and he sat straight up, knocking Caroline to the floor. He grabbed the cell phone and held it directly in front of his face. It rang again.

"Stop," he said to it, but it rang again, seeming even louder. "STOP!" he yelled this time, but it rang again, so he threw the phone across the room, where it shattered against the wall. Michael leaped from the bed and began screaming at the two women, "Get out, Get out! Get out of here NOW!"

Linda jumped from the bed with her hand over her mouth and ran for the door; in seconds she was out and running down the hall. Caroline stood frozen for a moment; Michael continued to yell, but she could not tell what or why he was yelling so she ran to the door and out, the door shutting itself behind her. Michael was breathing hard, his heart was pounding, and he felt sick. He ran to the toilet, barely making it in time to vomit into the bowl. He remained on his knees until he was sure his stomach was still. He rose and had begun rinsing his face when there was a knock at the door. He moved to the door and looked out the peephole. It was Caroline, still naked and holding herself as if she was cold.

Michael opened the door.

"We need our clothes," she said, as she came in almost casually. Michael said nothing. Caroline gathered her clothes, her small purse, and Linda's clothes. As she walked by Michael, she paused, fumbled with all the clothes, and rummaged around in her purse until she produced a pen. She took Michael's left hand and wrote her phone number on his palm. Then she kissed him lightly on the cheek, smiled, and left. The door shut loudly and Michael was alone.

Leaving

November 14, 2001

Michael pulled into the driveway. The streetlight across from his house made an illuminated circle encompassing the street, the curb, his mailbox, and the bottom of the driveway; its strange yellow light made everything that was familiar appear foreign and odd. Three days of newspapers were scattered on the ground near the mailbox, all still in their protective plastic wrapping. He stopped the car and got out to pick them up, knowing he was just going to throw them into the recycle bin. *There is never anything encouraging in the paper,* he thought, *I've got to remember to cancel this subscription.*

All the lights in and around the house were turned off, and he wondered if it was a message from his wife. *She probably just did not think about me coming home in the dark.* Michael was well acquainted with his surroundings so he did not need the light to open the garage or put the key in the door to unlock it and go inside. He was greeted by the dog, who always barked except when it was Michael—he had been silent, most likely recognizing the sounds that Michael made arriving home. He stopped to pet the dog, finding it much more comforting than he remembered. He needed the comfort.

As he sat petting the dog, he realized he was thinking about the night before. He did not feel guilty, and the fight had made him feel good. It was clean somehow, different from the fight he'd had months ago on the highway, but he wasn't sure why. He told himself that he probably was more in control this time. Then he thought about the two women, Linda and Caroline. He really did not feel anything where they were concerned. But the phone call had disturbed him. *I'm going to change my number when I get the phone fixed*, he thought to himself. The dog moved to his dog bed across the room.

"I guess it's that time, isn't it, boy?" he said to the dog.

He began the march up the stairs, half expecting his wife to meet him with questions: Where have you been? Why haven't you answered your phone? And why have you not called? But the stairway was dark and quiet. He slid off his shoes and walked into his bedroom. He turned on the light to see that his wife was not there and the bed was made. He checked on the kids and found his wife in bed with his daughter, *Just as well*, he thought.

He went back into his bedroom to undress for bed, and as he emptied his pockets, he pulled out his cell phone. It was in more than several pieces, and a couple of the broken pieces of plastic fell on the floor. He bent down to pick them up, and when he did, he noticed a box under the bed. Getting down on his knees, he slid the box out. It was cardboard but nice, like it had come from a nice store; he didn't recognize it.

He lifted off the lid, and inside the box were cards, letters, and notes. A blue rectangle, a green square, a white envelope, another green envelope, two red ones, and more, all addressed to the various names he used for his wife. Deborah Anne Tantalus, Mrs. Tantalus, Deb, Deborah, Debbie, Love, Lovey, Atilla (as in "the Hun"—this private joke made him smile). It looked like the box contained only cards that he had given to her, perhaps over years. He decided to read one, but when he turned it over to break the seal, he found that it was unopened. He picked up another, and it, too, was unopened. His pulse began to quicken as he went through them all, and every envelope was unopened. There were years of anniversary cards, birthday cards, Mother's Day cards, and sometimes cards for no reason, all unopened. He could not fathom what it could possibly mean, but his stomach dropped and he sensed that whatever the reason, it could not be good.

He rummaged through the box to see what else it contained and found a picture of himself with Deborah. *Probably before we were married*, he thought. They were both very young and the flash from the camera had illuminated them beautifully in the nighttime shot. Michael was wearing a dark, charcoal-colored shirt buttoned all the way up and a tweed blazer, no tie. His thick hair was short on the sides with waves piled high on his head; it appeared to be blowing in an unseen wind. *Late eighties or early nineties*, Michael thought, based on his own hairstyle. His waist was slender in the picture, and his chest was broad and full.

When he focused on the image of his wife, she was so lovely, he could not stop looking at her. Her hair was up and her eyes were soft and loving. He had his arm around her shoulder, while her arm was tucked underneath his, around his waist. She appeared to melt into him and her head lay gently on his shoulder. They were in love. He stared at the picture.

What he missed now, what he wanted now, what he felt he needed now, was in that picture. He was absorbed by the picture, looking at every detail. Deborah was wearing a white, lacy dress, and he remembered not only when she bought it, but also the first time she put it on. She knew it was beautiful, and she knew she was beautiful. It was in no way false vanity but simply the way she looked and the way she felt. Somehow he had forgotten how pretty she was. It was not loss of youth that hurt him now as he looked at the picture, it was the way her head tilted up to him and the look on her face that was there then, but nowhere to be seen now. He could not remember when he had last seen that look on his wife's face, and he was stunned. The small punches just kept coming; his decision to be honest was the toughest when he was faced with being honest with himself. And somewhere inside of himself, Michael knew why this picture hurt him so badly, but he did not want to let himself say it or even think it. He wondered how he could ever be honest or love honestly or walk in truth, if he could not be honest with himself.

His chest felt ripped open; his heart was exposed and all he could think of was how to cover it all up. *I need to drink something or smoke something or snort something or punch someone*, were his first thoughts. He put the picture back in the box with all of the unopened cards. He replaced the lid and slid the box back underneath the bed. Then he sat on the floor. *God knows I love my wife and I am pretty sure that she loves me*, he thought to comfort himself, but the picture was telling him something and it seemed that his body already knew what it was, but his mind could not put words around the feeling.

We love each other, he told himself, *but are we "in love"?* The question was in his mind, but he felt as though it came from the outside. *How could we have been together so long and done all the things we have done and had children together...* he was trying to answer the question that had appeared in his mind. *I know it wasn't all just youthful infatuation, that would never last, right?* he asked himself. *All that fades then real love begins, right?* The thoughts just kept coming. He felt weary and leaned against the bed, wishing he had not seen the picture, his heart felt as if it were breaking.

He thought about Jo and he felt sick. *Why had the relationship with her happened, what was he looking for? What did he think he was missing?* Was he "in love" with her? He felt that he was. *He had with Jo the thing that was in the picture. But he barely knew Jo and now she was...* Michael stopped thinking. He was sure that he knew what love was, but now he was not so sure. But there was something that he had once had with his wife, but did not have now, and he had had it with Jo. What was that thing that made him feel whole, complete? It was as though he were allowed a moment of heaven, a taste of bliss, and nothing more. But there had to be more, it was something bigger, something that encompassed everything else, but what was it?

Michael was tired of all the bullshit. He had decided to be honest with people, and he sat here now fearful of being honest. He was committed to it, but what he now faced was not about being honest with his wife and with everyone else, what Michal was facing was more difficult, what he was beginning to see was that he was not being honest with himself. He wanted to blame his wife for his relationship with Jo. *If my wife had only loved me more, the relationship with Jo would never have happened, and she would never have felt pain, she would still be...* Michael stopped his thoughts once again. This had nothing to do with his wife and everything to do with himself. And it was easy to hate himself, to tell himself that he did not deserve to be happy or deserve love. Yet he knew that self-loathing was just another indulgence. He could see it. Past failure meant nothing in this moment.

Michael rose and began to walk through the dark house. He pulled off his shirt and tossed it to the floor. He took off his socks, one then the other, and threw them on the floor. He was now bare-chested and barefoot, but he was not cold. His mood was dark. He could no longer stand his own compromises, and that was what the relationship with Jo had been, a foot in two different worlds. Running from one to the other, taking what he needed and damn the consequences. He walked around his house looking at things, televisions and stereos, fancy furniture, the chandelier that they had found in an antique store…and he felt loathing for all of these things, they felt like containment. His body burned like a hot, blue, and gentle but destructive flame.

He walked to his son's room. His son was sleeping, *Most likely dreaming,* he thought. Michael could see his small chest rising and falling as air came into and out of him like gentle waves coming onto the beach then slowly falling away. Life was watching his son breathing while he dreamt, life in this form was beautiful, innocent, and pure in a way that Michael longed for. His heart again felt heavy in his chest. *I tried so hard to be something or someone, but I forgot who I was,* Michael was thinking silently but intently to his son as though he were talking to him, *everything is so out of control.*

Michael moved to his daughter's room, she was being cradled by his wife. His wife was in deep sleep. *You look exhausted,* he thought to her, *you push yourself so hard, and you are a really good person, you deserve better than me. I just don't know what happened to me. I always prided myself for making people happier, for making their lives better, but now I see that that just wasn't true, I was just taking what I wanted. I am no good for anyone—you'll be better off without me.* He wanted to kiss her on the cheek, but he did not want to wake her up, and the way she had recoiled the last time he tried to kiss her was still fresh in his mind. *I know that you can't stand for me to even touch you. I know this is all my fault.*

It was easy to be honest in his mind, at least what he thought was being honest.

But he knew she was not happy, vacillating constantly between anger and indifference. *I think somewhere down deep you love me, but I am sure that you are not 'in love' with me, at least not anymore.* Michael kept talking to her in his mind. *You are always here handling everything, and I am always traveling.* He looked at her more deeply, trying to see in her the thing that he had seen in the old picture, but it just was not there. Michael sat beside the bed. *I've got to think this through. I'm married. It's the sacrament of marriage, and I committed to this, so I have an obligation to this.* He stood as though he had made a decision and began to walk away.

The institution of marriage is a structure of obligation. A contract with a person and a contract with society, and if it fails, so much more will surely fail; at least, that is the societal fear. But is intimacy a suitable sacrifice? Is it not the core? If that is gone, what is left of the obligation? Is one person's happiness a suitable sacrifice? Once a relationship has become toxic, can it ever be whole again? Then a small tickle in Michael's lungs exploded into a cough. He squeezed as hard as he could to suppress it, not wanting to wake his wife. He made it outside the door, then he bent over, letting the urge to cough take over, coughing out all his air. His eyes watered as his body tried to breathe.

He regained his composure and stood in the hallway for a moment before realizing he was cold. He walked into his bedroom and put on a shirt, then opened a suitcase on the bed. He went into his closet and pulled out his suits, figuring he would only take what he needed. He lay the suits on the bed, one after the other, black, navy, various shades of gray, pinstripe, and houndstooth. *I don't need these*, it was his own thought but it hit him like a train, and something in his stomach fell. He stood motionless for a moment thinking what to do next. He packed some jeans, underwear, and some socks. He could feel that his mind was not clear. *I'll come back later to talk to Deb and to get more things*, he assured himself, fumbling with the zipper on the suitcase; he was moving too fast and his hands shook as though they had raced ahead of his thoughts. And his hands would not obey his mind, they could not obey, they were swollen and ached.

His beaten and broken hands embodied how he was and took the brunt of his decisions. His hands told his story, *Dig hard through brick and steel to save someone, someone who cannot be saved, and when frustration boils, punch and keep punching and do not think.* It was a torrid story.

Michael picked up the hastily-packed suitcase and walked into the hall, where he paused. He moved to the doorway to his daughter's room, where he looked again at his wife. He just felt that something was not right. He wondered once again if she knew he had been unfaithful. *But it doesn't matter,* he thought, *I know I have not been faithful.* Whether she knew or not, she said nothing. *She just holds on to keep everything together,* he supposed, *by sheer will.* It was the way she did everything.

Michael loved her, admired her, and hated her all at once. All the things Michael wanted—the things he had seen in the picture—were things that he could not ask for. Asking for them would mean that he was weak, and no woman, no matter what she said, wanted a weak man. Michael wanted to be held and loved, and he wanted to cry. As he watched his wife, he recalled when they were young and in love. He realized that she was just as lost as was he, and the gulf between them felt too great; there seemed no way to connect, and she had just shut down. This life they were leading now was too hard and too heartless. Tough, hard days in a relationship could be overcome, but when there was no heart in it … *Well* then, Michael thought, *we are done.*

He wondered if Deborah needed what he needed. Maybe that was why the picture was in the box. Maybe she wanted what was in that picture as much as Michael did. *Maybe.* His sadness began to turn to anger, and then the anger turned to energy, as he thought, *You have ruined everything and you're a damned fool.* This thought, served now to give him the courage he needed to walk out the door. But he lingered a moment longer, because all that he had ever thought he wanted, all that everyone had told him to pursue in life, was right here: the wife, the kids, the house, the dog, the country club, the private school, and even the right friends. He tried to tell himself to hold on, but he could not. He felt again the urge to cough.

He walked downstairs when it hit him that he no longer had "the job." He was leaving his career and taking a menial job as a low-level analyst, just a small cog in a big corporation. And he was leaving his wife and his family.

Standing in the kitchen, the dog was waiting for him.

"No, boy, you can't come. Get back in your bed," Michael spoke lovingly to the dog. He put down the suitcase and petted him for a moment. Then the dog lowered his head and obeyed the command, walking slowly back to his bed. Michael walked outside and opened the garage door. He looked at his shiny new black car. It had certainly evoked envy from his neighbors. He felt richer when he drove it, but now suddenly it was not appealing.

He walked instead to his truck, which he had kept parked at the end of his driveway for years, a holdover from his teenage years. An old F150 Ford pickup, it was rusted and loud, but it was handy when someone need to move something. He climbed into the cab, finding that the windows had been left down. It smelled like the dog, but it was comforting. Someone had left a half-eaten apple in the drink holder, and the apple had turned brown. It made him think of Adam and Eve.

"The knowledge of good and evil and the fall of Eden," he said aloud as he threw the apple out of the truck window and into the bushes beside his house. *Was that it?* he wondered, *an evolutionary chip input into us all as part of the human condition, with the need to always strive to make things better?*

"None of this is her fault," he whispered. *It's the same thought in everyone, the same subconscious thought. The thought that something is wrong, that something is always wrong. I will never measure up, because no one can measure up. No one or no "thing" can ever be good enough: It's a zero sum game that can never be won. Forty years of wandering in the wilderness, and there will never be a promised land.* Suddenly Michael was aware of how loud the crickets were chirping. He listened to them until he remembered that he had left his suitcase in the house. He walked back to the house, and when he opened the door, his wife was standing in her pajamas, squinting in the light with sleep still in her eyes.

"Where are you going?" she asked in a sleepy, raspy voice that showed her irritation.

The conversation was a short one. Michael simply said that he was unhappy and Deb had said, "If you are going to leave, leave now, while there is still time for me to lose weight and find another man." Michael thought it was a strange thing for her to say. She followed her comment by pointing to the door, saying, "There's the door." Her voice never quivered and there were a few tears but not enough to indicate real devastation; it was as though she had expected things to come to this point and had rehearsed what to say.

"The kids and I will be fine," she had added.

What the hell did that mean? Michael asked himself. He wondered how she felt after he left. *Most likely she is just fine.*

Michael had found an apartment in no time. It had everything he was looking for—it was clean, relatively new, and had a pool—and it was cheap. It was not until he had moved in that he could see how stark it was, reminding him of the motel room where he had stayed the night he left New York a few nights after the towers fell. The décor was all in various shades of beige. Beige had always been a neutral color, or so he had been told, but now he viewed it with the utmost disdain. The plain, pale shades felt sterile, as though he were in a hospital recovering from some disease or terrible accident. There was nothing that said home. He had a blow-up mattress and a sleeping bag. There was no television or even a radio. He had a computer, but no Internet access. The kitchen and den together made one room and a small bedroom was the other. He had neighbors but he rarely saw any of them. They were mostly single men, alone. *Perhaps divorced or single*, Michael thought, *but he was not sure. They are all so quiet and docile, as though they have been severely wounded and are convalescing.*

Michael came into his empty apartment after a trip to the store. Long shadows of afternoon light from outside the door fell across the worn, short-cropped, beige carpet. He shut the door behind him and it was dark. He reached his hand out along the wall to his right and flipped the light switch: There was a click, but no light.

Somewhat sourly, he recalled that the switches just inside the door belonged to the outlets in the den and were meant for lamps that he did not have that would sit on tables that he did not have. He made his way gingerly to the kitchen and fumbled for the light switch there, eventually setting the groceries on the floor and using two hands to grope around until he found the switch and turned on the large fluorescent kitchen light. It buzzed slightly, making the silence seem greater, amplifying his loneliness.

Michael had always felt so strong, but now he was full of doubt and fear. He would convince himself otherwise, but the tightness in his gut pushed out any positive thoughts. *What am I doing? I should run home and beg for forgiveness.* The thoughts plagued him while he put the groceries away. First, he put one thing on each shelf of the refrigerator to make it look fuller, but it did not. Then, he opened a few cabinets to put away dry goods, deciding that he needed to organize the things on the shelves, but when he realized how little he had on the empty shelves, he decided there was no need.

When he was done, he sat on the carpet against the wall and watched the shadows coming in through the blinds. He had an urge to turn on the television to fill the void, then he remembered that he did not have one. He decided to fold sheets that went on a bed he did not have, then he put away all of his laundry, stacking most of it on the one shelf of his only closet and the rest on the floor. He realized that he did not even have hangers. He let out a sigh and began to laugh at himself. He could hear the sounds of birds chirping outside, and he could hear the wind in the trees just beyond the window. He wondered why the birds would be chirping in the night. He walked out onto his small balcony, seeing two large roaches scatter away from him as he stepped outside. He watched a carpenter bee boring into the wood siding. He moved closer but the bee was busy and indifferent to Michael. So many things that he thought were reserved for the daylight seemed to be busy at night, perhaps confused by the bright street lamps in the parking lot.

He walked back into the apartment and into the kitchen. The dishwasher had run, so he opened it and put away the two cups and one plate that were inside. Next, he thought that he would vacuum the carpet. As he vacuumed, he noticed that the clear catch basin of the machine quickly filled with a large amount of dust. He dumped the dust into the wastebasket when he was finished and sat again on the carpet against the wall, hugging his knees. The quiet of the apartment made the noise in his mind loud. Questions appeared in his mind and he tried to answer them one at a time.

Am I just passing time? No, I am getting my shit together. Am I running away? No, I am doing fine. Am I falling down, falling apart, am I missing some point? No, I am trying to live from my heart and live honestly to find out what is true. He imagined he could hear his kids down the hall laughing, and then he imagined himself getting up to investigate, as he always had. *Yes, I am falling,* he thought to himself, then added, *and I am definitely full of shit!*

PART 3:
The Search for Truth

If a man clings tenaciously to truth,
he ultimately realizes God.
Without this regard for truth,
one gradually loses everything.
If by chance I say that I will go to the pine-grove,
I must go there even if there is no further need of it,
lest I lose my attachment to truth.
After my vision of the Divine Mother,
I prayed to Her, taking a flower in my hands,
"Mother, here is Thy knowledge and here is Thy ignorance.
Take them both, and give me only pure love.
Here is Thy holiness and here is Thy unholiness.
Take them both, Mother, and give me pure love.
Here is Thy good and here is Thy evil.
Take them both, Mother, and give me pure love.
Here is Thy righteousness and here is Thy unrighteousness.
Take them both, Mother, and give me pure love."
I mentioned all these, but I could not say,
"Mother, here is Thy truth and here is Thy falsehood.
Take them both."
I gave up everything at Her feet,
But I could not bring myself to give up truth.

– Sri Ramakrishna

Living to Ride
in the Mountains

Five Years Later, 2007

Michael sat at the desk in his new cube. Stacks of files and reports completely covered the large, gray, laminate desktop, which extended from the cube wall to the back wall. There were drawers and metal filing cabinets underneath and above the desktop, and everything was some shade of gray; only the telephone was black. Every cube in the office was nearly identical, except the ones like Michael's at the outside walls of the building, which were slightly bigger and had dividers that rose an entire 12 inches higher. In cube farm hierarchy, a higher wall meant higher status.

The mailroom had already found Michael's new location, and there was a small corrugated box sitting on top of moving boxes in the middle of Michael's cube. "Senior Vice President Michael Tantalus," was printed on the box in bold letters. It made Michael laugh when he read it, remembering his father's words: "Vice President at a bank means you make more than $10,000 a year." At Universal Spectrum, it meant something to be a vice president, as there were only a handful of people who carried the title. But here at the bank, there were so many rows and rows of cubes of vice presidents, it was laughable.

Michael rummaged through one of the moving boxes on the floor until he found a pair of scissors and opened another small box. It was a glass cube and in the middle were etched the words "Five Years of Service." On the top in prominent letters was the logo for

Global Finance Bank and at the bottom in small letters was "Michael Tantalus," etched in neat block letters. *Five years?* Michael thought. *I can't believe it's been five years.* He began to do the math in his head and decided that it was actually closer to six years.

Michael looked out of the small window in his cube. For nearly six years he had not had a window to look out of. There was not much in the land of gray cubes to tell a good day from a bad day. Sometimes he would walk outside at the end of a day and be surprised to feel the weather outside. The air-conditioned and heated buildings felt much the same each day as they had the previous and will the next. But now Michael had a narrow window—only six inches wide—but it rose from the floor to the ceiling. He looked outside now, observing construction below and hearing a repetitive pounding sound.

Next to the building that Michael worked in, construction had begun on a new building. In fact, many new buildings had sprung up in the years that Michael had been in Charlotte. "Uptown," as it was called, was growing fast and changing every day. Michael chuckled to himself as he heard the word *Uptown* in his mind. There was no downtown or even a midtown to warrant an uptown, there were no boroughs or anything else that made Michael think of New York. But money was flowing into this relatively new financial center, and uptown sounded better for an up-and-coming city than downtown did.

Money was moving through Charlotte, and Michael remembered what he had learned from Bennie: When money moves, it makes money for everyone else. Plus, new money always is more visible than old money. The new money coming into Charlotte had added a lot of new things so far, including professional basketball and football teams with new stadiums and the feeling that Charlotte had arrived. On one of Michael's morning commutes to work he had tried to count all of the black BMWs that he saw, but he quickly realized that the effort was futile; it seemed everyone in Charlotte could afford a fancy automobile. Appearances suggested that everyone was moving up.

Even Michael had received a promotion, which came as a surprise. He had taken a menial job as an analyst and become part of the dreaded overhead of a major corporation. Five years earlier he had walked into a maze of cubes and lost himself.

Until then, Michael had always taken employment where he could "make things happen." But when he left Manhattan, he left something of himself behind. Michael knew that he was not the same, but it was only a vague feeling and nothing he could put into thoughts or words. Initially, he thought maybe he was just grieving and that he eventually would be his old self again. However, now Michael was beginning to realize that there was no going back to anything—moving forward was the only option. He thought evolving to something or going somewhere was the answer but he just did not seem to have the energy he used to. Or maybe he'd lost the ability to channel his energy into a single direction to "make things happen," so here he sat looking out his thin window at all the change that was happening outside.

Michael moved some boxes from his chair to the floor, then sat down to start getting organized. It was his job to look at the numbers and make recommendations. He was surprised to find out how few people could look at numbers on a printout and have some idea of what the numbers meant in the "outside world." It seemed that there were field people and office people and very few who could walk in both worlds. Michael had been chastised early by his boss, who told him to "slow down" and asked him if he was trying to make others look bad, suggesting that Michael was not a team player. All the analysis, he further explained to Michael, was done on behalf of the team, everyone together. It was utter ridiculousness to Michael, but he acquiesced. Michael quickly had assessed his teammates as having varying shades of incompetence or laziness, or both. He held no contempt for them but kept his distance. Substance and performance seemed to be in the background, while politics took the foreground.

Various ambitious people accused others of being "political," which usually meant that they themselves were political. And rather than stand on their own work, they endeavored to sabotage any of their coworkers they viewed as a threat. There were plenty of good, well-meaning people—and smart ones, too—but Michael could see that most of them worked in an environment that suppressed excellence and carried too much dead weight. There were so many capable people who would attend required meetings and keep as low a profile as possible, always afraid that they might lose their jobs.

Michael looked at the reports, took his time, fed everything to his boss, and watched the clock every day, leaving the stale office air as soon as he could to live a life on the outside that felt real and alive. He never saw the truth: "Michael Tantalus" was not just the sum of the moments in which he felt the most himself, but the total of his whole existence. So the promotion had come as a surprise.

He had no idea if anything had really changed other than the "Senior" placed in front of the "Vice President" in his title and a meager four percent raise in his salary. He moved three cubes down to a workspace with 20 square feet more space, a higher cube wall, and a window. He wanted to laugh out loud. He looked out of his fifth floor window, where a large, rusted red machine down below drove pylons into the ground. BAM, BAM, BAM. It was not too loud, but it was incessant. *I suppose like everything else, I'll get used to the noise and barely notice it after a time*, Michael thought. Suddenly, he felt as if he could not catch his breath. He wanted to cough but suppressed the urge. It was nearly time to go, so he searched under the stacks of paper and boxes for his black bag.

Michael knew that there would be a rush to the elevators precisely at five o'clock and thought he would get a jump on the crowd. If he left a little early he could avoid talking to anyone who might be waiting for the elevator, feeling chatty, asking some question that they really did not want to hear an answer to. Besides, it was Friday, and Michael was headed to the mountains. He stood holding the black bag with one hand behind him. Instinctively he was hiding the bag that held his change: a change of clothes that would bring a change of persona. He walked slowly and methodically out of his small, square office, down the small corridor to an open expanse of cubicles. *God, the air is terrible in here*, he was thinking, though no one else in the building had ever complained.

He crossed the corridor of perfect cubes, staring blankly at the bland, brown partitions. He could hear people on their phones and the tapping of thousands of fingers typing quickly on hundreds of keyboards. *Boxes of hungry ghosts, the true living dead,* he thought to himself. *Damn, I'm judgmental... but look at them, going about their appointed tasks, jumping at the phones, answering emails and texts, and not a single one of them has any idea how the activities in their small cube fit into or affect the functioning of the entire building, the entire company. Hell, how can I judge the poor slobs, I have no f'n clue myself. Nobody is thinking about what they are really doing. God, do any of them give a damn past the box they live in?*

At first, Michael had hated them and their shallow talk; it was painful to sit and listen to someone carry on and on about meaningless details of some file or email that had gone around the cubes. He wanted to shake them one by one to wake them up. He wanted to tell them things, but he was not sure what. He felt as if he was the only living person in the entire building. It made him feel lonely. And as he looked across the top of all the tranquillized boxes, he felt as if there had been a great killing sometime in the past: The hearts and spirits of these people had been killed, and for a moment he felt compassion and not judgment.

He kept walking though, hurrying toward the elevators. Unfortunately, the doors were closed, and he pushed at the button repeatedly, watching a distorted version of himself fidget in the brushed metal doors as he waited for them to open. "Freedom," he whispered as he heard the ding that signaled the elevator's impending opening, then stepped quickly into the elevator, relieved that it was empty. *Another damn box,* he thought, *like a moving coffin. Funny... coffin, the death of my business-self and the birth of my real-self...* But then the doubt set in.

Thoughts of New York came more and more often into his mind lately. This time, it came from the elevator, the smell of machine oil or some other unrecognizable mechanical smell. He thought of the day in the fall when he had awoken to his own life. He had been aware of a low level of discontentment since that day. Many days he was grateful for the awareness, but on days like today, there was nothing but doubt about the decisions he had been making.

The doors opened and Michael shook away his thoughts as he stepped into the grand lobby of the building. High, straight columns rose to what seemed like the sky, giving this space a bright majesty and the illusion that this was a tower he spent the better part of his days in. Michael walked to the large, heavy doors, which cast a shadow into the white marble lobby. *My eyes are wide open and I can see things with perfect clarity*, Michael told himself as he emerged from the shadows into the late afternoon sunlight outside. He had thought this thought often, for it seemed that he saw things more clearly than he had before the fall of the World Trade Center towers, but today, he just was not sure it was true.

Once outside, he listened to the sounds of the streets of Uptown Charlotte. The "Queen City" was just a small impression of "The City" of New York. Charlotte was much smaller, but it was also newer and appeared cleaner. There were tall buildings, but it seemed you could escape them easily by crossing a block or two at most. Michael looked up at the sky, then down at the naked, small trees that appeared so slight beneath the tall buildings. He found himself speaking reassuringly to the trees: "Don't worry, the buildings will be gone before long and the sky will be yours again, nothing stands for too long." Then he laughed, thinking *I can't believe that I talking to trees, or that I'm talking out loud to myself. Damn, people are going to think I'm crazy if they listen to me ramble on.* Suddenly, Michael realized that he was having a constant monologue. The only thing that kept others from thinking he was crazy was the fact that he kept the thoughts to himself. *Damn, maybe I am crazy!* He chuckled to himself, then continued walking down the sidewalk, which was becoming increasingly busy with commuters, toward the motorcycle parking.

Then the doubting thoughts came back: *What made me ever think I should try to discover Truth? If that's what I'm doing, it's doomed to fail. I just keep thinking the same stupid thoughts.* Then he laughed wryly to himself. *At least I'm still full of shit!* He turned to look back at the building from which he had emerged. Many more people followed him and the streets began to fill. Many of the men were wearing suits and ties, and they walked as if they were important. *Maybe they are important*, Michael thought. *Maybe I am the one who has this all wrong. I jumped off the corporate ladder for a crappy job: What the hell was I thinking? And I left my wife for what, an empty apartment? God, I am so full of shit. Maybe I just had a bad reaction to a trauma. Maybe I should have sought some sort of therapy, maybe everything I did was like an allergic reaction. Maybe.*

He thought again of the people in the office, caught in the "poppy fields." *What makes me any different?* he wondered. *I live like an ascetic. I read anything spiritual I can find, and I ride.* Then a cough came on suddenly. He stopped walking and bent over slightly, coughing into his fist. From one cough he went right into another, struggling to catch his breath.

"Sounds serious," said the young man waiting for him by the motorcycles, but he was only kidding Michael.

"Seems to linger, coming and going…but I feel alright. Must be allergies," Michael said.

"Hurry it up, would you! I want to beat the traffic up the interstate," the young man beamed as he verbally poked Michael. He was handsome and smart, but mostly he was young. Michael liked to ride with him; he rode hard and seemed to have no fear, so Michael had to push his own limits to keep up. Riding a little past his limits always gave Michael a jolt of adrenaline. A small amount of fear was just what Michael liked, it made him feel alive. Michael had told himself frequently that he and the young man were "really" riding. Neither man was interested in the gear or how it looked and they weren't trying to impress anyone; this guy was the real deal as far as Michael was concerned. The young man's leather jacket was worn, he wore faded blue jeans and dark riding boots, he was bare-handed, and he had on an open-faced helmet with dark sunglasses. None of his clothes matched and the green hood of a sweatshirt hung loose at his neck over the top of his jacket, but there was fire in the young man's eyes. From the outside, this young man and Michael appeared to be two of kind: Both pushed their limits and rode with an edge, like they were racing toward something or away from something. But they were quite different. The young man was named Spencer Davis.

It was a cool-sounding name and he had the good looks to match. What Michael liked about Spencer was that he raced hard and rode with passion, but there was a greenness to his thoughts. Spencer felt a rush at the pace but there was no fear; his young man's eyes glimmered at the excitement, but he knew little of living. Life had not broken him like it had Michael. Michael could see all this, but it did not matter to him; he preferred fast-moving company.

"Try to keep up today, old man," said Spencer with a wide grin.

"What's that you say, sonny?" Michael mimicked the voice of an old man. Spencer was already sitting on his bike, perched almost sideways with his arm resting on his gas tank in an impatient and awkward position. Michael opened the bag and threw some gear onto the pavement, then began to change on the sidewalk, attracting more than a few glares. He was swift and methodical, off with his button-down shirt then a sweatshirt over his undershirt. The silver cross on his necklace caught the sunlight and reflected it into Spencer's eye.

"Today? We are riding *today*, right?" the young man continued to tease Michael.

"Just keep it between the ditches," Michael said, smiling. Then, he put on his jacket, stuffed his work clothes into the bag, and strapped it down on the back of the motorcycle. Michael relished the routine, and he never wavered from it. Spencer was making eyes at two women sitting nearby at one of the outdoor tables of a restaurant. They were giggling, whispering to one another, so Michael waved as he strapped on his helmet, but Michael was out of sync and he awkwardly straddled his bike and struggled to pull on his gloves. He dropped one of them and had to get off the motorcycle to retrieve it. He knew he was being watched, making him fumble a bit with the zipper to his jacket, but he finally settled back on the bike.

"All ready, grandpa?" Spencer asked.

Michael ignored the jab. "I'll lead us out of town up I-77," he said, giving instructions before the machines roared to life, limiting any communication to gestures and signals.

"Sounds like a plan. When we get past the river, I'll take the lead and get us off the highway. I'm going to push it up the mountains until we get to the Parkway, so keep up!" This last was a challenge from Spencer, who began pulling knobs and flipping switches, but just before he started the engine he asked, "How hard do you want to push the switchbacks?"

"Hard," answered Michael, with an emphasis that surprised himself.

"Okay," answered Spencer mockingly, "If we get separated, I'll meet you at a place called Curly's."

"Okay, pretty boy," Michael said, loud enough for the two women nearby to hear; they were still watching the men, but their focus now was on Spencer. He is attractive, Michael thought, wondering exactly what made him so appealing. Was it his youth? *It's the damned bravado of testosterone: Women can't resist it,* Michael assured himself, then he coughed again. *Guess I better check it out with a doctor.*

Spencer hit the starter, and his motorcycle boomed to life loudly, echoing across the window fronts of the nearby buildings and startling the two women. Noticing them jump, he smiled and hit the throttle. Michael put his hands on the grips and thought about what to do first. After a moment, he reached his hand down to open the fuel valve. *Um, let's see, next is the um, on switch.* He stood the bike up, and it felt heavy and a little off-balance. He squeezed in the clutch and hit the start button. The bike clicked hard and the engine made a cha-cha-cha sound. Michael hit the starter again with the same result. *Ah, damn, forgot the choke.* He reached down, pulled out the choke, and then hit the starter again; this time the bike came to life. He let the bike idle for a bit then eased the throttle, sensing the engine was ready to respond. The engine roared, so Michael let it settle back down, then squeezed in the clutch, kicked it into first gear, eased out the clutch, and the bike began to move.

Doubt made one last attempt on Michael, but riding was like falling into alignment with the universe, even when everything felt forced and intentional. The vulnerability of being on a bike with no protection from other cars forced Michael to concentrate, and with no windshield, Michael could feel the elements, emphasizing the reality of his speed and acceleration.

Michael had pushed himself to be honest, pushed himself toward integrity, but his effort let him down constantly; however, riding never let him down. It never let him down because riding took concentration, and the concentration left no room for thoughts about what was wrong and what needed to be different. He simply breathed every breath and watched the gray blur below his feet. No judging of self, just watching and riding. Michael wondered if he could live the way he rode, falling into alignment with the road, pushing the throttle and letting the tires find the grooves in the roadway.

The rising tachometer caught Michael's attention, alerting him that the bike's engine was warming, so he reached down with one hand while holding the gas with the other and eased in the throttle, giving the engine strength. Michael looked into the rearview mirror, seeing the shaky image of the young man close behind him. The two men made one last turn and accelerated onto the interstate. The ramp was narrow, rising upward to meet the highway; as soon as they were at the top of the ramp they could see the oncoming traffic. Michael twisted the throttle only slightly, but it was enough to outrun any of the coming trucks and cars.

The two men followed their plan, and as they passed the river, Spencer buzzed past Michael and led them off the highway. Spencer rode aggressively and Michael stayed on his tail, and as they leaned into turn after turn, Michael's confidence grew. The trees blurred in his peripheral vision as they passed slower moving cars and trucks. Their ascent was pure joy and excitement—they had beaten the weekend traffic—and there were few obstacles to slow them down. Coming to a steep ridge, they began to wind back and forth, working the gears, the brakes, and the gas. Michael, close behind the younger man, wanted to go faster, so he decided to pass. When they hit a short straightaway, he roared past Spencer and they quickly came into a tight turn with a little too much velocity. Spencer took the pass as a challenge, hitting the throttle without regard for the coming bend in the road.

Adrenaline rushed into Michael and he tensed a little with fear for the intensity of the situation, but he looked where the road was headed, dipped the left handle grip, shifted his weight to the left side of the speeding motorcycle. He was leaning hard, and his left hand, right hand, and right foot all began to move together as he eased the gas, squeezed in the clutch, and downshifted, then let out the clutch and let the gears catch the speeding bike and slow it enough to make the turn. Michael kept his focus on the road and repeated the movement, downshifting once again as the turn tightened; as the road began to straighten, the adrenaline fueled the thrill while all fear left him completely. The road straightened and Michael came out of his lean, twisting his right wrist downward so the machine screamed to life as if it were being shot out of the turn. Michael threw his left fist exuberantly into the air and then hit the next turn back in the opposite direction just as quickly.

Spencer was catching up to Michael as they hit the turn. Spencer was higher in the bending road and carried more mass and velocity into the switchback. He instinctually got onto both the front and rear brakes as he noticed the loose gravel at the edge of the road. Almost instantly, his motorcycle was headed toward the focus and fear, even as he leaned away from the edge of the road. His fearful thought became his reality as first the rear wheel and then the front hit the gravel. The bike went down and slid out from underneath him, and he let go of the motorbike as terror filled him. He slid on his back across the curving band of gravel into the grass, then he began to roll down a soft hill. Suddenly, he came to a stop. He lay completely still for a few minutes, his heart beating wildly, the loudest thing he could hear over the rushing in his ears.

He looked up at the blue sky and began to pray for multitudes of past sins. He remembered many, some back to his childhood. Things that never bothered him before were now something that he must atone for. He rolled onto his side and began to check his body for breaks. He was shaking uncontrollably. Arms, legs, chest: *Everything seems to be okay*, he told himself. He sat up and his stomach lurched. He leaned over and vomited. After lying still for a few more minutes, he climbed to his hands and knees and began to curse.

The man was young and strong with fresh, keen senses and reactions. He had never had any reason to hold fear in his mind—and he was too young to know that the thoughts you hold in your mind are what you get in life, even if those thoughts are about what you do not want to receive.

Finding himself in the ditch, he blamed Michael.

"Where the hell are you Michael, you fucking asshole?!"

Spencer began to get back on his feet little by little, first one foot on the ground, then the other, then standing slowly, searching for his balance as if he were standing on a tightrope. Once standing, he realized how hard his body was shaking and noticed that dirt seemed to be everywhere: on his jacket, in his jacket, in his shirt, and even in his pants. He attempted to shake it out of his clothing.

"Where is that fucking jerk?!" Spencer said aloud. He took inventory of his body once again, and aside from the shaking, he seemed to be fine. He looked around for his motorcycle. It was not far away, and as he approached he could see that it was caked in dirt, adorned with small clumps of sod and grass. "Thank God for soft landings," he said as he began to take deep breaths, one right after the other. With as much strength as he could muster, he lifted up the heavy bike to find that one end of the handlebar was slightly bent and the left-side blinker and rearview mirror were both broken off. He put down the kickstand and leaned the bike to stand on its own.

He attempted to start the engine with far less confidence than ever before. It took much longer than normal, but the bike finally boomed a loud backfire then roared to life. Slowly, still shaking a little Spencer headed to Curly's.

Michael was sitting sideways on his motorcycle in the parking lot when Spencer arrived. Michael had removed all his gear and had a big grin on his face.

"What took so long? Did you get lost?" Michael asked, smiling big. He clearly did not notice any of the damage on Spencer's bike. "Let's have a drink, I'm buying," Michael added enthusiastically.

"No, I don't feel much like a drink," was all Spencer could think to say, still mad at Michael.

"I'm feeling beat—think I'll head home," he said, cranking the engine back to life. Then he yelled over the sound of his own bike, "See you Monday." But he did not mean it; he was through with Michael, his pride was bruised as much as his body was, and he blamed Michael for it.

"Hmm," was all that Michael said. He felt marvelous, so he stood and headed into the bar for a drink.

Curly's Place
Fall of 2007

Michael stepped out of the light of the day into the hazy bar. There were slivers of light streaming in through the dusty windows, even the cloudy exterior was brighter than the inside of the bar. Most of the people inside were bikers sitting against the shadowed wall, registering as silhouettes and shapes to Michael's unadjusted eyes. Curly's Place was permeated by a pungent mixture of stale beer, leather, and gasoline, a smell that was by-now familiar and comforting to Michael. He methodically scanned the bar, looking for a place to sit. The scattered tables were all taken and there was someone sitting on all of the bar stools except for one near the end. Michael moved towards the empty seat. He passed man after man wearing leather and jeans, some in sleeveless tee shirts exposing bulky arms covered in tattoos. They looked rough to Michael. *These are not lawyers and doctors pretending to be bikers*, Michael thought as he walked past, *these men are the real deal*.

Michael walked purposely towards the empty stool, unsnapping his leather jacket as he moved. The smoky warmth received Michael as he slid off the heavy leather jacket and sat at the bar. Michael looked to his right at the man at end of the bar. He was wearing a tweed blazer with a matching bowtie. He was an older man looking right at Michael and he had a slight smile, then squinted his eyes at Michael, and he looked as if he was about to say, *I know what you are thinking*. His mostly white beard was thick, but his long, silver wisps of hair had retreated high on his forehead, exposing several long, deep lines above bushy, white eyebrows. His eyes were deep blue and conveyed stillness, but they lay hidden behind large, round spectacles.

"Dr. Peter Stanhope, but please call me Doc," he greeted Michael formally and extended his hand.

"Oh, I'm Michael, Michael Tantalus, call me Michael," Michael was taken aback by the gentleman's appearance.

"Pleasure to make your acquaintance," he said and turned back towards the bar. Michael kept staring at the man trying to figure out what he was doing in a rough biker bar.

"You look like you…." Michael began.

"Like he's a handsome, sharply dressed gentleman," the female bartender interrupted Michael, finishing his sentence. "How are you today, Doc? I am always happy to see you," she addressed Dr. Stanhope and ignored Michael.

"Splendid, my dear, splendid," Doc answered.

"Your usual, Doc?" she asked.

"Yes, of course my dear, that would be lovely," Doc said as he gave her a small bow.

"Could I have a…" Michael tried to get in his drink order but the bartender had already turned and headed down the bar. Michael watched her: She was stunning, she had the kind of beauty that allowed her to be reckless with people. She was wearing a black, silky, sleeveless top and very tight blue jeans. Her hair was long, thick and wavy and auburn. Her face was petite and pretty, and her body was curvy. She returned quickly with a tall martini glass, chilled and full to the top with gin. She placed it in front of Doc, smiling, and waited for Doc's reply. He sipped the martini, cleared his throat, and said, "Perfect Lila, just perfect." The he motioned his head towards Michael.

"Okay, what do you want," her tone was considerably less cordial. Michael tried to think of something witty to say.

"One bourbon, one scotch, and one beer," Michael said smiling, obviously pleased with himself.

"Are you serious, or is that some pathetic attempt at humor?" she said to him.

"Um, yes, I mean, I think I am, no, well, yes," Michael said as he turned red. The bartender looked right at him for a bit longer and did not smile, then turned to get the drinks.

"Do you always speak in song lyrics," Doc asked Michael as he began to politely laugh.

"Sometimes, I guess, actually, no never. I think I panicked, she's a little intense," Michael said as he turned towards Doc.

"You mustn't get down on yourself, young chap, she has that effect on us all," then he sipped his martini. The bartender returned and placed two shot glasses both nearly full of an amber-colored liquid, one a little lighter than the other, and a beer in a tall, slender brown bottle.

"Doc, are you staying late tonight?" Lila asked, "I want to a talk a little 'Spiritual Smack,' later" she added then winked at the Doc.

"If we must," Doc answered. Then Lila looked at Michael and smiled, then brushed back a lock of her hair and tucked it behind her left ear. Then she turned back to the other patrons. Michael sat motionless.

"Oh no," Doc said as he looked at Michael.

"Doc, who is she, the bartender, maybe you should introduce us?"

"No, I do not think that would be prudent or wise," Doc answered.

"Doc, did you see the smile she just gave me?" Michael asked.

"Yes, my young foolish friend, I am afraid that we both just witnessed the devil herself. You see, she smiled at you because you are a man, she tempts all who cross her fancy," then Doc tipped his drink, taking a full swallow and not just a sip. "But do not take it to heart, she does the same to all men."

"You talk like you know her well," said Michael.

"Yes, my young precocious friend, I am in *love* with that young and beautiful maiden, but alas, I am gilded by age. Doomed to love but to never consecrate my deepest of desires," then Doc smiled and drank down the rest of the martini, taking out the olives and eating them one at a time.

"I really don't know what to say, Doc, I mean, we just met, I am feeling just a little awkward." Michael drank down one of the shots. It burned his throat and he grimaced, then reached for the beer. "Now I am more than sure that you should introduce us," he added.

"Who do you think I am, Jake?" Doc answered.

"What?" Michael asked as he turned towards Doc.

"Hemingway, old chap, Hemingway," Doc said as he motioned to Lila for another martini.

"As in Ernest Hemingway?" Michael asked.

"Yes my young friend, as in Ernest Hemingway, born in Oak Park, Illinois, 1899, I believe, voice of the 'Lost Generation'," Doc said as he peered over the top of his glasses, looking Michael up and down. "I would say you are in your forties, Mr. Michael Tantalus. I believe that would make you part of the 'Stairway to Heaven' generation," then Doc grinned.

"As in the song, 'she's buying the stairway to heaven' generation?" Michael asked.

"Well, something like that," Doc said and smiled at Lila as she set a fresh martini down in front of him. Then she smiled again at Michael. He was prepared this time and smiled back at her, it made her pause and they looked each other in the eyes for a moment, then she moved on to the other patrons.

"Doc," Michael asked, "Do you always talk in song lyrics?"

"Sometimes, I guess, actually, no never. I think I panicked, she's a little intense, don't you think?" Doc mimicked as he turned towards Michael, chuckling, his body moving but with no sound coming out. Michael laughed.

"So Doc, tell me about our attractive barmaid, what's her story?"

"That beautiful woman is 'Lady Ashley' as sure as my name is Dr. Peter Stanhope, and when a young buck like yourself asks me to introduce him to her, I feel just like Jake."

"Her name is Lady Ashley?" Michael asked.

"No, no, my dear man, her name is Lila but she is a 'Lady Ashley' most assuredly, as in Hemingway's The Sun Also Rises, do you not read the classics?"

"Well, yeah, Doc, I read plenty, but I don't think I ever read that one," said Michael.

"Better read it," Doc warned as he sipped the new martini. Michael followed his lead and drank the remaining shot. This one went down considerably smoother and Michael looked at the shot glass and wondered what he had just tasted.

"Why should I read it?" Michael asked, "Will it tell me something about Lila?"

"Read it because it is good literature!" Doc said the last word in a British accent, "And because it will tell you something of Lila." He said the last part in a near-whisper.

"So, what do you read?" Doc asked Michael.

"Search for Truth and the meaning of life kind of stuff," Michael answered.

"Oh, enlightenment!" Doc exclaimed, then added, "...a worthy pursuit."

A crack of thunder pounded loudly and the lights in the bar flickered and went out. The bar went dark and momentarily silent. Then a growing murmuring of voices grew, followed shortly thereafter by the sound of stools and chairs scooting across the room as people scrambled about in the darkness. A few people pulled out their cigarette lighters, flicked them alive, and held them up, giving a bit of light. Lila made her way to the door and opened it, and though it was beginning to rain, it was lighter outside than in the bar and the open door provided just enough light so people could see well enough to make their way out. Many got up to leave, and as they made their way to the door, Lila met them and scrambled to collect money. Soon everyone had left but Doc and Michael. They chatted in the dim light. Lila lit two candles, walked towards the voices of the two men and set the lighted candles between them. She stepped into the shadows momentarily and returned with another beer for Michael, then she put one elbow down on the bar and looked at Doc, nodding towards Michael. Doc sighed.

"If I must," Doc said. "Ms. Rorschach, may I have the honor of introducing you to Mr. Tantalus?"

"Lila," said the bartender as she extended her hand across the bar to Michael.

"Michael," he replied, taking her hand, which was soft and small but fit into his perfectly. He held it far too long and she pulled it away awkwardly. But she looked at him with soft eyes, inviting but at the same time keeping him at arm's length. There was an instant of familiarity that put them both at ease but also on edge. Lila poured herself a glass of wine and put it down on the bar between Michael and Doc. She sipped it and began to close up, putting away glasses and counting the money. Michael tried hard to think of something to say to her.

"Do you read," he finally asked Lila.

"You know, I've been meaning to learn, but ever since I started to run this," she paused and looked around her like she could not believe where she was, "place, I've just not had the time," she turned and headed into the darkness. Michael could hear the gentle chinking of glasses and bottles as she continued putting things away. Michael stared at the candle in front of him for a few minutes, watching it flicker in the moist wind coming in through the open door. Then he looked at Doc who was drinking his Martini and looking the other way. Michael sipped his beer then said,

"Well?"

"Oh, how did it go?" Doc responded.

"You were there, how do you think it went?" Michael asked.

"Well, when I pass a horrible auto accident on the highway, I usually turn away, especially if it looks to be one those accidents where there will be dead bodies and severed arms and legs with blood and such strewn about. I really do not sleep well enough so do not want any extra horror images in my mind," Doc said as he sipped his drink, then set it down, crossed his arms on the bar, and looked at Michael.

"That bad?" Michael asked.

"Was that your best stuff?" Doc asked as Michael scratched his chin then both men began to chuckle.

"God, she must think I'm an idiot," Michael said with a sigh.

"Thou shalt not take the Lord's name in vain," Doc said vigorously and held up a finger as if to make a point.

"Sorry Doc, are you religious?" Michael asked.

"Not particularly," Doc answered, "But I am somewhat of a pragmatist. You see, it is like this, I do not believe that the Third Commandment was put into the Bible because God feels confused or disrespected upon hearing his name called at an inappropriate time, such as when someone hits their thumb with a hammer. No, I think that this commandment is one of practicality for us confused masses searching humanity. You see, Michael, sooner or later, we all search. And when we have a word like God that we have used as an expletive, well that completely shatters any concept of, well, of God. Our subconscious just gets confused about for what exactly it is searching," Doc paused to drink.

"How many of those have you had, Doc?" Michael asked. It thundered again, this time the flash of lightning lit up the inside of the bar. It was beginning to rain harder. Lila brought another round of drinks.

"Michael, do you want your tab?" she asked. Michael looked out the open door; the rain was now coming straight down, it was uninviting but its sound was soothing.

"No, think I'll ride it out in here," Michael said, then he looked at Lila, "How late do you stay open?" he asked. She did not answer, she just stared at Michael. It was a look he could not read.

"Pardon the old man," Doc stood, excused himself, and headed for the restroom. Lila picked up an old rag from the bar and started wiping things down while asking Michael questions.

"Don't you need to call your wife or something?" she asked, not looking at him. He looked down at his hand; he was still wearing his wedding ring.

"No, I don't think she much cares where I am at this point," Michael answered, then took a drink of the beer and looked out the open door. She looked up at Michael and waited for him to elaborate, but he did not. She started wiping things again and asked her next question.

"What do you do, Michael Tantalus? No wait, let me guess." She stopped wiping and looked at Michael. He looked back at her. Their eyes caught for a moment and gazed at each other. It was not awkward this time, but it should have been so Lila began talking again. "You are a doctor, no wait, you are a lawyer, no wait, you are banker. That's it, isn't it? You are a banker," she smiled at Michael and he smiled back.

"What do you do other than, you know, this?" he asked her.

"What do you mean by that?"

"Well, I don't know, I don't really mean anything. But it just seems like you don't belong here, it seems like you belong, you know, somewhere else," he paused. The words did not make much sense but it felt like they were communicating on another level. Lila felt it too, normally she would take a man down a notch or two and she knew she could do it, but she sensed a gentleness in Michael, a quiet strength. His body language was so confident, she was not sure what it was that pulled her towards him, but pulled she was. But it did not matter, she would keep this man at bay, not let him in too close, but she was drawn to him, and he felt it too. They were quickly falling into a deep connection with each other. And it was the type of connection from which they would never be able to fully extricate themselves. They looked at each other in the candlelight; Michael felt something falling within himself and did not resist the feeling.

"The conversation looks deep," it was Doc returning from the restroom. It broke the spell between Michael and Lila, and she returned to her duties of cleaning and closing up the bar. "So Michael, tell me about your search for enlightenment," Doc said.

Michael began to expound on all the books he had read, he named them one after another, and he had been searching for years now, so the list was long. Doc nodded, or sometimes grabbed his chin. Sometimes he would make a comment on a book or two. Michael talked about various theories and recounted the words of many of the books. He rambled on and on from subject to subject, even contradicting himself. He finally paused and took a drink of his beer.

"Is that all?" Doc asked.

"Well I'm sure there's more, but I have forgotten a lot of what I have read," answered Michael.

"We are talking about enlightenment here?" Doc clarified.

"Well yes Doc, enlightenment, the search for Truth, answers to the big questions," answered Michael.

"You know, Michael, the journey to enlightenment leaves books behind, it leaves words behind, it even goes beyond thoughts," Doc looked straight at Michael and suddenly he sounded sober. "It is time to stop reading and thinking about enlightenment; it is time to go and find it, that is, if you really want to find out what's true,"

Michael looked back at Doc trying to figure out the old man; one minute, he seemed to be a drunken fool and the next moment, a sage. "Are you enlightened, Doc?" Michael asked.

"That, my young searching friend, is a trick question," he answered while raising a finger into the air. "Any part of me that would claim to be enlightened is precisely the part of me that cannot be enlightened," he said, then the smile went from his face,

"Wait, let me rethink that," Doc said and put his hand on his forehead, then he raised his glass with the other hand and sipped his martini. Michael chuckled.

"Doc, tell me, have you taken that journey beyond words, to enlightenment?" Michael asked in earnest.

"It is a worthy endeavor, Michael and I highly suggest it for you."

"Are *you* enlightened?"

"God no," answered Doc.

"Didn't you just say to not, you know, um never mind," Michael said, smiling and shaking his head to himself. He took another drink of his beer then started again. "So let me see if I have this right, you think I should take this journey even though you have not."

"I did not say I have not taken this journey, only that I am not enlightened," Doc answered, "And besides, it is a worthwhile journey and, God knows, someone here on earth needs to take the journey all the way to its conclusion," Doc was smiling again.

"Well, Doc, since you put it that way, sure, count me in," Michael said, looking around for Lila. Doc cleared his throat to get Michael's attention.

"Michael," Doc said in a serious tone, "I want to say it again to you, only clearer. It is time to put down your books and stop your conversations. It is time to stop thinking and talking about God, it is time to start experiencing God. The journey ahead of you is a required journey for everyone; the only choice is when you go, not if. The journey ahead of you, to find what it is that you seek, is a journey beyond words, beyond concepts, and beyond thinking."

"So Doc, you have taken this journey." Michael said, causing Doc to sigh. Then with some manufactured enthusiasm, Doc said,

"Yes, I have taken this journey. After years of study and exploration of the external world, I ventured inward!" Doc stood to emphasize his story and knocked over his stool. It made a loud noise and Lila stopped sweeping the floor and looked at him. "I journeyed to the abyss, and at the very edge I paused and peered into its infinite depth," Doc paused and picked up his stool. He sat and sipped his martini, took out an olive with a toothpick, popped it into his mouth, and began to chew with a big smile on his face.

"Well, what did you see?" Michael asked, both he and Lila looking at Doc.

And in a whisper he answered, "The abyss was peering back at me," and then he began to laugh and drank down the rest of his martini. Lila dropped the broom and Michael jumped. Doc began to laugh again.

"Michael," Doc's voice turned serious once again, "What is it that you really want? For what are you searching? Has something happened to you? Something that made you feel the need to be searching for something?" Doc finished his questions and looked at Michael, waiting for him to answer. Michael looked back at Doc for a moment then over to where Lila busied herself in the shadows. He took a deep breath and let it out loudly, making a funny sound with his lips.

"Well, Doc, I don't really know, I mean, I think I know. I guess it just dawned upon me one day that I was chasing the wrong things, living my life for the wrong reasons," then Michael stopped talking and took a drink from his beer.

"And what led you to this sudden realization? Was there some sort of trauma in your life?" Doc tipped his head downward and waited for an answer. Michael looked at Doc, perfectly still. He tried to think of something to say but no words came to mind, he simply was not ready to talk about what was in him. The sound of the rain filled the bar and Michael looked towards the door.

"So, you are in some sort of pain, or maybe you have a longing, and you wish it to end," Doc said matter-of-factly. "Michael, all of our pain and suffering stem from one thing and that is the fact that we do not know who or what exactly we are. So many of us are running, either away from something or after something. Perhaps you have done something that you feel is reprehensible, or perhaps someone has done something inexcusable to you, or perhaps, perhaps, perhaps.

It does not really matter, Michael. The search for Truth, for spiritual awakening, is indeed the answer, but it may not be the answer to what you have in mind. And if you take this journey, you have to be willing to take it all the way to its end, or it just becomes another thing. And we all already have too many things. And this thing, this journey, if it is truly what you are searching for is not about escaping anything, it's about just the opposite. It will bring you right into the heart of everything. So, think twice, if there is something you do not want to face, well then, run from this, because everything must be faced, and I mean everything, even some things that you do not even know are in you," then Doc stopped to sip his martini, his face lightening again.

"Doc, you make it sound like a bad thing," Michael said.

"Quite the opposite, my young friend: It's the best thing," Doc smiled. He and Michael sat quietly in the flickering light of the candles. The smell of the rain came across the bar on a light breeze. Doc rose and patted Michael on the back, then stumbled towards the door and into the rain. Then he was gone. Lila came out of the darkness and around the bar and sat on a stool next to Michael.

"Where's he going?" Michael asked.

"To bed," Lila answered and she looked into Michael's eyes.

"I guess you didn't get to talk spiritual smack," he said as he smiled at her.

"I got plenty listening to the two of you," then she laughed, followed by a slight but certain, serious glance.

"What an unusual old man. I am not sure if he is a drunk or some kind of guru or something," Michael drank the rest of his beer.

"Yes, something, but a sweet man. I don't see many real men in here," she said.

"What do you mean, there are always plenty of men in here," Michael said.

"Boys, just boys," she replied, "Where are you staying?"

"Well, I was hoping to get a room here," he answered.

"Sorry, all full at the inn," she said, smiling.

"Do you have a manger?" asked Michael

"No, no manager. So, would you be Jesus or one of the shepherds?"

"Maybe I am one of the kings," said Michael.

"Are you a King?" asked Lila.

"Um, that would be no," he smiled, and she smiled back at him.

"Where do you live?" she asked.

"Charlotte."

"Hmmm, kind of far," she said, dragging out her words. Michael stared at her lips in the dancing light of the candles.

"Especially in the dark and the rain," he said, motioning with his hand. Lila stared at his hand, the movement seeming to mesmerize her.

"Are you a gentleman?" she asked.

"Sometimes," he answered.

"You seem harmless, and the Doc liked you, so you cannot be all bad, and, well, if you are gentleman, I suppose you can crash at my place," she said it quickly, then stood and began putting glasses away on the shelf behind the bar. Michael walked to where Lila was, picked up a couple of glasses, and helped her put them away. The two quietly tidied up the bar, and after some time passed, the rain began to slow and Lila headed out of the door followed by Michael.

Behind Curly's Cafe was a long row of neat, square cabins. All recently built and identical, they were meant for summer rentals, with a few exceptions like Doc. Lila walked down a stone path between two of the cabins. It was dark but she was familiar with the path and had no trouble, Michael however, stumbled a bit on the uneven and barely seen stones at his feet. Her cabin was a bit farther in the woods. The path opened up and Michael could see the cabin and a few lights in the distance; it looked older, much older, and it looked as though it belonged here. It was a small one-story house, a farm house, Michael thought. Then it hit him, the bar was a converted mill. The house and mill were most likely more than one hundred years old. There was a yellow light on the porch with moths flying in circles; others landed and sat perfectly still on the porch rail, the house, and the door. As they stepped up onto the porch, she turned to Michael and said, "You are not expecting sex, right? This is no hook-up, I am just letting you crash for the night because I feel sorry for you, right?" She was emphatic.

"No, of course not, no sex, I appreciate the dry place to sleep," he said and smiled politely. The light on the porch illuminated Michael's face and Lila looked long on him. *He is almost handsome,* she thought to herself. His hair was thick and there was something attractive about him, maybe it was the way he walked, or perhaps the way he carried himself, he seemed to have a self-assurance about him, something that made her feel, she searched for the right word, *secure.* He was different than the other men that attracted her, she looked at him trying to see what it was. But try as she might, she had no idea what it was, but she was drawn to him, she admitted it to herself quietly, but still, she would keep him at arm's length.

Lila unlocked the door and they stepped inside. It was quiet and quaint. The inside did not match the mountain exterior. Inside, Michael thought that he could be in a flat in Paris, pretty and feminine things were all about the room. Against the back wall of the den there was a large mirror, taller than Michael and three or four feet wide. And pushed up against the near wall was an upright piano. It looked old, an antique maybe. Scattered about the square room between white, modern chairs and an armoire were more antique furniture and old tables, all dark wood with intricate detail. The contrast was stark but the mixture of old and new worked well and reminded Michael of Lila's personality, so modern in her thoughts but ancient in her presence.

There were shelves and shelves of books and small words such as Love and Faith made of silver and hanging on the walls, and many other small treasures, a small pig with wings and various things that Michael was sure whose value was known only to Lila. As Michael looked about, he could see that there was a depth to Lila, he could see her all about the room. He wondered where she grew up; there was one thing he was sure of, she was not from these mountains. He imagined that she was running from something, or perhaps, she was searching for something. *I guess that gives us something in common*, he thought to himself. He would soon find that they had far more in common.

"Excuse me a minute, why don't you make yourself comfortable, I want to get out of these 'bar clothes'," Lila said as she made her way across the small den, turning on lamps, then disappeared down a short hall to her bedroom. Michael walked to the mirror and stood in front of it. It was taller than his six feet and was maybe four feet wide, it had a heavy wooden frame and leaned slightly against the wall. It made the room look bigger, *Most likely its purpose*, Michael thought, but because of its lean, the reflection made the image of the room look slightly askew.

He stood in front of the mirror for several minutes before he noticed his own reflection. He was a little surprised to see what a mess he was. He was wet from walking under the dripping trees and his hair was matted down from having been in his helmet. His shirt tail on one side was hanging out and his jeans were too big, too baggy, and over-faded with holes, some with strings hanging down. Nothing seemed to fit him. *But the clothes were comfortable*, he told himself, *no suffering for fashion here*. It was little consolation. It was late and his whiskers made him look a little old and a little dirty. *Not much to look at*, he thought. He had not cared for his appearance for more than a few years and it showed.

He pictured Lila standing in the very place where he was. She was pretty so he knew that she had stood here looking at herself. He wondered what she said to herself when beholding her own image. Was she pleased or did she judge herself. Michael was betting on the latter.

"What do you do?" Lila's voice echoed from down the wood floor hall. It seemed to amplify the sounds she was making, and he could almost tell what she was doing even though he could not see her. "For a living?" she added.

"I'm a banker," he yelled it a little, as if she were far away.

"Ha ha, very funny," she quipped, "No, really, what do you do?"

"Really, I'm a banker," he was still talking loud and standing in front of the mirror as she entered the room. She stood quietly for a moment.

"Oh," she said, then straightened her shirt and stared at Michael. "Sorry, I didn't mean anything by…"

"No worries," he stopped her, "I feel the same way," not bothering to explain what the "same way" meant. He did feel the same way but for different reasons. He looked at her and smiled. She had dressed for bed, wearing an oversized tee shirt and a pair of tight gym shorts. She was wearing no makeup and had her hair pulled back into a ponytail. *She's naturally beautiful,* he thought. Michael turned and walked toward the piano, sat on the bench, and tapped a few keys to hear its sound.

"Do you play the piano?" Lila asked him.

"No, but I always wanted to learn to play just one song."

"Really, what one song did you want to learn to play?" she asked with some amount of attentiveness.

"Moonlight Sonata," he said. She did not reply, silent long enough to make him turn and look up at her; she just stood, expressionless, looking at him. They were melting together and both knew it, both felt it, but neither would say a word about it. She sat down on the bench next to him. "It's by Beethoven, I love it, but something about it haunts me," he said to her.

Lila put her hands on the keys and slowly began to play the sonata, her left hand and her right hand moving in different directions but together in C-sharp minor. With captivating emotion, her entire body was in slow but constant motion. She played the simple melancholic tune and moved her head in soft movements that were mournful and profound; it was dark, powerful music and it set the course for Lila and Michael. She slowed and bowed her head as the sad music played out in the sound of a certain hopelessness.

And when she finished, Michael and Lila sat looking at each other.

"Wow," Michael broke the silence, then whispered, "That was beautiful and moving. So, you play the piano, play something else," he said.

She looked at him for a long moment, not saying anything, then she said, "That's the only song I ever learned to play," and her eyes glowed. Michael stared at her. There was a feeling that they were very close, like they had been close for a very long time, and it was disconcerting to both of them.

"That's astonishing and unbelievable; it must mean something right? Don't you think it's crazy that you and I have always wanted to learn to play one song and that it's the same song?" Michael said breathlessly.

Lila looked at Michael, then said with a forced casualness, "No, I don't think so, I am sure it happens all the time. Are you hungry?" then she smiled and walked to the kitchen.

"Yes, I think I am," Michael answered while nodding his head, "Yes, I am definitely hungry." He could hear her getting out a pan, then the opening of a drawer and the shuffling of utensils. He could hear the sound the pan made as it was put on the stove, the sound of the gas stove lighting with a poof, then the smell of the burning gas. And then he could hear the opening of the refrigerator. He walked into the kitchen. It was small but had been renovated; the sink was new and the appliances were stainless steel. The counter hugged two walls around the square room, then jutted out with a raised area to form a bar with two stools. He sat down and watched her moving from one place to the next, like a choreographed dance, her hands reaching for things, not needing her eyes to tell her where the things were.

"Do you like grilled cheese?" she asked.

"Yes," he answered enthusiastically. "Could I have two?" Lila's dance seem to sharpen and quicken, she scooped a slab of butter and threw it into the pan, picked up the pan, and slammed it loudly onto a lit burner.

"I am so sick and tired of raising boys! You are all the same, you are looking for mothers. Well I am NOT your mother!" She continued to grumble and move in jerky motions, slamming the refrigerator door and the drawers shut.

"One is fine," Michael said to her quietly while her back was still turned. He did not know what had caused her sudden outburst but he was certain that it had nothing to do with him, he had obviously activated an older scene. He pulled out his cell phone to see if anyone had called, no one had. Lila turned and watched him looking down, his fingers flittering with his phone. Her shoulders dropped a bit and a smile returned to her face. She took out two more slices of bread and began to butter them slowly.

"Hey I'm really sorry that..." she began but Michael looked up and smiled at her. She smiled back, then moved a strand of hair that had fallen from her ponytail behind her ear and continued cooking. Michael stood and began to open cabinets one after another, searching.

"The cabinet next to the sink," Lila said, knowing what he was looking for. Michael opened it, pulled out a couple of plates and napkins, and set them on the tiled bar. Lila flipped the grilled sandwiches onto the plates and pulled out a jar of pickles from the refrigerator. She sat next to Michael and they ate quietly together in the kitchen. When they finished, they put their plates in the sink and moved into the den.

"I'm tired," she said as she opened a closet, pulling out a couple blankets and tossing them onto the small couch, "I am not getting up early, so if you do, do not wake me up," she said as she walked to the back bedroom to retrieve a pillow. When she returned, Michael had already kicked off his shoes and taken off his pants. He was standing in boxer shorts; it should have been awkward but was not. He spread one of the blankets on the couch while she stood hugging the pillow, watching him. He lay on the couch and it was too short. He folded his legs in but he was too cramped. He then extended his legs over the arm of the couch but this too was uncomfortable. He tried putting one foot on the floor and pulled the second blanket over him, then he began to slide off the couch. He rolled over and pulled himself into the fetal position and began to fidget. Lila laughed.

"Okay, a tall man and a short couch, not a good match. You can sleep on the bed with me, but I am warning you, you had better behave yourself," she was pointing her finger at him and he nodded. He picked up the blankets and followed her. She tossed the pillow onto one side of the bed.

"That's your side," she said, and he nodded again. He slid underneath the large heavy comforter. It was white with long pale stripes. He pulled off his shirt then punched the pillow a few times until he was settled. It all felt very natural to Lila, she knew she should feel awkward but she did not. Once Michael was still, Lila turned out the light. At first it was completely dark but Michael's eyes quickly adjusted and he could see the outline of Lila, first taking off her shirt, pulling it over her head, then pulling down and stepping out of her shorts. Then she pulled a pin from her hair and shook it loose. Michael watched as she walked nude across the room. He could barely see her but he could make out her hair, her breasts, and her long legs, all silhouettes against the dim light coming in through the window. He felt his heartbeat. She turned on a fan and its soft drone instantly made Michael sleepy. Lila walked back to the bed and slid under the covers. Michael lay on his back being as still as he could. He looked into the darkness above him and he could feel the soft moving air of the fan.

"Damn," Lila said.

"What?" Michael asked.

"Nothing," she said as she fidgeted, "I've got something in my eye, I think it's an eyelash and it's driving me crazy. I'm going to turn on a light, watch your eyes." Lila turned on a lamp beside the bed, then sat up holding the blanket over her chest with one hand and pulling on her eyelid with the other.

"Let me take a look," he said. With a finger still on her eyelid, she turned towards Michael. He looked for a moment but could not see anything. He climbed out of the bed and walked to the other side and sat down on the bed next to Lila. "Turn towards the light," he said to her. She turned and he gently held her head, moving it so the light would shine into her eye. But then he was caught in her gaze. They both remained completely still, looking into each other's eyes. Michael had the feeling that something inside him fell, it was a subtle sensation but significant and it startled him a bit.

"Well?" Lila asked.

"Be still." It was a quiet command but Lila completely complied. His voice was like a command that she wanted to obey.

"Ah ha," he said quietly.

"What?"

"Hold very still, I see an eyelash," he touched his middle finger to his tongue wetting it just a little. Then he touched the eyelash and it clung to his finger. He smiled triumphantly and showed to her.

"Thanks," she said as nonchalantly as she could, then they looked at each other for a moment longer. She was prepared for him to try something, and she prepared herself to say no. But instead, keeping his eyes on her the whole time, he slid off the bed, moved back to his side, and climbed back into the bed. As he lifted the covers, he glanced at her long legs but he did not linger: He rolled to his back and looked at the ceiling. She was not sure what to think. She turned out the light.

"You're married," it was not a question.

"Separated," he said.

"That's what men always say."

"Well, for me, it's true," his answer was convincing.

"Then why do you still wear your wedding ring?" she asked him. Michael tried to think of an answer but he could not think of one. He let out a sigh.

"I'm not sure," he turned towards her in the darkness.

"I never want to be a mistress, it never works out well for the woman," she was quiet for a moment, then she continued, "Though mistresses do tend to get lots of gifts, especially if the man is wealthy. Are you wealthy?'

"Terribly," he answered. She turned onto her side and looked out the window; it was raining again. He turned to match her; it was an instinctive move. She scooted backwards until her body was against his. He put his hand on her bare hip.

"Goodnight," he said quietly.

"Goodnight," she answered. The sounds of the rain and the fan were like a soothing lullaby and they both drifted peacefully off to sleep.

Finding Doc

Curly's Place, Spring 2008

The bright yellow bike buzzed into Michael's consciousness like a cold, aerodynamic hornet. The machine, built for handling and speed, had a high, menacing tail that tapered to nothing at the end. The rider was dressed all in black; something about him made Michael think of a "fire and brimstone" preacher. His helmet was full-faced and black, with a silver reflective visor that obscured his face. As the two men entered the tight turn, they leaned deep into the road, and for an instant when they were side by side, time seemed to stop. Then, the rider extended his middle finger towards Michael and exploded away, leaving Michael completely alone.

Michael was startled even in his already adrenaline-enhanced state. But instead of ramping up, he inexplicably relaxed. He slowed and eased off of his aggressive lean, coming out of the turn almost upright. Illusions began to fade. Like waking from an early morning dream into a cold room, a realization crept into the room of his mind through the windows of his soul: Suddenly, he could see that through all of his riding and pushing limits he was and had been chasing adrenaline, nothing more. Another veil fell away, and he could see deeper into himself.

Then anger replaced everything else. "Damn it!" Michael cursed as he took in a quick blast of air and then let it out as a long sigh. ""All that meditation, reading, sitting, disconnecting, connecting, riding, faster, FASTER, more sitting, more breathing, eating this, not eating that, riding, chasing, loving, passion, damn, damn, damn." He thought back to New York, everything he was doing and the way he was living his life kept leading him back to that day when death looked at him, squarely in the eyes. He thought aloud: "I panicked, that's all it is." Michael slowed the bike down even more, and as his mind churned, he lost connection with the bike, with the trees, with the road.

"I let go and let go, detached from everything, and there was no suffering, but what of passion, of living?" The falls kept coming as Michael came out of his dream-like state and thought his way into another, barely breathing in the cool morning air that greets those just awakening. Another veil would fall, another door would open, and once again, he was back to square one, ground zero. He was at nothing, nowhere, nada. The words of Hemingway played in his mind, mocking him, "Our nada who art in nada, hallowed be thy nada."

Michael grew aware of a ringing that was like the ocean sounding in his ears, and he began to laugh lightly. He needed to think, and he wanted a drink and someone for good, deep conversation. Realizing that Curly's was nearby, he slowed the bike and looked ahead to where the straightening asphalt main road joined a wide, gravel road which forked up into the wooded hillside. In just a mile or so, he could get a beer and likely find Peter Stanhope, "Doc," for some interesting conversation and possibly some reflective discourse on Michael's latest ride and realization.

Arriving at his destination, Michael coasted on his machine across the loose gravel and into a parking space at Curly's Café. He passed right by the bright yellow bike, silver-tinted visor on the black helmet sitting on top, seemingly laughing at him as he came to a rest. His skin heated up as he tried to suppress the feeling welling in him. *What made me angry,* he told himself, *was that I was fooling myself and not the man who sped by, not the man who made my mad rushing seem like child's play.* He kept trying to soothe himself. *Ah, hell, I hate the bastard who rides that bike!* he admitted to himself, *and I am going to tell the bastard if I see him!* He made himself relax a bit. It had been years since New York, but Michael was still a little afraid to let out anger.

He looked at his hands. *I definitely don't need to crack another knuckle on someone's head.* Then he reassured himself that he was completely in control of himself.

He walked calmly to the entrance of Curly's Place, a converted old mill that had most likely served several different purposes before its current one as a shot, beer, and biker hangout. Michael was still vibrating from the long ride as he climbed the wooden steps, holding firmly to the rails made of tree limbs still sporting bark. Above the entrance, carved into a wooden plaque, were the words, Hoka Hey! Michael paused at the words for a moment and mumbled to himself, *"Someday, I should probably find out what that means."*

Then, he stepped into the hazy bar. Michael methodically scanned it and was a bit startled to catch Doc's eyes. Dr. Stanhope was sitting in a tall chair at the end of a long row of mismatched stools, staring straight at Michael.

Doc's unwavering stare spoke volumes of questions. Michael straightened slightly as he spotted Lila, and he waved, a shy motion that Lila did not respond to. Her hair was long with natural waves and her eyes were dark; she was a stunning beauty unaccustomed to not being noticed and Michael had unknowingly walked directly past her without saying anything.

"Could I have a beer?" Michael asked meekly, "and whatever Doc's drinking?" Lila never acknowledged him, acting as if she was too busy to listen. "Hey there, Doc," Michael said as he nervously scooted his stool closer to the bar little by little. Once landed, Michael turned towards Lila, briefly catching her looking at him, but she quickly turned away and began talking to the man seated directly in front of her. Nonetheless, she slid a beer nonchalantly down the bar without looking, and it stopped directly in front of Michael. It was the first, but would not be the last, time that she would amaze Michael.

Doc watched the entire scene from over the top of his glasses. As soon as the beer came to a stop, Doc rolled his eyes and wrinkled his forehead, then turned slowly back to his martini.

"Doc, I have been thinking a little about our last conversation. Was it truth? No, it was freedom, right? I think I am ready to hear a little bit more about that." Doc turned back to Michael, looked over the top of his spectacles once more, then began to stroke his long white beard. Finally, Doc let out a deep, raspy laugh as he ground his cigarette into the overflowing ashtray.

"Well," Doc began, his broad smile preceding another chuckle. "In reality," Doc began again as Michael moved his eyes to the now-nearby Lila. "We are free only to the degree that we are enlightened." Michael instantly felt like he was back in college at a fairly interesting lecture, subdued by alcohol and frequent feminine distractions. Doc took a deep breath and lifted his martini, looking deeply into the glass as if the prisms of bar light and olives inside it held some long lost secrets of the universe. "Both as individuals and as a society…" Doc paused for air and another sip of his gin.

"Okay, Doc, free? What are you talking about? What do you mean? Aren't we all free in this country?" Michael was purposely provoking the old man; he was in the mood to listen to Dr. Stanhope pontificate. The disapproving look on Doc's face immediately brought Michael back to more serious conversation.

Michael sighed, then asked more genuine questions, "Okay, Doc, freedom: what are we talking about here? A way of experiencing life? Idealism? Because what I think you are talking about is marketing. The idea of freedom is what sells motorcycles. Some idea or concept that we think we need, just another way to get poor suckers like me to buy something. So, tell me what you mean, Doc. I have even looked it up in the dictionary. Freedom is in there but I still don't know what it means." Michael was now listening to himself ramble, wondering when he would stop.

"Well, to define the term, just like trying to define Truth, you have to clarify for whom and under what conditions. If you want to understand what freedom is, Michael, you have to experience it, not just think about it, or worse, read about it. It could be said that everyone is free to the degree that they believe they are and are able to accept."

"Tequila, please," Michael was able to get out to the quickly passing Lila. She wanted to ignore Michael but she was drawn to him. There had been no sex while they were together but she felt like the night Michael had stayed was intimate. It was comfortable having him there but she knew she did not know him very well. She wanted to ask him questions, but she wanted him to come to her and not vice-versa.

Michael sensed he was deep into it now with Doc, and as he turned to face the old man, a full shot of tequila slid to just in front of him. His left hand reached immediately for the glass, and he quickly downed its entire contents. "Ahhhh," Michael let out the toxic sound with some enthusiasm, beginning to feel comfortably warm. He liked these type of talks and he knew that Doc liked them, as well. He remembered Lila saying she wanted to talk "Spiritual Smack" with Doc; he wondered if she liked these kind of talks as well. Then Michael realized that he was thinking about Lila and not paying attention to Doc, so he refocused on the old man.

"Doc, are we talking imagination, a person's perspective, or something real?" At just that moment, a dictionary slid down the bar, finding its resting place in front of Michael, again. Michael turned, looked up the bar, and meeting eyes with Lila, said, "So you do read," as he tipped an invisible hat, gave a slight bow, and smiled at her.

"I think you are outmatched in your little conversation with Doc...thought you might need a little help," she said, smiling.

"Thank you for the help and I am more than sure that I am outmatched, but I'm up for the challenge nonetheless," Michael turned his attention to the large, dusty Webster's and began flipping the pages until he reached the "F's." Michael began reading from the book. "Let's see what ole man Webster has to say about the subject... Freedom: the state or quality of being free." Michael looked around to see who was paying attention. It did not appear that anyone was listening. "Well, I guess I better look up 'free.'" He thumbed back one page. "Free," he said the word with some emphasis. "Not in bondage, not under the control of some other person, or some arbitrary power; able to act or think without compulsion or arbitrary restriction; having liberty," Michael smiled as he read through the definition. Doc was trying to ignore Michael, but he began to laugh, making a wheezing noise.

"Do not look in the dictionary, Michael. We can see that freedom is defined in terms like you're reading, as desirable in terms of representing things of value or meaning, *or in terms of not having undesirable things of little value or meaning.* You see, freedom is defined in terms of human wants and needs, versus things we don't want and deprivations. It is obvious, Michael, that freedom, as defined, is subjective, reflecting the interface between desires and degrees of fulfillment. It is, therefore, a relative state of how people are. And so you can see that a person with few wants and/or aversions would feel more free. I mean freer," he corrected himself, "That person would feel inner freedom a majority of the time. And on the other hand, a person with many wants and/or many aversions would never feel free."

"Freedom is subjective. This is the state of Americans, in particular. Look at commercials, movies, marketing, the concept of keeping up with the Joneses...It bombards them every day via TV, radio, magazines, computers, the web, and billboards, all constantly reminding them of what they don't have or showing them something they should want. So, surrounded by everything, the poor American can never feel freedom, even though it is the one word that is promised to anyone that comes to this country," Doc cleared his throat took a deep breath and another sip of his gin. Raising his finger into the air, he continued, "Maturity. Michael, maturity is the word here. The level of a person's consciousness will determine the quality of his or her experience, which is personal."

"And then you have a government or society that feels obligated to fulfill everyone's expectations—expectations that are continually flamed and expanded by any kind of music or flashing lights of constant and ever-present media of all sorts. So, we now define social freedom in terms of accomplishments, but it's just not practical. Can a society expand its parameters so that no one feels uncomfortable in relation to their internal condition? Should the laws of the land be modeled after pathology? Or neuroticism and personality disorders?" Doc was now at a full smoky laugh, and he turned his attention to his martini. It seemed to Michael that somewhere along the discussion, Doc changed the subject, only slightly, but Michael was not sure he was following what the Doc was saying.

Michael looked at Lila, and she shrugged her shoulders. But then she smiled at him, and it was a smile like no other. It cracked within him in some way, so he considered her for a minute, then smiled back. Doc noticed Michael's attention to Lila. "Try to stay on subject," Doc's comment made Michael look away from her, but he could not stop smiling.

"I think I know what you mean, Doc."

"You do?" the reply was filled with an incredulous tone.

"Yeah, my great-grandfather, Papa Johan, used to say that to control a big bull, you had to put him in a bigger pasture," Michael smiled broadly at an expressionless Doc, who looked upward over the rim of his spectacles, thinking.

"In a strange sort of way, that does make a little sense." Doc assessed, talking now with an olive in his mouth. "Michael, to understand the relationship between the individual and society requires one to look at the mind, out of which dreams, desires, and aversions all come. Some people are uncomfortable all the time just because of who they are, and they have infantile expectations of being catered to. The higher a person's evolutionary development, the greater the chance that person has of experiencing freedom. So you see, Michael, freedom is real. In fact, for some people, it is a constant experience; for them, an inner experiential reality is independent of the world altogether. So this evolution, success, happiness, and freedom are all the gifts of realization, of Truth realization... of what some call enlightenment. That realization is the source of your own experience." "So, what is the source of your experience, Michael? That is the question you should be asking, that is what you are looking for. Your quest, Mr. Odysseus, is for this truth," and with that, Doc returned to silent appreciation of his martini once again.

Michael began to pick at the corner of the label on his beer. He watched Lila wiping the bar, then stacking glasses, hurrying occasionally to get someone a beer or a shot. He looked back at Doc and watched him fidget a cigarette out of its box and light it with two shaky hands, then stare off into the darkness, with his head tilted slightly backward.

Words, Michael thought to himself, *more words*. The veil of speed and adrenaline had fallen away in one hairpin turn in the road, and everything that it had given Michael was gone. He wondered what veil would fall away next. He loved talking to Doc, but he just wasn't sure if he was brilliant or another load of hot air. *The word source resonated, though. You could practically substitute it for the word God*, Michael thought to himself. So now he had two words: truth and source. Michael began to think of something to say to Doc, but then Lila walked quickly by, he could smell her scent and he smiled.

Confrontation

Spring 2008

A beast of a man arose from a chair in the back shadows, where men sat laughing drunkenly. He walked heavily, large boots echoing across the wooden floor as he approached Lila, who stood unafraid in his path. He reached the lacquered, liquor-coated wood bar and boomed his demand: "Bar wench, get me a drink!" The deep voice emerged from the cavern of his mouth, buried in a dark, hemp beard. His towering form seemed to block the few remaining streams of daylight that desperately penetrated the smoky shadows, and his brows overshadowed a weathered face. With breath reeking of sulfur and Jack Daniel's, he leaned across the bar to growl menacingly.

"Now!" he shouted as he slammed his fist on the bar, then he began to laugh. Michael drew in a breath; it was *him*, the man who had mocked him as he rode the mountain turn! His skin reddened, and his pulse quickened.

"That is no way to speak to lady." Dr. Peter Stanhope spoke with authority as he rose, clearing his throat and moving toward the foul man. The large man looked at Doc, and a smile slowly appeared on his face. Then, as suddenly as a clap of thunder, his face turned taut and he stared red-eyed, lowering his head like a wolf about to pounce on helpless prey. With the butt of his open palm, he struck the old man in the solar plexus, sending him over his high bar chair and into a line of stools against the back wall.

"Hey!" was all Michael could manage to say as he leapt between the reeling Doctor Stanhope and his aggressor. The beast began to laugh. Lila moved quickly from behind the bar, spewing curses directly in the large man's face. He put one hand on Lila's face and pushed her backwards so she landed hard on her backside. The man turned back to Doc, who was now on all fours, scanning the floor for his glasses. Just in time, he noticed Michael 's fist swinging towards his chin and managed to duck enough to turn the full-force punch to a glancing blow. Letting out a roar, the man charged, swinging both fists.

Michael ducked the first punch, but the second struck his left temple in an explosion that felt like a camera flash going off in a dark room. Michael was still standing but temporarily blind, so when he grabbed at the massive force that was aggressively pursuing him, he never saw the next punch. After he landed on the stale beer-sticky, swollen wooden floor, Michael found himself half picked up, and dragged out the back door and into the alley behind Curly's. The whole time, the beast had one arm locked around Michael's neck while he punched at him with his free fist.

Michael had only enough consciousness left to tuck his head, taking punch after punch on his forehead. All he could sense was darkness as he lost consciousness, barely sensing that he was in real trouble.

Deeper, there was a broader awareness in Michael, and it took him to what he thought was a memory but perceived as the present. He was sitting on a cushion in a bedroom of a long-ago-vacated home, where he had been in the silent dark for hours, his back aching with fatigue, but he stayed vigilant and focused on his breath, the feel of air coming in and leaving his nose, the soft rise and fall of his stomach. Then there was a moment—an ordinary moment—when time stood still, and that moment and this moment were the same. So, while receiving blow after blow of a massive fist, Michael was having the experience of being everywhere, with no substance to identify as himself, as a center. And he heard a question within himself, "What was there in the quiet solitude that also is here now in violent chaos?"

"STOP NOW, you motherfucker! You have two barrels about to end your pathetic life!" Lila was loud and demanding as she pointed a shotgun with two barely steady hands. The man stopped mid-punch, turning to Lila and smiling. "The State Patrol is on the way," she added. The man easily tossed Michael, limp, against the outside wall with the garbage.

"You didn't call nobody," the man replied. Then he turned towards the barely conscious Michael, "Lucky for you, I like you, and Angel here wants to see you spared." Then he began to laugh. Shaking off the pain in his punching hand, he stood, pushed out his chest fully, and walked proudly back into the bar.

Lila and Doc moved swiftly to Michael, helping him to a sitting position as he slowly returned to a waking state of consciousness. Michael could hear Lila mumbling at him, but he was still a bit hazy and could not make any sense of what she was saying. The two helped Michael to his feet while he began to take inventory of various wounds and the condition of his body. His head ached and his nose was numb and trickling blood to his lower lip. He felt the side of his head: There was a small gash across the center of a swelling lump, and the tenderness of the wound caused Michael to remove his hand quickly. The fog in his thinking was beginning to lift, and he became aware that both Doc and Lila were talking to him, but it still registered only as noise.

"You idiot," was the first thing he understood Lila to say. "I can handle that monster! I don't need anyone getting themselves killed in my bar!" Lila was now shaking slightly, but she continued to chastise Michael in a stream-of-consciousness tirade. Michael had the odd sensation that some if not most of what she was saying to him in this moment was something that she meant to say to someone else from her past.

Michael wobbled and staggered from the pain in his head as Lila and Doc walked him back into the bar and onto a stool. Lila wrapped ice in a towel and placed it on the side of his head. His eyes widened and he winced as the towel made contact with his still-growing wound. The beast had returned to his seat, glowing in the flashing red of a nearby bar light endorsing drinking and "being manly." He was sitting among the other Visigoths who acted as his friends because they feared him; they were all drinking, smoking, and laughing, living as though they were not scared. One was looking at Michael, causing the beast to notice that Michael was back in the barroom.

"Hey, pretty boy, you best leave before I decide to kick your ass," he jeered, pausing for a moment before saying, "again!" Then, he laughed and turned his attention back to the other men, who all joined in the laughter. Michael turned to face the laughter in what seemed like slow motion, then he turned back to Lila. She wore an empty expression, but something deep in her brown eyes was staring into Michael's heart. He paused to feel her gaze, and then he rose and moved toward the door while some of the men continued taunting him, feeling brave in the path of what they thought was a retreating man. But he was not leaving. Michael walked methodically to the jukebox, which was just inside the front door.

He pulled a dollar from his pocket, unfolded and flattened the bill, then fed it into the slot on the machine. He leaned two hands onto the glass, scanned the titles, and pushed a button. Drums began to beat like those of a primitive tribe summoning the battle gods. Michael slowly backed away from the music machine and stretched his arms out and back like the unfolding of large wings as he let his head fall backwards and thrust his chest upwards deeply, filling his lungs with something more than the stale smoky air of the bar. He turned, and as Curly's began to echo with pounding music, something also turned inside Michael. The violence of moments earlier summoned demonic and angelic powers within Michael, and whether it was genetic memory or absorption of hatred from the terrorists during the attacks, an energy returned and built within him.

Michael bore no emotion, no anger nor fear, and the energy that was building subsumed his identification as an individual body. He filled with an unseen strength, walking steadfast but with no vengeance in his heart. He stood in this bar, in this realm, but he walked almost in a dance of remembrance of ancient powers from another realm. He was, without knowing it, in abidance and alignment with divine will, and he moved only to subdue a darker presence, a shadowy soul. So he was unencumbered by the weakening forces of thought of free will or of consequence. Michael felt clean; there was no pain in his head or in his heart as he stepped to the bar.

Lila watched Michael carefully. He was walking differently: His step was slower, steadier. Her heart began to pound as fear and lust entered her body simultaneously. Her mind was still trying to assess the moment while passion welled in her, goose bumps running across her arms and a tingling sensation moving up the back of her neck into her hair. Michael walked toward her, but he was not looking at her. He stepped behind the bar and began to lift bottles of liquor one by one until one seemed exact; he grasped it firmly, then moved out from behind the bar.

"No, Michael, no," she was whispering over and over, "No, Michael." She reached out her hand, then withdrew it and covered her mouth as Michael moved towards the mountainous, foul man. Michael brandished the bottle like a heavy sword and then thrust it into the air behind the beast. The men across from the large man were looking up, signaling him to turn, and although he did, he had no time to react to the blur of brown glass and liquor as it exploded on the side of his face, opening a large gash on his head and driving him immediately to the hard wooden floor.

The other men leapt to their feet, knocking over their chairs. The beast began to scramble to his feet, but Michael kicked hard, slamming the left heel of his boot into the man's ribs. The force of the impact drove all air out of his lungs, and he sucked unsuccessfully for air while reaching for his revolver. But Michael was still in motion— now his rounding right boot swung into the man's forehead, causing him to pull the gun free but sending it spinning across the wooden planks of the floor. Michael walked slowly to the revolver and picked it up, first pointing it at the scattering, stunned men, making them all stop abruptly in their tracks.

None of them moved nor uttered a sound. They liked the predictability of bully rules, where brutality and force were king, but here now was unpredictability. Though not a one of them could put a word to what left them frozen and motionless, they were experiencing true power.

Michael squatted next to the beast, who was rolling over onto his back, sweating, as air slowly began to ease back into his lungs. Michael pushed the cold hard steel of the barrel into the cleft on the man's chin.

"Who the fuck are you?" the deep, hoarse voice asked between heavy labored breaths.

"The hand of God, you foul beast," Michael answered, "A fucking Archangel, you dumbass or should I say dumb ox? …I am not sure," Michael turned his head, giving the man a sideways glance as if peripheral vision would reveal what or who the man truly was. Michael turned back to the man and looked into his dark eyes, "You spent millennia climbing out of the slimy pits of hell, and this is how you want to live, you poor pathetic beast. Do you want to die here like this and return to the fiery pits? Is that what you want? You are blowing it; you are a slight pull of a trigger from returning to that dark oblivion that I am bound by the heavens to return you to…"

"No, Michael."

Lila's quiet, sure voice brought Michael back to himself, back to the smoky bar, back to where there was thought of right and wrong, back to the knowledge born of a single apple, back to the world of judgment. Michael stood, then looked at the gun and the man lying on the floor.

"A 38 revolver—very dependable," Michael began talking in a calm, easygoing voice. "I am going to keep this. This is my gun now. Are you okay with that?" Michael asked the man, who didn't move. "Thank you," Michael said as he turned back toward the bar. In the next few short steps, feelings of shame, fear, and depression almost took over Michael. His mind began to run the programs—the false, limiting internal beliefs—the controlling voices that said the things he believed, the things that kept him where he was, how he was, who he was.

An incident of violence and acting as a warrior threatened all that, so the voices began chanting, trying to regain control just below the surface, repeating, "You are scared! They will find out you are not the man they think you are. You are inadequate," and then the big one, "You are not worthy of love." He was returning quickly to who he thought he was: that limited, failure of a middle-aged man headed quickly to the grave without love, with a closet full of shameful skeletons that he kept in a small place deep in his psyche to fuel the fire of the judging voices.

Michael approached the bar. Lila's eyes were unblinking, burning into Michael, her lips pursed like those of a disapproving mother. She extended an open hand and he gently handed her the gun.

"How many crimes do you think were committed here tonight?" Michael asked, trying to ease the tension.

"Nine crimes, at least," Lila answered as she held the gun firmly, opened the revolver, and spun the chamber, seeing each with a bullet. "You give your gun away when it's loaded?" Lila asked Michael.

"Archangel of death?" Doc asked mockingly. Michael shrugged his shoulders sheepishly, and both men began to laugh uncontrollably, releasing their tightened nerves.

"I should throw you both out," Lila told them as she locked the gun in a drawer in the bar. Michael picked up the ice-filled towel and walked it over to the man who was now sitting in a chair. He flinched as Michael handed him the towel.

"Light pressure," Michael told him. Michael was now fully back to himself, and his mind began to race as he stepped over beer and blood, some of it his own. As he sat, a bottle of beer magically appeared in front of him and a crisp martini appeared in front of Doc. Michael looked straight ahead into the darkness and began his confession to Doc, but he knew he also was within earshot of Lila.

"Doc, this day broke gloriously as I pushed my machine to the edge, the edge of something undefined," Michael looked to make sure Doc was listening. He was, but he turned to sip from his martini, then refocused on Michael. Michael took another drink as well, cleared his throat, then turned back to the darkness of the bar and continued, "I was chasing the wind, and something, something unseen— I could feel it, sense it—was within my grasp, close to my soul. I just knew, Doc, I was living life fully, truthfully, honestly. I pushed my bike and myself hard, pausing only at the Continental Divide. I got off my bike and looked west into the distance where I was headed, where all the answers lay, then I looked back east at the gold and red rising sun, from where I had come. My body was pulsing, and the silence was broken gently by the sound of a sudden gust of wind bending the soft, tall green grass in broad serpentine arcs in my direction. Then the breeze danced with me for a moment, fleeing across the road and into the trees, having tasted all that I had attained," Michael paused to see if Doc was still listening.

Michael turned to Lila, who quickly began drying glasses with a towel, pretending she wasn't listening. "I had started back down to the flat plains, back to the city, when it happened. A devil of a man dressed all in black passed me on the inside of a tight turn. And as the evil spirit passed me, he calmly looked at me and gave me the finger, then accelerated out of my view into the next switchback and he was gone.

"And Doc, here is the deal: something, *something* inside of me happened, I don't know what it was exactly, but it was familiar, it has happened before." Michael paused a moment, stopping himself from going down the path of a different story. He took another drink then continued once again. "It was like a veil of something unreal, something that covers deeper truths, was pulled aside, revealing something deeper. And that deeper something rendered that former outer veil—the outer realm, the outer truth that I was living— rendered all that I was living to be but a shallow dream… nothing more than a deception, an opiate. This veil, Doc, was the something I had attained, it was the sweet air. That damned bright fire of life that I have been chasing was nothing more than adrenaline."

This time, Michael tipped the bottle up and let the rest of the beer pour down his throat. Lila was already bringing him another before he put the empty on the bar. He looked at her from his vulnerability, something that he had always believed made women scramble away like bugs on the kitchen floor when the light comes on. But Lila seemed to be looking into him, and encouraged him, "Go on."

"Well, I realized I have been chasing an experience, a heightened state, nothing more." Michael held up the empty beer bottle and looked through it at the colored neon of the bar lights, distracting himself from what he was feeling, trying to minimize the revelation even now as he retold the experience. He felt once again all-too-mortal, dying, a powerless man lying in the cold bed of an absent lover. And recognizing the feeling, he held his mind from returning to memories of feelings of inadequacy and of failure.

Doc took a deep drink of the gin and began to stroke his beard, clearing his throat several times. "Michael," Doc began as if he was going to tell a long story, "I was taught at the university that using Greek words in our teaching and in our lectures would make us, as professors, appear over-intellectual and pretentious. That said, I would like to tell you the Greek word for removing of a veil. It is the word, apocalypse. Interesting, is it not?" Michael turned to Doc and then stared ahead. Both men sat in silence for a brief time and then they burst into laughter.

"Apocalypse," Michael said aloud, "Yes, Doc, that is very interesting. Apocalypse," Michael whispered the word one more time.

The chuckle was just subsiding for Doc but his broad smile turned expressionless as his next words came from a place like a still ocean, reflecting the blue glow of a sacred moon, whispering the secrets of the cosmos. "My friend, I think you are ready."

"Ready for what, Doc?" asked Michael.

"Ready to listen, to listen to a little story, and I want to offer an observation."

"Sounds serious, Doc—I'd better have another beer."

"When I was in India pursuing some research on the early Christian church, I met a man there with an interesting story. He told of a secret order of monks, which was founded by the Apostle John after writing his 'Apocalypse.' The secret order was hidden in the Himalayas, where the monks were preserving the true teachings of Christ. And hidden until now, this teaching contained seven crucial understandings. The man told me that the monks maintained that St. John had predicted that all of humanity would learn these seven, and that it would give birth to and nourish the prophesied new millennium, creating for our world the first true civilization."

"That's a nice story, Doc," Michael said with a patronizing tone.

Doc took another sip, never smiling. He simply looked up, stroked his beard, and began again. "Right, to the point, yes, yes. Right, you are my warrior-turning-into-shaman friend. Let us draw our bow and take aim: here it is plain and simple, so listen and see if this strikes at the center of your being. You *can* transform your human life into a constant perception and knowing of *divinity* within your heart." Doc was no longer looking at Michael. Michael turned to look at Doc, then reached once more for his beer, putting the firm cold glass to his lips but not drinking. He looked across the bar through blue bands of neon light to find Lila. The blue shone brilliant on her long, shiny hair; she gave him a brief smile and continued with her work. Doc continued, "Yes, truth. We have talked of truth, Michael, but let us talk about your goal. For you so eloquently expressed to me moments ago that you have not found that for which you search. So let us discuss that for which you are searching."

Michael took a deep breath and let out a long sigh. "What am I searching for, Doc?" he asked as he blotted a bit of blood from the side of his head with a bar napkin. Doc smiled once again.

"Michael, look deeper: what is the source of your life or the goal of your life? You see, the mind, in what is called the 'waking state' is filled with opposing thoughts. Truth, perfection, is not something to be found after you die. Heaven is not some far-off state or place, and you do not get there or attain it by living a good life. Michael, the secret to the great mystery is that heaven is at hand. You are standing this very moment at its gate, and you do not even perceive just how close you are. It is a reality that can be attained. Let me say it better: a reality that can be experienced, noticed, and perceived, here and now. Heaven is possible in the present." Doc paused, letting the words ease into Michael.

"Okay, Doc," replied Michael, humoring him. He looked again

over to Lila, who was fastidiously wiping and cleaning the bar, the sink, the fixtures, and the glasses.

"Michael, this realm, this universe within which we live, this dream that we call reality, is in constant change. And this change appears to be either constructive or destructive. There seem to be two great natural forces at play in our universe: evolution and devolution. But Michael, when you examine closer, you will observe that every moment of devolution is not without purpose, for it opens the doorway for more and greater evolution. It is only when the bud is destroyed that the flower emerges. Michael, destructive forces have moved into your life. Your evolution is about to begin, but you had better be paying attention." As Doc finished, the look on his face lightened, and he returned to his martini.

"How many of those have you had, Doc," Michael asked with a smile. He sat quietly now, chugging his beer and staring once more into the darkness beyond the neon glow of beer lights above the shelves of multicolored liquor bottles. Michael played the one sentence again in his thoughts: "Destructive forces have moved into your life." He tried to shake the thought from his conscious mind, but he knew it was true. However, he had been of the opinion, until now at least, that it was he who was destroying his own life. Doc reached for a napkin, pulled a pen from his pocket and began to scratch a name and phone number. He slid the napkin slowly to Michael and said, "Call the number, Michael. It is the number of a teacher who can teach you techniques to experience what I am talking about. Stop reading and thinking and talking about finding truth, Michael; it's time to go find it."

Michael peered at the napkin, folded it, and put it into his pocket. He looked again at Lila; she was leaning against the doorway talking to an unseen person in another room. Her arms were folded and her hair hung straight down her back, her weight shifting against the door jamb so that it pushed her hip outward, accentuating the curve of her bottom. Michael was seeing how beautiful she was, slowly, as though it had been inexplicably hidden from him for some ancient reason or rule of multiple lifetimes. *God, I'm beginning to sound like Doc*, he chastised himself.

Then he coughed, hard and productive. There it was again: Everyone goes about their business as though death is never there, never looming. Living as though the earth isn't spinning, as though the darkness will never come. Then it shows itself, entering in the tiniest of places. We never think of how it will come—in a crash of speeding metal, or via a single cell gone astray, spreading is deception as it reproduces devolution, or old and in our sleep after all thoughts of anything have retreated to infancy. *Coming and going, that's all it is,* Michael attempted to reassure himself.

"I've got to head out, Doc. As always, it was a pleasure; let's pick up the conversation soon." Doc nodded and sipped the gin once again. He looked towards Lila, who was still engaged in conversation with someone in the other room. Michael quickly picked up his jacket and headed out the door. Lila noticed that he was leaving and walked over to Doc.

"I could so teach him a thing or two," Lila said in tones sultry enough to make the old man blush.

Doc looked at her over the top of his glasses, then offered a returning smile that broke into a boyish grin. "Oh, go ahead and get it over with."

Searching Backward for the Fork in the Road

Early Spring of 2008

After Michael returned to Charlotte from the mountains, he decided to have the wound on the side of his head examined. He had been having headaches. But the doctor had been more interested in Michael's cough and had him return for more tests. Michael did not like the tone of the doctor's voice after they looked at the x-rays of his chest. He had simply walked out of the doctor's office before hearing the dreaded diagnosis. Michael had a search ahead him, the pursuit of a path to his source was more important than what anyone might tell him that would lead him down a different life path. *So many people want to guide you down a path that is good for them and I have tried that. I want to find a path that has my own heart in it*, Michael told himself. He sat in his truck and decided upon a different direction. He searched his pocket for the number written on a napkin by Doc. *What do I have to lose?* he thought, and as his mind began to answer his own question, he stopped thinking and dialed the number. The telephone rang until an answering machine picked up the line.

"We're not here, so leeeeave a message!"

There was nothing special about the voice, and Michael laughed a little at himself, *I guess I was expecting chimes or an Asian accent of some kind*, Michael left his name and number on the answering machine, with an awkward description of why he had called, then hung up. His head began to pound. He had not had any coffee before the doctor's visit and felt sure he was getting a caffeine withdrawal headache. He reached over to open the glove box, shuffling through the overstuffed compartment searching for an aspirin.

A thin book slid out and fell onto the floorboard, but Michael ignored it, continuing his search for the aspirin bottle. Not finding one, he began impatiently stuffing everything that had fallen out back into the small compartment. He paused when he finally picked up the glossy, dark-covered novelette: *Don Juan.* He leafed through the pages, stopping when he came to words that were highlighted in what was now a faded yellow. He began to read the words that had seemed important enough back then to mark for some future purpose. *Perhaps now?*

For me there is only the traveling on paths that have heart, on any path that may have heart. There I travel, and the only worthwhile challenge is to traverse its full length. And there I travel looking, looking breathlessly.

— Don Juan

Michael smiled. *What an opportune time to find this*, he thought. The visit with the doctor left him restless and with no small amount of apprehension about going his own way. So he sat back and started the engine of his truck with a loud roar. As the engine settled to a comforting hum, vibrating his whole body, he began feeling the slow relief of the best pain reliever that he knew: driving.

As Michael found a downward-sloping on-ramp, he stepped on the old truck's accelerator, matching the speed of the other vehicles on the highway, then accelerated once more until he was passing them. The faster he went and the farther he moved forward on the dark asphalt, the quicker and deeper he moved backward in time into his memory. He rolled down the windows, the hypnotic white noise of the rushing wind gave assistance to his self-imposed excavation into his own history. He was looking for that imagined wrong turn, hoping to travel backward in his mind to discover where he had missed the road that he had intended to take.

There was, he believed, a point where he took that wrong turn. Maybe he missed something. Perhaps he made a compromise he shouldn't have. Was there some unintentional grab for something of comfort? Steadily Michael plumbed the universe of his mind, first skimming, but then delving deeper, exploring past good times and bad times, analyzing past good decisions and bad decisions.

Whether it was the result of doubt, discontent, or fear, it didn't matter to him why he was in this mood. He was trying to figure out where he was with everything in his life. *Who am I? What am I doing? Why am I doing this work?* He laughed to himself. Scratch that: this occupation. Michael was convinced that there had been a schism in his life somewhere.

He thought of the passage he had read, a path of heart. *Am I on a path of heart? Do I know what's true?* He knew so many people for whom these questions would have no meaning. He wondered if it were those who never questioned or people like him who asked "too many questions" that were off the path?

Michael took a deep breath, feeling the smooth vinyl of the steering wheel vibrating in his hands. He looked out the window to see the blur of pine silhouettes under a deeply reddening sky.

Recalling the words *a path of heart* gently shook him like a loving parent wakening a slumbering child. What awoke in him was a long-buried feeling, a sweet melancholy for a time not so long ago, really, when he ached for his own future. It was a time when he wrote songs, strumming his fingers across a dark wooden guitar that he held like a child holds a doll, singing away the nights alone, sitting by an open window under the dim lights of the busy city sidewalk just below. He remembered the curtains dancing passionately to the wild wind and to his song, and he etched notes and lyrics until the streets quieted and the morning sun broke into his small, dank apartment. He had had so little, but as he thought about it now, he knew he had been on a path of heart.

The memories rushed in now as Michael drove on, reliving the first nights with his wife Deborah during their early courtship, reading his poetry to her, listening to music together, sipping wine and tasting everything sensually: an apple slice, a grape, her lips. Sometimes they talked, but often they just sat in silence, holding hands and looking into each other's eyes by candlelight. Back then, they lay for hours tangled on the couch in soft light, listening to the passing conversations that ebbed and flowed on the street outside the window, feeling each other's warmth and dreaming of what would come.

Michael's mind returned grimly to the now-dark road, and he watched long white lines appearing out of the darkness beyond his headlights. He had been in love, and he had been on a path with heart. He took a deep breath, then let it out slowly, feeding the coming rationalizations born of life's experiences of loss and disappointment. *This is how life goes: That deep, heart feeling I experienced was nothing more than Mother Nature, who was, after all, a bitch, casting her spell for procreation. She just wanted us to keep the genes moving, nothing more.* But he just could not quite convince himself that it was true.

He longed to be lost in love.

He thought about it now, and it occurred to him that any attempt to get back to that time, to that feeling, was always sabotaged by the plans they had already made and were executing. A quiet moment became a discussion about bills, money, and the always-present stress of "not enough." He wanted to connect, he looked at her with admiration, but she was tired. Tired of him, tired of kids, tired of work, tired of everything.

He knew he loved his wife, and could only say that, even though he had left her, he was still wearing his wedding ring, owing to some vow that he barely remembered. And he always wondered, "What was the higher path? Sticking to what you said you would do, or chasing every passing butterfly and changing horses midstream?"

But what he knew for sure was that he longed to find his own heart. During those too-few moments alone with his wife at night, they nearly always succumbed to exhaustion, and the thought of crossing a desert of a few short inches of mattress and sheets only to meet a continental divide of accumulated disappointments and shortcomings felt like folly. The last time he did reach across that empty space—to touch, to stare into her eyes, to feel her warmth—had become years ago without him noticing.

Michael realized he could not remember exactly when, but at

some point, she had simply stopped coming to bed. There were the kids, of course, who needed her, but now he wondered why, for nearly ten years, she had never returned. So then he thought of the picture that he had found in the box under the bed and admitted to himself: *One thing is missing and it's the one I want.* That was a word that caught his attention: want. One thing he had learned in his years was that wanting surely was a path of suffering. His thoughts turned to Lila.

Longing for love? Where does that lead? Michael's thoughts rambled. *The pursuit of love, gaining love, losing love, then the experience of heartbreak?*

So, am I looking for an experience? How did I get off the path of heart? Michael was trying to separate his need for love and success into two distinct categories. Although he couldn't see it yet, all of his questions pointed to the same thing: *Something was missing, something was wrong.* Beneath his tumultuous thoughts, driving the hot ocean of his mind into a southern squall, was the idea that something was wrong with his life. *What is the root of my dissatisfaction and restlessness?* The question was just beginning to come to Michael's conscious mind.

Again Michael turned to what he thought was important: *Let's see, what are the "facts" about the things that have and have not happened in my life?* Michael was looking for solid ground as he re-ran the internal mental tapes of his dissatisfaction. *So, she never comes to bed anymore, she never reaches for me, never hugs me, and resists any time I try to kiss her.* He was hearing all the negative relationship tapes, affirming some unstated knowledge or fact of unworthiness, and the collection of thoughts and memories worked their purpose as they always did: He was feeling less and less loved, less and less worthy of love. But his thoughts did not stop there; with what he remembered as the facts, he carried on in his mind, making assumptions that he considered facts. *She does not want to be married to me, she does not love me, she does not care.* The thoughts ran on and on, barely conscious to Michael's working, thinking brain, but enough to have their effect. And as his thoughts became heavy, he caught himself. *Are these thoughts true, are these crazy thoughts true?* He was able, for the moment, to stop himself.

Actually, at this moment, if I don't project… he paused… *I am fine.* There it was: In this precise moment, he was fine. Fear of what the doctor might say was stirring every fear he had.

"I like to drive," He told himself, "I am a very good driver in the driveway," he mimicked Dustin Hoffman in the movie Rainman, making him chuckle at himself and allowing him to begin to relax a little. He remembered the last colors of the setting sun, and though it was now dark, there was still a glow in the horizon. Then he noticed his breathing, and for the next moments he perceived his own breath, in and out, in and out, and he grew more fully relaxed. He did not feel crazy, not right now. For Michael, occupation, work, life, and love all twisted into some kind of a crazy game.

Indeed, a storm had broken loose in Michael, and that storm at this moment was as a soft sentimental rain. As he thought of love as the reason for his turning the steering wheel down a different road, he quickly moved to his career. It was easier to look at and far easier to judge. He felt a need to return again, later to confront his own heart where it concerned love and desire, but for now, there remained a veil, a sweet, self-deception that fed his dream, the "big dream."

Michael leaned forward in the darkness of his truck and fiddled with the knobs on the radio, rolled up the windows, then turned the radio off, leaving him in dark, quiet stillness with only the dull hum of the road. His thoughts slowed and he began to realize that there was not one wrong turn to be excavated and/or corrected, no single moment of choosing greed over substance. His decisions, his path, were innocently chosen, but he had chosen over and over to turn away from the path of heart. The turn from art, from the "work," his work, his life's art, to occupation was constant and consensual: One thought, one decision right after another by an acute mind, searching for solutions and answers to imagined problems.

Hoarding, planning, conceiving all to placate some created or imagined fear, so many times, for so long, that the thought of God, the thought of the divine, of a life of a path of heart became lost, hidden, and deviant. That's where everything changed for me, and the most natural and easiest of endeavors became, in some strange twist of fates, imagined as the most difficult path. And even my point of view became warped, I judged that being a true man of God was the path of a wandering fool.

Michael's thoughts rambled on for a bit longer and then slowly settled to a moment in his past. He had been sitting on the warm grass, squinting in the bright sun, watching the graceful shadows of a nearby tree as its branches alternately praised and bowed to the glowing sun that warmed all below. College was complete, he had bills to pay, and he needed a job. He had been offered a job at the manufacturing plant across town, and he was pondering what at the time—early in adult life—seemed like a standard post-college question, "What do I want to do?" Michael realized now that he had been trying to choose a profession, but he actually was up against what would become a great divide in his life.

Back then, he dreamed of music, of writing songs, of singing. *And that had not been going too well,* he smiled to himself. At the time, though, he thought it was going great: staying up late at night, softly strumming his six-string, laying into minor chords and letting his voice mix and tangle into smooth riffs, adding words and anecdotes that were trite and unappealing to anyone but himself. The feeling he created within himself was marvelous; but no one echoed or shared his love of his crooning short ditties.

When he was very young he had once had a chance to play his guitar and sing for a famous country-and-western singer; in fact, it was his boyhood idol. An uncle, the editor of a fine country-and-western publication, had devised the plan to get young Michael in front of the celebrity, a legend in the industry. Most likely preceded by other young aspirants coming to the mountain, teenaged Michael clutched the neck of his guitar and approached the table of laughing men in a dark, smoky bar. He noticed they were eating chili and drinking tequila, presumably eating before the night's show to come (or more likely eating after a full night of howling at the moon). Michael's eyes met his hero's dark, steady eyes, just visible under the broad brim of his hat.

"Well, I guess I know why you are here; you best get to it," the famous singer said calmly. Michael lifted his guitar strap over his head, looked down at the strings and began to play, coming in strong with his voice on-key and on the beat. His heart was beating hard and mixed up within him, tied with the rhythm of his left hand so loudly that Michael was sure everyone at the table could hear.

All the men at the table kept eating, except the singer. And as the song came to an end, the man waited for a moment, then looked down to take a sip of his tequila. Then, without looking up, he said, "Son, keep your day job." At that, all of the men at the table began to laugh quietly, attempting to hide their amusement at the boy's demise by tucking into their food or looking away. Michael bowed his head, deflated and defeated, and turned to leave.

The famous singer lifted his head and watched as the boy walked away dejectedly. "Hey boy," the man shouted at him. Michael turned and saw a bright swathe of light shining in through a high, rectangular window, making its way across the floor, the table, and his hero's eyes.

"I am going to give you some advice that someone gave me a long time ago. If you are going into music to be rich or famous, well, it just doesn't happen. But if you are going into music because it is all you want to do, all you can do, well, son, then you are going to go into music, no matter what I or anyone else says. So whether I like your little song or not, or whether I or anyone else thinks you have any talent or not, well, it just doesn't matter. It's the wrong question, the question is what is in your heart, and what do you want to do. It's a rough, gravely road out there and it's impartial, it doesn't give a damn who makes it and who doesn't. Do what you love and success, as measured by others, won't matter: You will have found your own heart."

All the men at the table went still, listening. Michael could not tell if they were looking at him or not: All he could see were his hero's eyes... intense, open, and offering him wisdom from having surely traveled on that road. As Michael thought about that moment now, he was sure the advice was made possible by a long road of experience. Most likely, his idol had seen a lot of musicians come and go.

The words of the cowboy musician had always stayed with Michael. In fact, he had kept singing, playing, writing for years after, but he had decided to go to college. Rather, it had been decided for him: There was never any thought that he would do anything else. College seemed designed to feed graduates to some unknown, large institution, most likely a well-known corporation. Business school and interviews with food companies, furniture companies, accounting firms. Companies came to the college, and students were prepped for the coming interviews. Everyone had to be ready for the "real world." Looking back now, he thought of how they had been herded like cattle, branded and sold in market, with little resistance or fanfare. It was all accepted as the way things were supposed to be.

And now, here he was driving along Interstate 77, years later, thinking about his music. It was what he had wanted to do. *You may not have had a job, but you would have had a life.* Now there was wisdom: If he had followed his path of heart, things most likely would have turned out very differently. He thought about one of his college buddies who had indeed taken that path, living not knowing where his life was going or how it was going to turn out. At the time, the "not knowing" seemed like an unbearable predicament.

His buddy worked at a craft where there were few jobs, and rather than find a career or success, he had found the bottle, never making much of his life (at least as everyone else watching had judged him). Michael wondered now what his friend had seen, for he traveled the road that the singer was talking about, hadn't he? What had he done and what had he experienced: Had his friend found his path of heart? He had no idea where his friend Dallas McKenzie was now. The more Dallas had traveled that road, the more he drank, the more he changed his women, the more he moved around, and the less Michael and Dallas talked.

Dallas had shown up every so often, in wrinkled clothing, usually with a new girl who laughed too loudly and drank too much for Deborah's liking. He would stay for a day and then be on his way. The gaps between visits had grown until they stopped completely, and rather than try to connect, Michael had always said, "Dallas will find me when he wants to." But now he wondered about Dallas as he wondered about himself.

Michael had always felt that he had lived a better life, not necessarily superior, but in some small way he thought he had done things the "right way." He laughed a little to himself, wondering how Dallas had viewed him. As the friends drifted apart, Michael had always believed that Dallas had changed, but at this moment, he could not say for sure who had changed.

Michael had decided to take the manufacturing plant job and continue his music, convincing himself he could write and play at night. He believed he always would work at his art, but there was no money in it, so to live, he took the job. Choosing the job took a low degree of effort in his heart relative to his music. And over the years, with little resistance, his music made steady progress as it moved from the den coffee table to the kitchen table to the bedroom desk to the closet to a box in the attic into the garage, and, one day, into the garbage. Thinking about it now made Michael's stomach drop, bringing him instantly back to the darkness of his truck.

Instinctively he reached once again across the darkness to slam the radio knob with the back of his hand, making the speakers jump as the music popped loud against his ears. A sacrilege. His thoughts and emotions were now in full gear together: *That was sacrilege for my youth, for my heart.* Art was his "work," while employment was "just a job." But because he did well in his job, his employers rewarded him with higher positions and more to do, and always with more money. There was nothing he could point to that was creative, or even intellectually difficult or challenging about his job, but there was always more to do, and he had to give more, more of himself to the job. Every time he gave, he was rewarded with a higher salary. And the more he had, the more he thought he needed.

Newer commitments had cut down on his free time, warm moments of love and music became fewer and fewer, eventually fading altogether into a sedated complacency, until one day he did not even notice that the true work of his heart had become clutter.

Michael turned the music even louder to drown out the

thoughts. He wanted to let the music and the road medicate the new realization. Until this very moment, Michael had thought of his "successful" career path as a life accomplishment. Now, it was an empty place in his life. His breath felt labored and his thoughts for just a moment returned to the spots in the x-ray. He slowed the truck and looked for an exit where he could turn around: He wanted to go to sleep and he needed to get home. As he slowed, angling the truck down the off-ramp, he looked into the now-dark sky. There was a dull, shimmering band far above and he wondered, *Am I looking at clouds floating in the night sky, or am I looking at the Milky Way?* It felt better to imagine he was looking at the Milky Way, so he imagined it as so, and could see broad dancing bands of stars in his mind as he turned the truck back, toward home.

Meditation for Warriors

Summer 2008

Michael hung up the telephone and looked out the slender window of his cubicle. He could see the road extending in the distance and he longed to be on it. It was not yet five P.M. but he did not care he felt jubilant. He was going to do it: His plans were now in place to attend a meditation retreat. The idea was intriguing, but Michael suddenly was struck with the need for reassurance. Not surprisingly, he thought of Doc, so he hopped on his bike and headed for Curly's, sure he would find the old man there at the bar sipping a martini. Perhaps he would also find the lovely Lila. A short ride later, he was rolling into the gravel parking lot. He slid the motorcycle into an open space near the wooden shack, turning off the engine as he halted. His steps were quick, like those of a young boy with something he wanted to show off to a friend.

Michael bounded up the steps, slowing only as he moved into the dim light of the pub. He stood just inside the door, and when his eyes adjusted to the darkness of the room, he saw Doc sitting near the back in his usual spot. He had turned toward Michael and was looking over the top of his glasses at him, grinning. Michael began to move toward him but Lila intercepted him, crossing his path but pretending not to notice him. As she passed close by, Michael caught her scent. He stopped and turned to her.

"Hello," he said, but it came out deeper than he intended and Lila turned, smiling. Lila looked at the side of Michael's head, examining for the wound he had endured defending her and Doc.

"Mmmmm," was the only sound she made, but she was sufficiently satisfied that Michael had healed properly. Looking into his eyes affected her. Everytime she had been with Michael her view of him had changed, from the almost shy man she let stay with her while it rained to the aggressive fighter who had defended her. And now she knew he was headed to a meditation retreat. She was definitely drawn to this complex man.

Michael just stood there looking at her, and although he was never at a loss for words, he was straining to find something to say to her.

Finally, she helped him out: "Doc says that you are going to a meditation retreat." She combed her hair a little nervously with her fingers, making Michael smile.

"Yes... Yes, I am," Michael responded, still trying to find the right thing to say.

"Sounds interesting...tell me about it?"

"Well, I am pretty sure it's some kind of meditation, but they don't call it meditation. All I really know is that I am going to be doing it, whatever it is, all day," he said, making quotation signs with his fingers as he said the word, it, then continued, "They have already given me some basic instruction about how to sit and meditate, but I've never been able to do it for more than 30 minutes or so. I just don't seem to be able to sit still. So, I am little nervous about it." He put his hands in his back pockets. "Let's see," he said, looking upward as if there were words on the ceiling, "Oh yes, they said 'no alcohol, no caffeine, no red meat,' and there was something else... oh yeah, 'no sex.'"

Lila smirked and let out a little noise at the last word. He grinned back at her, and he suddenly found himself in full flirt mode, with Lila flirting back. Neither mentioned their night together nor the fight. Michael had left and had not gotten her phone number, so there was no stress about when or if he would call. However, now that he thought about it, he wanted to ask her for her number, but it didn't feel right just now. The feeling she and he had known each other in a past life was even stronger now; there was something so familiar about her.

Lila's eyes stayed on Michael as she continued on her way, and when she eventually turned away, he noticed that she had a copy of the Bhagavad Gita stuffed into her back pocket.

"Lila, are you reading the *Bhagavad Gita?*" he asked, showing only a little surprise. She stopped and turned back to Michael.

"Yes, I am re-reading it; it's one of my favorite books."

"Really?" Michael said. "Mine, too, how unusual that we both love the same book... and the same song." He forced astonishment and waited for her to agree.

"Really? No, I think it probably happens all the time." Lila smiled as she responded, then turned and walked into the next room. Michael watched her walk away then continued to the back of the bar where he sat on the barstool next to Doc. Doc was waiting, wearing a knowing smirk but not saying anything.

"Doc..." Michael began the conversation.

"Yes, my young friend," Doc said as he folded his arms.

"I want to ask you about this meditation thing—you know this retreat thing you got me into?"

"Yes, my young, naïve friend, what would you like to know?" Doc's voice was raspy, more fit for an aged rock-and-roller than a distinguished professor in a dark sport coat and brightly colored bowtie. The more Michael looked at Doc, the more he thought he looked like he belonged in a university, sitting amidst stacks of books, having important dialogue with other intellectuals; not holding up in a bar at the end of a dirt road where there were more catcalls and grunts than the uttering of complete sentences.

"Doc, what you are doing here at Curly's?" Michael's question made Doc laugh.

"That's what you want to know? You come into this bar from wherever you were, looking all serious, to ask me a question, and it's, why I am here?"

Michael smiled.

"Well, I was going to ask you the meaning of life, but, you know, I figured that one out on my own. So, yeah, Doc, I want to know what you are doing in a place like this. Look at yourself—you look like you just walked off the grounds of Oxford University, looking for a pipe store or something."

"I have no idea what you mean. I think I look rather like a mountain man, just like Grizzly Adams or Jeremiah Johnson," Doc replied, making Michael chuckle.

"Well, that is a manly-looking beard you have there," Michael teased. "Doc, look around you: These men all have untrimmed beards, tattoos, and scars… and they smell like meat, cheese, and beer."

Doc smiled, then looked over at Lila; Michael followed his eyes. "Yes, that's another one who doesn't belong here. I'll figure her out next," Michael said, grinning.

Doc began to laugh. "So you think you are going to figure that one out?" he said as he motioned at Lila with his head. "Why don't you stick to the unknowable truths of the universe; you know, the easier questions," Doc said, making Michael chuckle again. There was a slight pause, and Doc took advantage of it to sip his martini. As he did, Michael noticed that there was a beer in front of him; he had not seen Lila bring it, and he wondered for just a minute if she had been listening to their conversation.

"Well, my young warrior friend, I'll tell you why I am here at Curly's."

"So now I am a warrior?" Michael asked.

"In more ways than you could possibly discern," answered the Doc, "And I am not talking about your little fisticuffs the other night. You see, those who seek truth—what we will call enlightenment—are spiritual warriors. And *that* I can help you with. But as for the truths of Lady Ashley, I mean Lila? Well then, you will have to go to someone else, though I fear there may be no one to help you with figuring her out, or any other woman for that matter."

Doc let out a raspy cough, then took another sip of his Martini and rubbed his chin. Doc's cough reminded Michael of his own incessant cough. He first felt an itching deep down at the base of his throat, almost as if he could feel his bronchial tubes constricting, then a deep cough came. He rushed to cover his mouth with his hand, then suppressed the aftershock. It was like swallowing a grenade. Doc raised his eyebrows but said nothing of the cough. Instead, he continued on with the conversation.

"Michael, do you know the name of this place?"

"Yes, of course, Doc, this place is called Curly's."

"Do you know who Curly was?"

"Ummm," Michael looked up, searching his mind but finding nothing, "No, Doc, I have no idea, but I'll venture a guess: the bald Stooge named Curly?"

Doc gave Michael a look that said, "Be serious."

"Ever hear of an Indian named Crazy Horse?"

"Yes, of course, the Sioux warrior," Michael answered.

"Well, before he took his father's name of Crazy Horse, that young warrior was called Curly. And the Sioux—or rather, the Lakota—called him their 'strange man of the Oglalas,' which was the tribe from which he came. And yes, he was a great warrior, and also a reluctant leader of his people."

"I thought he was their chief?" Michael interjected.

"Well, not by birth, and not as elected by other heads of other tribes. But Crazy Horse was the people's choice to lead them. Young braves were drawn to him because he was brave and ferocious in battle and he never left anyone behind. He once rode into the face of bullets and arrows to kill a suffering horse. The older peoples of his tribes and the helpless ones were drawn to him because he took care of them, and it is said that he left all who made eye contact with him with a smile. But more, he was the son of a holy man, being to be a holy man, and all Indians around Crazy Horse could sense that something holy was happening around him," Doc took a deep breath then continued.

"For the longest time, he resisted going to the reservation. Many Indians and many of the Lakota tribes were attracted to the white men who, on behalf of the President of the United States—"the great father"—promised the Indians food, blankets, shelter, and safety. All they had to do was to give up their way of life."

Doc paused for a moment as if he was thinking about what he had just said.

"Lies," Michael said.

"Well, whether or not it was offered in good faith, in the end, yes… lies," Doc agreed. "But you see, the Indians' way of life was hard for many. There were no guarantees that they would eat, for they depended on the land and the game, and a cold winter or an elusive herd of buffalo meant no meat and no hides. Many lives were lost during the hard times. The promise of food and warmth in the winter was enticing, especially to a group of people who were not inclined to lie so had no need to doubt the word of others," Doc took a drink of his martini.

"But none of this mattered to Curly, the young Crazy Horse. He loved the Lakota way of life; to him it was a sacred walk. He wanted to roam the open plains to be free and alive like his brethren animals. And that was the life he pursued—he did not want to live on the reservation. And you see, my young warrior friend called Michael, your friend sitting next to you does not want to live on the reservation."

"Doc, that is all very odd, I must have told you about my dreams the other night when we were drinking," Michael said to Doc.

"Do you remember telling me about your dreams?" Doc asked.

"Well, no, not exactly…So how did you know about my dreams?" Michael asked.

"What dreams?" Doc asked.

"I didn't tell you about my dreams?" Michael asked.

"No, but let me guess, you are about to…" Doc said and smiled.

"Doc, I have been having these crazy dreams. Sometimes I dream I am an angel, and sometimes I dream that I am an Indian—Crazy Horse to be exact."

After Michael finished speaking, Doc peered at him to see if he was kidding. Doc took another drink of his martini while continuing to observe Michael; he could see by his facial expressions that Michael was serious and wanted more information, so Doc sighed, then continued.

"You see, Michael, our government is much the same now as it was then. Promises are made, handouts are offered… but now it's not for the Indians, it's for what they call the poor or the needy. Men lose their way of life—they are on the reservation and they don't even know it, because the government's hand is in everything they do. I am not proposing revolution, mind you, I am much too old for that. I just do not want to live on the reservation. So the entertainment, the food, the welfare—all the things offered by the government—suck people in and deaden their instincts to live, to live free. They feel safe. The government makes them feel safe, watching over us. For God's sake, someone has legislated that wearing your safety belt is the law, and your car will beep you into insanity if you try to drive without a seatbelt buckled. Someone has decided to make decisions for you," he paused for a moment searching for words, "I just do not want to live on the reservation. I want to live out here where things are not so certain, where danger lurks, where men do what they want. Nothing is safe, nothing is guaranteed, but this is the life I want to live. And I think that it's the life you want to live as well."

Doc finished his lecture, then took a deep breath before asking, "So, should I start calling you Crazy Horse?"

Michael smiled as he turned on his stool to face the bar and reached for his beer. This was not what he had come to talk to the Doc about. He looked at Lila behind the bar, and he could feel something far beyond mere sexual attraction suffusing his entire body. She noticed his lingering glance, but she flashed a quick, polite smile and turned to talk to another patron, pretending as though his gaze had not affected her in any way. However, he knew that it did, because he saw that she smiled, then she turned back ever so slightly to see if he was still looking at her.

"So Doc, let's get this conversation to what you call the greater truth. And yes, I am looking for what's true, what's real in this life… I want to look deeper. Tell me more about this meditation retreat that I am about to embark on, and tell me what great truth does it lead to. What am I pursuing? How am I to live?"

"Well, my friend, *now* you are asking some very interesting questions, and you have come to the right place. I tell you now, Michael, you must live—live like a warrior. I think that maybe this is the reason you are dreaming that you are a warrior. The image of a warrior resonates deeply with the experience of meditation. A warrior views life as a challenge. He sets out to see things for himself, he does not complain while on his journey, and he lives without regrets. He travels lightly, for he knows that he is on a long journey. What matters most to the warrior is what is in his own heart, and the thing that is in a warrior's heart is *gentle strength*. It is the strength in his heart in which he puts his trust, and he follows what he feels there—not what others say to him. And like a warrior, Michael, you are undertaking a noble task. In this great journey that you are undertaking, you will be moving yourself away from hatred, away from greed, and dispelling your own illusions. You will need to ground yourself in wisdom, and—even more powerful than wisdom—you will need to ground yourself in love."

Doc took a breath and looked into Michael's eyes to gauge his attention, then added, "And you will need to walk in compassion. You need a vision, Michael, and if this is your vision, well, then it is a rare thing, a noble endeavor. Everyone needs this: People are hungry for a leader. You could be a leader, Michael. Perhaps you could show people the way—it is a rare walk indeed. This is important, so let's talk more about it."

Michael began to laugh nervously, "I don't know, Doc. First of all, I am not much of a warrior, and second, I have no idea what I am even looking for! I'm just trying find out what really matters. Maybe I'm really just a coward trying to escape."

"Are you a coward, Michael?" Doc asked, and his eyes bored into Michael.

Michael looked back at Doc then answered, "No, I am not a coward, and I want to hear more about this retreat and meditation."

"Okay, let us talk about meditation. Have you ever read the story of Siddhartha?"

"No, I have not."

"Do you know who Siddhartha is?"

"Yes, Siddhartha was the name of the Buddha, right?"

"Yes, so let me ask you what three traits you think it takes to be a warrior, and what three traits you think that Siddhartha learned that helped him become the Buddha, the enlightened one?"

"I have no idea," Michael smiled as he answered, wondering quietly if Doc was wise or just a crazy old man.

"He learned how to have patience, how to be brave, and how to fast. So let's talk about these three strengths or traits. First, like a warrior, he learned to wait. Young warriors chase after the first game they see, often chasing off the larger herd or prey. And too, the impatient warriors would ride out prematurely into battle, giving away a carefully-planned ambush. So in meditation, he learned how to watch his own thoughts and how not to get caught up in the tracks of his mind's movements, even the well-established thoughts of his conditioning, his beliefs. He learned how not to be swept away by the constant river of thoughts. So this first trait or power gave him clarity.

"The second trait the warrior and meditator needs is courage, and I do not mean the type of courage to punch the big guy," Doc laughed and Michael smiled. "I think punching the big guy is closer to foolishness."

Now both men chuckled.

"I have to agree with you on that one, Doc," Michael chuckled, then sipped his beer. He glanced over his shoulder at Lila, but quickly returned his attention to Doc.

"Michael, I am talking about the kind of courage to let go of everything that you think you know. The kind of courage to go inside of yourself, to go deep, and when you think you have gone as deep as you can go, to keep going to explore and discover the deepest parts of your mind, beyond the limits of your body. This journey, Michael, will more than likely be troubling. Like everyone else, you have over the years developed a lot of comfortable habits. Some of the habits are self-destructive, and this you can see, but even these bad habits have embedded within them some secret payoff that makes you comfortable. But you must learn to let go and experience the flow of impermanence. And Michael, you have to have the courage to face your own insecurities of this mind/body process that you call, you. To confront the fact that, every moment, what you think you are dissolves completely and there is no place to take a stand. Michael, what I am talking about is the courage to die. I am not talking about the death of the body, but rather the death of the concept of who or what you think you are. To experience death while you are still living takes courage: This is what is called the 'Big Death.'"

Michael stared at the Doc and almost started to laugh.

"Is that it? That is just two traits, you said that there are three? Is that all you got?" Now Doc laughed. It was a serious conversation, but it felt a little like nonsense to Michael.

"Okay, if you think you are ready, the third trait is the ability to surrender," Doc continued, "and this trait takes energy, effort, and strength. It is the act of giving up, renunciation. What can you let go of, Michael? You see, there is a simplistic beauty and joy in a life where you are unencumbered by possessions or the need to take strong positions, by strong opinions that must be defended because they are the concept of who you think you are. This need to be right can be more difficult to give up than any other desire."

At that moment, Lila sighed out loud as she passed by, prompting both Doc and Michael to follow her with their eyes until she disappeared into the next room, then they looked at each other and burst into laughter.

"Michael, there may be a few desires that you might want to explore before you traverse this road," Doc joked. As they both laughed again, Michael reached for his beer and looked again at Lila as she walked back into the bar. This time, she caught his glance and it was he who quickly looked away.

"Doc where does all this lead? What kind of road is this?"

"Michael, you are on the road to veracity and to yourself. It is the greatest adventure of your life, and it is the toughest road you will travel, but it is the greatest endeavor you could choose for a lifetime. Giving things up, Michael, does not have to be overwhelming, but rather a simple letting go of old habits, and as you give things up one by one, you will experience a spaciousness. A spaciousness that grows exponentially as you let go of your attachments. In other words, Michael, you will be fasting. It is one of the oldest ways to reach within yourself. But I am not talking about fasting from food, but from everything."

Michael smiled and nodded his head as if to say yes to everything Doc had just said. Doc simply turned back to his drink. Michael looked at Lila; now she was looking directly at him. She went about her work wiping down the bar, but now he could see that she was smiling. Michael could feel the energy growing between them. He let his head tilt backwards as he swiveled, turning on his barstool away from Lila, resting his elbows on the bar behind him. His thoughts turned to more shallow endeavors and he felt pleasant, feeling the music playing on the jukebox beat through him. Doc reached over and slapped Michael companionably on the back.

"It is good to see you, my friend," Doc said, then returned to his drink.

"Yes, it's good to see you, too, Doc," Michael smiled.

"Come find me when you get back from the meditation retreat… I look forward to speaking with you."

"I look forward to that conversation myself, Doc."

Om and Touching Eternity

The Meditation Retreat

Michael left his apartment early in the morning, deciding to travel by truck rather than by his preferred mode of two wheels. Without all of his usual protective gear—gloves, heavy leather jacket, helmet, and boots—he sat in the seat of the truck, feeling vulnerable and with a strong sense that he was forgetting something. He pulled the folder of instructions for the retreat from the duffel bag next to him on the passenger seat and thumbed through the papers for the fourth (or maybe the fifth) time, wondering to himself why he felt the need to read them over and over.

In bold type were the rules: **No Alcohol.** *Okay,* he thought, then he wondered how long it had been since he had gone a day, much less a week, without having a single drink. He was not sure, but he decided that it had been a long while. *When did I start drinking so much? Well, it's not so much that it is all the time,* he tried to reassure himself. The rules were making him reassess himself, something he had not done in quite some time. Next on the list: **No Red Meat.** *Okay, fine with this one,* he thought. Then: **No Caffeine.** *This one is going to hurt.* **No Sex.** *A shame that this one is not a problem,* he thought, smiling wryly as he put the folder back into the bag. He felt more secure and was pretty sure he had everything he needed, so he started the engine, buckled his seatbelt, and put the truck into drive.

The retreat was situated within a 100-acre wood on a high Tennessee mountain lake, a less than four-hour drive from Charlotte. Michael decided to get off the highway and take backroads; it would add a little time to his drive, but he liked driving through the small towns in the foothills. After several hours of driving, the road changed from straight to soft arching turns, then to sharp bends as it crisscrossed back and forth, ascending the highlands. As the road climbed, he drove through countless narrow passes of exposed rock. When he finally reached a fairly straight stretch of road, he decided to stop to stretch his legs. Assessing where he was, Michael realized that he had already spent enough time driving to be at the retreat already, but he was not yet halfway to his destination. He wondered why he was making such slow progress; typically, he rushed to complete each new task ahead.

Michael noticed a small trail leading away from the road near the open space where he had parked—a trail that he would never have seen while driving. He decided to see if it led anywhere, and it did: After just a short walk, he was rewarded with a long view of the valley below. The wind made a swooshing sound across the trees, and Michael's ears were filled with loud chirping and whistling of many birds. *What the hell am I doing?* he asked himself. He thought about his conversations with Doc. He thought about his children. He had given up time with his kids to go on this retreat, and he was feeling a small amount of guilt. His wife had taken the opportunity to jab him about it.

His wife: he and she just could never seem to say anything nice to each other. He looked at his wedding ring, wondering not for the first time why he still wore it. He took it off his finger and held it up in the sun, where it sparkled brightly. He had an urge to throw it over the side of the mountain and the urge sparked a small pang of fear, but fear of what Michael did not know. So he put the ring back on his finger, then he felt resentment.

Michael decided to walk further and came upon a meadow, where he walked through the tall grass and looked across the rolling hills below, which looked soft and darkened in shades of deep blue and gray. Michael thought of Lila, mostly because anything beautiful reminded him of her. And then his thoughts turned to Jo, and what started as a small shiver grew into a shudder as it moved through his body. He folded up his collar as if to ward off the cold, but the breeze was gentle and mild. He felt an itch in his lungs, then an urge to cough, but it was easily suppressed.

"I'd better be going. I'm already running late." He said this to the view as if it were a companion before getting into the truck and hurrying up the road. As he followed the directions, the road first began to narrow, soon turning into a gravel road that followed the natural contours of the land. The trees grew in height and girth as Michael neared the retreat center, and he began to wonder if he was lost and was considering turning around. Finally, he saw a mailbox with small numbers on the side: 1012. It was the retreat center, and there were no other signs to indicate he had arrived in the correct place.

He was not sure what he was expecting to see, but he had imagined something more elaborate, a large stone archway or something. Instead, there was a long metal swing gate suspended over the rails of a cattle guard, much like he would see in Texas at the back entrance to a ranch or perhaps the front entrance to a small farm. There was a short chain looped over the end of the gate and an adjoining post. Michael looked at it for a few minutes, then got out of the truck to lift the chain and open the gate. He drove the truck through the gate and onto what looked like a dirt road that meandered up and down small hills beneath tall pine trees. The road seemed very long, as do many trails when they are traveled for the first time. He rolled down the windows and the smell of the pines filled the truck. The road dipped down sharply to a creek, then up steeply. As Michael came over the hill, a house appeared in the distance. As he drew near he could see that it had three stories, brown and white with intricate trim, like a Swiss chalet.

The dirt road ended at the house, where fifteen or so cars were parked haphazardly on the grass, the edge of the road, and further into the trees. Michael could see what looked like the only space left next to another car under a large pine, so he pulled in and parked. He stepped out of the truck and put his hands into the small of his back, leaning backwards, then bending over to touch his toes, stretching to release the back of his legs. As he stood, he came face to face with a woman who was so close that it startled him.

She introduced herself as Govinda, one of the teachers. Her hair was curly and gray, and she walked with her hands low and outward, a gesture that he has seen his grandmother use.

"Well, hello!" she welcomed Michael warmly.

"Sorry I'm late," said Michael.

"Don't worry about that," she said in a whisper, smiling. After Michael had called it was Govinda who had called back and guided him to a local teacher where Michael could learn this teaching over a weekend. Govinda was warm and genuine and seemed to have a Texas accent, reminding Michael of someone from where he had grown up, making him feel like he was home. He was aware of the feeling, and in a rural setting, it was magnified and very comforting; he could feel himself beginning to relax.

"Let me show you to your bunk," she said, still speaking in quiet tones. "What can I help you carry?"

"I think I've got it," Michael answered as he pulled two bags out of the truck: a large duffel bag full of comfortable clothes, which he slung over his shoulder, then a backpack full of books, mostly about meditation and similar topics.

Michael followed Govinda past the main house and down a stone pathway that led to a long rectangular bunk house in the woods. They had walked quietly up the wooden steps and into the bunk house, when Govinda turned back toward Michael to whisper, "Don't let the screen door slam behind you." There was a long line of beds down one wall and a stack of suitcases and bags against the other wall. "This is where you will sleep," she said, pointing to one of the beds. It looked comfortable, but it was not very private. Next, she showed him the bathroom and gave him a stack of towels. There was one other man in the bunk house, sitting on a large square cushion next to his bed. He was sitting upright, perfectly straight, with his legs crossed and his eyes closed. Michael stared at the man but was careful not to disturb him. When he looked back at Govinda, she had her palms out and she looked as if she was laughing, but she made no sound.

"So, do I just start doing the technique and meditate until dinner?" Michael asked in a whisper. The teaching had a name. But it was nothing more than a series of techniques for direct experience of the deeper levels in the mind. The technique was simple: When Michael noticed a thought, he was instructed to think a thought designed with input from himself that was specifically for him. And that thought acted like taking a new thorn in hand to remove all the old thorns. A thought to replace the other 60,000 thoughts Michael would normally think throughout the day. Michael had heard one of the teachers say, "What we pay attention to grows." The technique was a simple and gentle turning of his attention to something else. The previous weeks and months, Michael had endeavored to see clearly what was real in his life, and as veils of illusion began to fall away, he began to see "what is." And the teaching was a natural next step. It was a means of turning his attention away from what is and, instead, to the *source of what is*.

"Yes, that would be lovely," Govinda said, "but we don't call it meditation; it's closer to prayer, but we don't call it prayer either. The words meditation and prayer conjure up concepts and preformed ideas, so we call the technique the 'teaching.' Both words— prayer and meditation—can be misleading. Take prayer: for most people, it is connected to religion and belief. There is nothing to believe here, just do the technique and let whatever happens, happen," she said, smiling. Michael just nodded, and Govinda turned and left the bunk house. Michael removed his shoes, climbed into the bed, closed his eyes, and began the technique, but then he fell asleep.

The loud clang of a bell announced dinner, jolting Michael awake. The bunk house was empty of people, so he slid on his shoes and headed to the main house, which was bustling with energy, a commotion of people greeting one another and shuffling between the kitchen and a long wooden table on the porch. As Michael entered the kitchen through a screen door he saw the teacher. Her hair was completely white, her eyes were sky blue, and she was looking right at him.

Michael could sense a dissonance and tried to put words on the feeling; it was a strong sensation, but he was not sure what it was. He stood awkwardly just inside the kitchen, fidgeting. First, he folded his arms, then he put his hands in his pockets, then he clasped his hands behind his back. The teacher smiled at Michael, calm and serene. The dissonance that Michael felt was in no way uncomfortable—just striking—as he stood next to the teacher.

"Hello, Michael, I trust your travels were uneventful."

"Yes, sorry I'm late."

"Well, you are here now," she smiled, and while it was not the same big, enthusiastic greeting Govinda had offered, it still was comforting.

"You start here," she said, pointing to a large bowl, "and you work your way around the island." She was giving Michael dinner instructions, "And there is humus, fruit, and water on the table." Michael looked at the food. *Nothing too crazy*, he thought. He was not sure what he was expecting, but he was certain the food would be more exotic than salads, fruits, breads, cheeses, nuts and other various healthy-looking but otherwise simple foods. He browsed and filled his plate.

He moved to the table on the porch and sat down, then he began to look at the other people at the retreat. They, like the food, were much more ordinary than he expected, as if shaved heads and robes were the norm for a meditation retreat. Introductions were being thrown about the table, and Michael attempted to keep track. Tina, Richard, and Suzy, he knew, but he also knew he would not be able to remember all the names, so he stopped trying. Dinner was pleasant and the conversation light, and soon everyone began gathering in a large den with a high ceiling. There was a large stone fireplace in the center of the room against the inside wall of the house, while the opposite wall was almost all windows, affording a grand view of a large lake with mountain vistas on the far side of the water. Michael was momentarily mesmerized by the vision as he stood in the middle of the room staring out of the window, unaware of the others. Someone bumped him gently, bringing him back into the room, and he quickly and quietly found a seat.

Soon after, the teacher and Govinda entered the room and sat on cushions on the stone hearth. Everyone quieted down and the teacher looked about the room slowly, making eye contact with everyone one at a time.

"We have a new arrival and it's his first time coming to retreat," the teacher said while looking at Michael. "This is Michael Tantalus." Various people began to greet him, saying their names and what they did for a living; they were yoga instructors, Sunday school teachers, a professor, a Catholic nun, an ordained minister, a writer, a chef, an accountant, and others. They were all here on some sort of spiritual quest or another, even if they called it by a different name—enlightenment, search for truth, find God, find themselves, be one with everything, Samadhi, or many other spiritual terms, some of which Michael knew and some he did not.

"Would anyone like to voice a concern about or an expectation for the retreat?" the teacher asked.

"I am worried I will not be able to get close enough to God," said Tina, and as she spoke the teacher smiled.

"Michael, any worries or concerns?" the voice itself was equanimity, and Michael heard himself saying the first thing that came into his mind.

"Well, I was reading the rules and guidelines, and I can't remember going a single day without a coffee, a beer, and a hamburger, so I'm a little worried what my body's reaction will be." Laughter filled the room, but Michael was not trying to be funny and his face turned red as he smiled. Then a soft-spoken woman asked, "What is this teaching? What is it really, what are we doing?" The teacher smiled as she brushed back her white hair, and with deep penetrating azure eyes, she looked into the face of the lovely, inquiring woman and began to speak. There was a light ringing in Michael's ears as he listened to her speak. He was listening to the sounds of her voice, the vibrational sounds; her words were nearly secondary to him, and he felt exceedingly calm.

"This teaching is a way to realize the objective of this mortal life, a way to experience 'The peace that passes understanding.'"

"Do you mean oneness with God?" a man asked.

"That would be one way to say it," the teacher answered.

"Enlightenment?" another woman asked.

"That would be another way to say it," she answered.

"What is enlightenment?" the woman asked.

"It is sometimes easier to understand something's meaning by looking at its opposite," she said as she put out her hand, then turned up her palm. "Ignorance or the state of ignoring something that is already there."

"Who can be enlightened?" the man asked.

"Anyone. It is a basic right of the human condition," she answered. "All we have to do is dissolve the obstacles that prevent us from knowing and experiencing this." She moved her hand in an arcing motion with her palm upwards, saying, "We begin our lives in the pure wisdom of innocence, but then we quickly establish beliefs and belief systems. And the things we believe act like barriers that hide from us the Truth of what we are. Eventually, we begin to identify with the beliefs, as if the barriers themselves are who we are," and she smiled as if she were on the verge of laughing.

"Where do these beliefs come from?" another man asked.

"Our parents, our families, and our larger society, and many come from personal experience. Our beliefs in made-up limitations and our belief in separation from our source is what we call the ego or the false-self. These belief systems are like programing in a computer, they give you your output, your life experience."

"So are you saying that the programs are the false or made-up self and that, truly, we are the computer?" a man asked, making the teacher smile again.

"In this made-up analogy, your mind and body are the computer, the ego or false-self is the programing, and you are the programmer," the teacher chuckled.

"You say we must dissolve the barriers. How do we do this?" a woman asked.

"Since the mind is dominant and the body secondary, it is possible to reverse the internal programming and return life to the perfect innocence in the present moment," then the teacher smiled again. All eyes in the room were on her; the room was quiet and still. Then she continued, "And this is what we call the teaching, where we use the technique to go beyond the conscious thinking level of the mind."

As the teacher paused, a man asked, "Is this what we are to believe?"

"There is nothing to believe here," she answered, "this process is simple and natural, just do the technique and let whatever happens, happen. It is our emotions that most dramatically change the level of our consciousness, and though we can use the technique with our eyes open or closed, its greatest value comes from closing our eyes and moving inward, using the technique as a tool for meditation." Then the teacher leaned forward, saying, "Let's close our eyes together now and use the technique."

Michael shut his eyes and scooted down in his chair, fidgeting a bit until he was comfortable. After an hour or so, he realized he was sleeping and roused himself enough to head back to the bunkhouse. He felt exhausted but the cool mountain air was refreshing. The crickets were chirping so loudly that it sounded like song, and the stars were brighter than he ever remembered seeing, giving off enough light to guide him down the stone path.

Michael moved up the steps and quietly opened the screen door, careful to not let it slam behind him. There were already a few men in the bunkhouse, but everyone was quiet. Michael reached the bed, collapsing into the pillows and the warm blanket. It was an old, soft mattress, but it felt marvelous. It occurred to him that for years now, his body's sensory system had been in overload: years of driving himself hard in every way, years of listening to loud music, years of watching all kinds of violence in movies and on television. And, too, living and working within the demented and delusional environment of the corporate world, where he had to keep his guard up continually. When he had searched to find love, instead he had found the push and pull of manipulative relationships. Add to all that the constant punches of everyday living, and it was a wonder he could feel anything at all.

For years since 9/11, he had pulled himself in tight, little by little, day by day, to protect himself, and now that he opened himself even a little and let down his defenses, it was as if he was beginning feel it all, to experience things as if it were for the first time. And as this new process was pleasant in the beginning, it was now beginning to expose and release tension and accumulated stress from years before, and this was not a pleasant process. His nervous system had been pulled in and held tight, walled and dulled, like hearing a recurring sound in your house, like a loud refrigerator, for so long that the body and mind no longer register it. A noise immediately noticed by a stranger but unheard by him in his own house.

Such was Michael's body, and in the silence of the retreat as he began to touch places deep within his mind, he began to be aware of all the noises and thoughts in his body and in his mind. Michael was in no way prepared for what was beginning to come out of him. He began to feel the most painful experiences of his past: He was feeling the feelings, but by introducing his new thought, he was not indulging in the story of what happened. And as thoughts surfaced like a fever, he continually introduced the new thought he learned in the teaching. And as the *"what is"* of his life surfaced, and the elements of an emotional past, he would simply turn his attention to the *source of what is*. And he was beginning to notice things by their absence. Exhaustion eventually surfaced and took Michael into a deep sleep and he slept for the better part of the next three days.

Early on the fourth morning of the retreat, Michael awoke while it was still dark with a stiff body and aching muscles; no one else was stirring. He tossed back the covers and stretched his arms and legs, then stacked a couple of pillows to prop himself up a little, hoping to relieve his aching back. He shut his eyes and continued doing the technique. He watched his thoughts pass by, seemingly eclectic in content —coming from everywhere, memories from a few days ago, his childhood, a car ride, Lila, Deborah, a dog he had as a child—they kept coming out of what Michael perceived as nowhere, passing easily as he watched them float through his mind, then let them go.

Then he became interested in the content of distant childhood memories that were vivid. Smells came to him, first that of his grandfather's timeworn car, the dusty and musty mixture that meant old and pleasant to Michael. His memory was of riding with his grandfather in the country, the window down, and he was on his knees with both arms folded on the open window's edge. The air was blowing across his face and through his hair, and he could remember the difficulty in breathing in the fast-moving air. The smell of the grasses and the trees completely filled him, and he could feel sun's rays coming in though the open window warming his arms and his face. He felt marvelously pleasant. Then again, he chose a thought of gratitude.

After a few hours, light began to creep into the bunk house through the windows and the screen door. Michael decided to stop meditating, because he felt groggy, his head ached, and he felt a little dizzy. He sat up and began to think of all the things he had done in his life to find peace, and in this suddenly alert state, he realized that nearly all his endeavors involved numbing himself in one way or another. Excessive exercise, alcohol, and sex were the first things that came to his mind, and as he sat in the increasing light he began to feel restless, and then the feeling began to grow. "No drink, no exercise, and no sex...no damn wonder I feel a little crazy," he whispered quietly to himself. *Damn, I could use a drink.* This last thought came as a response to his growing restlessness, but then he admitted to himself that, lately, alcohol only left him feeling agitated. And sex did not seem like a possibility right now, at least while still at the retreat. There was the old, reliable "think of nothing," he told himself, but as he attempted to not think, his mind became an echo chamber of negative thoughts: voices of failure, failure in everything he did. It felt as if the failure thoughts were assaulting him, and the longer he sat, the louder they became.

That's it, I'm splitting, I've got to leave this place. Michael picked up his duffel bag and began to stuff clothes into it. He decided in an instant that he would pack his truck and he could be out of the 100-acre woods before anyone knew he was gone. It was always Michael's first urge, and it had always served him well: *run!* But then he saw the urge for what it was. *Yes,* he said to himself, *I can always run, but I think I will stay and see this thing through. I want to evolve, and this may all be a bunch of crap, but I'm here, so I might as well give it a chance.* However, his restlessness had grown so acute that he needed to move. So he put on his shorts, his socks, and shoes. He was in such a hurry to get out of the bunkhouse that he put on a tee shirt as he was going out the door, the screen door slamming loudly behind him. The sound jolted him and he paused, waiting for someone to yell a complaint, but none came.

He started out with the intention of a rigorous hike, and he was in such a hurry that he did not warm up or stretch. Michael chose a path that immediately started up a steep incline. And very quickly as the path ascended the mountain, the terrain became so steep that the trees appeared to be leaning inland. The loose dirt and gravel of the pathway began to give way beneath the strenuous push of his legs and feet. Though he was exerting a substantial amount of effort, the outcome seemed to involve more sliding than progress. Michael tried to estimate how far he had gone, four miles maybe, but he did not care: He needed the strain more than the miles, and it was not long before his effort was rewarded with gasping lungs and aching legs. Despite the effort of his strenuous hike, he could soon see that there would be no reward of a distant view. And without the pull of a reward, his hands soon found his knees and he bent over, gasping for air. After a short amount of time, his breathing slowed and he stood, feeling small beads of sweat running down his brow as the endorphins began to take effect. His body was relaxing, and his mind began to relax as well and thoughts in the form of questions began to appear in his mind: *Had anyone ever searched and found what they were looking for? Had they been able to satiate the restlessness? Had anyone ever really evolved and found enlightenment? Was enlightenment real or was it just a myth? Was there really a place of perpetual peace?*

As Michael's breathing and heart beat slowed, his thoughts slowed as well and he once again began to notice things. First, a large, yellow and black butterfly floating effortlessly to a flower, slowly opening and shutting its intricately decorated wings. Then, the crackling of a bird and a large heron descended toward the lake. The wind rushed through the branches of the birch trees above, causing the leaves to shudder and spark in the filtering sunlight of the deep blue sky. Then Michael noticed himself noticing. He became aware of awareness itself. And after pausing there for a few minutes, he turned and began walking back down the pathway to ask the teacher some questions.

Michael found the stone path that led around to the back of the house, where there was a large stone patio that stretched the entire length of the main house. The teacher was sitting in a chair, her white locks of hair moving gently in the breeze. She was drinking hot tea, and looking out across the lake, where the sun sparkled across the small ripples, but she turned to watch Michael as he came closer. He approached without speaking, and sat in the chair next to her.

They both sat in silence, hearing only the sound of the wind through the trees. Michael closed his eyes and began using the technique, his breathing became even and easy. After a while, he opened his eyes, wanting to ask the teacher a question, but he could not recall what he wanted to ask. He searched his mind to find a good question, and when it came to him, he asked it, albeit a little awkwardly.

"Are we evolving?" he asked. The teacher turned to look at him, and Michael felt a need to elaborate, "I mean we as individuals, you know as biological response/stimulus machines… are we evolving in our own life times, and is this the process of what we call attaining enlightenment?" The question caused the teacher to smile so broadly she looked as if she were about to laugh.

"This is what you want to ask?" the teacher asked in a teasing tone.

"Yes," he answered, but then thinking more said, "I mean, I think so." Michael then smiled, feeling as if he had asked a silly question.

"Yes, of course," she said, "all this could be called evolution, but I am not sure why it is important.'

"So the mind and body are evolving over our lifetime as time passes?" Michael asked again, making the teacher laugh gently. He tried to rephrase the question: "I guess I am asking who— or what—evolves, and what is it evolving to? Enlightenment? And why? What is going on exactly?"

"All there is, is 'Consciousness.' That is all you really need to know. And consciousness has simply identified itself with an individual, an individual response/stimulus machine," she smiled, looking at Michael. They locked eyes for a moment, then Michael looked out across the lake, then up into the trees.

"Why would Consciousness do that?" Michael asked. He noticed that he was relaxing, and he had the sensation of watching himself ask questions. He knew the words had meaning but he was experiencing the conversation as sounds; he was sensing and experiencing vibrations as the teacher spoke, her voice like pleasant waves. He had the sensation of feeling refreshed after drinking cool water, and he could feel that his restlessness was subsiding. Then the teacher answered his question.

"So that this *'Lila,'* this dream can happen, like going to the movies to see an earth drama play out in the most entertaining manner."

" Lila?" he questioned.

"Yes, Lila is used in ancient Indian texts and writing. It means the illusion, the dance, the cosmic game that the consciousness of the universe plays, or as you like to say, as it evolves," she said and once again looked into his eyes.

"Ironic," he said, "the word 'Lila' I mean. I know someone, a girl, I mean a woman, and her name is Lila," he wanted to explain but he was drawn into the teacher's gaze and a certain peacefulness resonated through him.

"Consciousness identifying with individual biological machines has been going on over and over for a very long time. And it continues today. New people—or should we say new biological response/stimulus machines—and only the new ones—have been slightly upgraded, they change as the demands of an impermanent world changes," the teacher continued, and Michael began to laugh at himself as he heard his own description of a human being. "The newly slightly upgraded ones are being created continually, and in them, consciousness identifies with the new body. It goes on and on in what you and I are calling evolution, but then the plot thickens!"

The teacher paused and lowered her voice to a more serious tone as she leaned toward Michael. "The fun begins, and it can happen right now in this individual life: The mind simply tires or becomes bored of reaching outward towards the stars and turns inward." Then she sat back into her chair, sipped her tea, and matter-of-factly finished her statement. "The process of disidentification begins, and consciousness simply becomes aware of itself or returns to itself, or enlightenment or whatever concept you want to create."

Their conversation was interrupted by the loud chattering of a nearby raccoon sitting atop the rubbish heap. It was picking through various pieces of garbage—a banana peel, egg shells, and wilted lettuce—and suddenly looked up, aware that he was being watched.

"Hello, sweetie," the teacher said to the raccoon, which scooted down the hillside and disappeared into the woods. The teacher returned her gaze to the water. Michael looked too, the sun sparkling off the water was spectacular.

"Why are you here, Michael?" the teacher asked.

"Well, to heal a little, I guess," was the first thing Michael thought to say. He surprised himself with his answer, because he had always been purposeful in everything he did. So he thought a bit longer, then answered the question again.

"I needed some time and space to figure out where and when my life got off-track. Things just don't seem to be working out for me right now. Or, I guess it would be more accurate to say that the way I am living right now makes things not work out for me. There is always this feeling of discontent. It's like a little voice in my head constantly judging me, telling me how much I am screwing everything up and how much I'm screwing up the lives of the people around me. So I think that the reason I am here is to discover something or to learn something, some new process or way to live so I can be better, better for me and for everyone around me."

Michael was satisfied this time with the way he answered the question, but then he leaned forward and said something else that took him by surprise: "But honestly, I have done so many things wrong in my life that I am not sure that I deserve any better." Then, he sat back and let out a big sigh.

"Michael," the teacher said directly, "this is not a place to gain things, this is a place to lose things." Three black crows circled through the trees and landed on the ground below the patio. They began to caw loudly, bobbing their heads up and down, and hopped about the grass looking to stir up bugs. As Michael watched them, the teacher began to speak again.

"You are a child of God, a creation of an omnipotent presence of love. You are worthy of joy, of health, of happiness, and of love. By grace, you are worthy of miracles in your life. Stop believing you deserve to suffer: God has a different plan for you."

"I guess I believe that," Michael said, "but it just seems like I am losing everything," then Michael looked down. "Nothing seems to be changing for the better in my life."

"Michael, your life will begin to change on the basis of new experience, not because you 'believe' something. Do the technique Michael, turn your attention. I am a testament that it works," she said, then paused, watching him for a moment before continuing. "As you shed layers, it can look and feel like loss," she paused again, thinking of a way to explain it to Michael. "If you have always believed that a fancy car would make you happy, and that having that car would make you feel successful, then losing that car will cause you suffering. But losing the belief that you need a fancy car is freeing."

"And to take it further, Michael, to a deeper-rooted belief, let go of the belief that you need someone to love you, and you will experience freedom."

"How do you know that I want to feel loved?"

"It's not uncommon, Michael."

"But I feel lonely already, and this searching for what is real, for truth, seems to be a pretty lonesome path," Michael was amazed at how open he was in sharing what was inside of him and what was coming out. The teacher looked upon Michael with compassion.

"It's the karma of loneliness. When you make things about you, there is only you. And when there is only you, you are lonely. Narcissism, the human condition. Do the technique Michael, the teaching cuts through all of that. The mind thinks the endgame will be awful, it conceives of a dark blank, a nothing, but it's freedom. The process of clearing out the vehicle can look like losing, like suffering, but it is necessary. When the gift is seen as mine, there is something in the way, ruthless choosing for God takes care of it! We find ourselves asking 'Who am I without these things, without these thoughts, without these beliefs?' But you see none of these things were you or yours in the first place, and they will come back. The strong identification with what we think is essential gets in the way, so the nonessential is revealed. What feels necessary to our survival can look different. As things fall away, it may not look like a blessing: Life will bring you what you need, not what you want. But in the end, what you want will be what you need. We are taken care of." At that moment, the crows began cawing loudly again, taking flight one after the other over the bluff, catching a warm updraft from the warming cliff, gliding easily upward, disturbing the flight of a passing egret, who screeched his displeasure at the crows.

"How does this teaching work? How does it transform?" Michael asked.

"As you touch the silence within you, it begins to erode the self-destructive habits of mind. The internal tapes, that constantly talking voice of self-judgment that you speak of, becomes replaced by a constant appreciation of the outside world. It is literally seen as the divine world."

"Sounds wonderful," Michael said, "But it also sounds lonely."

"Some paths in life we have to walk alone. The path to discover truth is one of these paths, for truly it is a path to one's own heart and no one can accompany you. However, once established in truth, you discover the place of pure love within your own heart, and once there, you discover you already have everything and everyone. There are no longer thoughts of need, nor thoughts of loneliness." The teacher stopped talking and closed her eyes. Michael closed his eyes as well and soon his awareness was deep into very subtle places of his mind. So deep was his meditation that he did not notice the teacher get up and walk into the house. After a long while he opened his eyes, noticed he was alone, then calmly looked out across the lake.

Michael was feeling a deep sense of peace, and he closed his eyes once again and meditated. He spent the next remaining days of the retreat with his eyes closed as much as he could. His deep feeling of peace grew, and he felt clearer than he had in a very long time that everything was okay, and would continue being okay. Soon, it was the last evening meal and the last talk with the teacher. Michael was packing to prepare to leave the retreat the next morning when he heard his phone buzz, signaling that a text message had arrived.

"That's strange," Michael said quietly to himself. "I have not had a cell signal my entire time here." He reached for his cell phone and read the text, which was from Lila.

"I hope your retreat is going well. I don't know why but for some reason I cannot stop thinking about you while you are there. I look forward to seeing your sweet, smiling face." He read the text again, and it made his heart beat. "Hmmm," was all he said aloud, but now he could not stop thinking about Lila. He heard the large bell and realized that he was late for dinner, so he tossed the phone into his duffel bag and hurried to the main house. He swung the door open and hopped into the kitchen, catching the eye of one of the women at the retreat.

"I can see a lot of heart in your eyes," she said to him, and he just smiled. He filled a plate with various foods. He was beginning to like the simple cuisine, and it was compatible with his digestive system and conducive to an equanimous disposition. He found the last remaining open space at the table and sat down, realizing that several folks were already engaged in a discussion.

"God," a man began, "Our 'Source,' 'The Source,' is the space within which things exist, it is the essence out of which everything is created—your thoughts, your feelings, this chair, this table, this cup." The man held up his green mug, making Michael giggle a little picturing the cup as God.

"Are you talking about the 'void,' the 'nothing'?" a woman asked. The teacher listened, only barely amused. Michael looked at her, and she immediately sensed his glance, turned, and looked directly into his eyes and smiled. Michael looked at her stark white hair and her crystal-blue eyes. He felt that there was something deep in her gaze, something profound—an invitation of sorts—but he knew she always behaved as though all was ordinary, even when her effect on others was so extraordinary. He heard the others speak of things the teacher had said or done, that she had healed them or known what they were thinking. Sometimes they would bring it up in the meeting and she would just shrug and sometimes laugh. Michael looked at her now and he wondered about her.

"This is not a void as many have imagined," the man answered emphatically, "It is not empty space, and it is not nothingness. It is the Presence, it is God, a state of fullness, of Infinite potential energy out of which everything is created, *Everything*," he emphasized. "*Everything* comes from *this* and exists only because of *this*. Nothing exists nor could exist outside of *this*, *everything* is composed of *this* and its essence is continually flowing in and out of existence." The man went on and on enthusiastically as Michael listened to him calmly, watching him wave his arms while he spoke.

Michael watched his own thoughts with his eyes open, and as he noticed a thought he would choose a thought of gratitude. He ate food and drank water, but he felt no compulsion to speak. Soon the meal concluded, and everyone pitched in to clean up before gathering in the big room. People began to sit, making themselves comfortable, some with a blanket or a spread across their legs, some sitting up, and others lying down on the floor. The teacher sat down and everyone closed their eyes and meditated together for nearly an hour. Eventually, the teacher opened her eyes and people began to ask her questions and share their observations of the retreat.

"I feel so peaceful," one woman began, "I do not want the retreat to end! My life out there is so crazy and chaotic." There were other similar sentiments shared. Michael sat back in his chair, looked at the ceiling, and listened.

"There can be 'contrast' when we return to our daily lives, a re-entry so to speak. But if you do the teaching *ruthlessly* all will be fine," affirmed the teacher.

"Why do we have to go back? Maybe I could just stay," said a young woman sitting at the back who was normally quiet.

"You could stay: Many do come here to stay. But ask yourself why you want to stay. For many, this begins as a running away from pain. On this pathway they learn to say, 'I am not my body, I am not my mind, I am not my personality, I am not this or that, they close their eyes and plunge into this teaching, finding comfort and relief from their stress. The path becomes transcendental as they experience openness and expansiveness, and it appears that they have found the freedom they have sought. But then they wake up one morning back in their body and it hurts. However, while they are still in the life situation that they ran away from, they *are* different. There is with them in the midst of their life's drama a certain freedom, a different kind of freedom than they imagined.

The Christ walk is our model. God incarnate as man, walking the earth, feeling pain and engaged in drama…yet walking the divine walk of God. God incarnate to show us how. So we come back from this transcendental state, back into our bodies and back into our life situation to begin our life journey of living our life, but with the ability to turn our gaze to our source, to choose God. Our response to life becomes a response of praise, of gratitude and of love."

As Michael was listening and doing the teaching, a thought entered his mind, *I need to go to New York and face Jo's husband.* The thought shocked him and he immediately disposed of it, but the more he resisted it, the more it persisted. He sat up and refocused intently on what the teacher was saying.

"'Everything is okay,' becomes the ground rule to live by, and there is never a reason to hold back. By meditating to transcend, we are still trying to control things, to make them the way we want them to be, to escape all pain. Try instead to simply do the technique and let whatever happens, happen." The teacher looked around the room as she stopped talking. Michael was beginning to shake; it had started as a small quiver and grown quickly. His entire life, he had run from one thing to another, away from one thing to another, and the thought of making a stand was as disturbing as it was foreign.

"Awaken to your heart's telling story. Absolute honesty opens the heart. Any place we do not allow ourselves to experience within ourselves is a closing down. It takes grit and honesty to let all your false beliefs fall away. Do not worry, though, for if you do not have true grit, or if you do not want to be honest with yourself, it won't matter. Once the process has started, it will find its end naturally, so if we cling tightly to our cherished beliefs, they will be ripped from us."

In conclusion, the teacher smiled, almost laughing, then she closed her eyes and everyone else followed her lead. As the evening wore on, people began to rise and find their way to their beds. Eventually, Michael did as well, and he kept doing the teaching as he drifted off into a deep and restful sleep.

Michael awoke early the next morning; he had never been good with goodbyes, so he liked to wake before everyone else and be on his way. He put his duffel bag into the passenger seat of the truck, and as he closed the door the teacher was standing there. She gave him a warm, heart-to-heart hug.

"Thank you," he heard himself say, then she gave him a warning.

"Michael, be careful. This is the stage where many fall in love, then go traveling with that person; it is a way to avoid themselves." *What a strange warning,* he thought. He gave her another hug, then looked into her eyes and hopped into the truck and was on his way. He soon reached the bridge over the lake, where there was a beautiful morning mist rising from the water. The sun brightened everything and Michael felt nothing but joy. He rolled down the truck window and leaned out his head to feel the rush of air through his hair, feeling not a care in the world.

Falling Again

Summer 2008

Michael arrived at work early, like he usually did on Mondays. It had been a long weekend and he wanted to plan out the week's work. Most of the cubes were still dark, with only a few scattered lights here and there, and the smell of fresh coffee brewing permeating the air. For so long, this place had seemed toxic to Michael, but today its familiarity seemed warm and comforting. *Perhaps it's a side effect of all the meditation*, Michael thought, *but everything and everyone is so pleasant.* This feeling was about to change, but he did not see the coming blow. He sat at his desk and pulled out his computer, and while he was still turning it on, his desk phone rang. It was unusual for it to ring so early, so he sat staring at it for a moment before answering.

"Hello?"

"Michael, it's Robert." Michael's boss said with an ominous tone. "I saw you come in. Will you come down to my office? I need to talk to you."

Then he hung up, not giving Michael any chance to ask any questions. So Michael stood and began to walk across the floor to the far corner, where Robert's office was. He began to think of all the things that could be wrong; it did not take great instincts or great insight to know that something was up, but he could not think what. He ran a few conversations and the latest projects through his mind, but couldn't come up with any red flags. *No, nothing wrong, everything has been progressing pretty well*, he thought to himself.

He knocked on his boss's door, and could see through the etched glass that Robert was sitting immobile in his chair.

"Come in," Robert said softly. Robert looked pale, and while he was looking out the thin sliver of a window he did not seem to be focused on anything. Michael sat in one of the chairs in front of the desk. Robert turned to face him, forcing a smile.

"Michael, you have been one of my best guys…"

Well, that was an ominous start, Michael thought.

"Robert, just tell me what's going on."

"We are being shut down," Robert answered, his voice cracking a bit.

"What do you mean, we are being shut down?" Michael asked.

"The whole department, the word came down that HR will be here soon—everyone is in the R.I.F.—everyone."

He stopped talking and looked out the window again.

"That's not possible! How can that be?" Michael asked in disbelief.

"Michael, where the hell have you been? You're smart…you're intelligent, but you have had your head up your ass. You had to know that this was coming," Robert's response was agitated.

"How could I know this was coming?" Michael asked, but he was not genuinely at a loss. Michael was smart and he could see the mortgage disaster coming, he could see the growing defaults and what was behind it. But somehow he never thought consciously that what was coming would overrun him, but just now, though he denied it, he had felt it all along in his stomach. Robert turned toward Michael and sat up straighter in his chair.

"Let me see if I can think of anything. Oh yes, Labor Day 2008," Robert began, "It was a Sunday, Fed takes over Freddie and Fannie… that's more than a little ominous; the government taking over anything can never be good. So let's see, was there anything else? Oh yeah, September 15, I believe, Lehman

Brothers declares bankruptcy, sending a shock wave of fear through everyone in banking…except you, Michael. You come in to do your thing, then split to God knows where."

Robert stood, walked to the window and looked out. "I don't fault you for not paying attention, Michael. I suppose I am just jealous. I am sure you will find something else—you are very talented—but this place is all I know…"

He let out a big sigh, then sat back down, folded his hands, and dropped the sarcasm, continuing in a very professional tone: "The Federal Government strong-armed us to take over a large investment firm, then deemed the insurance companies too big to fail and gave them $120 billion, maybe more for all we know. The news media blasts the message that the country's banking system is going down the tubes and *fear* alone degrades stability, so there is a run on banks. People rush to pull out hundreds of millions of dollars in cash from their bank accounts. Big trees fall, stalwart banks fail…WAMU, Wachovia, and suddenly the entire economy is on the brink of collapse."

Robert paused to take a deep breath, and Michael raised his eyebrows in response. Robert sat back into the chair and lowered his voice, "Then the Dow begins to fall from 14,500 to 11,000. The TARP money allocated to hold things together begins to look like it is failing; the rescue just does not look to be enough. The Dow drops another 800 points, one trillion dollars in losses, Michael. People begin to hoard food, water, and bullets, for God's sake."

Robert looked out the window then back at Michael. "Two hundred and twenty-five lenders go broke, then the Dow drops another 1,800 points in one week. Twenty-one percent of America's wealth disappears like that," Robert snapped his fingers. He walked to the whiteboard, picked up a marker, and began to write as he spoke.

"So, $13.5 trillion in Dow losses and $8.6 trillion in home equity evaporates." He wrote the 8.6 directly under the 13.5 like a math equation, then added them together, writing $22.1 trillion, underlining the sum with double lines. He gently put the marker down and sat on his desk facing Michael. "Over $20 trillion in losses, Michael, and mortgage is at ground zero, the epicenter of disaster." Robert folded his arms. Clearly done talking, he stood and walked back to the window.

Two times in the same life, Michael thought to himself, but even though his boss had used the words "ground zero," this in no way felt as bad to Michael. Then he stood and walked out of the office to the elevator; he did not want to wait for HR. He could just imagine the way they would look at him and talk to him. He was not willing to expose himself to someone younger, talking to him like they knew what he was going through—how could anyone ever know what he was going through, *Hell, I don't know what I'm going through?*

So he took a reading of his own state of mind. *I think I feel just fine*, he thought. People were beginning to come into the office and there was loud whispering; the word was already out and the air smelled like fear. Michael went down the elevator and walked out of the building and up the street. His job had never seemed important to him, but thoughts of what to do were running wild through his mind; the hushed panic in the office had been contagious. The farther he walked from the building, the better he felt.

I think I'll go find Doc, he thought to himself, but he knew that he really wanted to find Lila: Her text was still on his mind.

Michael reached his place, went inside, and started to pack a bag. *Funny, I just can't think of anything I really need.* He sat on a chair in his den and closed his eyes; he did the technique and everything was soft and warm. He felt like he should be panicked but realized he was not. He went outside and looked at his motorcycle, then thought, *I think I'll take the truck.*

Michael's truck reminded him of himself. It was dusty, dirty, and dented. He had clocked more than 250,000 miles. The seams of the seat were frayed, coming apart in places. Michael's sense of self—who he believed himself to be—was worn and weary from the miles and the years, his career was in the shitter, and his marriage was, well, he could not even think of a word to describe it. It was done, he was sure, but he was holding on for reasons he did not fully understand. He was sure that Deborah was no longer in love with him, but there were kids, and there was family, and there was the one word he always feared but always obeyed: obligation. Men forever were tagged with the idea that they could not commit, when for most, the opposite was true. They could never let go of anything.

Michael's outer world was in various states of disrepair. And lately, his only refuge had been found in the tiny but growing state of peace within him. However, it lay tangled up in the state of despair that grew within him at the same time. The despair was entirely related to ideas of who he thought he was, where he thought he was supposed to be, and what he was supposed to have accomplished. It all was measured by how much money he was "supposed" to be making, but to Michael, this money was necessary to pay for things he no longer believed in. The outward persona of Michael Tantalus was deteriorating, while at the same time, deep within him, he was aware that there was a place, a source of something growing.

Michael's fear of *not measuring up* was beginning to succumb to his exhaustion. It was like the inevitable ocean of "everything" was coming in like the tide, soothing his struggle. And as he took inventory of how he felt, there was sadness for sure, but he also felt love. And without a notion of its true source, he attributed it to Lila.

Michael turned into the parking lot of Curly's. The sound of crunching gravel under the tires of the truck brought back a warm summer memory of driving at night near the lake, his girlfriend sitting close to him. He smiled, then gave up the memory and climbed out of the truck to walk up the steps of the bar. He stood just inside the door and looked down the length of the bar.

"He's not here."

It was Lila. Michael looked at her and smiled. A feeling washed over him, different from the feeling he had had as a boy in love. The feeling was so strong that he tried to put words on it as he looked at her, but everything sounded corny or inadequate: It was as if part of the earth had fallen away, and he now was partially suspended in nothing. It was like part of him was gone, not some essential part; more like something he had been carrying had been cast away. It was such a strange but pleasant feeling that he lingered in the moment.

"Well, aren't you going to say hi or something?" Lila smiled at him.

"Hi or something," he said to her, smiling back.

"What are you smiling about? You look like the bird that ate the canary."

"I lost my job today," was all he could think to say.

Lila started to shake her head, saying, "It's always the people the bank needs that they get rid of."

"Well, apparently everything was crashing around me and I wasn't paying attention," he said.

Lila looked at him for a minute. "Why don't you sit down, and I'll bring you a drink."

"You know, I really don't feel like a drink, I feel like driving somewhere instead," he said, then flashed her a smile.

"Are you running away because you lost your job?" she asked.

"I guess it sounds like I am running away, but I feel like I just want to go see some things...you know, travel around for a bit," he shrugged.

Lila looked at him for a minute trying to read him.

"Where would you go?" she asked.

"Well, let's see, I've been to D.C. many times for business, but I've never really toured...I think I want to see the White House."

"What about the Lincoln Memorial?" she asked.

"Well, of course—all the memorials. How many are there?"

Lila considered the question with a thoughtful expression and pursed lips, then said, "I don't know?"

"Have you ever been to D.C.?" he asked her.

"No, I never have been to the nation's capital."

"Come with me," he said with abandon but no desperation, and it caught her by surprise.

"Are you asking me to leave my job here and go to Washington, D.C., with you to look at monuments?"

She feigned a lack of interest, but truly she was thrilled.

"No." Michael watched to see her reaction, and seeing none he continued, "I am asking you to leave your job here and go to Washington, D.C., with me to look at memorials." He was on the verge of laughing.

"Okay, when do you want to leave?" she felt powerless, and it was marvelous.

"When does your shift end?"

"Whenever I want it to," she said, suddenly back in control. "You know this is a no-sex junket," she added sternly, trying to mask her complete complicity with anything he might ask of her.

"Of course: hotels with two beds, I promise," he smiled again.

Shortly thereafter Lila began closing down Curly's for the night. There were only a few patrons and most everyone was ready to leave so she offered friendly encouragement to get them all out the door. Michael followed her to her cabin, sitting just inside the door fidgeting with his hands, resisting the temptation to wander about her house. He could hear her on the telephone, presumably making arrangements to be gone.

Lila packed quickly and was still on her cell phone as she came into her den. She looked at Michael as she spoke.

"It is just a friend trip—stop worrying," she reassured someone on the other line, perhaps her boyfriend. She began to get irritated with him and showed it in her short, curt replies. "No," she answered, then "Yes, no, no okay," Then she hung up and smiled at Michael. He had the strange thought that one day, if he were on the other line, wondering what Lila was doing, getting short answers to questions, he would know that she was moving on to someone else. It was a strange thought and he shook it from his mind.

"Wow, what a truck! I love trucks—I grew up driving a truck," Lila said, throwing her bags into the back as she continued talking rapidly without ever pausing for a reply. She climbed into the truck and smiled. She was having thoughts about what she was doing and why she was traveling with this man she barely knew. And though her mind was busy and she initially had been very chatty, the drive began quietly. The truck was old, and the gearshift was on the steering wheel column. Lila watched Michael's hands as he shifted the gears, noticing that the winding road kept Michael's hands busy on the steering wheel. Again she thought about what she was doing. She was so comfortable with this man, as if she had known and loved him for a very long time. She tried to muster some sort of a defense, but finally she let herself relax into the drive.

Michael felt good. He knew he should be bothered by having no job, and he wondered what Lila was expecting from this trip. But he was feeling a moment of clarity. His awareness had shifted in some way since the retreat. His experience of who or what he was had changed; Michael could not say what was different, but he felt no compunction to force his mind down typical lines of thinking, so he simply enjoyed Lila's company. He looked at her in the seat next to him, fidgeting with the truck radio.

"No disc player," she said out loud but more for herself. Then she began to sift through one of the bags she had brought and pulled out what looked like a cassette with a wire attached to it. She put the device into the cassette player in the truck, then connected the wire to an MP3 player, and the old truck was filled with music.

"Voilá," she said, pleased with herself. Michael smiled back at her; just having her in the seat next to him made him feel stronger, more self-assured, and peaceful. Song after song, mile after mile, Michael and Lila connected through music. Neither one noticed, but each song had a purpose—one song for general mood, the next for the lyrics that became a discussion between them—and each song was a catalyst, accelerating and deepening their connection. An easygoing pop song was followed by rap music, then alternative rock, then something obscure, then something from Michael's past:

an old country song that made him feel warm and connected to everything. The music was not a sharing of something new, but a replay of some past, reminding Michael and Lila both of who they were as individuals and who they were together.

"Gadsden," Lila said breaking the momentary silence.

"Gadsden, Alabama?" Michael asked.

"Yes, that's where I grew up…population 36,000 I think, but it felt smaller. My father was a local hero, a football coach, so everyone knew him, and we were like celebrities. So how many?"

"How many what?" Michael asked.

"How many people were in the town where you grew up?"

"One thousand, two hundred and six." He looked at her, and they both laughed.

"I knew you were a little red," she said, "So where? What town?"

"Seronia, Texas," he answered, "I played football, cut hay in the summer, and dreamed of one day owning more than ten cows."

"That's quite a dream," she said. "Ten whole cows. A bit ambitious, don't you think?"

"Well, I've always been a big dreamer," he said with a grin.

"And football… so you are a big dreamer and an athlete," she said mockingly, then added, "…dangerous combination."

"Well, I was a little small and a little awkward, but they needed one more to make eleven to have a team, so I was conscripted. Coach liked me, though. He used to say, 'Tantalus, if you had a little ass, you'd be dangerous.'" Michael laughed at his own memory.

"So, you like football?" he asked Lila.

"No, not particularly," she said. Lila asked question after question. She was still trying to reconcile how good it felt to be with Michael with how little she knew about him.

After a while she just played music as they made their way northward towards Washington, D.C. Michael had one hand on the wheel and looked relaxed. Lila, as was customary, let what was on her mind spill out of her mouth.

"So, why did you get fired?" she asked. Michael sat up straighter in the seat and cleared his throat as if he were about to give a speech.

"Our entire department was let go," he said dispassionately. "I am in the mortgage business and apparently it is falling apart. I guess I knew it was falling apart, but as I watched it happen, somehow I did not connect that it was my world that was crumbling."

"How many people?" she asked.

"Well, they came in the morning and let go some 2,000 or so unsuspecting, hard-working people. That sounds like a lot, but I have heard numbers of upwards of 100,000 people from the mortgage business have either left the industry or lost their jobs…it's crazy."

"So they came in one morning and let Seronia go," she said casually, but it struck Michael like a train.

"I never looked at it like that before: poor Aunt Melba and Uncle Harlan," Michael replied in jest, trying to keep his mood light, but Lila kept a serious tone.

"That's the problem of big corporations. To them, 2,000 people are just a little overhead. They need to cut back on expenses, so they cut back on 2,000 people here and 3,000 there… but to you and me and everyone else, it's Aunt Melba and Uncle Harlan."

Lila paused until Michael looked at her.

"Maybe you're right," he said, but he was met with a stern, accusing glare. "I mean, yes! Yes, you are right, definitely right, most blatantly, obviously right."

He was prepared to keep going, but she stopped him.

"That's far enough," she smiled. Then, after a moment of silence, she asked, "Do you really have an Aunt Melba and Uncle Harlan?"

Michael smiled, then said, "Yes, I really do. You should meet them sometime."

"I'd like that," Lila responded. Then, suddenly feeling their deepening intimacy, she looked down at her music player and searched for a song. Finding it, she hit the play button and they drifted together accompanied by a soft, winding song as the scenery rushed by. After a while, Lila asked another question.

"Why do you drink so much?" She watched him, waiting for an answer, but none come immediately.

"Well, I am not sure," he said, hesitantly, then glanced at her and continued driving. But she was not going to let him avoid the question like he had before when she asked about his marriage.

"Do you like to drink? Does it make you feel good?" She was trying to draw him out. He knew he could not put her off, and that was something he liked about her. He felt he could be honest with her and she would never use his own words against him. So many people asked you questions, and experience had taught Michael that if you are too honest, they store away the information and one day will use it against you.

"I used to drink to have fun. It did, at one time, make me feel better," he said to her.

"Used to?" she was looking at his hands while she asked him questions. He was gesturing with one hand while he talked to her, and he noticed that she followed the moving hand with her eyes, so he moved it back and forth more. She followed it with her eyes for only a moment, then looked right at him.

"Very funny," she said.

"You like hands?" he asked her.

"Don't change the subject," she commanded, and he smiled.

"It's strange now. Starting, I think, when I began to meditate or whatever they called it at the retreat. But I swear I can feel the alcohol in my system, like some residue of poison. And that's not all. Now when I drink, I feel like I am letting myself down somehow." He looked her, then added, "That must sound strange to you."

"No, not at all, it makes complete sense. And yes," she said the word very quietly.

"Yes, what?" he asked her.

"Yes, I like hands," she said curtly, then continued, "…So you feel the residue of alcohol in your system: poison, you call it. And then you judge yourself. You are *letting yourself down*, you said. You just expressed several thoughts, several concepts, and several beliefs in one sentence. First, let's take the concept of the word 'poison.' Poison can come in many forms. Sometimes we eat or drink something that damages the body. But sometimes we consume something into our mind, perhaps the impact of seeing something—a trauma, like in a war, a car accident, the local news, or maybe watching a horror movie that goes too far, or maybe a terrorist attack."

She paused for a moment. The last words she said had shaken Michael, and he felt that she was somehow sensing him. He was sure that he had not said anything to her about New York. *Hell*, he thought, *I don't even think about it myself*, but that was not true; he often thought of it. And just now the image of Jo appeared in his mind, and he realized he wanted to tell Lila all about it. But he was quiet and kept listening to her instead. She was different than any woman he had ever been with before. There was something about her; she seemed to look into him. She seemed to know things about him. She continued talking.

"Sometimes it is just the spoken word. Something said a little too quickly to a child or maybe the rejection of a lover. A criticism from someone we respect, or an insult from an angry stranger. The poison in this case is a thought we dwell on, carry inside of ourselves. Telling ourselves that something is wrong when in truth we are just fine, but the thought continues like drinking a mortal potion."

"I saw a bumper sticker one time that said, 'resentment is like drinking poison and waiting for the other person to die,'" he smiled as he said it, trying to lighten the mood. Lila smiled, but she did not laugh. She continued as though he had not interrupted her.

"…but the most destructive poison is a subconscious thought that plays over and over, an unquestioned negative belief about ourselves, a belief like, *I am not worthy or I am not loveable*. So there are my thoughts on poison." She looked down at her music player and selected a different song.

"So now," she continued, "Let's discuss your thought— or should I say *judgment*—that you let yourself down."

Her voice was soothing and matched the music. *I would be content to just listen to the sound of her voice even if she spoke a different language*, Michael thought to himself. Something about her cadence felt pleasant to him, like a mother's voice to an infant who doesn't understand any words but knows instinctively and completely what the tone is conveying: love. Lila was unaware of how her voice washed over and affected Michael.

"The deadening effect of alcohol, as with so many other things both physical and mental that relax a person who is in a perpetual state of high agitation—or better said, living with constant anxiety— is such that the person experiences the alcohol as soothing, almost a gift of God that eases the pain of living. But as a person begins to consciously advance, their vibration rate, for lack of better words, begins to rise. What at one time soothed their agitation, now acts in the opposite direction. Alcohol indeed will lower the vibration of a consciously advancing person, raising the level of agitation. Perhaps alcohol does not serve you anymore."

Lila changed the music again, then continued, "Which brings me to another point. In between your words, it feels as if you have judged alcohol as bad. So, is alcohol bad? Is chemo bad, is the poison given to a dog with heartworms bad? You see, the element is the element, neutral in a world of judgment. There is a saying in yoga that even non-practice is practice: feeling tight, sore muscles is a helpful way we know we are growing. So the dissonance you feel is not that you let yourself down, but that you—in your current state—value the choice of a higher vibrational state, a state closer to God. You are choosing God over the choice of a lower vibrational state away from God. What a wonderful realization: *You love God*."

Then Lila went quiet. Michael was not completely sure what she had said, but he knew he liked to listen to her talk. He repeated to himself in his mind the last thing she said, *I love God.*

Once again Michael's attention returned to the road. He looked at the passing signs to see where they were. He saw a mileage sign with Washington, D.C. on it and turned to Lila and said, "Not too much further."

They drove in the ease of pleasant music and each other's company. As the highway spilled into Washington, they passed the Pentagon. It was on Michael's side and he looked at it as they passed. Conceptually, Michael should have known that he would pass the Pentagon, but as he passed it, it caught him by surprise, much as it had when he fled New York. He had not seen it since he left New York back in 2001. When Michael last looked upon the Pentagon, it was smoking. And now, in the near darkness, it looked peaceful. *Peaceful,* he ran the word through his mind several times. There was something in the word, and then it hit him: He himself felt peaceful, he was perceiving things for how he felt inside.

Lila noticed a mood change in Michael; it was not something he said, for he was quiet. And there was nothing in his body language to suggest anything different. She simply felt what he was feeling, but she did not know what to say, so she said nothing. They crossed the bridge into D.C., and Michael drove toward the National Mall. He turned on Constitution Avenue and began to circle the towering marble obelisk of the Washington Monument.

"Stop the truck," said Lila. Michael pulled close to the curb and slowed to a stop. Lila opened the door and hopped out without bothering to put on her shoes. She ran joyfully and danced across the soft grass like a jubilant child. Arms extended, she twirled, and her long hair flowed through the air. Michael abandoned the truck and followed her. He caught her and grabbed her hand; they twirled around each other and laughed. They slowed to a soft spin and were looking into each other's eyes. Michael wondered if he had ever looked into anyone's eyes as much as hers. She pulled her hand free and began to run again. Michael followed, and there was a sudden, bright flash across the sky, followed a few seconds later by a loud clap of thunder. They both froze for a moment, then laughed, turned, and ran back to the truck. Once inside, they laughed and laughed. Michael drove slowly until he found a place to park, then they ventured out once again to walk along the Mall.

The coming storm held back but the air was suddenly cooler and there was a breeze that smelled of rain. They strolled side by side easily without talking, ignoring the lightning that flashed across the sky every few minutes. They slowly made their way to the Vietnam Veterans Memorial where the names of the missing and the dead were inscribed upon the V-shaped granite. As they walked, the memorial arched up and the etched names increased in number. It was dark, but there were several people standing, touching the Memorial— some touching a specific name—quiet in contemplation, some with silent tears.

Michael ran his fingers across the names on the wall. He was filled with a feeling of respect and reverence. He hated violence, but there was something here that was different. Violence was different from what was left behind; what remained was *holy*. *Holy* was the word that came to Michael's mind, but he was sure that it was the wrong word, so he tried unsuccessfully to put a different word on what he was feeling. It was like he was trying to remember people he never knew. In a way, it was like New York. He wondered how each person whose name was on the wall met their end, what they were thinking as death came. He resisted thinking about that day, but thoughts came of their own accord, more now than before. He wondered if the retreat had opened him, making it harder for him to keep his thoughts inside. He wondered if he had just relaxed, and he considered that relaxing and letting things go were not good.

Keep it together, he told himself. Then came another memory— a moment of utter panic, strong and present. Things seemed extremely loud and clear in the memory, but he could not remember what he was thinking: He had grabbed his brief case and everything fell out, then he ran. He searched the memory again for what he had been thinking, but there was nothing—even though he could clearly recall his awareness at the time. *Perhaps I was not thinking consciously about anything at all*, Michael concluded. He pulled his hand away from the wall, and he was back at the Vietnam Memorial. He looked around for Lila, who had wandered farther away; when he finally spotted her, he walked swiftly to catch up with her.

Lila was already on her way to the Korean War Memorial. The sky flashed again and the thunder rolled gently afterward. Again they walked side by side with a naturalness that felt like they belonged together. They were just getting to know one another, but it felt as though they were seeing each other again after spending lifetimes together. They walked into the memorial and beheld large statues of soldiers, as if on patrol—the mist and the darkness made them feel the tension of walking in a war zone. And throughout the entire walk, Michael and Lila remained silent but ever aware of the other, moving and experiencing as one.

After making their way through the Lincoln and Jefferson monuments, Lila and Michael considered where to go next. Lila was trying to control what she was feeling for Michael. Nothing was making any sense to her, but she knew she felt completely content so she stopped trying to figure everything out and again relaxed. It felt good to be standing next to Michael so she stepped just a little closer to him.

"Do tell, are we going to the memorial for Franklin Delano Roosevelt?"

"You have heard of him?"

"Everyone knows FDR," she said, looking down her nose at Michael, then putting her nose up with an air of mock snobbery. They drove down Ohio Drive, again finding a nearly empty parking lot. Inside, the memorial was divided into four outdoor galleries, one for each of Roosevelt's terms in office. They walked through the maze-like spaces, passing various sculptures depicting him.

"Funny," Lila began, "Someone decided what was important in his life, and this is what we see, but it is likely not what was most important to him."

"What do you mean?" Michael asked.

"He was in love," she said.

"You mean with Eleanor?" Michael asked.

"Well, I would guess that, at one time, he was in love with Eleanor, but somewhere along the way, he fell in love with someone else. Her name was Lucy. She was the love of his life. Eleanor found out about it, and there was a family meeting. Because it would ruin his political career, he left Lucy. Franklin made a bargain with Eleanor, but it was clear through letters that he never stopped loving Lucy. And they say that Eleanor never forgave him and that they never slept in the same room after that.

"When Franklin learned that Lucy had married another man, the shock was almost more than he could bear. I think about it sometimes: What must it have been like for him and for her?

"But years later, after Lucy's husband passed away, they were together again. She was with him at the end when he died. And too, I think of Eleanor. The affair crushed her, but also, it may be part of what made her the woman she was. These things, so relevant to Franklin and who he was, but kept in the shadows...I think of these things, sometimes."

Going silent, Lila looked at Michael, then down at his hand with the ring on his finger, but she showed no emotion. The sky flashed lightning, so they turned and hurried to the truck.

"I'm hungry," said Lila.

"Me, too. Let's drive to the hotel and check in, then we can get something to eat. I know a place close to the hotel." They checked into their room—with two beds as Michael had promised—dropped their bags, and hurried back down to the street a few blocks to an Italian restaurant, where they were greeted warmly when they entered.

"Hello, Mr. Tantalus, it has been a long time!"

The maître d' recognized Michael and shook his hand vigorously. "We have your reserved table ready, Mr. Tantalus... please follow me," he said, walking them past a dozen or more people waiting to be seated. As they walked to a table near a window, the maître d' was making rapid arm motions, signaling other staff, while a waiter met them at the table, already pouring water as the maître d' pulled out the chair for Lila.

A different waiter brought bread, while the sommelier approached Michael. "Nice to see you again, sir. Wine tonight?" he asked.

"Yes, red, and please choose something nice for the lady," Michael responded, smiling at Lila. The sommelier looked at Lila and smiled, too, twisting his mustache pensively.

"Yes, of course, something nice for the lady."

"What was all that?" Lila asked. "Did you call ahead and make reservations?" Michael began to laugh.

"No, I am afraid not. I really didn't think they would remember me, it's been such long time since I was here. I was surprised to see that the same maître d' and sommelier were still here."

At that moment, more waiters came to the table and began to scoop up all the tableware, which were quickly replaced by finer china, crystal glasses, and expensive-looking silver. Michael watched the brigade of waiters bustling about the table, and his smile was so big, it was clear he was about to laugh.

"What's so funny?" Lila asked Michael. "If you are trying to impress me, I think you went a little over the top. I am really not the kind of girl that needs all this…"

Michael interrupted her. "Well, I am afraid that this is going to be a very expensive meal," he said, still smiling from ear to ear.

"What are you talking about, Michael?" she asked.

When the waiters left the table, he leaned over to whisper to her: "The last time I was here, I was a little drunk and I messed up the tip a little."

"Messed it up how?" she said the words slowly.

"I tipped them $1,500."

"$1,500!" Lila said, too loudly, and Michael's eyes got big.

"$1,500 is more than a little messed up...what are you going to do?"

"I think I will use my credit card," he replied, then began to laugh as the sommelier brought the wine, cradling it like a baby. Michael had never heard of it before and he only imagined how expensive it was, but he nodded his head in approval. It was quickly opened and the cork handed to Michael as the sommelier puffed up his chest, then poured a small amount. Michael swished it around and smelled it, then tasted it, watching Lila the entire time.

"It will do," Michael said to the sommelier in a tone that Lila had never heard from him before.

"Very good, sir," he answered, then poured a glass for Lila and bowed slightly as he left the table.

"So what if I don't like wine?" Lila asked.

"Do you like wine?" Michael asked her.

"Why, yes, I do like wine," she answered, beginning to laugh. The evening was set, and they never saw a menu; the chef came out of the kitchen to explain what he was preparing for them, and it was all spectacular. At the end of the meal, Lila watched Michael intently as he signed the check without ever showing the slightest sign that the amount was unusually high. Michael stood and smiled, and as they walked out they were sent off with farewells from the entire staff.

Once outside, they both laughed so heartily they found it hard to breathe. They walked close to each other for several blocks in the wind, then turned into the stone patio of a lively cafe. There was music inside and lots of people, but the chairs on the patio were empty except one, which was occupied by a large woman who sat smoking and watching Michael and Lila as they approached. Michael looked at Lila and joy filled him; the flashing lights and neon signs blinked their colors across her face, and as he looked into her eyes, he could think of nothing he needed or wanted. Lila looked back at him, realizing dimly that she had never felt this intimate with anyone before, and there hadn't been any sex, just this growing closeness.

Michael leaned in to kiss her, but when his lips touched hers, there was no response. Lila just kept looking at him.

"Why did you do that?" she asked him.

"Because you are in love with me," he said to her.

"Eros is prone to delusion," she replied, her expression remaining the same.

"You think I am deluded?" he asked as he smiled. "Don't make me do the hand thing again!"

Lila tried unsuccessfully not to smile. Michael looked at her; she had just rebuffed his attempt to kiss her. Any other time he would have felt awkward and recoiled. But somehow it did not matter to him that she had resisted him. Michael loved her in a way he had never loved a woman before. *I love her, damn,* Michael suddenly realized with clarity, and he began to laugh at himself, puzzling Lila. She continued to hold the line—after all, she was in a serious relationship, and Michael was still wearing his wedding ring. She wondered why he did not take it off.

Michael let his new realization play around in his mind, thinking that he should be panicking, but aware that he was not. The usual questions like, *What will I do if she does not love me back?* had no weight in his mind. He loved her if she loved him back, and he loved her if she did not. The mere fact that he loved her was enough for him. He did not need her to love him back. He did not need anything from her. This was something new for Michael and for Lila too. *God, he makes me feel like I am okay. How does he do that? He just seems okay with me, and damn, that feels good,* Lila thought, but remained silent.

A live band began playing their first song, the drums pounding a happy beat, with the rest of the band soon joining in. Michael began to move his body to the beat and he could hear *Jesus* and *Buddha* in the lyrics. He began to hop and snap his fingers.

"Dance with me," he said to Lila, but she just looked at him, still trying not to smile.

"I'll dance with you, Romeo," said the woman who was still sitting on the patio smoking. She put out her cigarette, stood up, and came to take Michael by the hands. Michael began to kick his legs and spin with the woman.

"What kind of dance is that?" Lila called out to Michael.

"He is doing some kind of wild, Irish jig," the woman laughed. She let go of Michael's hands and twirled in her own dance. Michael began to kick his feet wildly and awkwardly across the uneven stones of the patio. Then, the large woman linked her bent arm with Michael's and twirled him into the café. People were sitting at tables, sipping drinks, and the twirling pair spun their way to an open space in front of the band. Michael kept kicking up his feet, and the people at the tables began to clap to the beat of the band and to the rhythm of Michael and the woman's Whirling Dervish-like dancing.

Suddenly, the woman let go of Michael and put her hands in the air, screaming,

"Woo-hoo!" Michael nearly fell into a nearby table as she let go of him. Lila followed the pair into the café, and watching this, she put her hand over her mouth and began to laugh. A woman at the table where Michael landed stood up, and she began to dance with Michael, while the woman Michael had been dancing with took another man by the arm and he began to dance, too. The festive mood engulfed the entire café, and one by one people got up and began to clap and dance. Michael felt one person, then another link his arm and twirl him about, sometimes a woman and sometimes a man, until nearly everyone in the entire room was clapping and dancing; even some of the waiters and waitresses had joined in. Michael felt a small hand grasp his and gently pull him to the side. It was Lila, and she led him out the back door and into the alley.

The alley was broad, clean, and well lit, but as they stepped outside the sky let loose and the rain came down in sheets. Michael put his hands into the air and tilted his head back, feeling the cool rush of the rain on his face. Lila's hand reached up around his neck and gently grasped the hair on the back of his head, guiding his face down to hers and his lips to hers, beginning a kiss that would last for what felt like eternity. The rain washed them both as they kissed and kissed. Lila's heart beat wildly, and she fell completely into Michael. His arms around her made her feel clean and whole, this was the happiest she ever remembered feeling.

Lila took Michael by the hand and led him toward their hotel, but their passion could not wait, so they stopped every ten or twenty feet to kiss. They were not far away and once inside, Lila pulled Michael's wet shirt up over his head. She let him struggle for a moment with his arms and head all tangled in the wet shirt, then laughed and pulled him free. Michael was overwhelmed by the sudden and instant intimacy, and his heart began to drum a primal beat. Lila's pupils relaxed and opened to take in every bit of light and every bit of Michael. Michael pulled off her wet top and she shed her jeans, then they moved to the bed. The slight but glimmering light of the city came in through the window and revealed in its shadows Lila's exquisite beauty.

Michael ran his fingers lightly across the skin of her back, and then, still barely touching her, he ran his fingers up the inside of her thighs, across the front of her hip and onto her bottom, then back to her slim waist, up her spine, and into the warmth of her hair, which was still wet. When he finally kissed her again, Lila's skin leapt to his touch, and her body and head fell back almost helplessly onto the bed. She kept her eyes on his as he climbed onto her; they both were laid open, with all of their hopes, expectations of love, and wounds.

As he entered her, he rested his chin over her shoulder, but she put her hand onto his heart as if stopping him. He paused for a moment trying to read her, and she looked into his eyes. She leaned up to kiss him and again he entered her, putting his chin over her shoulder. But again she put her hand to his chest and pushed him away gently. This time she put her hand onto his cheek and cradled his chin, then she put her other hand onto his back, pulling him to her but keeping his eyes locked with hers.

"Look at me. I want you to look at me," she whispered sensually. And he did.

"How could you know?" he whispered to her, then loved her as all words disappeared and all wounds were healed. Their connection overrode everything. For both of them, sex had always been how they connected with their past partners, but this time, with each other, they were connected first, then intimate. They held tightly to one another through the night and into the dawn, both feeling a stillness they had never experienced before, and knowing that as long as they held each other, nothing could destroy it.

Love and Fear

Summer 2009

Michael was on his motorcycle riding into the mountains as fast as he was able; he wanted to see Lila. There had been a sudden storm, fueled by the intense heat of summer. Fresh green leaves were scattered across the wet and winding road, and occasionally he saw large branches and small trees that had been tossed about in the ferocious wind. The storm had absorbed every bit of energy in its path, and in expending it had destroyed nearly everything in its wake. But now there was only stillness and a raw, deep-blue sky.

In the months since Michael and Lila had returned from Washington, D.C., he would visit her on the weekends but go back to spend the week in Charlotte. He always told Lila it was because he needed to be with his kids; he sometimes stayed at the house, sometimes Deborah was there and sometimes she wasn't. His leaving began to bother Lila more and more, and every time he left, problems between them grew. However, they shrank again as soon as Michael and she were together. They just were not good when apart. Lila had deep hope and fathomless love for Michael, but she had begun to realize it was imperfectly cloaking a growing and profound despair.

Michael pulled into the gravel parking lot and rolled to a stop, in such a hurry that he left his keys in the motorcycle.

"Dude," a young man in the parking lot called to Michael, "You left your keys in your bike," then smiled.

"Thanks, man," Michael said, walking back to the motorcycle to take out the keys. He stood for a moment looking at the bike to see if he had forgotten anything else. Deciding that he had not, he took a deep breath and walked into Curly's. He knew the deal with Lila: She would be a little mad at him, maybe even ignore him for a little bit. But he knew, too, that she would not be able to keep away from him for long. Once inside, he spotted her right away and smiled at her when she looked his way. She did not smile back, but he knew everything would be good—when they were together, nature took over.

Lila was engaged in a conversation with a man at the bar, but she was aware of Michael's presence. Michael was not possessive, so he took a seat down at the end of the bar. Lila had always wielded her power over men flippantly—she was like a child playing with dolls. She always referred to her past relationships as having been with "boys," and to her they were just that: boys. She was constantly pursued by men and had been in a number of serious relationships, loving each of her partners for different reasons. But Michael was different from all of them. This was the first time she was "in love," and his constant leaving was taking a toll on her. She was not used to feeling this way. When she looked at Michael, there was certainly nothing remarkable about him, physically. He was slight and not overly handsome, but he seemed in some way to her more of a man than she had been with before.

When she told Michael this, he ascribed it to her inability to manipulate him. Michael was fooling himself, though, for Lila easily controlled his feelings and thoughts. He was in love with her, he knew for sure, more deeply than with anyone he had ever loved before. And he knew she was in love, too. This was something that neither had expected, and it, had come on so suddenly and powerfully that they both were caught in it and both were scared of where it might lead.

She tried to control him, the way she had always controlled other men, but when she began to twist him, he always backed out. It was a dance they did now, unconscious to both of them, but never had either experienced such a deep connection and the thought of losing the other was debilitating to both. Passion always brought them together, and once they were holding one another, all problems vanished. The intensity of their connection emblazoned their passion, but also increased their fear.

"Hey," Lila said to Michael as she slowly made her way down the bar.

"Hey," he said, breathlessly.

"What do you want?" she said to him.

"You. I mean, you know what I want. I mean…" he stumbled over his words.

"How do you do that? I am mad at you," she said, even as her irritation began to melt. Michael smiled at her.

"Why don't you wait at the house? I'll be there soon," she said, and Michael nodded and reached out to touch her hand. She squeezed his hand and smiled before releasing him.

Michael had been resting in a chair in Lila's house for only a little while before the door swung open and she leaped onto Michael and they kissed. She laid her head on his shoulder and rubbed his arm, and her heart soared. He sat up and cradled her as he stood, walking her to the back bedroom and gently tossed her onto the bed. They undressed and climbed under the covers and held on as tightly as they could, they just could not get close enough to each other. They made love slowly and lovingly, then slept as though they never rested when the other was away. They had fallen asleep early, and Lila awoke in the middle of the night. Moonlight was coming in the window, and a band of bright light crossed Michael's chin. Lila looked at him, feeling that everything was always good when he was here with her. She jostled him until he woke.

"Hmmm," he mumbled groggily as he rolled on top of her.

"Ahh, you are heavy," she said, pulling herself out from under him. She kissed him and he smiled. She bounced out of bed and he could hear her feet pattering across the floor.

"What are you doing?" he asked.

"It's a beautiful night, let's go for walk."

"You have far too much energy," he said.

"Come on, lazy."

"Okay, okay, what time is it?" he asked.

"Time to take me for a walk."

Lila began putting her clothes on, so Michael rose and began to dress quickly, trying to catch up with her. They went out the back door of her house into the dirt driveway and were instantly engulfed in bright moonlight. The willow trees shhhhed softly in the breeze, and the dark silhouettes of cabins in the distance near Curly's were distinguishable from the trees only in their angularity and stillness. The light of a single light bulb shone on the hill in the distance, its yellowish tone washed over the path below but everything else was washed in the overwhelming blue bands of moon rays.

"What a beautiful night," he said.

"Feels magical," she said and moved closer to him. Her presence was as pleasant as anything he could remember. He began to have memories of enjoying the soft rain on his grandparents' ranch when he was a child. Everyone sitting together on the porch, sipping coffee, laughing, resting in their unspoken gratefulness for the rain's assurance of a good life through another season. Why was it that whenever she was near him, his mind wandered to pleasant childhood memories? Perhaps it was the familiarity about Lila, an honesty about her, that let him explore his own mind and his own heart; he was fully aware of how his present life contained no honesty, no openness, and no pleasant simplicity.

"Do you want to go back to the house?" Lila asked. Her hair, dark and blowing in the wind, tossed sparkles and streaks of blue, and she looked like an angel. *And she feels angelic, too*, Michael thought.

"Let's keep walking, the night is so pleasant," Michael replied, feeling that his words were not expressing the moment. "I just want to keep feeling this." he smiled to himself at the realization that he would rather walk than go to the bedroom with a beautiful woman. There will be time enough for loving, he assured himself, but then wondered what made this woman so different. He had always rushed a woman to the bedroom, then counted the moments until he could run. *But I do run from Lila*, he thought, but reassured himself, *I just have family and obligations in Charlotte, and I always come back to her as soon as I can. Maybe I'll ask her to come back with me.* But he never said it to her.

"Want to walk down to the river?"

"Yes," Michael said, tilting his head back as he breathed in the bright night sky, "Baby," Michael felt open and safe and began to express his thoughts, "I am so tired, I feel a weight on my chest. The years have taken their toll and I feel weak. I sit in fear some nights, lying awake for hours."

Lila reached to his hand and just looked at him. She did not speak, which drew him out more. He did not often speak this openly.

"I feel as if I am wounded—I mean, I think I may be sick." Then he stopped, feeling a thickness in his chest that he wanted to cough out but knew that he could not. "And then I clumsily stumble back to your arms to sleep, to rest, to feel your warmth, to breathe your breath. I am so tired, but I love you, I just wanted you to know." Lila pulled him tightly to her and held her heart to his, her tears rolling silently down her cheeks, unseen in the night. Eventually, she let him go and they continued walking.

"Baby, 'I have been your angel whose only job up until now has been to make sure you don't get too comfortable and miss your life.'"

They both laughed as Lila quoted a card she had given Michael not too long ago.

"That card did not make sense when you gave it to me, but now, standing here with you….it still makes no sense," Michael said and they both laughed.

"Well, maybe now my job can be just to hold you while you rest, while you sleep." Lila's heart felt as if it was beating roughly and sporadically. She began to think of all the things that this man had shown her, in such a short time—she felt as if he owned her.

She was not sure what he was telling her. She had heard the way he coughed, and she had asked if he had seen a doctor. He always said yes and changed the subject. A thought passed through her mind, *He is me.* This was a connection that she had desired, wanted, ached for, yet never thought existed. It was some young girl's idealistic fantasy of what could exist. But it was here now, and it was real, tangible. Suddenly, a fear of losing him gripped her. She was caught between the depth of love that she thought could not exist (yet did!) and the dark, heavy realization that this man might really be sick—might even be dying. She could not possess him forever.

Lila's thoughts ran to the future. *Perhaps he is not dying. Maybe he just wants to leave me...maybe he wants to go back to his wife.* She felt a contraction of fear, but instead of giving into it, she let it go through heartbeats and in soft tears. She assessed the situation in the present, knowing that she was right here in this night glow, waiting to be taken, spun around and looked at from every angle in all its gold, shining glory—or maybe to be dropped at any moment, broken and shattered into a million tiny pieces that could never be put back together—or perhaps to be put on a shelf, a bright, beautiful bell, a memory, to look back at, to envy, to want to touch but never to hold. She longed for this man, desired Michael, his hands, his lips, his arms, his laugh, his smile, and oh, his heart! The thought came to her once more: *He is me,* she heard in her thoughts. *I already have him.* It was here, for the first time in her life, that she just held the grace of love, pure love, with no thought of what it would become or not become, she just beheld it and allowed herself to hold this love. It was enough, total and complete.

Lila was struck by her own discovery that she had been creating her own reality, and even now her mind wanted to run, to create a story of something needed, and she smiled at herself, wondering what she had been thinking all these years, how much life had she missed, how much love had she missed? She felt an urge to be angry at an impending loss, but that thought was met by grace, and she was grateful instead. *He is me,* she thought to herself one more time, and it was enough. Lila stumbled as she walked in the glowing grass.

"Walk much?" Michael said, laughing gently at her.

"Very funny."

"Your presence, your dancing, innocent presence, is more beautiful than anything I have ever encountered. But…"

"Oh, here it comes," Lila said playfully; they both loved word play. "No one has ever accused me of being innocent, well, at least, not in a long time."

Michael stopped walking and turned to her.

"Your awkward grace is always swallowed by and lost in your laugh, your smile that is as brilliant as the sun. I have been thinking about it, and I think I know why your feet stumble. Sometimes when I see your graceful, dancing, divine body moving across the room, I realize that you are an angel and are just not used to walking." Lila's smile broadened until her lips pursed in fake disappointment.

"Is that all you have?"

"Damn, that is my best stuff! I know you are a sucker for anything poetic, I know it's working, just try to hold out." Now Michael was smirking.

"Want to go back to the house?" Lila asked slowly and quietly.

Michael just smiled, and with one arm, firmly pulled her to his chest, paused, then kissed her deeply, passionately, as if Lila was the only woman he had ever kissed. Michael struggled to take a breath, but he found that he did not care. The first light of day peeked through the woods, and dawn had advanced so slowly that Michael had not noticed. Objects obscured by the night began to appear in the growing light. "No, I have to get back."

His words struck her like a blow, and she pulled away from him. She was so open and so in love that the blow went deep. They walked silently toward the house. Michael realized he had been abrupt, he did not mean for it to come out that way. They had not talked, and he was sure that she had expected him to stay the entire weekend. The peace and grace of the past few hours were lost.

"Why won't you be with me?" And in an instant Lila went from complete openness and the warmth of "he is me," to a convulsive contraction. *If he will not be with me, then he does not love me, and if he does not love me, how can I exist?* Her thoughts raced under the surface from love to an imagined world of no love and suffering. Michael could not see or understand what was happening, and he could not react to it in a way to assuage Lila's fears. Michael and Lila fit perfectly into each other's subconscious patterns, stepping into and all over each other's subconscious fears.

"Hey, baby, I am here with you... I love you... I just have obligations back in Charlotte."

Lila felt she was losing him. She looked at his finger and the ring was still there. She could not understand why he kept it on. He must be lying to her. She had to find a way to get back in control of herself. She felt sick to her stomach.

"Go. I don't care. Go!" she said harshly. Michael took a deep breath, then sighed and turned away from her. Lila stood dumbfounded; no man had ever treated her like this. They walked back to the house quietly, neither speaking. Her anger grew, and as soon as they walked back into the house she began to clean vigorously. Michael packed up the few things he had brought. He wanted to tell her something, but he did not know what the right thing would be, so he just said, "I'll call you in a bit. Sorry I have to run. I'll be back..." His words trailed off, and he walked out the door. None of this made any sense to Lila. Her stomach ached. She walked to her bedroom and lay on the bed, tears filling her eyes as she tried to think of ways to bring him to her, to make him hers.

Too High and Too Fast

December 2009

Michael was riding up the Enola Highway into a slight headwind, the winding road still wet from a light rain. The highway began to bend sharply back and forth as he gained altitude on the way to Curly's Café. He hurried—he and Lila had not communicated much during the week and he needed to see her. Michael ran his relationship with Lila through his mind, trying to sort out where they were. He could see addictive qualities in both of their behaviors, but he was sure that they were perfect for each other; they were so much alike, it was if she were a female version of himself.

Michael was also aware that he was trying to hold on to many things. He wanted to be with his children, he wanted to make his extended family happy, he wanted to have Lila, and he wanted to experience the overpowering love that seemed to engulf them. He and Lila had fallen in love, he was sure: He had recognized it immediately. At first he was afraid that it was only him, and he had considered the things that Doc had told him. He had, after all, met several men at Curly's who had said they were in love with Lila, and perhaps they were; she seemed to have a hold over men in a way that few other women did. She could use her power over men. Michael was sure that she was not even aware that she was doing it. It made him wonder from time to time if he was just one of them, thinking that Lila loved him when in reality he was just under her spell.

Lila had been married before, she told Michael. She said that she had loved her ex-husband in the beginning, that he had offered her some amount of reassurance, a safety net, and was always a call away for her. She needed to feel like she had options so she kept in touch with him along with other men just close enough, but she was not "in love" with any of them, or so she said, and Michael believed it.

Michael kept thinking about Lila as he rode, not watching the road, not seeing the wet leaves on the turns; he was lost in his thoughts. He considered the idea of loving, but not being "in love." What did that mean exactly? It made him think of Deborah. He loved his wife, he was certain, but there was nothing more. Was he unrealistic to expect or want more? Was the "more" that he desired simply nature? Was the feeling he was chasing something that was forever fleeting? What was it exactly that was missing? When he talked to his wife, they always talked about something— one of their children, or a bill, or the leaky kitchen sink—but never to each other, not like they used to. Michael could not say or express what exactly was missing, but he was certain that whatever it was, it was gone. When he talked with Lila, though, there was definitely something more there, a connection he didn't feel with Deborah. *Did I used to feel the same way with Deborah? And if I did but don't feel it now, what does it mean? I just don't know.* But what Michael did know was that when he and Lila were together, everything was heightened, more important, and more substantial.

Michael suspected in the very beginning that Lila was falling in love with him, but she resisted. She had even told him that she loved him early on; it had just slipped out, and she was surprised to hear herself say it. For the most part, though, Michael felt that she held back, maybe because Michael was still wearing his wedding ring. *But too, by holding back*, Michael thought, *Lila had slipped ever deeper into Michael.* (What Michael did not know was that she had unwittingly gone so deep that she was having trouble distinguishing herself from Michael and the thought of losing him meant her own death. The stakes of the relationship for her had become high, and so was her dread.)

As Michael sped along, thinking of Lila, the narrow road bent sharply to the right, and he entered the turn too high and too fast. The motorcycle pushed to the double yellow line directly in front of a large, yellow truck coming down the mountain from the other direction on the road.

Michael dipped the handlebar, turning hard. He instinctively hit the brakes, and the back end of the motorcycle began to slide across the solid-painted middle lines toward the fast coming tractor-trailer. The truck driver tried to swerve to his right to steer clear of the motorcycle, but there was very little shoulder before a steep decline on the side of the winding mountain road. Michael let go of the brakes and twisted the throttle to full in an attempt to accelerate out of his slide, but he braced for a horrific impact. The wheels responded, and the tire rubber grabbed the pavement just as the truck's wheels nudged off the road and it began to slide in the gravel. By the smallest of margins, Michael cleared the truck, and as the passing truck driver regained control of his rig he blasted the air horn, adding insult to near-death. The vortex of air trailing behind the huge truck grabbed at Michael, jerking him about.

Michael immediately slowed the bike. There were no more thoughts of Lila; he was only aware of his pounding heartbeat and shaky hands. The motorcycle felt awkward on the road, and he struggled to keep the bike balanced. Michael rode the rest of the way to Curly's Café slowly and methodically. Before, he had shifted gears without thinking, but now it was difficult and unnatural—he just could not seem to match his speed with the right gear. Near the café, Michael was glad to be off the main road, but he felt uneasy and vulnerable as he rode across the loose gravel of the parking lot. When he glided to a stop and turned off the motorcycle, he could not think what to do next. He put down the kickstand and leaned the bike into place. He pulled the keys out of the ignition and promptly dropped them. Then, when he swung his leg off the bike and bent over to search for the keys, he bumped his helmet on the handlebars. He stood, feeling unsteady on his feet and reached a hand out to steady himself on the motorcycle, taking a deep breath to compose himself as much as possible.

Michael hurried into the bar, looking for Lila. He scanned the room quickly, soon seeing her sitting on a stool engrossed in conversation with a tall, heavy man. He let out a sigh of relief and smiled just to see her. He felt almost giddy as he moved quietly to the stool next to her, hoping to surprise her with his presence. However, she never turned to him; instead, she kept talking to the man. Michael cleared his throat to get her attention, but he only caught a glance from the man.

"I think you have a customer," the man said to Lila. She looked at Michael but then turned back toward the man, seemingly engrossed in their conversation.

"Can I get myself a drink?" Michael asked as he leaned into Lila to get her attention. She turned again to him, this time smiling.

"Michael, this is Franklin Alexander Cade, THE Franklin Alexander Cade!"

"My friends call me F.A.," he said, stretching out his hand. Michael grabbed the hand, noticing that for a big man, it was small and weak.

"Michael, F.A. was the quarterback for Alabama when my dad was coaching high school ball in Alabama: F.A. knows my dad!"

Lila was like an excited schoolgirl talking to her idol.

"F.A. Cade... yes, I think I remember you," Michael said, but he quickly realized he was not being included in the conversation. Standing slowly, he was not sure what to do. Lila and F.A. were engrossed in their conversation. Lila was nodding enthusiastically to everything he said. Michael listened to the conversation, football, Alabama, banking, football, "I" this and "I" that. *Nothing special or very interesting* Michael thought. Nothing spiritual, which is what Lila always talked about. It was perplexing.

"I'm going to chat with the Doc," Michael said. Lila waved her hand without looking at him. Michael began walking, looking the whole time at the two engaged in deep conversation. Doc watched Michael walk in his direction, pulling out a stool for him to sit on. Michael sat down, still looking at Lila and F.A.

"Don't worry about that," said Doc.

"I suppose you are going to call me Jake?" Michael said, finally looking at Doc. Doc smiled a warm smile.

"It is just an opportunity to see things as they are, Michael. An opportunity to see what you told me you are searching for… Let's see, what was that thing? Oh yes, Truth," Doc said, seriously.

Then, he said, "Michael, tell me about your retreat."

Michael turned away from Doc and looked again at Lila, muttering, "I don't think I like this."

"We never do, Michael."

Doc put his hand on Michael's shoulder. "Michael, how long have you known Lila?"

"A year? Maybe a little longer," Michael answered.

"How long have the two of you dated?"

"Almost a year…why do you ask, Doc?"

"Michael, I have never seen two people fall into each other so quickly and so completely as you two have."

Doc turned to look at Lila, then back to Michael.

"When Lila opens her mouth, I hear your voice, and when you open your mouth, I hear her voice," he said, then sipped at an already-empty martini glass. Michael looked at him as he continued talking.

"You see Michael, Lila has an image of a person, of a man, a 'true love,' she calls it. An image of someone special, someone smart, someone she can talk to… a man with means who makes her feel secure, someone who is spiritual, someone who fits her and makes her feel special. You fit that image, Michael, almost perfectly."

Doc was looking at Michael so intensely that he unconsciously turned away to look at the back of the bar, but he did not focus on anything.

"And Michael, tell me about Lila: What is it you like about her?"

Michael turned again to look at her.

"I am not sure right now," Michael said, smiling, but when he turned to meet Doc's eyes, he saw that Doc had a straight face. He took a deep breath and then looked up into the darkness of the ceiling. As he thought about Lila, he said, "She is so beautiful and smart. I love the way she smells, and I love her intuition. I love the way she turns in the bed every time I turn. I love the way she talks, I love the way she thinks. But mostly I love the way I feel when she is near me."

"Tell me more about that," Doc said.

Michael thought for a minute, then said, "I like the way she makes me feel about myself."

"Aha," said Doc quietly as he raised his eyebrows.

"You see, Michael, you also have an image in your mind. An image that Lila fits, nearly perfectly. I am not saying that the two of you are not in love...you may very well be."

Doc sipped the empty glass again.

"What are you saying, Doc?" Michael asked.

"What I am saying is that you have an image in your mind— partly inherited, partly conditioning, and partly created by you. It's the 'you' that you think you are, and Michael, Lila reflects the image of the 'you' that you want to be. But it is not real: To find out what is real, you will have to give up that image."

"Doc, are we talking about enlightenment again? About a higher consciousness? Because if we are, then you should know that I don't believe in enlightenment. I know how Lila makes me feel, and I believe in that, Doc."

"Michael, how does Lila make you feel right now, here in this moment?"

Michael pursed his lips to exhale forcefully. Then he looked at Lila, whose attention was still focused on F.A. Cade.

"Okay, Doc, I think I see what you are saying," Michael said, then looked at Doc to ask, "So, what next?"

"Well, Michael, you do not have to believe in enlightenment or higher consciousness. You just need to believe in a better life, with more love and happiness that is sustainable and real. Believe in that, Michael, if you need to believe in something. Go back to the meditation, do the technique, and see what happens. That is all: Keep the search for your source first, keep diving back into that deep silence."

"What about Lila? I mean, Lila and me?" Michael asked. Doc looked over at Lila and F.A. Cade.

"I do not know, Michael, but I am fearing this is going to be painful for you, and I am afraid it is going to be even more painful for Lila," then Doc crinkled his face and squinted his eyes, it was a pained expression, as if he were feeling what was ahead for Michael and Lila

"I hope you're wrong, Doc," Michael said, then rose and walked back to Lila.

"Hey Lila," he said, but she did not turn, either not hearing him or pretending not to.

"What do you need, pal?" Franklin asked a little menacingly, but then he turned toward Lila and said, "I've got to piss like a race horse." He stood and headed toward the restroom, bumping Michael as he passed, stumbling a bit on the way. Lila watched him until he disappeared into the bathroom, then she turned to Michael.

"He is so interesting. We're having an important discussion, and he really needs to talk to someone," she said, and then she took a deep breath. "Why don't you wait at my house?" She reached into her pocket and pulled out a key, then handed it to Michael. Michael looked at the key, and then at Lila.

"Okay, I guess I'll see you in a bit."

Michael turned and slowly walked toward the back door. Franklin stumbled out of the men's room, looking up as he passed Michael and flashing him an overly large, lecherous grin.

"Good night, Doc," Michael said as he passed Doc. Doc waved but did not smile. Michael walked out the back door and into the cool night air and shivered. The light on Lila's front porch was on, and he easily made his way through the woods. Once inside Lila's house, Michael began to turn on lamps scattered about on tables and shelves. He had never noticed that she had so many lamps. While collectively they made the room bright, his mood was dim.

He turned on Lila's stereo and then perused her music. He did not find anything he wanted to listen to in the same music collection from which Lila always was able to find song after song that matched the moment precisely.

After sifting through her music collection, he moved to the bedroom, which was quiet and still. The room had always seemed alive, but now it felt sterile. Michael took his wallet and his keys out of his pocket and set them on the dresser. Then, he took off his pants and folded them neatly, putting them on the chair in the corner. Next, he took off and folded his shirt, pressing it down with his hands as he put it on top of his pants. After removing and folding his underwear, he slid naked under the covers. Exhausted, he fell asleep with the bedside lamp still on.

Michael awoke with a start. He was sure that he had heard a loud noise. He listened intently but heard nothing. It took him a few minutes to realize where he was. *Where is Lila and what time is it?* Michael looked at the huge decorative clock on the wall, seeing that it was past 3:00 a.m. *Where the hell is Lila?* Michael threw back the covers and leapt to his feet. His nudity was a shock to him, and he felt more vulnerable than he ever remembered feeling. He quickly dressed and walked out the front door of Lila's house. The front porch light was the only light Michael still on.

He quickly made his way through the woods, past the guest bungalows to Curly's Café. The lights were out, but Michael still climbed the steps and pulled on the handle of the door, finding it locked. He stood looking at the door handle, not knowing what to think. He turned slowly and headed back to Lila's house, but as he faced the bungalows, a door opened and Lila backed out, smiling and laughing. She turned to see Michael standing there. He was smiling, glad to see her, then the meaning of the whole scene dawned on him. It was a punch that Michael had not seen coming, and he had not tensed enough to take the blow. He turned and half-walked, half-ran to his motorcycle. Lila ran after him.

He reached the motorcycle then stuck his hand into his pocket, searching for the key to the bike. "Damn it!' he swore as he realized he had left the keys on Lila's dresser.

When Lila caught up with Michael, she was short of breath. "Nothing happened," she said.

Michael did not look at her; he just sat on his motorcycle and stared straight ahead. Then he took a deep breath, folded his arms and looked up at the stars, then he looked down at the ground.

"Are you going to say anything?" Lila asked. "Stop whatever you are thinking! We were just talking!" She stomped her foot, then made a growling noise and turned to walk away. Suddenly, she stopped and turned back to Michael.

"Are you coming? If you were any other man, I would just leave you here. You are being ridiculous!" she feigned anger.

Michael stood and swung his leg off the motorcycle and began walking toward the house. Lila let out a little breath; for just a moment she thought they were getting past what she considered a small indiscretion, but Michael was experiencing it as the end of his world. Michael walked past her and she followed him, but neither said anything all the way to the house. They walked inside in silence and went into the kitchen.

Michael and Lila stood looking at one another. They were trapped. Trapped by having truly fallen in love with one another, yet having come into the relationship through the ravaged landscape of failed past marriages. They had been playing unconscious games from the beginning, but now the stakes were high, they were exploring a relationship that was deeper than either had ever expected.

Neither knew what to do next, and both were scared.

Michael looked into Lila's eyes. The feeling of shock at seeing her come out of another man's room was subsiding, but now, deeply, deeper than before, he knew that he loved her. *The deeper the pain, the deeper the love,* he thought wryly. *Loving someone completely is as close to dying as any other human struggle.* His stomach ached. He just stared at her, sensing that he was at a crossroad. The universe was conspiring with his deepest desire to find out what was true, and this punch to the gut was making him pause to look at what was true.

There was desperation in Lila's eyes; she knew that something had changed.

"Nothing happened," she said again, still feigning anger, which had always been her ally. Michael could barely hear her, and his eyes drifted to focus on nothing. He neither felt solid in his body nor solid in his thoughts.

I was born for freedom, born to find the portal out of this mind and this body. I was born to find a way out of this cycle of birth and death. This idea, this endeavor, the purpose of this birth is to break through. It was divinely given; it is my birth right to find the way out of Plato's cave and to leave clues, markers for the travelers behind to follow. There are ancient pathways, but most of the clues are well covered by dogma and canonization. It is time to find a new path, and right now I am at the crossroad that sent too many before me adrift into the wilderness. Michael seemed frozen, watching the scene he was in as if he were a witness, not a participant. He was sensing, feeling things in his stomach, and whether by divine guidance or a keen gift of intuition, he felt an energy building that would help him break through. He thought of the retreat and the teaching. He was sure that it would get him through this, but he chose instead a thought.

The thought was that he wanted her more than anything he had ever wanted. *I love her, exactly as she is,* he told himself. This sentiment had been their mantra, but suddenly he could see that this path of loving her always would lead back to this moment. She would always drift, her sight would roam, her attention would be caught by something shiny— a young man, a tall man, a smart man, or a spiritual man—and she would be mesmerized, even if only for a moment. It would always bring suffering, and here was the sign that he was looking for: suffering.

Desire, consummation, loss, pain, fear, consummation, dream, desire, consummation pain. The cycle would be endless, and he would never find peace in this kind of love. He would reside in the part of what he imagined was him: It was the part of his self-created illusions, and that part would die, for it had been imaginary all along. But the draw to this drama—to her—was greater in this moment than he had ever experienced. His thoughts drifted back to Hell's Kitchen and the junkies. They lived all around him, and he pitied them. Once they had experienced the needle and the spoon, and let heroin into their blood, it never left them. No number of years of being clean, they told him, were enough time for the thought of that high to dissipate to nothing. It stayed always in their thoughts. They were forever weakened to its draw and likely to fall to its grip, never to own their own lives. They could only hope to avoid her, the dragon of all highs.

And here he was, feeling the same way: Lila would always be in his thoughts, he would be forever weakened to her draw. His only real hope was to avoid her, because, after all, *I was born to be free.* As long as he was with her, he would never be free but would remain locked in the illusion of finding completeness in another's arms. He began to laugh, and she smiled, feeling like they had gotten past something, past what was in her mind a small carelessness. She was not fully seeing, or perhaps she did not want to see, that she had in a deep way wounded Michael.

Besides, she thought to herself, *I am not his until he is mine. I am not beholden to him until he is free and clear of his wife. Until he has devoted himself to me, there is no need for me to devote myself to him, and the sooner he sees what is at stake, the better.* Then, she worked to get back her sense of control, using her sexuality. She touched her forefinger to her lower lip, pulling on it gently. Her eyes began to penetrate him, and when he resisted, she amplified her allure by letting out a soft breath. Michael weakened and began down a treacherous path.

Michael had the sensation that had become familiar to him: He was falling, even if only ever so slightly. Michael watched as Lila walked toward the sink, then reached into the cabinet and pulled out two glasses. She slunk sinuously towards the refrigerator, and Michael's heart quickened as he listened to her drop ice cubes into the glasses. He watched Lila's every move, and everything was beginning to intensify and speed up. She moved sensually, sexually, as she made their drinks. His body responded to her body, but he felt as if he was watching everything unfold from afar. She touched her hair lightly, head lowered, then looked up at him as she moved closer. She handed him a glass and he sipped from it; the liquor bit at his tongue, but he swallowed down a gulp, then another. Lila tasted the alcohol when he kissed her, and although she had initiated this connection, her first instinct was to withdraw. Michael seemed different, and she felt a small pang of fear. She decided to push on, feeling that she needed to connect with him, and though they were not connecting with talk, she knew that she could pull him in with sex. She reached out and tugged at him. Then she pushed him in the chest, teasing him, smiling even though something felt lost to her. Again she pushed him.

"Come on," she said. He stared into her eyes and stood like stone. "Come on...Let me have it...you know what I want," she insisted, then licked her glass.

"Rough sex," he said. She had brought it up before, jokingly at first but often enough that Michael knew it was what she wanted. His body responded, but it was not a pleasant feeling, as if something inside of him was sinking. He could not turn from her, though, and he could not think of anything to say, while things began to speed up within him again.

"Come on," she whispered.

"You want it rough?" he asked.

"Everyone wants it rough," she said, poking her finger into this chest then shoving him with the palms of her hands. He leaned into her with his mouth close to hers; he could smell her breath.

He took another drink, then downed the rest and hurled the glass across the kitchen, where it exploded into small shards against the far wall. The suddenness of his violence assaulted her senses, and she stiffened as he leaned her into the wall, pushing all his weight against her. The hair on the back of her neck stood up, and she could barely breathe against his mass. He had never seemed so large to her. Her eyes widened with a heady combination of excitement and fear, and he shoved her to the ground, knocking the breath out of her. As she began to scramble to all fours, Michael reached down to pull her sweatshirt over her head, then broke the thin strap of her bra as he pulled at her clothes. Her left breast spilled out and her shirt got tangled in her hair as he tried to jerk it off, and he began dragging her—partly by the shirt and partly by her hair. She tried to scream but she still did not have enough breath. Trying to think, she was having trouble discerning whether or not she was in trouble. She was not sure; none of this seemed like Michael.

Now her arms became entangled in the shirt and she felt buttons popping. She struggled to get her feet under herself, but Michael dragged her into the den, banging her into the doorway then into the wall. Fear and adrenaline surged through her body. He spun her onto her side, then with one arm scooped her up and threw her over the back of the couch. She bounced off of the couch, crashed across the coffee table, and landed on the floor, hearing a lamp shatter. She clambered to get away from Michael, but he was on her in an instant, lifting her by her hair again, and shoving and pulling her down the hall, her feet dragging and scraping across the hardwood floor. He flung her on the bed facedown and ripped down her pants and panties. Then, he unfastened his pants and dropped them to the floor, climbing onto the bed where she was squirming to get away. He quickly reached down and scooped under her stomach to lift her and thrust himself inside of her in one fierce motion.

The image of a falling, burning man flashed through Michael's mind. He crashed his hips into her, slamming into her again and again. Then he knocked her over and grabbed her by her arms, pulling her onto him in the bed. Another flash of memory— Michael's fist cracking upward into a man's jaw—and he reached up to seize a fistful of her hair.

Lila was utterly overwhelmed, helpless in Michael's frenzied clutches. He slammed himself into her over and over. A flash of a woman played across his inner vision, tumbling and tumbling downward, then Michael was aware of himself with Lila, and then his mind showed him the image of himself slamming his fist into the back of a man's head as he lay sprawled across the hood of a car. Again he returned to conscious thought in the bed, locked in ferocious intercourse with Lila, but then there were the hot, loud cracks of bullets and the faintest awareness of hot lead sizzling past his skull, flashes of fire and small, deadly explosions of smoke—in his mind now he could hear bones splintering. At that, Michael released his grip from Lila, throwing his arms into the air, thrusting out his chest, and screaming like a wild warrior. He saw a vision of himself, first as the war-painted Indian Crazy Horse, then as himself screaming, brandishing a liquor bottle over a man who lay on the floor, and then with the wide, white, outstretched wings of an archangel.

Michael reached down with his right hand and grasped Lila by her hips to rip her away from him, throwing her off the bed forcefully against wall. Her back slammed into the plaster, and her legs were in the air. The sweatshirt was still tangled over her head as she fell headfirst between the bed and the wall, almost in slow motion as one more scene played through Michael's thoughts: The jukebox shattered and silence found the battered barroom, where smoke drifted in expanding round clouds. And as Michael collapsed into the jukebox in his mind, he collapsed into the bed, his heart pounding. He was covered in sweat, and he rolled over onto his back, chest heaving. He convulsed into a seemingly endless cough. Then stillness.

"Fighting, fucking, and falling...they're all the same damn thing," Michael whispered to himself. He was physically spent, but he felt no relief, no satisfaction, and no contentment. And the very place that once felt so much like home now felt like hell. Where once he thought true love resided, now also was home to anger, desire, fear, and desperation. His place of rest had become a place of restlessness, and all his feelings of guilt and loss returned, stronger than before.

Lila poked her head up from behind the bed and pulled her sweatshirt down. She looked at Michael, smiling broadly—a broader smile than Michael thought could have fit on her narrow face.

"Did you say something?" she asked.

"No, nothing."

"Wow, my God, I thought you were out of control," she said, climbing back onto the bed towards Michael.

"I was out of control," he said, mostly as a groan.

"Oh. Well, we should have a safe word then," she said to him.

"A safe word?"

"Yeah, you know, like a word we use when we are not feeling safe—a word either of us can say to slow things down when we need to." Lila smiled at Michael and snuggled as close as she could.

"A safe word like what?" he asked.

"Oh, I don't know, I have a girlfriend who uses the word *banana*."

"Banana?" Michael repeated.

Lila pulled off her sweatshirt and climbed on top of Michael, kissing him softly on the mouth, then slid onto him. Michael put his chin over her shoulder and looked at the ceiling, and had the sensation that he was falling backward into himself. The very action—with the very woman!—that had opened him, now closed him.

He closed his eyes, and he could barely feel her; Lila sensed it, as he lay perfectly motionless. After a while he propped himself up, but she kept her ear on his chest over his soft and irregular heartbeat. Eventually, they looked at each other, realizing they were trapped. Trapped between truly having fallen in love with one another and having come into the relationship through the ravaged landscape of failed past relationships. They had been playing subconscious games, but now they were past that, deeper than either had ever explored, and now neither knew what to do next. Michael got up and began to get dressed.

"Where are you going?"

Lila's question was low and ominous.

"I don't know, I need to get some air—I need to go," Michael answered, knowing it would upset her even though that was not his intention. He tried to sort things out in his mind: He felt shattered:

He could not stay, and he could not rest. Then, he felt another cough building and he doubled over as he coughed hard, the feeling of glass in his lungs. He was sure he was in love with Lila, and he was sure that she was in love with him, but just now it did not seem like enough to know that they were in love. *Something is wrong*, was all he could think.

If he left now, they might never have a chance to be together, but he knew that if he stayed, they would never have a chance either. *We are so much alike*, he thought again, wondering if she could see it. Lila wanted love—love to save her—but she could not love herself, just as Michael could not love himself.

And when they were desperate they reached to sex to connect, but it was a terrible replacement for the real connection they both really wanted. There was something in what they were building together that was greater, but it was more than either felt they deserved, driving the highs higher but the lows lower and lower. Again, Michael told himself that for both of their sakes, he had to leave her.

Then a veil lifted, only this one did not fall away in a slow dawning, it was ripped away from him, leaving him feeling bare. He now saw with clarity that he had counted on another person's love to make him feel like the person he wanted to be. It was not the loss of love he feared, but his attachment to what it meant to who he thought he was, the kind of person he envisioned himself to be. Love could never save him, and it could not save Lila. At least this kind of love, the kind of love that feels like addiction—it is tied to so many other things, attached to needs and desires and fears. Lila came after Michael, suddenly dizzy and sick to her stomach. Things had turned so quickly, and she was confused. This felt so strong and so powerful, but she was disoriented, suddenly feeling as empty as she had ever felt.

Michael thought of the teacher from the retreat as he stood near the doorway. He had expressed the common contrast between the calm of the retreat and the chaos of the "real world." Michael remembered now how it made the teacher smile, and he recalled her response: "Michael, the real world is inside of you and the outside world is a reflection. The chaos and the suffering that you see on the outside are an image of what is on the inside. You will never find what it is that you are looking for 'out there' or in someone else." Then she touched Michael's heart with two fingers, "Look there, mind your thoughts, choose the technique, choose the attitude. What you seek is on the inside."

Then Michael's memory was shattered by Lila's voice.

"Are you running back to her?" Lila yelled. "Has that been it all along—you never meant to leave her?"

Lila was shaking as she stood before Michael, confronting him and her own deep fear. "You still are wearing that damn ring...I am such a fool."

She turned away and looked down at the floor, then turned back to Michael with pleading in her voice.

"She does not love you anymore, she has abandoned you, you are nothing to her... you told me so yourself. How can you hang on to someone, to something that is dead."

"Don't say that! Jo is not dead! She never abandoned me, she loves me—forever—she..." Michael heard his own words, and almost could not believe them. It was a shock. He looked at Lila and she at him, with tears filling her eyes.

"Who is Jo, Michael? Is she the person you love? What are you doing here, Michael?" Lila paused for a moment, then with barely any energy in her voice, she said, "I think you better leave." After he walked out the door, Lila shut it gently behind him, but it sounded like a cell door to a jail clanging, leaving him locked inside. But he was outside and Lila was inside.

Inside, Lila sat down on her chair. She pulled her legs up and wrapped them in her arms. She was unprepared for the painful feelings. *Has this all been some big mis-calculation?* She had the sensation of being completely raw, but in one of the ironies of life, grace came to her. Her love for Michael, for what she had thought he could give her, had wounded her and opened her. She thought of past wounds, of the guilt of not loving men who had loved her, the guilt of manipulating others, and the things that other men had done to her, and she had in a strange way manifested everything as shame. As she watched Michael walk out the door, everything began to come out of her in soft convulsions, waves of weeping came across her, and the grace of this burning pain purified like fire. She had been looking for love to save her, but it was pain that would be her salvation.

Outside, Michael paused as he walked down the steps. He had always wanted to make everything right, but now, standing open with his own guilt, he was confused. What had he blurted about Jo? She was not alive, *Jo was dead*. And the thought submerged Michael into near-total darkness.

Then he began to walk away again, thinking of Lila. He felt as if he were in a movie house, watching himself walking away from the greatest love he had ever experienced. *Turn around*, he shouted to himself from an imaginary red velvet chair. But he kept walking. *Just keep walking*, he heard himself say, and he looked down at his feet. Another memory: his wingtip shoes, covered in ash, one step in front of the other, each foot heavy and with huge effort he made slow progress…then there was the sound of a growing wail, people crying out, and he turned to witness the North Tower crumble into itself. As he watched it fall within himself, he felt again that feeling and braced for the vibration and impact. None came, though, and he begged God for the impact – because the impact signaled the end.

Then he found himself in his body again; he had wandered off the stone path in the darkness and was stumbling across tree roots and fallen branches. He did not turn back to Lila, but instead looked toward a lone streetlight in the distance near Curly's Café. He walked toward it, and it guided him out of the darkness. Michael felt a burning low on the surface of his chest. It was not in his lungs, it was where the bullet had pierced him. He put two fingers to the spot and rubbed it, the burning somewhat subsided. He thought of Lila once more. *She was perfect for me. She has flaws, but they are the same as mine.* He could never hope to find another who was such a perfect match. He turned and looked back to the house. *I see that her love cannot save me.* He turned once again and headed toward his motorcycle.

Michael felt wounded, but more than just a new wound, what he experienced with Lila had reopened much older wounds. He had blurted his love for Jo—Michael had not seen that coming. He did not see that inside of himself; he thought that he had scarred and healed, but now he felt like a weak and weary man. He felt he had no strength, no moral character, and he judged himself harshly. *Did Lila really love me? Yes*, he told himself, *and I love her.* He turned again toward the house and began to walk. *She loves me— I make her feel secure.* This was a thought meant to reassure him, and he continued in his mind, *She just wants shelter from the storm.* Then he stopped walking as the realization hit him: *I am not her shelter, I am her storm. She loves me for what she thinks I can provide her, but long term I cannot give her security. Long term, no one can.*

"I am strong, I can move past this," he whispered to himself. Michael could see what it was that he could not give Lila, but he was not seeing what it was that he wanted from her that she could not provide. Michael could not see that his own strength was the thing that got in the way of his seeing.

With great resolve, he turned one last time and walked away. He felt a stream of sweat run down the side of his forehead, so he raised his arm and wiped at it with his sleeve. As his shirtsleeve brushed past his nose, he smelled Lila. He closed his eyes and sniffed it again deeply. A pleasant memory of her breathing lightly on his neck while they slept tangled eased across him and he felt joy, then his stomach tightened at the thought of perhaps never again having that sensation. Their connection was undeniable and unmistakable. And it was an opening to such a depth as to expose them not to *who they truly were* but to *what they truly were*, only neither could see the blessing nor recognize the significance of the opening, or allow the depth of the connection to reveal the place where everything is one thing.

And though both would at times feel the connection and both at times would try, neither would be able to close the gateway. The opening could be ignored for a time, but only ignored. Never forgotten and never closed, for once the cosmic egg of false identification is cracked, then birth—or rather rebirth— is inevitable. Never to return to the smaller limited false sense of self.

And now they separated from one another physically, wounded, with neither getting what they thought they wanted: a true love. Instead, they got what they needed: an opening, a chance to see what was true. The gift of their wounds was that they were doorways to the transcendent so they could learn that the search for what was true, the search for themselves, would not take them beyond the heartbreaks of their lives, but would rather be a journey into and through their own personal dramas.

Michael walked slowly across the gravel to his motorcycle, which was parked under the lone streetlight in the parking lot. He put in the key, pulled out the choke, and started to warm up the machine. He saw his cell phone inside the saddlebag that he had left unfastened. He reached down, picked it up, and turned it on, and then everything got worse. Missed call alerts began to flash across the face of the phone: his father, his wife, his sister, and his father again. He pushed the button to replay the first message, and he held the phone to his ear.

"Son, this is your father," the voice said, soft with little energy. "Please call me tonight, I have something important to tell you."

Michael's heart sank.

Carrying Things

January 2010

The thrust of the jet pushed Michael backward into the seat cushion. Quickly, the plane lifted off the ground and Michael was on his way to Texas. He had always considered it "going home," but the pleasant remembrances of the familiar constant dry wind and smell of mesquite trees that had always brightened his mood was different today. *A lot can happen in a day*, he thought. *I lost my mother, I lost Lila, and I found out that I have been holding on to Jo. I guess I never really dealt with losing her. I guess I never really let myself think about it. I guess I never let myself feel her loss. I guess things don't just go away. I guess...* As childhood memories began to run through his mind, he spoke quietly to himself: "I am not ready for this." He thought about who would be at his mother's funeral, and the first person that crossed his mind was Deborah, his wife. Suddenly, he felt lonely.

I suppose I never let go of any of the women in my life, but now I think I have lost them all. He wondered why he had held on to Jo. If anyone had asked if he thought about her, he would have said no, but now he could see that he was always thinking about her. He closed his eyes, and another childhood memory came to him: climbing from the tree in his backyard to the roof of his house when he was maybe six years old. There were wet leaves on the wooden shingles and he lost his footing on the sloping roof. He hit the roof, then rolled off, landing in the soft grass, but hard enough to knock all the air from his body. He lay in his child-thoughts sure that he was dying.

His mother had seen him fall and was running in an instant. She scooped him into her arms and cradled him.

"My poor baby," she said softly, with no hint of panic or fear. She held his head against her breast, gently looking into his eyes as air slowly came back to his body. As soon as he could breathe, he let out a sob. "Now, now there, you're okay, you are okay," his mother soothed. As tears ran down his cheeks, he knew he was okay.

Sitting in the airplane, now nearly forty years later, he fought back tears, but he smiled. His mother always made him feel certain that everything was okay. She saw the best in him so he wanted to be the best for her, always. That was the worst part of her being gone. *Mom, I'm really just a mess, my work is a mess, my marriage is a mess, I think I love someone, and well, that's just completely a mess, and I can't even think what kind of father I am, and if there is a heaven and if you're looking down…well then, now you know: I am really just a big fat fake.*

Then he thought again of the women in his life. They had all given him something in the beginning, but now it seemed that they just wanted something from him. Because he was feeling more and more empty as time passed, he had nothing left to give. Now his mother was gone, and what she had given him—what he always had known was there— was gone, leaving a huge empty place. He wanted to stand in this desolate place, but he found that he had to float. He did not feel sorry for himself, or weak: He felt strong, but not in a good way. He did not feel like a good person, just a person who had fallen short in everything, and that made him harder and more distant. He could feel himself pulling away emotionally from everything.

He needed to be held. Perhaps by Deborah? No, that was unrealistic. It was not in her to offer him any softness, and he did not know how to ask to be held. Perhaps Lila? Yes, she would hold him, but then there would come a storm. *Wow*, he thought, *she is my storm, and I am her storm. I am her and she is me: Damn, Doc was right.* As the thought dawned on him, he laughed quietly to himself. Desire for Lila came over him like an addiction; he wanted to tell her about his mother, and he was sure that she would be able to tell him something that would make it better. He struggled to resist the impulse to call her, then was strangely relieved to remember that he was on a plane and could not.

That left him with Jo. He had to get past her: She was just a ghost, an image, a thought, a memory. But he missed her, and he missed his mother. *Damn*, he thought, *I miss Deborah, and I miss Lila, too.* He sighed deeply, crossed his arms, and felt a little more objective.

Lila will take me back, he told himself, *even if for the wrong reasons. The wrong reasons... the wrong reasons....* He mulled this thought over several more times. *I cannot be with Lila, even if I love her, but how in the hell do you love someone enough to leave them?* Then he thought about his wife again. *Maybe it's time to move back home. I know I miss the kids. I do love Deborah, and although I am not so sure that she loves me, as long as I have a job, she'll take me back.*

"Damn," he said out loud, then looked to see if anyone was paying attention. No one was. Michael had completely forgotten that he was supposed to respond to a couple of potential employers. He had been interviewing for months and had a two offers on the table, one in sales and one in management. Michael considered the jobs. *Sales: In sales, you only have to worry about yourself, but sales is a young man's hustle and I am not so young.* Michael unfolded his arms, back in his thinking work mind—with a practical task at hand he felt much more comfortable. *Management: the second job. I know I'm a good manager, but managing people is a pain in the ass. When you manage a team, there is always someone with a problem, and if one of your folks has a problem, then you have a problem... so you always have a problem.* Michael chuckled, then he sighed and looked out the plane window.

Guess I have to make some choices sooner or later, he thought as he looked out at the clouds. *Later maybe?* Then he laughed at himself, *When did I get so damned indecisive? Should I meditate or have a drink? Should I go back to my wife or to the woman I love? Should I go into sales or management?* He laughed at himself a little louder and this time someone noticed—a young girl in the seat next to him smiled at him. He smiled back at her, then looked out the window again. In every aspect of his life, on the inside and on the outside, everywhere, he had a foot in two worlds, he was riding the fence. He could see that by trying to be everywhere and with everyone, he was nowhere and with no one.

Michael sighed, pushed himself back into the seat and pushed the button on the armrest with his thumb to make the seat recline, but it would not work.

"They don't go back when you are in the last row," said the girl.

"What?" he asked, turning to her.

"The seats," she said matter-of-factly. "They don't lean back when you are sitting in the back row."

She never looked at Michael but instead reached forward to lower the seatback tray in front of her. Then, she pulled a sketchpad and several pencils, each a slightly different softness of lead, out of her backpack. She turned to a page on which she had already drawn an image, and began shading the edges of her picture.

"What are you drawing?" Michael asked.

"An angel," she said, still not looking at him. "I draw angels, then I meet them," she clarified, this time looking up at Michael.

"Oh," he said and locked his fingers, then stretched his arms into the air and arched his aching back.

"People with upper back pain are just feeling where their wings used to be," the girl said, then she smiled at Michael and went back to shading her drawing. "The pain should stop in a few years. There is some kind of ascension thing coming, that's what my mother says, anyway."

"You seem to know a lot for a young girl—how old are you?" he asked.

"Fifteen," she answered.

"Michael Tantalus," he said and extended his hand toward her. She reached out and politely shook it.

"Tabitha Seer," she said and smiled, then returned to her drawing. "I draw angels, then I meet them," she repeated.

"What are you working on now?" Michael asked. She kept shading the drawing for minute longer, then she held it out to look at, and deciding that it was finished, handed it to him. It was a beautiful sketch of a young male angel with a boyish face, long hair, and large hoop earrings. His entire right arm was wrapped, with his hand hidden behind him as if it were holding something, a sword perhaps. He wore a skull cap and tennis shoes, and had a large symbol on his chest, *Sanskrit or perhaps Hebrew?* thought Michael.

"This angel is called Wish. He has one dark wing turned downward and white wing turned upwards. He is torn between two worlds."

"His yin and his yang?" Michael asked.

"Maybe," she answered, "He is an interesting one, this angel Wish. He thinks he has to choose a path and he is trying to discern precisely the right one."

"We all face crossroads—it is a part of life—and finding our way, the right way, is part of our own personal journeys. Perhaps this angel Wish is just like the rest of us." Michael was more than pleased with his response to the young girl.

"Maybe," she said, looking at the drawing and apparently deciding it needed a little more shading, took it back from Michael. "But I think it does not matter what path you," then she paused and looked up at him, "I mean he… it does not matter what path Wish chooses, because even if he chooses the wrong path, well, you will end up on the right path… in the end, I mean," she said, looking directly into Michael's eyes.

"You are most unusual, young lady," he said to her.

"Yes, I hear that all the time, but my mother says that I am the normal one and most everyone else is unusual, so I should be patient with them."

She smiled and handed the drawing back to Michael. He looked at it and the words that she had written around the picture. There was the angel's name, "Wish," and underneath the name she had written, "second chance and torn between two."

"What does the symbol mean?" Michael asked.

"I don't know," she answered, "I just draw what I see." Then she pulled out another piece of paper and began another drawing. Shortly thereafter, the pilot came over the loud speaker to announce that the plane was about to land. Michael said his goodbyes to the young girl as the plane landed and taxied to the gate.

He moved quickly past security to find his father standing across the concourse waiting for him. He was glad to see him, and they hugged, holding each other longer than was usual. They spoke often and communicated deeply, so sometimes things could be felt between them with no need to verbalize. His mother's death was one of these things; her loss was heavy on both of them, but there was nothing that either of them needed to say. They were glad to be with the other, feeling stronger together. They headed back to the house, where Michael's sisters had taken care of most of the details and duties: Calling family, making arrangements, and taking care of others while sifting through their own memories and feelings.

The next morning before the funeral, Michael and his father met in the kitchen, both tearing up; they did not need to speak. The moment passed and soon, Michael, his father, and his sisters were riding in a long, black limousine alongside a narrow, winding creek that led down to a meadow and the old graveyard of a small, white church. The land was mostly flat and the only trees visible on the horizon were the large cottonwoods and pecan trees that lined the creek. Michael looked at his father, who was nearly eighty but never seemed old to him, realizing that he still was the strongest element in Michael's life.

His mother had been ill for some time, and though Michael knew conceptually that she was dying, it had not seemed real to him. Now it was all sinking in. She had been an invisible pillar supporting him in so many ways, and he wondered who might provide what she had for him. She had been his spiritual source since he was a child— not a source of dos and don'ts, but a model for how to hold your own heart. She had always adored and loved him unconditionally, and now he was beginning to see that she had taught him how to love. He wanted someone that he could love unconditionally, and he wanted someone to love him the same way. He had always told himself that the women he loved tired of him and stopped loving him. But now he could see that he had it upside-down, he had grown tired of them because he was not getting what he really wanted. Of course, they could not possibly give him what he really wanted, but he would simply stop loving them.

He thought of Jo, who was now very present in his thoughts. He had never gone to her funeral—there had never been any closure—and he did not even realize that he had been holding on to her until he yelled it at Lila. *But one thing I know,* he told himself, *is that she loved me until the very end and I love her still. That was my chance at true love—what we had was different and it was forever, nothing can ever change that.*

He thought of Lila, who was still fresh in his mind; he had thought he smelled her scent on a shirt he had packed for the trip. He craved her and the comfort she would give him. Their relationship was raw, and the more he thought about it, the more he was sure that they could never make it over the long haul. But still, he wanted to call and tell her that his mother had died. Then he thought of Deborah, who was in the car behind him with their children. There was love there, but not the kind that would give him what he felt he needed. She would not offer comfort. Whether she was incapable of it or unwilling to do so, he did not know, but he was certain she wouldn't.

The long line of cars came to a stop, and everyone began to get out. Michael walked to the hearse, and the men his mother loved lined up to carry her casket to her grave: her minister, her brother, her husband, and her son. Without talking, they slid out the long black box, hoisted it to their shoulders, and walked to place it onto the lowering device that would gently carry it down into the grave. Michael stood and watched as people began to surround the gravesite. His mind drifted to another memory: This time he was four, the car door had shut on his thumb, he calmly tried to get his mother's attention, and when he finally did, she snapped into action, opening the door to free his thumb and picking him up to hold him in her arms. And though there was throbbing pain, as his mother held him tightly he knew all was okay. Then the memory faded and Michael was left with the sadness of never being able to get that feeling from his mother again.

I have fallen in love with three women in my life, one who has been the everyday of life, one who has been the excitement and the passion of my heart, and one who was a ghost, just an idea—a thought—and now I have lost all three of them. I lost my wife to the mundane drain of the everyday toil of living, of maintaining a house, of raising children in an endless grind. I lost Lila to the fear in my own heart, the fear of not being enough of a man to meet the intensity of the desire that we created. And I lost Jo to the brutality of ignorance and hatred, but at least I will always have the memory of how we were, forever locked in the height of passion and love; she can never leave me nor can I tire of her.

But then Michael realized that truly, he never had any of them. They had all come needing something, whether healing, security, or something else. He had held them for a while, getting whatever it was that he thought he needed. And trying desperately but unsuccessfully to give them what they needed. And when he began to feel that he was not receiving what he needed—that comfort, that feeling that it was all okay—and when they became dissatisfied with what Michael was able to give them, *Then I destroy it.* The flash of the memory of the bathroom door being kicked open in New York came across his mind. *Damn, he thought, my mind makes everything pretty and behind the door is what is really going on, damn.* Then another veil fell away, *I—who am stuck on "I am not good enough"—is married to or engaged in a relationship with someone who is never satisfied. I'll be damned.* And the realization lead him to what inevitably happened next: "You ruin it," he whispered. It was his own voice, but he heard it like a voice from somewhere else, and it came as a punch in the gut. *I'm chasing something I think I need or need to give? And when I figure out that I will not get it, nor will I be able to provide it, I run!*

More cars were arriving, bringing more friends and family members. Michael was amazed at how many people were coming. He stood next to his father greeting people; some of the faces were familiar and some were not. He had prepared himself for his mother's funeral the way he prepared for everything, in his mind. But now that he was standing here, he could hear words, and he could hear himself replying, but what he had not prepared himself for was that everything was happening in his gut. Despite everything Michael thought and believed about the mind, about the heart, and about being, it was the gut where he met life. In this moment, it was the most substantial part of who he was, a place to hold onto. It was contracted tightly as though he had taken a deep breath and was holding it in, and it allowed him to stand and to greet people. Suddenly, a strong contraction came over him and he bent over double, coughing. Feeling his father's hand on his back, Michael stood and reassured him, "I'm okay."

Michael's eldest sister had three kids, all adults now, and one of her sons had two children, ages four and five. Their mother brought them in just as the service was about to begin to minimize any distraction they might cause. They were bright and attentive and glad to see their grandmother. They rushed to sit beside Michael's sister and began asking questions.

"What's in the box?" the youngest, a boy, asked earnestly.

"Gammy, Gammy is in the box," his older sister informed him.

"Gammy is in the box?" he shouted his surprise. His mother grabbed his hand to quiet him, but the somber occasion was lightened briefly by quiet laughter from those who had heard the boy's question.

"Mom would have loved that," Michael's sister whispered to him, and he smiled and nodded in agreement. Soon everyone sat and Michael found a place next to his wife and kids. Both of his children leaned on Deborah; his daughter lay her head on Deborah's shoulder. The minister cleared his throat and began to talk about Michael's mother, speaking calmly about death. As the minister told stories of things past, Michael's stomach continued to speak to him in small contractions of fear—fear of pain, fear of not being, fear of nothingness, fear of dissolution at death.

But then Michael looked at his wife, who was comforting the children. A soft breeze moved through the trees along the side of the church, and as the branches and leaves gently bent back and forth, rays of sunshine filtered through and the light danced across Deborah's face. And while Michael was looking at his wife, the light seemed to sparkle about her, illuminating wrinkles across the tight skin on her forehead and around her eyes. She wrapped an arm around each of his children a short distance away, but Michael sat alone. He began to pray for his mother, then he prayed for guidance. Then he looked at his wife again, and as her beauty washed over him, his heart leapt as if he were returning from being dead. When she turned and saw that he was looking at her, she smiled, her quiet strength and her steady giving of herself to the children was suddenly evident to him. *Then why could she never give herself to me?*

Deborah's gray-streaked hair was gathered into a bun, exposing her neck, which was still long, thin, and beautiful. Michael felt his heart contract and then slowly begin to warm. *How selfish of me to want something*, he thought. There was no doubt he could see how the years of self-sacrifice, the years of working hard taking care of the children, had aged her. But as he looked at her now, he could see the young woman he had fallen in love with and married. His sensations momentarily moved from his stomach to his heart, and he felt nothing but love for his wife.

"Perhaps I have been wrong, wrong about everything," he whispered to Deborah but purposefully too quietly for her to hear.

Michael turned his attention back to the minister, who was beginning to sermonize. Michael knew that this man had been his mother's pastor for years, and as such, the man no doubt had been under duress from time to time when dealing with Irene Tantalus. She was tough on ministers, demanding that they be more than mere men full of frailties. She molded her ministers the way she had molded Michael, with love and with expectation of them being more. The man was tall and thin with a compassionate face covered in wispy gray whiskers. He likely had been handsome when he was younger but now was prematurely aged, his hair thinning and his skin leathery and wrinkled, most likely from too much exposure to the harsh Texas sun. His dress was more Western than church-like; instead of a tie, he wore a bolo, which was gathered in the center with a large topaz surrounded in silver; his shirt was crisp white with both shoulders covered in a colored, quilted material that reached halfway down his chest; and he wore a dark jacket with matching slacks and black cowboy boots.

"I met Irene Tantalus when I was just out of the seminary. I was young, naïve, and ambitious, ready for anything. Anything, that is, until I met Irene. She was not your ordinary matriarch. She did not want to dominate or control, but she ate young preachers for lunch," the minister began, and his comment sent a wave of laughter through the crowd. "I learned a lot about being a minister from Irene Tantalus," he said in that pitchy voice that ministers always used to invoke emotion. "She always had a sense of ethics, expecting more in a time of change when everyone around her was compromising what they believed. But Irene never doubted her faith. She had a sense of who she was and where she belonged. She had a strong connection to her parents and her grandparents, their lives, their stories, and their actions as they moved across this rugged country while it was still open, wild, and unsettled. She always knew where she came from and where she wanted to go. She never searched for her calling, because for Irene Tantalus, her calling was apparent and simple: never give an inch, but always lead with your heart and always lend a hand."

"She never backed away from a fight either," Michael's father whispered to Michael and his sisters. Michael tried not to laugh, and as he looked at his father, he realized how much he missed him and wondered why he did not travel to see him more often. Then the preacher brought the sermon to the audience.

"Who are you? Where do you belong? And what is your personal calling?"

Michael looked up to find that the minister was looking directly at him.

"Your being did not begin at your birth and it does not end at your death, look around you," the minister looked up across the rows of chairs, pointing his finger slowly across the rows of people sitting there. "Look around at who you can see, your parents, your grandparents, your children, your grandchildren, great-grandchildren. How far can you see? Your life extends past your vision in either direction in this journey we call life, from where you came and to where you are going, you are the connection, you are the connecting link. Many of you know this, you know that you are a link in the chain, but you are also the chain not just the link. What is your generational vision, what is your calling?" his voice had become loud with feeling, so he paused and looked down as if to calm himself.

The preacher took a deep breath and began again, but more quietly. "Sometimes life can put us in a trance-like state. Recently, I saw a man whose car had stalled in traffic. He needed assistance, but cars were going around him, rushing by most assuredly on their way to some important tasks. The man attempted to get out of his car, and as he opened the car door, he blocked a car from passing. The driver of that car leaned on the horn until he closed his door. His misfortune had become someone else's inconvenience. We as a people have become disconnected with the wider realities and responsibilities of our lifetime. Irene Tantalus would have stopped to help that man," the preacher paused again and looked out across the audience. "Space and time, for those of us growing up in this technological era, have become smaller and smaller and more restricted. We are not seeing the larger units that we are part of and are part of us. In our trance-like state and with our focus on the fleeting reward of instant gratification, we as a people have fallen asleep and forgotten who and what we are. We belong to and are part of the universe; we are of the dust of the stars and the dirt of the earth. And we are the ancestor, each and every one of us. We are the parents and we are the children. Irene Tantalus never forgot that and she never lost her faith, she knew her job as a link in life. Each of you are the link between your parents and your children. Pass on love and pass on peace."

The preacher then bowed his head, saying, "Let's pray in silence."

A few moments into the silence, a recording of Irene Tantalus' favorite songs began to play. People rose and began to file out. Michael stood beside his mother's grave along with his father and sisters.

A man lowered the coffin into the grave and then two men lowered a large square of cement over the top, and just as they shoved it into place, a puff of air whooshed out of the grave. Strangely, hundreds of ladybugs came up with the air, many landing on Michael and his dark gray suit.

"Mom loved ladybugs! Look at them, they are all over you! You always were her favorite," Michael's sister teased. Michael held out his arms, and slowly one after another, the ladybugs took flight upward and out of sight. After the graveside ritual, Michael's sister linked her arm with his and they walked back to the car, followed by Michael's father, who had his arm around the other sister. They all quietly climbed into the long, dark limousine and headed back to the house. They drove in silence for only a few minutes, then began to talk about small things, to ease their tension; the weather, details about who was coming to the house, and what food had been laid out. The car soon pulled up to the house, and as they got out of the car, they were met with greetings and embraces from family and neighbors. All had stories about Irene that they told with gusto. Some of the stories had been told many times before but everyone enjoyed re-living Irene's past deeds and daring acts—she had left her imprint on many.

After a while, Michael found himself looking around the house, as if seeing it for the first time. He'd never noticed the drapes the entire time his parents had lived in this current house, but now he looked at them with keen interest. The material was heavy and substantial, an off-yellow covered in designs of blue flowers and paisleys, and the curtains ran from the ceiling to the floor. Michael realized the drapes were a remnant of his mother, something she had chosen; perhaps they made her feel happy, so he stood for a time looking at them, trying to see them as she had seen them.

As he walked through the kitchen and dining room, which were crowded with people eating and chatting loudly about various things from cattle to how fast time flies, Michael saw that every available surface was covered with more food than could possibly be eaten. He moved through the crowd, hugging and chatting politely until he reached the den, where he found his daughter sitting on the couch with his great Uncle Clovis.

Clovis was Michael's grandmother's youngest brother, a war hero who had been awarded many medals, including multiple Purple Hearts and the Silver Star. He fought in the Pacific during World War II, and though nearly 90, he was in good physical shape and mentally sharp. Uncle Clovis and Michael's daughter were watching the memorial video loop of Irene Tantalus. Picture after picture came across the large screen while Michael's mother's favorite songs played—Baptist hymns, country and western songs, and musicals. Every image evoked an emotional memory, powered by the music. So Michael sat on the couch with his Uncle Clovis and his daughter to experience memories of his mother.

"Dad?" his daughter spoke up.

"Yes, honey?"

"What is the greatest fallacy of mankind?" she asked.

"Such a serious and thoughtful question," Michael said as he turned to her, "Let me think about that for a moment," putting two fingers to his chin and looking upward. After a moment, he answered, "I think mankind's greatest fallacy is its inability to discern truth."

Michael smiled at his daughter, more than a little satisfied with his answer.

"No, Daddy," she said simply, "It's the inability to lick your elbow."

She stood as she gave her father the answer, kissing him on the forehead, then bouncing out of the den and into the crowd of people in the kitchen. Michael watched her hop away, then bent his arm trying to get his mouth to his elbow, then bent it the other direction with equally futile results. He turned toward his Uncle Clovis, who was laughing, silently at first, then out loud.

"Damn kids!" Michael said, joining Clovis in laughter.

"I loved your mother, Michael. She was such a pistol. And always she adored you. You were such a wild young man, and now I see that gene in your daughter... she is quite a young lady, so full of spirit, that one." And just at that moment, a passing relative blew out a nearby candle and its serpentine smoke winding upward drew Michael's attention. Clovis noticed Michael's reaction.

"Michael, when you were in New York, back at 9/11, did you smell any burning bodies?"

The question caught Michael off guard—his uncle delivered it directly and without emotion. Michael pursed his lips. "Well, that's what some people were saying, but I don't think so. There was an odd, acrid odor all over lower Manhattan, and some were saying that it was the smell of incinerated bodies, but others were saying no. Just an awful burnt smell."

"Do you ever think you smell that odor now? I mean, sometimes in places other than New York?"

"Yes, sometimes I think it is on something in my closet. You know, shoes, shirt, something," Michael answered, waving his hands.

"Can't find it, can you?" Clovis asked, looking directly into Michael's eyes.

"No, sir, I can't," Michael answered.

"It's not there… and don't worry, you are not going crazy," he said, then he looked at the floor and added, "Phosphorous does a hell of a thing to a man."

He looked up at Michael again. "Michael, do you still carry things?" Clovis asked, causing Michael to shrug his shoulders.

"I am not sure what you mean," he said.

"Have you been back to New York?"

"No," Michael answered, then added, "Well, once, but that was just after and I had to go to…to take care of some things, but I haven't been back since then."

"Over the years, some of my buddies have returned to battlefields: They say it is liberating, but some say it's painful."

"What are you saying, Clovis?"

"Well, if you suspect that you are carrying anything, then I might think about going back, but don't go alone. It's got to be the right time and the right friend, or friends. Then afterwards, if it were me, I'd find myself a right good honky-tonk and have myself more than a few belts."

Clovis looked at Michael for a moment, then slapped him on the leg, and stood up. As he got to his feet, he began to chuckle again. "That is some daughter you have," he said as he headed into the kitchen.

Michael found himself alone, looking at the pictures on the video, many of which featured himself as a child, always smiling. *Where is that kid, is he still inside of me?* Then he thought about what Clovis had said to him. *Am I carrying anything?* He mulled the question around and it made him think of his wallet, so he reached into his pocket and pulled it out. He used his wallet many times a day, but never looked at it carefully. He inspected it closely now, seeing that all the grooves on the leather were worn thin and it was crushed flat at the ends. The seams were a little frayed, it looked like something you might find in a garbage pile. *Why do I hold on to things so long? I think it's time for a new wallet.* Opening the wallet, he searched for the small piece of paper that he was not even sure was still there. He did not see it at first, so he opened the wallet further, almost turning it inside out. He could see the folded paper tucked deep into one of the corners, still in the same place he had put it years ago. He retrieved it and carefully unfolded it so it wouldn't tear. He looked at the number written there. He could not have remembered the number, but looking at it now, it seemed more than familiar, instantly available for his immediate recall.

At that very moment, Michael's wife Deborah flopped next to him on the couch. She leaned in and kissed Michael on the head. She was willing to forgive the emotional distance between them for the time being. She had been close to Michael at one time and she knew he was close to his mother. And she wanted to be supportive to him the best she could.

"How are you holding up?" she asked.

"Good, fine," he nodded. "Well, okay," he added.

"Not very convincing," said Deborah, putting her hand up to Michael's cheek. "It is okay… I mean it will be okay." It came out a little oddly but Michael disregarded how it sounded. He looked at his wife, there was something different about her and he felt his heart beginning to swell: She looked more beautiful to him now than she had for a very long time. Her hair, her makeup, her dress, everything contributed to make her look prettier than he had remembered her ever looking. He scooted closer to her and put his arm on the back of the couch just behind her.

"Deborah, I was thinking that when we get back to Charlotte, I would come by the house."

Michael was smiling while he said it, but his wife Deborah sat motionless, her face blank. Michael cleared his throat and continued, "I was thinking that maybe it is time for you and me to go to dinner, and maybe it's time for you and me to talk and spend a little time together."

He flashed his broad smile at her, the smile that never let him down. Deborah's face showed no emotion, as she searched for what to say.

"Michael," she began, trying to smile, "I know that this is not the right time nor the right place to talk about this but I'll just say it: I am seeing someone." Deborah smiled broadly, unconsciously for just a moment before catching herself. "I think the relationship has become serious—he is such a good man, steady and patient, and he has been there for me."

She looked down and then up at the pictures of Michael's mother's life. As she did, an image of Michael with Deborah and the kids flashed across the large screen. Deborah looked back at Michael as if trying to say something more.

"Right," he tried to mask his surprise. "Of course."

Now Michael was looking for the right thing to say, but he had been knocked back on his heels. The words "serious" and "such a good man" were like daggers. He sat motionless, looking at his wife.

Then, Deborah leaned closer to Michael and whispered, "Michael, I love you… I probably always will. I waited for you to come around for years. I cried for months after you walked out the door. But I am over all that hurt and confusion now. I have moved on. You should move ahead with your life, Michael."

Deborah forced a smile. "I am really sorry about your mother, Michael. I think you are just missing her and that's okay." Then she stood, kissed Michael again on the head, and walked to another room without looking back. Michael looked down, still holding the piece of paper in his hand. He looked at the number and his stomach tightened. Then a large close-up of his mother came across the screen. Michael smiled, then whispered to the image of his mother: "Should I go to New York?" Then the image changed and his mother was gone.

Impulsively, Michael pulled out his cell and tried to call Lila. The call immediately rolled to nothing, no voicemail nor anything, so he assumed that she was blocking his calls. He decided that he could not blame her. So instead he closed his eyes and did the meditation technique, easily touching the silence within himself. After a moment he opened his eyes and a picture of Michael appeared on the screen. He was four, jumping into the pool; in the photo, the water looked frozen as it splashed upward and outward. Michael's arms were stretched out wide, an exuberant expression on his face, and his mother was behind him with her arms stretched outward, too, her face pure joy.

Michael fumbled with the piece of paper. He looked at the number once again, peering at his handwriting as if checking it to see if it was a forgery. *I am sure that the number doesn't work anymore, but I suppose I have to try it.* He stood and headed out the back door where he could be alone. He stood beside the pool and dialed the number.

"Hello."

The voice was curt and deep, and it stunned Michael so much it took him a few moments to say anything; he had just dialed the number without thinking about what he would say.

Finally, he spoke: "Hello, this is…"

"I know who this is," said the voice on the other end, cutting Michael short.

After a pause, Michael firmly said, "I think we should meet."

Now, there was a pause on the other end.

Eventually, the man said, "Alright."

PART 4:
The Surrender

"Human existence is not pre-destined; every man is given free choice [will] to accept the Divine plan of existence or to follow the path of ignorance and misery."

Bhagavad Gita, Verse 47

"See, I set before you today life and prosperity, death and adversity; in that I command you today to love the LORD your God, to walk in His ways and to keep His commandments."

Deuteronomy 30:15

"See, I am setting before you today a blessing and a curse."

Deuteronomy 11:26

"Furthermore, tell the people, this is what the LORD says: See, I am setting before you the way of life and the way of death."

Jeremiah 21:8

The New York Gravesite

Late summer 2010

Light from the already setting sun reflected off the top of the thick thunderclouds visible through the plane window next to him. Michael looked at his cell phone, where 9:11 P.M. shone brightly on the screen.

"Perfect," he said sarcastically. The plane began to descend into the thick, dark clouds below, and Michael let his thoughts access the tender memories and places of sorrow that were precious, sacred, and often hidden deep within his mind. It had been almost nine years since Michael had been in Manhattan and his unconscious provided him with a steady stream of feelings of loss and guilt. The plane shook and shuddered as it sank into the thickening dark clouds. Rain appeared and ran in long, tear-like streaks across the small window while Michael allowed himself to think of the last night he and Jo were together.

He had given her a ring—not a terribly expensive one, but a significant one—with little diamonds embedded into arches that bent across the top and crossed beautifully, forming the symbol of eternity. Michael had not been searching for a ring but he had come across it one afternoon while walking in the city. He saw it in a shop window and immediately knew it belonged to Jo, so he impulsively bought it and gave it to her late one night on the 52nd Street Bridge. Jo's hair blew about in the wind, and her eyes momentarily welled with tears.

"What does it mean?" she had asked.

"Nothing," he had answered, "I just wanted you to have it." She had stared long into his eyes, reading his every thought and feeling.

"I don't believe you," she had said as she reached for his hand and began walking. He was unconsciously nodding his head, and as they walked he began to speak.

"I know we are both married and we both have lives with kids and family." He stopped for a moment, took a deep breath, then said, "This ring means forever, and it is for the time when we can be together, always, when…" Then he lost his words.

"Are you asking me to marry you?" Jo's voice came out loudly, and she stopped walking.

"Well, you know, I mean that, well…" he struggled.

"Okay, I'll marry you," she had said plainly, "But you have to put it on my finger." Michael smiled, then took the ring box from her and took out the ring, got down on one knee, and placed the ring on her finger. They looked into each other's eyes for a long time, then he stood and they embraced, kissing softly.

"I love you, Jo," he had said to her quietly, earnestly.

"I love you, Michael," she replied, allowing herself to melt into him, laying her head on his chest as he sheltered her from the wind.

Suddenly, the plane lurched in the storm, jerking Michael out of this memory. Several people shrieked while the plane fought against the unseen resistance of the swirling storm.

There are so many things I wish I would have told her, things I felt but never said. Michael stared out the window as the plane finally emerged from the great thundercloud. He could see speckles of sunlight and a few patches of blue sky over the top of the next large cloud. As the jet headed into this next storm cloud, Michael saw a large flash of lightning streak across the clouds with very little gap between the arresting flash and the crackling boom of thunder.

And he thought that the total of what he was seeing was like the women he loved, givers of sunlight, givers of life-confirming rain, but capable any moment of a sudden strike of deadly lightening. It was all beautiful to him. *Yes*, Michael thought, *love can take you across the blue sky and into the stars to reveal deep secrets, but it's equally and more likely capable of a sudden strike of energy leading to your destruction.* Then Michael laughed at himself. *But either way*—he thought of Jo, then Deborah, then Lila—*life without the power of love is merely counting time until death.* And then a thought came to Michael; he heard his own voice in his mind but felt that the thought came from somewhere else: *To love with everything you are is death.*

Michael sat back in the seat of the rocking plane and closed his eyes. He began to think small compact thoughts of love and gratitude when he remembered something that the teacher said, "Love is the deepest possible acceptance of what is." He tried to reconcile his competing thoughts. Michael continued to think thoughts of gratitude while trying to hold on to his thoughts about what he imagined love was, but the teaching kept taking him deeper into the subtle parts of his mind.

The plane jolted Michael into alertness again as it touched down hard. Within moments, the airplane reached the gate, and passengers began to stand and depart. Michael stood and pulled his suitcase out of the bin above his seat. He walked, in no hurry, to the car rental counter. Always before, Michael had taken taxis while in New York, but he had plans to drive to out to Long Island to see Jo's husband. He drove trance-like from LaGuardia Airport to the Midtown Tunnel and across Manhattan to his hotel, leaving the car with the valet outside.

"I won't need the car until the morning" he said to the man, handing him a ten-dollar bill. He checked in, then went up the elevator to his room and collapsed on the bed. He considered whether or not he was "carrying" anything emotional. And taking a self-reading he decided that he did not feel anything at all, so he took off his clothes, throwing them onto the chair next to the bed rather than taking the time to hang them up, and turned out the lights.

Following his Uncle Clovis's advice, he had plans to visit Ground Zero. And he had also followed Clovis's advice to not go alone; he had called a friend whom he thought would fit the category of "right friend," even though he admitted to himself that he had no idea what that really meant. Michael's old friend J.B. Heckem knew Michael's history, including all his experiences in New York, so he knew he would not have to explain anything. J.B. would not ask Michael any questions, but he would be willing to talk if Michael wanted. In addition, he had some depth and was capable of introspection and perspective, two things that Michael respected. And most importantly, J.B. would be more than willing to drink with Michael, so Michael surmised J.B. would be the "right" friend—actually, the more he thought about it, he decided that J.B. would be the "perfect" friend for this task.

Michael thought about what it might be like to see where the towers had been, and he had a strange sensation that he could not identify, so he instinctively and quickly stopped thinking about it. But to stop his thinking was different from meditating. Even though he tried to control his thoughts, the strange sensation continued.

So he decided instead to think about his plans for the next day. He had arranged to meet with Jack Kelleher—Jo's husband had agreed to meet him in the morning at a diner out on Long Island, Jack's home turf for sure. Michael considered calling to cancel the meeting. There was a tightness in his stomach. *Why stir up the past, would any good come of it?* Then Michael did the technique again in purposeful movements. In essence he thought a thought of gratitude. And his mind could only think one thought at a time, so by thinking a thought of gratitude, he replaced the thought of anxiety over his coming meeting. *Damn, this technique is going to change me*, he thought, *I need to be ready to protect myself, because no telling what he might want to do to me. If I am thinking praise, gratitude, and love instead of "watch out for a fist," I might get clobbered.* Michael went back and forth, but he kept doing the technique, and beginning to feel better, he relaxed enough to drift off to sleep.

Michael was already out of bed when his alarm began to buzz. He always faced conflict with intention and readiness, but the meditation had left him calm. *How could he meet Jack Kelleher with love?*

Michael's drive to Long Island was peaceful. He easily found the diner, and driving not far past it, he found a place to parallel park the car. It was well into the morning, but it was still dark and the rain was coming down in sheets. Walking in the rain toward the door, Michael tried to imagine how the meeting would go and decided that if Jo's husband tried to hit him, he would let him, but only one punch. But then he thought further, *No, I will let him hit me as much as he needs. I won't fight back.*

Michael stepped into the diner. It was a local place and Michael was an outsider. He did not yet know where Jo's husband was or what he looked like, but he knew standing just inside the door dripping that Jack was looking at him and knew exactly who he was. Michael started at one end of the diner and methodically scanned the room for the man he was here to meet. The darkness outside, coupled with the incandescent lighting on the inside of the diner, bathed everything in varying shades of sepia tones of red, yellow, and orange, giving the scene the feel of an old movie. The diner appeared dirty, not because it had not been cleaned, but because it was old. Then, across the diner sitting in a booth Michael saw a man glaring at him, and he was eye-to-eye with Jack Kelleher. Jack had a broad, tense, unshaven face. His neck was thick and leathery, his shoulders were broad, and he looked powerful, unsmiling. Michael walked slowly but purposefully to the booth and sat across from him. The two men sat for a few moments without speaking, the sound of the rain was loud even through the closed window.

Without taking his eyes off of Michael, Jack reached into a folder beside him on the seat and pulled out a photo and put it on the table.

"This is Jo's and my daughter Morgan. She's fifteen," Jack said to Michael. When Michael took the photo and looked at it, it hit him like a sledgehammer. "My God! She's the spitting image of…" Then he stopped himself. He stared at the photo, he could not believe it. It looked like Lila. And it looked like Jo.

"My God," he said again, "She looks just like her mother," and as he said it, he looked up. Jack's eyes were full of tears. Michael looked away from him, but it was too late and tears began to fill his own eyes.

"For years I fantasized about hunting you down and killing you," Jack said, his voice beginning stern and angry, but then starting to crack. "But now I see you as just another person who loved Jo. I could see it on your face the minute you looked at the photo. And I guess I know that she felt something for you," he said, then stopped talking to wipe his face. Michael handed the photo back to Jack, who took it and placed it back on the seat beside him.

"Your daughter is beautiful like Jo," Michael started, then stopped himself, not sure what to say or what not to say. He had come prepared to say some things, to take punches if necessary, but this was not going as he had imagined, and he could think of nothing that needed to be said. Then Jack began talking again.

"I miss her, I love her more now than when I had her, and sometimes when my daughter is talking I think I hear Jo and I call out to her. I am so full of things that I cannot understand or settle. For so long I told myself that if it were not for you, I'd still have her, that she would at least still be alive, and her daughter could talk to her about boys." Jack tried to keep himself together, but his voice began to weaken and pitch upward as he spoke through his tears. He lowered his voice and leaned toward Michael. "Morgan's so great, she wants to talk to me about boys, and I don't know what to say. I just keep thinking and wishing Jo was here." Then both men teared up again.

Suddenly, Jack reached across the table, grabbing handfuls of Michael's trench coat at both shoulders, crying, "I know it wasn't your fault. I want to hate you! But you are something she loved, so now you are something I value because you are a part of her." He bowed his head as he said it.

Michael reached up to Jack's shoulders as tears ran down his own cheeks. "My God, I am so, so sorry, I just, I just…" but no words came for Michael as the two men pulled closer together over the table. At that moment, the waitress approached, but as she looked at the two men crying and grappling with each other, she said, "Maybe I should come back at a better time."

As she walked away, both men let go and their tears turned instantly into laughter, easing the tension. Jack sat back in his seat, sighing heavily.

"I know this was not your fault," Jack finally said as he looked at Michael. "And for a long time, I hated Muslims and those damned hijackers and those bastards that sent them. After Jo's funeral, I was determined to join the military, but then Jo's mother walked me to Morgan's bedroom and we both watched her sleeping, and I knew that I had to stay for her. And over time, the more I thought about it, I realized that the terrorists came because someone else told them we were evil, that it was their duty to God to kill us. We are all from the same place and what kind of God orders you to kill another? No God. I realized this was a delusion, and then I realized that for me to think that they were evil and that I should go kill them was just as delusional. Religious leaders telling young men to kill in the name of Allah, the name of God: ridiculous. I had all this hatred bottled up inside of me, then every morning I would wake up and see my daughter's big, beautiful eyes looking at me, needing love and not just the love of one, but of two. I had to be even more love for her. And being love, even if only for her, changed me. Then it hit me that no matter what, no matter who did what, no matter what they did to who, my response had to be love. It had to be." As Jack finished talking, a soft smile came across his face.

"I wish I could go back… I wish it all the time. I ask myself why, why the hell did I have to meet her?" Michael began to ramble, but Jack put his hand up to stop him.

"Look, you can't go back and make it all okay, and sometimes our past is just a bunch of shit. You called me. I'm not sure why, but if it's because you need forgiveness for you to move on with your life, then okay."

At that moment, Michael suddenly bent over, convulsing into a cough, coughing hard again and again. He reached for the napkin holder on the table, and in one awkward motion he pulled out several napkins to cover his mouth. The coughing slowed, but his lungs now burned and the urge to cough again was strong. Michael felt a little dizzy with the sensation that he was slowly falling. As he sat up straight, he felt as if the ground was shaking and then there was a slight flash of falling beams and debris crashing to the ground. It was only an instant, and then he felt as if he could perceive one bad cancerous cell passing on bad information to another cell, and then one thought of hatred transferring to another thought. But then there was a thought of gratitude, and it replaced the bad thoughts, and the chain was broken by one single thought. All the other thoughts of hatred and anger were replaced as Michael imagined a single ray of light penetrating through all of his thoughts. The light began to accumulate in his heart, and as his heart quickly warmed, the urge to cough subsided.

"That cough sounds bad," said Jack.

"I used to think so, but now I think it may be okay," answered Michael. The two men looked at each other for a moment. Jack reached to the folder on the seat beside him and pulled out an envelope. It was white and sealed, but it was wrinkled badly as though it had been wet and then dried. Jack slid it across the table to Michael. There was a brown crescent stain of coffee on one end and written across the front in large letters was Michael's name.

"I don't know what's in this letter, and I don't want to know. It was in Jo's pocket the day she died." Then Jack slid another piece of paper across the table with an address on it. "This is where Jo is buried. I wasn't sure you would want to know, but now I think you do." Jack then lowered his head, took a deep breath, and asked, "Did she die alone?"

Jack's question came like a hammer at Michael. "No," he answered in a near-whisper.

"Did she suffer?" Jack looked up at Michael as he asked.

Michael's face contorted slightly as he answered. "No, she did not," he said, bowing his head as memories of that day began to flood into his mind.

"You don't need my forgiveness. You need it from the big guy upstairs, and I am sure that it is there for the asking. So that leaves only one bastard who tortures you and won't forgive you... and that poor bastard is sitting across from me," Jack said, then stood and walked out of the diner and into the rain.

The waitress came back to the table holding a carafe of coffee. She stood with her weight on one leg, looking at Michael. He reached to the upside-down coffee cup and turned it over; after he set it gently onto the saucer, the waitress filled it with coffee.

"Anything else?" she asked.

"No. No, thank you," he answered, and she walked away. Michael poured a little cream into the coffee and watched it swirl around in the cup. He sipped just a little, then folded a $20 bill and slid it under the saucer. He picked up the letter and the note with the address of the cemetery. Then he stood and headed out into the rain to go see Jo.

As he drove, the rain began to let up. The address was in Central Islip and the GPS on his phone told him that he did not have far to drive. There was very little time to think. Michael came to a crossroad, where he turned and quickly came upon a large brick sign that read All Saints. The clouds were thinning and moving quickly; small breaks in the clouds overhead began to appear as sunlight began to stream down, first in front of Michael then to his side, then all about him. He parked the car at a small, brown brick building. There were few windows and a large cross on the front of the building. Michael walked into the building, where just inside the door he was greeted by an elderly lady.

"May I help you, sir?" she asked.

"Yes, I am looking for the gravesite of Josephine Kelleher."

The woman shuffled slowly to a map on the wall and pointed a shaky finger to a location with a number on it. Then, she carefully walked to the door, opened it, and pointed Michael in the right direction, then tilted her wrinkled face upward to peer at Michael with a loving smile.

Michael walked down a narrow asphalt road until he reached a stone pathway, where he turned and began to read the headstones. About halfway down the row of headstones, near a tall tree, Michael came to a large, flat granite stone. It had a brass faceplate with the words "Josephine Kelleher, Born October 12, 1969, Died September

11, 2001, Beloved Mother, Sister, Daughter, and Wife, We will never forget you." Michael bent down and touched the brass inscription. Everything was still and peaceful, and the only noise was the soft ebbing and flowing of cars passing in the near distance. In Michael's hand was the letter, and he finally opened it. Across the top Jo had drawn three large hearts.

My Dearest Michael,

The past months with you have been the greatest times of my life. And you have helped me learn so much about myself. I now see the whole job/career thing for what it is, that spell is broken. My daughter means everything to me. And I've learned that we don't stand alone, there is something within us that is not separate, heart strings connected to hundreds, maybe thousands. Family roots to be sure, but further to friends and communities. And anything I do that uproots those connections affects the entire community. But for me, what I want, more than anything is to be with you. And there just doesn't seem to be any way to reconcile these two thoughts.

I have fallen in love with you, perhaps being in love for the first time—no, most certainly for the first time—you are the first and only love I have ever had. I feel crazy when I am with you, but crazy in a way that feels like I am really me. And when I am with you it is as if it is not just me thinking but us together and I am filled with nothing but you.

My husband is a good man in so many ways. He is good to me and he is a good father. But passion makes me want to leap into nothing and hope I have wings to fly. And right in this moment I am filled with love for you, but too, I am filled with despair, for all the strings, all the roots, all the mess I would leave behind in the wake of passion's sake.

My mind tells me that passion cannot last and that anything that burns this bright and this hot will consume itself. I could not sleep last night knowing we were to meet, my heart would not be still. So I walked to my daughter's bedroom and watched her sleeping, the sweetness of her face, the scent of her hair, and I listened to her lightly breathing. And I knew that I just could not rock her world, even if it means walling off that place where my heart and soul reside, and the end of that part of me that believes in fairy tale endings.

Please forgive me, I do and always will love you and long for you, but I have to stop seeing you. I feel you more in me than anyone I have ever known. I am sure that none of this makes any sense, but please don't try to talk me out of this decision. And please understand. I have no right to ask this but: Will you hold me one more time?

I will forever cherish our times and feel grateful for falling helplessly into you, so unsettling, but never have I felt such a depth of being alive as when with you, so dangerously close to destroying my life and so dangerously close to divine rapture! Perhaps baby, I am just scared, please forgive me.

Michael stopped reading and looked at the headstone. A cool breeze caressed his back as the clouds moved out to sea. He looked back at the letter, and he could see three small roundish places where water had dripped and the ink of her writing had blurred. Jo had circled the spots and drawn an arrow to the margin where she had written, "Can you see where my tears have formed three hearts!?"

Michael looked again and indeed, in all three places, her tears had left what looked like roundish hearts. He smiled, then let out a little air from deep within his lungs. Then, he continued reading.

Again, I have no right to ask, but please be with me one more time. You are like a storm that has moved into my heart, filling me with excitement, with passion, and with possibilities. But too, I am full of fear, as though we are flying so high and I am scared of the fall, and all the things around me that would fall, all the strings to my heart, all the things I hold dear, all the things I believe myself to be, the good wife in me, the constant and loving mother in me, the pleasing daughter in me, the stable, supportive sibling—so many depend upon me.

All this makes me so sad, sad for me and my heart. Losing you will be like a death to the person that I think I am or rather the person I think I can be. The thought of not having you leaves a pain in my heart, and empty place where I cannot breathe, but this empty place will be my most treasured place of refuge in my heart. I know I keep contradicting myself and this all sounds so strange and all I can think of to write is to ask you to hold me one more time until I am in deep sleep, then quietly leave me, for I cannot bear to watch you walk away. I will love you forever!

Love,

Jo

Michael put down the letter and stared off into space, letting Jo's words sink into him. Love had failed him; or more accurately, his own idea of what love was had failed him. The veils just kept falling. *When would it ever end?* he asked himself. And all that was there was the sound of cars and trucks passing on the highway. After a time, he tried to think of what to do next. His body took over, and his impulse was the same as always, to keep moving, never slowing, always seeking the swirl of chaos. He longed to be in the soft roar and vibrating hum of an engine and passing pavement. *Yes*, he thought, *in the car and passing miles and possibly the grace of a steady rain.* That's what he told himself, *I need to drive, and feel the motion.* Perpetual motion to stay ahead of the nightmare of memories— sweet, but wrapped in despair. He had to keep moving always to stay ahead of the ever-present darkness that trailed him.

"No," he said aloud, thinking, *I came here to end things, to put things to rest, and if I don't go through with this now, I'll just have to come back.*

Michael pulled his phone out of his pocket and dialed.

"Hello?" answered J.B. Heckam.

"J.B.!"

"What's up, buddy? When are you heading to Hell's Kitchen?"

"I am ready to do this thing. I'm headed to Eighth Avenue now—should be there in time for a late lunch."

"Great, I'll be there waiting with the boys," J.B. told him.

"J.B."

"Yes?"

"Better bring your liver!" Michael laughed, then hung up the phone and thought about Jo.

Then he let his mind move to the day back in 2001 when the planes came. For years, bits and pieces of the day—a smell here, a sound there, a flash of memory—had pushed their way through and over the fragile dam that had been erected to store the most intense part of that morning. And now, with his heart ripped open by Jo's letter, Michael was headed to where the Twin Towers had once stood. And with very little effort, he let the memories of the day unfold from his subconscious into his present thoughts.

Day of Days

September 11, 2001

It was just after 9:00 A.M. when the Port Authority officials broadcast orders to evacuate the World Trade Center's South Tower over the speakers of the building's public address system. The occupants had initially been told to remain in the building, but tens of thousands of people now were evacuating the massive towers, pouring into the street. Chaos and confusion grew as the North Tower billowed dark, thick smoke. Michael could not see what was happening, but he knew from the radio that things were bad and people on the street were distraught. Then at 9:03 A.M., terrorists crashed United Airlines Flight 175 into the World Trade Center's South Tower.

The loud, fiery crash sent a vibration reverberating up and down Michael's spine. He began to walk toward the calamity, walking in stunned silence until he could see the gaping black hole in the South Tower, smoke and flames pouring out. In a slow-motion, dreamlike state, Michael moved closer as people pushed by, running and screaming. He stayed close to the building to let them pass, but he kept moving nearer. He found a place to watch the streets fill with hysterical people, police cars, and fire engines.

Michael lost his sense of time. "It's snowing," he heard himself say softly, then realized it was ash and debris he saw sparkling as it descended in the bright sun. Michael held out his hands and turned a little, then looked up into the dark hole in the building.

"Michael!"

"Michael!" Thomas yelled again, but it had no effect. So Thomas ran toward Michael; when he reached him, he grabbed him and shook him. Michael looked down, then back up into Thomas's eyes, finally snapping into the reality of the moment. Michael's eyes grew wide and panic raced across his face. He reached for his mobile phone and began to dial Jo's number frantically, having to start over three times before he could punch the buttons properly to place the call. A busy tone came across Michael's phone and its digital screen spelled the flashing letters c-o-n-j. Michael ended the call and tried the number again and again.

Michael began to run toward the tower through the throng of evacuating people. One woman passed, screaming, with her hands covering her ears. A man passed, blood on his white business shirt, as he walked slowly by carrying a briefcase. Michael darted through the panicked crowd with Thomas running close behind him. He crossed Cedar Street, and when he reached Liberty, he stopped to scan the people walking about.

"Hey, brother," a man said to Michael, "Do you have a cigarette?"

"No," Michael replied, then heard a loud, unidentifiable crash. He heard more screaming. Thomas caught up to Michael, out of breath.

"Are you looking for the rest of the team?" he said, gasping for air.

"Damn," was all Michael said as he began dialing his phone again, number after number, as if another number might go through.

High above, people stuck their heads out of broken windows. Thick, dark smoke trailed out of the window above their shoulders. One after another, they began to ease themselves further and further out of the windows to escape the fires, trying not to make the decision between fiery hell and falling. But then there was no choice, and as Michael and Thomas looked up, tiny pieces of debris began to fall.

"Oh, my God. Oh, my God. Oh, my God." Thomas repeated it again and again, recognizing that the debris was human. And as a person falling came closer to the ground, the realization finally hit Michael—what had appeared at first to be fluttering debris became flailing arms and legs. The two men stood transfixed in shock and horror. Then another person jumped, falling slowly at first, then quickly accelerating before crashing loudly.

"Lord, have mercy," Michael uttered. As the men watched, a third, then a fourth jumped. And as the people fell, something simultaneously fell within Michael.

"The hell with this, I can't watch anymore," said Thomas as sirens screamed. The recognition and sounds of the people witnessing those falling were unmistakable as more fell and tumbled.

"You gotta go! You can't stand here!" a policeman was shouting. The smoke kept pouring, and there were more sirens and more screaming and another person falling, crashing to the ground.

"Be damned, be damned," Michael said. The policemen were moving people away, and Michael and Thomas began walking, but then Michael stopped to watch another fall. It ripped its way into his memory, and all the horrendous sounds swirled cacophonously around him.

"Damn it! Don't look up!" yelled Thomas, as he pulled on Michael's jacket to keep him moving.

"I have to find Jo!" Michael yelled to Thomas. Then, another man fell from the Tower, looking almost peaceful in the midst of the chaos. Pop! Bam! A large piece of debris hit the street, jolting both men.

They passed a man who was hopping in rapid circles yelling, "Oh, my God! Oh, my God! Oh, my God!" Throngs of people moved in all directions. A bus blared its horn, trying to push through the crowd. More screaming sirens. Michael looked up again at the billowing smoke that was filling the sky. A large truck honked, then the incessant whine of a passing ambulance's horn temporarily drowned out all other sound until it had passed. People were walking quickly. Some ran away, knocking others over and not bothering to stop to help them up. Still others came running toward the chaos to help in any way they could—ordinary people with no thought of themselves, like small lights on a dark day. Thomas and Michael were forced to keep moving.

"Let's get the hell out of here," said Thomas.

"I've got people here somewhere, and I've got to find Jo!" shouted Michael, then added, "You go! I order you to go!"

"Hell, no, I'm not leaving you. There are people dying everywhere, but I am sticking with you," he said evenly. Thomas was beginning to calm, and it helped Michael compose himself.

"Okay," said Michael, "But we have to find Jo and anyone else, so let's keep circling. Maybe we'll get lucky."

"Go home…. everyone go home!" a man was shouting.

As Michael and Thomas turned a corner, they came across a place where some firemen were bringing people out of the buildings on stretchers and setting them down. Many of the windows of the buildings around them were broken out. There were fewer people here than on the other street and it was a little quieter. Policemen and firemen were talking into microphones, exchanging information and calmly requesting help as they called out coordinates and codes that Michael did not understand. Michael watched as they brought people and set them down behind red tape that was stretched from a light pole to a street sign. Two men set down a woman—she was burned black, her skin or clothes or both were dark and oily, and Michael was so close he could smell her burns. Another man was carried by two firemen—part of his skin was gone and he was shaking. An ambulance came and loaded as many people as possible into it, then drove off. Michael watched the first responders working, doing their jobs, not giving in to the chaos, but clearly distressed and in danger of being overwhelmed. The police had cleared many of the people, but the near-empty street where they stood was covered in debris. Michael and Thomas walked on, and as policemen pushed them further and further, their circling perimeter widened. But as they kept moving, they were able to move closer to the spot near the South Tower where Michael was supposed to meet Jo.

The two men rounded the corner of another building and could see an open parking lot covered with more and larger debris and a burning car. As they walked, music somewhere played a soft, mellow melody, and Michael could hear firemen talking calmly, calling orders. They ignored Michael and Thomas as they walked by. In a deserted market where papers were blowing about, they could see people gathered just inside a building. Two men carrying a woman passed by, a priest walking close behind, but they did not appear to be in a hurry. Michael and Thomas rounded another street corner, but there was a crowd of firemen there, so they turned back and headed down another side street. Just as Michael realized that he had completely lost track of where he was, he saw her.

In the distance, Jo turned and saw him. They ran toward one another. Michael's heart began to race, and he felt a jolt of relief and a rush of joy, then there was a roar like a great tidal wave and the popping of floor after floor exploding, and the sky darkened as a half-million tons of debris came crashing down. The ground was shaking, and Thomas was running close behind Michael, gaining ground. The noise from above was growing louder and louder as they ran past a man lying in a fetal position against the building. There were firemen and a few others running across their path on a side street. A blast of swirling air blew off the firemen's heavy hats, then lifted all of the people into the air. There was a bright flash, and everything slowed down for Michael: He knew that he was about to die.

Somehow in the moment, Thomas caught up with Michael, and grabbed him by the back of his shirt and his right arm. Though he was shorter and much stouter, Thomas picked Michael up and dove with him to fall into a doorway for cover. The stone archway of the old building held under the onslaught of the falling building of glass and steel.

Then there was a temporary but infinite silence.

"South Tower down. Repeat, South Tower down."

These words were the first thing Michael's mind was able to discern, and the voice of a shaken but professional fireman brought him back to his senses. Michael attempted to get to his feet, but it was still dark and hazy, and he was shaking. The acrid dust of pulverized cement and other materials burned his eyes and lungs. He struggled to breathe, and as he coughed, he drew more dust into his lungs. He coughed uncontrollably for a few minutes, covering his mouth with his jacket as Thomas stood, pulling on him. Finally, Michael was able to stand and move from the doorway in the direction where he had last seen Jo. He tried to run but faced mountainous piles of rubble.

"Jo!" he shouted, "Josephine Kelleher!"

Michael struggled to make progress through the mangled debris, and as he passed ghostly figures in the thick smoke, he moved close enough to them to make sure that none were Jo. He imagined that they were firemen, policemen, civilians, and angels. Michael coughed again, but he did his best to suppress the urge as he moved. He heard a soft hissing and crackling as he passed a dull glow in the dark shadows of the destroyed street. Michael looked closer at the soft light and realized it was a twisted beam standing vertically, popping with more crackles. He moved on frantically to find the spot where he thought Jo had been running, but he was disoriented. It was still eerily quiet as he crawled over the heavy rubble. The skin on his forehead was pulled taut, as though his entire scalp was tense and could not let go. His body had experienced more input and intensity than could be processed, and a feeling of helplessness came across him as he tried to find Jo. But he kept shouting as he moved.

"Josephine Kelleher!"

"Michael," said Thomas, "Let's get the hell out of here!"

"I have got to find her," his voice was shaky.

"Okay, let's find her," Thomas said, still not sure who they were looking for. The air was still smoky but beginning to clear ever so slightly. There were some cars crushed along the street and they saw a fire engine flipped on its side. The devastation was complete.

"Josephine Kelleher!" Michael shouted.

"Josephine Kelleher!" Thomas echoed.

"I am sure we are close to where she was standing," Michael said desperately to Thomas.

"Michael?"

He heard a chillingly weak voice. And though small, the sound hit Michael with immense impact. His stomach dropped, and he threw himself into the broken bricks, the cement, and the hot metal. Thomas fell at Michael's side and they dug and clawed into the debris with their hands, trying to uncover the feeble voice. As Michael dug frantically, his heart raced, and his lungs sucked in more dust—clouds of it at a time. Finally, he reached Jo. Her head was caked in blood and ash. She stared up at Michael, but she was barely breathing. He tried to pull her out of the rubble, but she was caught on something. Thomas turned to run for help.

Michael cradled Jo. "I've got you," he said to her, "It's going to be okay."

Jo convulsed, but she kept looking at Michael as a puff of air came out of her lungs and a single tear rolled out of her eye. She stopped breathing. Michael stared at her for a long moment.

Then, he shouted, "No! Be with me! Be with me!"

He tried to breathe air into her lungs, and as he took another breath, a large man forcibly lifted Michael out of the way so several other firemen could move the rubble with a pry bar. They lifted Jo out, put her on a stretcher and began to run, with Michael and Thomas running right behind them. Through and around the rubble, the men ran until they reached a church, and they took Jo up the steps. Several men worked to save her life, but soon, they all looked at one another and relaxed, knowing there was nothing they could do. When they stopped, no one said anything, but one of the men made eye contact with Michael, communicating with no words. There was a loud ringing in Michael's ears. Then, an ambulance pulled up, and as they loaded Jo into the back, he tried to climb in, but a fireman held him by his arm.

"I am sorry, but we cannot spare the room," he said to Michael and loaded more people into the ambulance. They shut the doors, and as the siren screamed, Michael watched the ambulance drive away with Jo inside. Barely 20 minutes had passed since he had seen her running toward him, and he struggled to grasp the reality of what had just happened. Thomas put his arm around Michael's shoulder.

"They say we have to move out of here," Thomas said to Michael as easily as he could. Michael looked at Thomas and he nodded. "I am really sorry," Thomas added, then stopped talking. Michael instinctively led them westward toward the Westside Highway. The two men walked in silence like ghosts. Soon they re-entered the crowds of panicked, screaming people running in all directions. And when they reached the Westside Highway, they turned north, where they saw throngs of firefighters and police swarming toward the North Tower, which was still in flames.

A wail went through the crowd standing on the streets watching, and Michael and Thomas turned to see the North Tower of the World Trade Center collapse. Screams and cries of those watching mixed with the sirens. Michael did not want to see any more— he felt as if he simply couldn't see more. He already had seen and experienced more than he could bear—so he turned and headed to the hotel. Each step was conscious and difficult, like he was walking for the first time. Thomas followed, and the two men slowly walked in the unrelenting sun, covered in ash.

"Michael," Thomas whispered, "Look at your hands." Michael looked down and was surprised to see all of his fingers covered in ash and dried blood. He did not feel anything. So he kept walking.

Back to Ground Zero

Fall of 2010

Michael found a spot to park along the street. It was a modest walk to the pub where he was to meet J.B. and a few friends. Across from where he parked was an empty lot covered in broken cement with small strands of grass pushing through here and there, and littered across the entirety were different-colored glass shards. The lot sat between two large brick buildings and a high chain-link fence closed off any entrance to the empty lot, yet inside the space a woman in tattered clothing sat against one wall.

With knees pulled up and arms wrapped around her dirty legs, she lay her head on her even-dirtier arms. Michael looked at her and wondered how she had come to be in this fenced-in area. She reminded him of an animal he had once seen in a zoo, and although Michael had only been a young child in the memory, he remembered thinking that whatever the animal had been like in the wild, it was not here now. He had felt compassion for the animal, knowing intuitively that this was not how a wild animal should live.

Surely she can get out of there, Michael thought, then he wondered how she had come to be in this condition. He wanted to help her, but all he could think to do was to give her some money. He looked in his wallet and found only a $100 bill.

"Hey!" he shouted through the fence. The woman sat up with an empty look in her eyes. "Come here! Come over here!" Michael said it like a command, and she obeyed, struggling for a few moments to get to her feet, then stumbling her way over to Michael. She wrapped her stringy hands around the chain link to hold herself to the fence. Michael folded the $100 bill in half lengthwise and stuck it through the fence. She took it with one hand and looked at it, as if trying to discern what it was. Michael waited for some sort of recognition or acknowledgment, but none came. There was no change of expression on the woman's face; she did not even look at Michael, but instead turned to shuffle back to her place against the wall, holding the bill carelessly and with no regard for its value. And once back at her spot, she sat and laid her head back on her knees, the $100 bill falling to her feet. Michael watched her for a while, wanting to do something, but he just did not know what. After again surveying the area and seeing no way in and no way out, he turned and headed to the bar to meet his friends.

J.B. and several others were sitting outside joking and talking about baseball. Michael knew why he was here and J.B. knew as well, but there was nothing said about it.

"What's up, buddy?" J.B. asked as he stood and greeted Michael, extending one hand in a handshake while leaning in and patting him on the back. It was a kind of hug, warm but not intimate—a decidedly masculine greeting. Each of the other men stood to greet Michael, too. Michael asked the waitress for water, but by the time he greeted everyone and sat down, there was a beer in front of him. Soon, chicken wings, nachos, and other bar food appeared, and the conversation was light and everyone laughed easily. From where Michael was sitting, he could see the empty lot. He could not see the woman, but he watched as people walked by the chain-link fence, never looking in and never seeing the woman. All the people walking were decidedly headed to some specific place, and they would find seats at bars or keep walking on down the street to their destination, and the woman they didn't see was nothing to them.

"Okay," J.B. announced, "It's time. Let's head to Ground Zero," he said casually. There was no discussion about it but everyone knew what they were doing; Michael felt a little as if he were being watched. He was still raw from Jo's letter and not much time had passed between so many recent heartbreaks, but he had the same feeling he had at his mother's funeral: He felt strong, and in this moment Michael felt as if there was nothing left within him that could break and there was nothing left for him to do. He thought about what he was feeling and decided that it was not apathy, apathy left you weak, and right now Michael felt as though he could take on anyone or anything.

But strangely he had very little awareness of his surroundings. Michael was in the flow of his friends and was quite content to be ushered into a cab and look out the window as they headed south down the Westside Highway towards Ground Zero. Michael began to think about what to expect, and there was an increasing roar in his mind but no discernible thought. The men in the cab were all talking but it was all background noise to Michael. He rolled down the window and let in more noise from the city, and it all blended together, the noise of the city, the noise in the cab, and the noise in his head.

In no time the cab pulled over to the curb, more words, J.B. and the cabbie exchanged money, a large bill from J.B., a few smaller bills back to J.B. Michael stepped out of the cab and was completely swallowed by the busy city. The sky had cleared and was an amazing blue while the sun steadily dried puddled water here and there left by the rain. The men all watched Michael, giving plenty of space. He struggled to get his bearings. He searched for a place to cling to, where he could take hold and measure his next steps, but instead he felt like he was tumbling into the area where the towers had once been and did not know where he was.

They walked as a quiet group towards where Michael thought the North Tower once stood, but he was not sure. There were fences and construction, it had been nine years since Michael had walked these streets and he was disoriented, nothing seemed as it was supposed to be, or at least how Michael remembered it used to be. Where he thought he remembered there should be a building, there was none, and in other places stood edifices that brought no recollection, so he kept walking, kept moving, hoping to find a place to land.

Michael meandered around the outside of a high chain-link fence, behind which were many people and trucks and cranes all very busy working on the 9/11 Memorial. The last time Michael had wandered outside the fences, there was nothing but destruction and fire and everything was dusty, but now the odd smell was gone, things seemed cleaner and clearer, the streets even seemed broader, and Michael felt there was a certain amount of rebirth here in the place where there had once been so much destruction. *This is how it always is and always should be*, Michael thought, *rebirth where the old shit becomes fertilizer feeding the next thing.* Michael turned away from the fence and saw many people walking around. *Tourists maybe*, he thought. Everyone looked so ordinary to him.

"I think we are coming in from where the North Tower once stood," Michael said to one of his friends, *But I don't think this is the way we escaped.* He felt the need to explain some things to the others but to keep some things to himself. J.B. spotted a table with books with a man standing behind it, talking to passing tourists. J.B. approached the table and Michael followed, then the rest of the small group. Michael looked at the books; they were bright, shiny and glossy, and all about 9/11. Picture books of the terrorist attacks and of the destruction.

"What are these?" Michael asked the man. He had dark skin and thick black curly hair. He answered Michael in a clear but thick accent that was unrecognizable.

"Memorial books, look, please," and he handed one to Michael. Michael turned to his friends and they were beginning to look through some of the books as a policeman pushed his way through the small crowd, bumping Michael hard as he moved towards the table.

"Whose books are these?" the policeman yelled, "Are they yours?!" The man behind the table began speaking a foreign language. "Oh now you don't speak English?!" the policeman yelled as he angrily overturned the table, causing the pretty books to bounce across the pavement. Michael stood motionless for a brief moment, then tossed the book he was holding onto the others on the ground, then turned to walk away, followed by J.B. and the others.

Michael turned to look over his shoulder at the policeman and the man that had been behind the table. The policeman had him by the lapels of his jacket and pushed him to the ground; he was rough and Michael could no longer hear what either man was saying.

"Like Jesus and the money-changers," J.B. said to Michael.

"What?" Michael asked.

"Profiting off the sacred," he answered. Michael looked at J.B. and then back at the man and the policeman. The man was now face down in the street and the policeman had his knee in the man's back. "We are walking on the sacred here," J.B. added. "Probably means nothing to the poor bastard being busted, but profiteering on 9/11, can you imagine? I bet that policeman knows someone who died here on that day." Michael stopped walking and looked at J.B. "This ground has gone from profane to hallowed," J.B. said and Michael nodded as the men continued walking. Michael's mind felt surprisingly clear but he could tell that there was much going on deeper inside his head. It was like the way he took shallow breaths so as not to disturb the damaged lung deeper down. There was also plenty in his body that had been locked there for years and now it was starting to come out. He was beginning to shiver, but it was not cold. He kept a little distance from the others so they would not notice. A cough came and bent Michael over before he could suppress it and he reached out to steady himself on a light pole. As he stood, his first thought was about Jo. He wished he had the letter. He wanted to read it again, just to feel her presence, to hear her words. He wished he had not thrown it away. Then he thought about what he would do if he came to the place where they had been together the last time and decided to avoid that place.

J.B. and the other men sensed that Michael was trying to move away from the group and they let him. But soon they came upon a store front that said, 9/11 Memorial Preview Site. Michael was a little distance away but he followed the other men into the memorial museum and was immediately hit with emotion. There were many people milling about, and as Michael felt water in his eyes he sought somewhere to be alone.

"Damn, this is tougher than I thought," he said to J.B. "I'm going to wait outside, you guys take your time," and he quickly left the museum. It was still bright outside and Michael took a deep breath then crossed the street to where there was some shade under a few trees next to a church. There was a slight hill and Michael scampered up it and sat down unknowingly amongst tombstones that were aged enough that their engraved names and dates were barely legible if at all. *I should have come alone*, Michael thought. *No, I should have come with Lila*. He craved her in this moment, he wanted to bury his head into her breast, he wanted to feel her heat and hear her heart beat. He lowered his head and watched the dancing shadows across the sidewalk that the sun made as the light came through the leaves of the trees. He wanted to read the letter again, he tried to think what it said. He remembered disposing of it but now he could not remember why. He pulled out his cell phone and tried to call Lila, but the call would not go through and it would not roll to voicemail. Guilt was growing within him and he thought of his children, and now he wished he was with them in this moment, and he thought about his mother, where was she now? He thought about his father and imagined that he was talking to him there among the graves.

"It wasn't all death," he whispered to his imaginary father. "I have heard it said that time heals all wounds, but I don't know I think we just learn to live with however wounded we might be. But I wonder Dad, by surviving do I owe something to the dead, should I be living a certain way for those who are no longer here?" And then, as if his father was there, he heard answers in his mind. It was the wisdom of his father speaking to him, things he had heard him say, and things that he imagined were the way his father would answer.

"What we call our wounds are merely part of what we have become. We do not live for just the good things we have experienced, we are living for the experience of living itself, both good and bad, for those we have loved and those we have lost and those we have battled, it is all part of the experience of life, that is what we live for. Some wounds never heal, nor should they, but they become part of who we are and what we carry forward. And as far as owing anything to the dead, well, the dead are dead. It is for the living that we live for, we live our lives for ourselves, and for 'ourselves,' I mean all those around us, everyone."

Then Michael's body twitched hard, the acrid smell of something burning crossed his senses, then the sound of sirens, bwop! His entire body jerked and he felt the urge to cough. He struggled with flashes of images, of difficult memories and buried feelings. He wondered if he was better to resist or to let them flow, then he thought of Jo and tears ran down his cheeks, he did not resist their course but lowered his head so no one would see and he felt ashamed. Thoughts surged through Michael, memories of sound, of hard vibrations and the concussion of impact, and Michael was lost in the content of his past until suddenly and to his surprise, his mind did the technique by itself. His thoughts turned to the teaching and he began the rote repetition of the words and thoughts of the technique. One new thought replacing all his old thoughts.

Michael sat doing the teaching, the larger context of what he was, the observer within, watched itself as he introduced a thought of gratitude, then came a thought of running through the debris that had been in the streets and then a thought of gratitude, then a thought of the roar the moment everything came down, then a thought of gratitude.

"Let's find a pub," it was J.B.

"I thought you would never ask," Michael answered.

"I'll let the crew know where we are going, they can catch up later," he said as he crossed back over the street and disappeared into the Memorial's preview site. Michael stood and stretched, the memories ebbed like the tide and his mind was quieter. He noticed that he felt pretty good, surprising since he had prepared himself to feel terrible, and he was grateful to feel just a little sound. And the thought of gratitude in his mind acted like a thorn removing all the old thorns, the old thoughts that had been so deep so long, thoughts that had putrefied. And now, having them out, he felt better, lighter, not happy or giddy, but in some way a little relieved.

J.B. crossed the street toward Michael and they began walking and circling the Memorial construction. They turned down Liberty Street and the two men walked slowly about watching all the busy, fast-walking people. *They seem to have such purpose*, Michael thought. They came upon a firehouse, and as they walked alongside Michael paused. He thought of the firemen and the policemen, the men and the women, which he had watched going into the North Tower after the South Tower had already collapsed. It was the bravest thing he had ever witnessed. The memory warmed him, then again he was filled with gratitude. FDNY Engine 10, FDNY Ladder 10, Michael read on the firehouse then he saw a memorial on the long wall. Fifty, maybe sixty feet long, it was a brass relief sculpture depicting firemen in action. Michael reached out to touch it, he ran his fingers across the wall, and again he felt warmth in his heart. Michael smiled in gratitude.

"It was the year of 2001, in the distance in the blue horizon, in the morning of September 11, a plane appeared in the sky," Michael turned to look at the man that was speaking out. It was a tall willowy black man wearing tattered pants and sandals, bare-chested with a cloth bound to his head making him look like a shepherd from biblical times. He brandished a long wooden staff and pointed it toward the sky as he spoke. He turned directly toward Michael, then pointed his staff at him and said, "Why have you come to me, my son?" Michael looked about to see who the man was speaking to and then realized it was him, but Michael remained silent, not sure what to make of the man. "Do you seek absolution?" he bellowed out like an evangelical preacher. "Then choose God, my son," he said, lowering his voice and his staff. "You suffer because you have one foot each in two different worlds, you have to choose, my son. Be not of this world. Choose God with every thought and every action and every moment, ruthlessly choose, my son, and all your suffering will end," then the man turned back towards the memorial construction and once again raised his staff, "It was the year of 2001," he bellowed. Michael felt a tug on his arm,

"This city is full of crackpots," J.B. said, then he put his hand on Michael's shoulder and led him into a bar.

Michael turned and walked into O'Hara's Restaurant and Pub. Inside it was bigger and more spacious than Michael expected for a bar in Manhattan. It was clean and well-lit inside, and looked as if it were almost new. The broad bands of wood across the restaurant were stained but not too dark, exposing the long beautiful runs of the grain of the wood. There were large wooden beams with no small amount of detail in the trim and carpentry. Something more likely to be in an old, stately hotel than a financial district pub. The brass beer taps stood tall and were bright and shiny. The pub itself was in two levels, the men entered into the lower level which was nearly full with what looked to Michael to be New Yorkers. And standing there was a man with a white shirt and suspenders; he had a small towel over his shoulder and directed the men up a half flight of stairs to the upper bar room. The upper level was even more open and hospitable and was speckled by an eclectic gathering of people. Michael turned to J.B and said, "I think we have been banned to the land of the tourist," and then he laughed.

"Brother," said J.B., "We are all tourists, and as long as the beer is cold then all will be well," and he laughed. Against the far wall was a long window where the men could see people walking along the sidewalk. Michael walked to the window and watched the busy people walk by only a short distance away.

"Must be reflective glass," Michael said as he made funny faces at the people as they passed, "They don't seem to be able to see us."

"Did you consider that maybe they don't want to see us," said J.B.

"It's like one of those natural habitat zoos," said Michael.

"The wild animals of Wall Street," said J.B. then he faked a shudder of fear and both men laughed. Suddenly J.B.'s expression turned serious as he looked first at Michael then the bar. Both men, acting more like two little boys, scrambled to beat the other to the bartender. Michael reached the man first. The bartender also had a white shirt with dark suspenders. He was a large man with black hair and a big belly. He leaned toward Michael, putting his massive knuckles on the bar.

"What'll you be having?" asked the barman.

"Stout," Michael said sternly. The barman put a large glass under the tap filling it only partway then let it settle.

"You?" he nodded towards J.B.

"I'll be halving de same," J.B. answered in his best Irish accent, which was not the least bit amusing to the barman. "I'll be thakin' ya fer gittin the first round," J.B said to Michael.

"Was that a pirate accent?" Michael asked.

"Arrrgg, very funny and don't make me say 'shiver me timbers,'" answered J.B. The barman started another tap for J.B.'s beer then finished filling Michael's glass and slid it across the bar. Michael put more than a few bills on the bar and slid them to the barman. He looked at the pint of stout in front of him and in the head of the beer he could see the image of a rough shamrock.

"Now that's art," said Michael as he picked up the glass put it to his lips, and began to gulp, he tilted the glass and he tilted his head until the last of the beer went down his throat then put the glass back down on to the bar a little too loud.

"Arrrg, another," he said in a poor imitation of a growling pirate.

"Oh, so that's how it's going to be," J.B. said as he picked up his beer. The barman finished filling the glass again for Michael and as he slid it across the bar he gave Michael a warning glare, the kind of look that says, "I'm not going to put up with any of your shit." Michael looked directly at the large bartender and promptly chugged the second pint of stout. Only this time Michael put the glass onto the bar gently and quietly, exaggerating his care, and then he slid it across the bar to the barman.

"Friend," Michael addressed the barman, "May I please have another?"

"Maybe we should take it a bit easier and slower, *friend*." he said to Michael in a quiet tone. Michael put both his palms on the bar and was about to say something but J.B. interceded.

"Look," he said in a near whisper to the large barman, "This is my friend here's first trip back to this place since 9/11." The barman looked at Michael.

"You were here?" he asked Michael but Michael said nothing, his face blank. The barman poured Michael a beer and slid it across the bar,

"Here you go," was all the barman said, then disappeared downstairs.

"Thank you," Michael said as the barman walked away. Michael picked up his beer and both men walked back to the window and watched the people outside the window. Some were walking by in dark suites and bright ties, there were sharply dressed women walking swiftly, some in high heels and some in tennis shoes. Those walking weaved their way in and out of other casually-dressed people standing in the middle of the sidewalk, looking all around, some carrying cameras and some taking pictures with their phones.

"Lost my Mom," Michael said unexpectedly.

"I heard, sorry brother, I lost my Dad last year. Tough, that time of life I guess, but doesn't make it any easier," J.B. said as he looked out the window, then sighed.

"How's the family?" J.B. asked.

"The wife, I mean the ex, is seeing someone, she says it's serious."

"Is that a bad thing?" J.B. asked

"Do you feel like you know your kids, J.B.?" Michael asked changing the subject a little. This time J.B. looked at Michael, then he drank the rest of his beer. "It doesn't feel like I am here," Michael said, changing the subject again.

"What do you mean?" asked J.B.

"I don't know what I was expecting, and I don't know how to explain it but this place doesn't feel like where I was back then, everything is different, and I guess I am different. I just had expectations in coming here," Michael drank down the rest of his beer.

"Yes, that is when the problem arises, when there is an expectation," J.B. was searching for the right thing to say so he added, "The whole world is different now."

"You're up," said Michael.

"What?"

"You're up, your round, I want another beer," said Michael.

"Michael, I am your friend, and as your friend it is my duty to tell you that you don't need another beer," J.B. said it in a solemn tone.

"I don't?" asked Michael and looked at J.B.

"No, Michael, what you need is a shot," J.B. said while keeping a serious facial expression.

"That is so beautiful and that is why you are my friend," said Michael and put his hand on J.B.'s shoulder.

"Yes, it is my job to be your friend and I take my job very seriously," J.B. said as he slapped Michael on the back and walked over to the bar, returning shortly with two hefty shots of Irish whiskey. The men clanked the shots together and drank them down. J.B contorted his face then put the empty shot glass down upside-down on a nearby table. Then he looked at Michael more seriously and said, "Yes, I feel like I know my kids."

"I've been gone so much," Michael said, "Too much," and that was all Michael said but his face showed more and J.B. knew not to ask. Then the barman approached Michael and J.B. with a large, overstuffed picture scrapbook under his arm and two mugs of beer.

"Bring it back when you are finished," he said to Michael then he set down the beers. "These are on the house," he said, never smiling, and turned and walked away. Michael and J.B. began to turn the pages of the book of photos and newspaper clippings, and memories began to come back to Michael. He looked at the pictures of the white and gray debris that was in the streets and in the fire escapes and lodged into and onto every nook and crevice. And the pictures let Michael know where he was and he slowly began to get his bearings. He looked out the window to where he and Jo had been and everything stopped like darkness had encroached on his every awareness, then he shuddered. Michael picked up his beer and turned away from the window, away from anyone's eye.

And as he faced the wall, within inches of his face was a patch, a fireman's emblem stuck to the wall. And next to it was another, one, and another one and then his vision widened. A policeman's patch then another, then a firehouse emblem then another and all along the wall to the ceiling and across the beams, *How did I not see these?* he asked himself, then another shiver ran through Michael. He turned back towards J.B., who was now looking at all the patches too, and a feeling of respect and reverence came over both men. They continued looking through the picture book in silence then Michael returned the book to the barman who gave him a slight smile and knowing nod.

At that moment the rest of the men in their party came into the bar loudly and there was another round of shots and more beer. The mood was festive as they began to tell stories of things the others had done through the years and there were more drinks. After a while they moved to another bar further in up on Wall Street and as they continued to drink and laugh, other people joined them, attracted to the good energy of the group. They began to move from bar to bar, some people would drop off and others would join as they all laughed and teased and flirted with anyone nearby.

J.B handed Michael another shot, but instead of drinking it Michael set it down on the bar. He looked at the shot and it occurred to him that they had been drinking quite a lot and that he should feel drunk but he did not. He felt clear and clean in his mind and he pushed the shot away and turned toward J.B. "I'm done," he said plainly.

"Done drinking?" asked J.B.

"With everything, I am done with everything," said Michael, "As long as I can remember, we have always been chasing something."

"Yeah, like girls and beer," said J.B. as he drank his shot then Michael's, and both men laughed.

"Yes, like girls and beer and good times, then we chased jobs, then careers, then love. Right? Then 'the woman,' a marriage, then family, then more pleasure and more good times, but then, J.B.," Michael paused then said, "I had a shock. Then nothing seemed right, it was like I could see right through everything in my life for what it was and what it wasn't and suddenly nothing seemed to satisfy, so I refined the chase. I thought I should live a certain way, the right way, I began to chase true love, enlightenment, and I sought Truth, whatever the hell that meant. I was expecting something, I am not even sure what I thought was going to happen, but whatever it was, it was going to be great!" Michael paused and looked at J.B.; he was listening as intently as he could to Michael but his eyes were a little glassy and he swayed a bit.

"So you're done," J.B. repeated.

"Yes, I am finished. And you were right when you said that problems arise when we have expectations. All this struggle for so long, I feel like I have lost so much. When I came here to drink with you it was because I was coming to terms with giving up. I have always heard that you never give up. But there just seemed like no reason to keep thrashing about trying to get somewhere. And then I had a realization."

"Tell me," said J.B.

"In that precise moment of giving up, what was experienced was surrender. I was not giving up, I was surrendering, and there is a difference."

"How so, how is giving up and surrendering different?" J.B. asked. And as Michael answered he had the feeling that he was hearing at the same he was speaking.

"If you are in a fast-moving stream and you have the idea or expectation that you should be upstream, then your experience of your life is struggle, you are bound to get beat up. Giving up is when, in exhaustion, you stop struggling, but suffering continues because you still have the idea that you should be upstream. Surrender is letting go and letting the stream carry you ahead. And your experience is no longer struggle and no longer suffering, and it might even be exhilaration. It could bring fear, or love, or anything, but you let the stream carry you and you joyfully participate in your life accepting *what is*.

"So what of your search for truth and enlightenment?" asked J.B.

"*Truth is simply what is*, and the more we search for it, the more we chase after it, the more we think about it and talk about it, the further we get from it. And *Enlightenment* is complete and total acceptance of what is. And there is one more step. You accept what is, but your focus of your awareness is not on what is, but the source of what is. Enlightenment is surrender and focus on source. It's that simple," Michael said all this while looking into the eyes of his friend and J.B. felt overwhelmingly peaceful as he looked back at Michael.

"Okay, you're done, what next?" asked J.B. Michael looked out the window of the bar and pointed at the big brass Bull of Wall Street.

"I am going to ride that bull," he said and walked outside, with J.B. J.B laced his fingers together to give Michael a boost up and onto the bull and once on top Michael mimicked a cowboy in a rodeo on a real bull. He put one hand down and one hand into the air and said, "I'm strapped, open the gate!"

J.B. put his hands together in a cone at his mouth and made a noise that sounded like a horn. "Burrmp!" J.B. made the noise loud enough to garner the attention of passersby's.

"Yahooo!" Michael screamed and kicked his legs as if the bull had come alive and was kicking and bucking. J.B. clapped and cheered as Michael rode the bull with god-like composure, staying balanced and centered on the bull as it kicked with all its strength to throw Michael in the wild contest with the beast, and Michael rode him for the eight required seconds without being gored, kicked, or torn to shreds.

"Yee haw!" he yelled until J.B. made another sound of an ending horn and as Michael slid down off the bull the expression on his face was joy.

"What next?" asked J.B.

"I think I'll go for a walk," he said, "Thank you J.B.," Michael said as he put his hands on J.B.'s shoulders.

"Don't go getting all misty on me, burr burr," J.B. said, then he grabbed Michael and pulled him in for a hug, unusual for J.B., "Keep 'em rolling, Michael Tantalus."

"Take care of that family, J.B.," Michael said as he smiled and then turned and headed into the night, walking south. Michael wondered for a moment what time it was but his curiosity was not enough for him to check and he kept walking instead. He meandered his way through the streets until he found himself on Water Street and he knew where he wanted to go. He wound his way to Battery Park. There was a breeze off the dark water and a street lamp lit a small circle where he found a bench and sat down. He could see the lights on boats as they passed and he thought he could hear birds chirping, a sign that the sunrise was not far off.

Soon an elderly woman came upon Michael. She was bent over and shuffled her feet as she walked. As she came into the small amount of light of the street lamp, Michael could see that her hair was in tangles and she was dirty. She was wearing several layers of clothes with long underwear extending beyond her skirt and with mismatched socks pulled up to her knees. She sat politely next to Michael and looked out over the water, her hair stiff against the more than fair breeze. She was singing quietly or perhaps humming, Michael as not sure. The tune was familiar to Michael, *Ah* he thought, *Silent Night*.

"Silent night, Holy night," Michael tried his best to sing but he had very little air in his lungs and it came out like a melodious whisper.

"What's your name?" the woman asked Michael.

"Michael," he answered curtly trying to act annoyed so she would leave him alone; it was an unconscious response by Michael, after years of learning to put up boundaries it had become his natural response. But tonight was different, Michael was letting go, so he relented, more out of exhaustion than any consideration. "I am

Michael Tantalus," he said, more friendly this time, and extended his hand to the woman. The old woman giggled as she shook his hand.

"What's your name?" Michael asked.

"Harold," she answered.

"Harold," Michael repeated, "That an interesting name."

"Harold B. Smith, to be exact," she said with no small amount of emphasis. "Want to see my identification?" she asked as she produced an old, worn, brown wallet. She unfolded it and pulled out a driver's license and handed it Michael. He examined it with difficulty in the dim light. He could see the picture of a balding middle-aged man and he read the name on the license out loud.

"Harold B. Smith," then Michael looked at the back and handed it back to the old woman.

"Well, Harold," Michael said, "What brings you to Battery Park?"

"It will be light soon and you can see angels at sunrise," she whispered, "For some reason, angels like it here at sunrise," she said it matter-of-factly as she put away her wallet. "And what brings you here, Mr. Tantalus?" she asked Michael, smiling broadly as though she were about to laugh. He looked up into the softly lightening sky and let out a big sigh. "Let me guess: You are looking for true and pure love!" she said with a little excitement and pointed a finger at Michael. Michael looked at her and said nothing, but he smiled. "I am a love expert, I can spot a romantic in a heartbeat," she said. "Yes, I am sure that you have been looking for love. But you don't *look* for love, silly, you *Be Love*," she held her hands out, palms up as she said it. Then she stretched and yawned and said, "Daddy, I am sleepy, and very tired." And then the woman laid her head on Michael's lap and closed her eyes. And though his nose filled with the smell of urine his heart filled with compassion and he stroked her dirty hair. It was soothing to Michael and he easily drifted off to sleep.

Michael swiftly fell into a deep dream state. *High on a stone cliff at the end of a long and deep valley there was a cave. The cave led into a maze* of catacombs deep into the rock. Michael walked carefully, he was bent so with age that he looked at the ground as he moved along. His clothing was coarse and scratched his skin, a reminder of his state as a human bound to the earth far beneath the heavens. And the rough cloth pulled and caught on the ridges of scars and fresh wounds across his back. He jolted as he heard yelling and the shrieks of other monks. He moved as swiftly as his crippled body would allow, shuffling his bare feet across the smooth stone floor. He reached the mouth of the cave and looked out, and in the horizon he could see three winged creatures flying towards the monk's lair.

He turned to run in fear but before he could get far into the catacombs the winged beings were upon him. He flung himself to the ground against the cave wall and covered his head, trembling before the massive winged beings.

"Mich'El, you are needed," the voice was deep, bitonal and lovely, like a melody that vibrates the entire body and mind. Michael turned to see that the creatures were angels. There were three of them and they were massive and one of them was extending a sword to Michael with the hilt towards him. Michael as a monk stood and extended his hands outward and blood began to ooze from wounds on his palms. The large angel placed the sword gently into Michael's frail hands; its weight was overwhelming. But as he looked at the large steel sword he began to recognize ancient, sacred symbols etched into the metal. And as Michael began to whisper sounds that corresponded with the symbols. The sword became lighter and lighter.

Michael grew instantly in strength and size, and as he stood straight he felt wings at his back.

"I have wings," he said simply to the three angels. The three angels took flight and headed out of the cave and Michael followed them carrying the sword. They flew down the deepening valley, staying in the crease of the land and just above the trees. Soon the acrid smell of sulfur flooded Michael's nostrils. Deeper and deeper into the earth the valley fell and as they reached the bottom there was a dense, noxious cloud of dust and debris, like a caustic lake. And around the edges the trees were burned and jagged shoots of tangled steel beams protruded from the ground.

Michael flew into the dense, cold cloud with his sword aimed out ahead of him. He was instantly besieged in all directions by slimy bulldog-like creatures, only they were winged, their front paws had long menacing claws, they had no *hind legs, and their tails were like the tentacles of a squid. The dense cloud was dark, blinding Michael, and the creatures were on him like piranhas, biting him everywhere with large angry mouths. He swung his sword to no avail for the creatures were too close in to fight them.*

Michael turned and began to wing his way out of the toxic fog. He crested the dark cloud and flew up into the clean air of the deep green valley. Suspended in the blue sky, Michael scanned the large trees for a hold. Spotting an ancient oak and with one swift overhand throw, Michael sheathed the sword into the middle of the massive tree nearly to the scabbard. Then he circled high above the hellish dense fog, facing the sky upwards towards the heavens then folded his wings over his body like a sarcophagus and let himself drop into the dense cloud. Farther and farther he fell. Falling and falling, in total surrender. Past the slimy beasts into the fires of hell, encased within his wings like a butterfly in a cocoon.

His speed increased faster and faster and he did nothing to resist his fall, the heat intensifying around him as if he were an asteroid speeding into the atmosphere. Sensing no bottom and when he could bear it no longer, he suddenly knew it was time to come from his shell. He extended his prodigious wings and instantly halted his fall. He turned and began to ascend, upwards he flew in pursuit of air. He swiftly flew out of the acidic air and landed near his sword, embedded in the oak tree. Michael was completely encrusted in a thick, black, charred layer of what he thought was skin but it was deeper. And as he tried to move, pieces of the charred exterior began to crack. He balled his hands into fists and banged his chest, and a large chunk of incinerated matter fell away, then another piece and then another, and he had the sensation that it was himself that was crumbling away. And as the crusted shell began falling away, brilliant bands of golden light burst forth until everything but light fell away. And the light that was himself blended with all the light that was there.

And then Michael's head fell, he quickly caught himself, the feeling of falling awakened him. Michael stretched out his arms and noticed that the old woman was gone. He stood and walked to the railing next to the water. There was light in the sky in great arcing bands announcing the coming sun. And beyond the water in the distant horizon was a slender strand of land, and above the land was an orange sky. The water was still and reflected the dawn. Above Michael the bands of light were rapidly expanding in a glorious sunrise, and at the edge as far as Michael could see, the land formed a barely perceptible and disappearing line between what was real and what was reflection. Michael felt overwhelmed by the bright, luminous bands of sunshine coming across the water. And he watched in awe all that was unfolding before him. And as he scanned the horizon to take it all in, to his right he saw the Statue of Liberty some distance across the water, and it looked as if she were facing the morning sun, standing straight, taking in all its splendor.

"Hello, Ms. Liberty!" Michael shouted and waved to the statue. He breathed in several deep breaths and watched the sun begin the day. And as he stood he realized that his wallet was not in his pocket. He searched frantically for a few moments, and when he turned back to the bench where the old woman had been sitting he saw it. He picked it up and looked inside, all his credit cards and all his cash were still there.

"Everything is still here," he said aloud, a little surprised. But then he noticed something was missing: his license! And Michael began to laugh.

Racing in the Streets

Spring morning, 2011

Michael Tantalus and two other men started out as the light of the rising sun broke across the flat plain, just slightly illuminating everything. In their increasing speed, the wind felt hard and icy across their leather suits, and it chilled bare creases of exposed neck between high, tight collars and the hard expanse of plastic helmets. Each followed the other close, staying as much in the invisible draft of the man ahead as possible and out of the turbulence of the other rapidly advancing machines. The motorcycles were covered in chrome adornments that sparkled in the pale but growing light as each man rode in silence, isolated by the rush of the wind and the roar of their engines.

The lead sat atop a Harley Panhead; it was old, rusty, and worn underneath but clean and polished where visible to others, with a fresh, light covering of oil splatters seeping from ignored, aging gaskets. Branded just right and hanging low were black saddlebags carrying peanut butter sandwiches, water, and mobile phones.

The two riders with Michael wanted to be wild and free— free of attachments and free of fear, and also feared by others. But somewhere on each of their bikes, the riders carried elements of the life they rode to ignore, or at least pretend that they didn't live. The men they really were revealed in their wallet photos of perfect families, their bleached white undershirts that were soft and clean, their neat and polished fingernails...but also in their thoughts of being right, thoughts of knowing.

These two men with Michael exhibited signs of living but they were sleepwalking, only imagining thoughts of being alive. Believing a commercial and living the mythical images portrayed in their own minds that they were something other than what they actually were. And it should have been their clue. Yet all but one of the men, Michael Tantalus, were totally unaware they were sleeping through their lives, ignoring their wake-up calls, their own inner knowing that truly, what they knew was all a farce, everything they believed, everything they said, everything they did; all that is but Michael. Perhaps that is what attracted the other two men to Michael. Otherwise, they had very little in common. The two men had only recently met Michael. They were drawn to him, but neither man was sure why.

The three men pressed on, out of the city and into what appeared to them as empty countryside, roaring past cows that turned to run a short distance from the road, giving some support that their illusions of strength and indomitability were real. Just a slight roll of the throttle gave them all a feeling of power, pressing them into the wind, and it felt like....living. And neither of the two men with Michael could see the vultures, gliding high above the continually moving sun. But Michael could see them and had made peace with them within himself.

The three motorcycles rose and fell like the tide as the flat road began to climb and roll into the foothills. The wind pitched rebelliously and the temperature began to fall sharply. The men had traveled westward in anticipation but now turned sharply north and began the serious task of attacking the mountains. After only an hour or so, substantial clouds rolled over the sun and the streams along the highway became edged in jagged, new ice. The rolling rubber that so confidently grabbed the pavement just moments earlier now felt slippery on the rising, bending road. As their trust in their engines' horsepower dwindled, they slowed, making less progress against the switchbacks and the high, winding road toward the glorious mountain views they were imagining up ahead.

"Let me lead." Absorbed within the padding of his helmet, Michaels's voice had the effect of a loud thought. Michael raised a fist and motioned as he passed the man ahead. The man who had been in the lead sat straight on his bike and motioned with a "go ahead" with his left hand to Michael, who had already begun the pass. Michael passed with steely intent; he was riding for a different reason than the other two men, and he was determined to keep the pace set earlier in the flat lands.

Michael dipped his head, and with only a slight easy twisting of his wrist, he drove fire into the V-twin engine, waking the horsepower and torque of 1200 ccs, converting any restlessness still left instantly into adrenaline and a lurching two-wheeled machine. Michael was accelerating hard as he hit the first turn, laying his body as low as he could on the motorcycle, downshifting quickly with the lever under the toe of his boot, letting the gears of his bike scream and wind as the thick cogs and inner steel wheels violently slowed the man and machine now acting as one entity, challenging gravity with faith in the friction of an induced marriage between the rubber of the tires and the sharp curving asphalt of the road. The road now drove north and west, twisting higher upward on the mountain.

And still, hanging over the mountain and now over the three men, long, dark bands of clouds signaled a threat of harsh weather and treacherous roads ahead.

"Easy!" The third man yelled a caution that never left the bubble of his own helmet; even if it had, it would have been lost in all the noise. "There is no reason to hurry," he said, but by now he realized he was only talking to himself. He eased off his throttle and began slowing little by little each time the road reversed its course and increased its pitch. The twisting road gave Michael a thrill, made his heart pound, gave him the feeling of being alive, but he focused on the source of the feeling. A thought a gratitude played itself across Michael's mind.

To the other two men, racing up the road was the very thing to avoid. True danger was to be avoided and the road was to be traversed slowly and cautiously, to survive to live on as if life did not contain death, and if he ignored death, never faced her, that somehow he would be allowed to stay in his current state forever. *They don't know they are falling*, Michael thought.

Michael had the gift of having looked death in the eyes, stared deeply into her abyss of nothingness, and having become aware of her existence, he could not ignore her. He thought about her every day. And now, the vast mystery of the unknown was creeping deeper into Michael's being and closer to his heart, closer to his soul. The man now second on the road tried to keep pace with Michael, but his heart was beating at an uncomfortable pace. Compensating by holding too tightly to his grips, he leaned forward to look into his rearview mirror and caught a shaking, shrinking image of the third man receding farther and farther behind. Now aware his eyes were off the road, the second man jolted, jerking his attention back to the view ahead, tensing but without moving a single muscle in any of his limbs. His eyes were now back on the road, he was in no danger, he was not running off the road, but that slight instant of not knowing where he was or where he was going or what was about to happen had sent fear washing over him. Anxiety knotted his stomach, and feeling the g-force of the next turn while still in fear he did not lean the bike over enough and found himself too far upright and too wide in the turn: His wheels began to find gravel as the bike lost its firm confident grip of the road. The man's heart was racing and sweat squeezed out of his pores but he did not panic and instantly rolled off the throttle, slowing quickly on the rising road. The safer speed began to gently ease the beating of his heart.

After only a few switchbacks, Michael—who had been working the turns and stretching his skills—had put distance between himself and the other two men. He anchored himself to the seat and squeezed his knees tightly against the hot machine, shifting his body in a tucked lean into the turns and the wind. His hands and feet were all working different functions but all together in a rhythmic orchestration of body, mind, and machine. Michael's left hand was quickly squeezing and releasing the clutch, his right hand worked the gas and the front brake, his left foot worked the rear brake, and his right foot rapidly downshifted under his toes, deep into the arching bends of the mountain road. Then, as the road straightened for a short stretch, he slid his boot under the gearshift, changing to higher and higher gears, gaining as much speed as possible. Everything worked simultaneously without thought, Michael and the motorcycle, two separate machines, one organic, one of steel, but at the same time, everything was one, both two and one at the same time.

Eventually, Michael began to ease his speed, having wound his way up the side of the mountain and through a gap between two ancient and worn but still majestic peaks of the Smokey Mountain chain. The end of the small, winding road spent itself abruptly at the Blue Ridge Parkway, widening into large gravel landing areas on both sides of the road. Michael glided gently across the gravel, being mindful to not make any sudden changes on the loose surface. He braked and turned off the motor, pulled a round flat piece of plastic out of the front of his saddlebag, and dropped it onto the ground, pushed down the kickstand, and aligned its foot to land perfectly onto the plastic plate. He leaned the bike to stand on its own, then swung his leg high over the back of the bike like he was dismounting a horse. His body was still pleasantly vibrating from the long ride, the bumping of the uneven road and the after-effects of adrenaline and endorphins all combined to give him a gentle high. He pulled off his helmet so the cool mountain breeze could caress the back of his neck lightly.

The air felt so clean, so pure and inviting, that Michael gave in to his natural inclination to take as much into his lungs as possible, but the deep breath was caught short in his itchy lungs and he suppressed a growing urge to cough. Sometimes it was better to not stir what was inside; he did not resist it, it was part of him, but he left it alone. So he leaned back, looking at the glorious blue sky being chased by the coming storm. It was all so beautiful.

Michael pulled at the snaps around his neck then tugged the long zipper, peeling off the tightly-fitted leather jacket. Seeing the large dark clouds and the crystal blue emptiness all at once gave Michael the feeling of seeing the whole universe in one shot, and he stood motionless taking it all into his awareness, and gratitude filled his mind. He began to wonder about his traveling companions. He looked down at his watch and it hit him like it always did: 9:11 A.M. 9-1-1, that number.

He wondered how many times had he looked at it but not seen it in his life before that day. And now, the number stood out, quietly, but always there, always a reminder. Something he could never separate from himself, it was a part of him, it, was in him.

The pounding of Michael's heart in his chest gave him the feeling of filling his entire torso. There was joy as the light broke unevenly between the calm and the storm in jagged bands of gray and deep, dark blue. Streams of color lit the bare trees, whose branches reached gloriously into every direction, stretching to meet every ray of sun as if in conscious praise of the light. The melting of the aging, crystallized snow revealed millions of tiny prisms, turning the clear white edging of a shallow stream into merging rainbows of color, awakening all of the sleeping life from their winter dreams.

With eyes open, for just that moment, there was no death, no suffering for Michael. His awareness moved to the dancing swirls of his still-rapid breath in the cool mountain air. Michael felt good; he felt content. There was a tiny voice in his head that said, "Don't let it go." And that tiny pleasant moment reintroduced Michael to fear in a momentary contraction. He quickly relaxed, but the voice made him once again, Michael, the man who was living, but also the man who was dying.

It was some time later that the other two riders methodically made their way to where Michael was resting against a worn, decaying wooden structure, almost out of sight of the road. The building was a square two-room shack with a deep front porch and overhang. The wooden planks had shrunk and separated from each other, leaving clear gaps to the inside, revealing the emptiness. The grain of the weathered, gray wood extended outward like the veins on the overworked forearm of a lean ranch hand. Michael was sitting on the porch, leaning against the skeleton of the once living house. He had eaten his lunch and now stared at the rapidly darkening sky.

"What a ride!" the second man yelled out as he and the third man turned off their engines and took off their helmets.

"You got it, brother," Michael answered. No one would mention how Michael left them behind; no one wanted to break the sensation of living wild and free of their own controlled lives, and neither of the other two men wanted to wake from their dreams. Michael felt no urge to shatter any illusion for anyone else because he was still trying to break free himself, from what he did not know and to what he did not know. *The longer I have searched, the less I seem to know*, he thought.

As the men sorted through their packs for their road lunches, Michael rose and walked to the stream, where he bent down and cupped his hand for a drink of the cool water.

"I wouldn't drink that water!" the third man yelled in caution.

"Better than city water," Michael barked back.

The second man chimed in, explaining all of the bacteria and various pathogens that were present. The third man added his opinions, but it was all lost on Michael as he kept drinking from the stream. The two men knew much, read extensively, had earned many degrees between them, and they were experts in many fields. But they didn't realize how by knowing so much—being so sure—their minds only allowed them to consider limited and few possibilities.

But in the grace of his tragedies, the grace of his falls, Michael was no longer sure of anything. *"Turns out Chicken Little was a prophet,"* he thought, not knowing where the thought came from, but chuckling to himself nonetheless. Michael questioned everything, but mostly his beliefs, and as it was turning out, nearly everything he thought he knew was a belief. The teaching had required no belief and it had by now become so natural that thoughts of love and gratitude came often, effortlessly, and of their own accord. Letting go had in the beginning been disorienting to Michael, but as he let go more and more and "knew" less and less, he was seeing things, discovering things like a child. And regaining a childlike approach to everything had allowed his possibilities to become many.

It was getting darker now as the clouds of the storm passed overhead, and both of the men with Michael retreated into their own thoughts. Michael noticed that the shadows of the trees that earlier crossed the road had receded back to their source and now were beginning to fade entirely as the clouds raced rapidly overhead.

The rush of the ascent was now gone, leaving a little sadness in Michael. He had come so far, but when he was still, the aching caught up with him. He had convinced himself that he was different now, living differently, but still, there was something calling to him, he needed to go further. He felt the volition to move. Looking back down the road into the valley, he could see the flat plain below, misty and layered with soft bands of color. The distance increased the intensity of what he was feeling, so he reached for his long, black gloves.

Behind him, Michael could feel the whispering wind of the coming storm. The anxiety of avoiding the storm always was more than the discomfort of the cold, wet reality, but still Michael moved quickly out of an old but still partially present and unconscious belief that he could succeed in outrunning the storm. He crouched like a tiger and took hold of the throttle grip with his right hand, simultaneously hitting the ignition with his thumb. The bike roared to life as Michael snapped his wrist on the gas, startling the other two men. Michael stared at them both and said nothing as the back tire clawed helplessly for friction on the soft shoulder, throwing gravel into the trees while searching for some solid ground. As the tire grabbed hold of the earth, Michael's heart beat faster, there was fear, there was excitement, there was still a dream, but there was no awareness of pain. He roared down the valley, pushing the switchback, and out of sight of the others.

"What's his problem?" the second man asked the third.

"The hell with him if he wants to kill himself," was the matter-of-fact answer.

"Damned mid-life crisis if you ask me."

"Nah, he just thinks he is a kid," Both men chuckled, "Some men hear, 'go farther,' but Michael hears, 'go faster.'" It was a thoughtless comment and would have accurately described Michael a mere year earlier, but now was nowhere near the truth. Now the men were laughing—not looking deeply, not asking, not wanting to know, not questioning the way things were—laughing away the things that did not fit the way things were "supposed to," but then one man asked. "Why do you ride with Michael?"

"Oh, I don't know, some kind of death wish, I guess," and then he tried to laugh but the other man had a serious look on his face.

"I really don't have anything in common with Michael," the man said, "And I really don't like to ride with him, I mean, who wants to go that fast, crazy really," the man paused and was looking at the ground then he looked up, "But when I look into Michael's eyes, I feel peaceful."

"Yep, that's what I feel too—perplexes me," the other man said, "I come back from these rides feeling in some way content." They supposed that Michael lived differently because he thought he was dying, not ever considering for one instant, that they too were dying. For ten, twenty, thirty... maybe forty years they live quietly, pretending that they don't hear a noise in the closet, pulling the covers over their heads with a scotch or an expensive coffee, even riding themselves to sleep.

Michael did live differently, and maybe it was the grace of his personal trauma, of having stood so close that September a few years back as death fell to the ground all around him. *I imagine that nearly the entire world awakened at the moment the towers came down, many have fallen back to sleep, but if only a few remain awakened, then mankind is better off today. Waking up is easy, staying awake is hard,* Michael thought.

Michael Tantalus's quest had not yielded any absolutes or answers, but he was experiencing a certain comfort being in the state of absolute not-knowing. He had thought the quest for life's meaning was impossible. But what Michael did not yet see was that in the beginning, he had been avoiding facing death in these wild rides up the mountain, but now he rode for the sheer feeling, the experience of pleasure—he now embraced everything and met it all entirely with love.

Michael sat up on the seat and eased off the throttle. As the bike slowed, he could feel the ever-pursuing storm at his back, could see the treetops bending and thrashing in the strong winds. He had the sensation of dreaming, and he was not afraid. He also recognized the beauty of the coming change in the weather, his coming personal change, the inevitable, and he smiled.

Michael brought the bike to a stop. He had come to a crossroad. The Enola Highway lay before him in a wide and inviting dark and new asphalt, it was smooth with fresh, brightly painted yellow lines. But crossing the main road was a hard-to-notice old and winding road. There was a small sign that did not look official or like it had been placed there by the highway department. It was made of wood and pointed up the barely maintained road: "Old Enota Road."

Michael dipped his head and turned down the ancient looking pathway. He then leaned forward and twisted his wrist, throttling the motorcycle onto the road into a destination unknown.

EPILOGUE
The Final Veil

Spring Evening, 2011

Michael had been riding for hours but his hands were light on the handlebars, and he was relaxed listening to the pulsing mantra of the engine humming and the wind blowing in his ears. There were peaks as far as he could see, one fading into the other in shades of blue and gray, blending softly into the pale sky. The gently bending arcs of asphalt meandered below his feet and there was nothing but an eternal view above. Turns required merely a slight leaning of the bike, not engaging fear or any emotion—just enough bend in the road to occupy his mind. The storm was nearly past, and in the near-distance was the promise of clear skies.

Michael's spirit soared and expanded into the sky; his mind was still, hearing none of the incessant judging voices that kept him locked into his body. In that moment, everything that lay before him stretched into infinity and everything within him stretched just as far. Destination and source became the same. He was not experiencing or living in the moment, he was the moment. He was eternity and he was source. He needed nothing: no lover, no alcohol, no technique.

The sun had begun its setting, and Michael slowed, turning to ride down a less-traveled gravel road as lengthening shadows pointed to the coming darkness. Farther and farther he traveled away from the main road until the gravel gave way to dirt. His motorcycle was made for the pavement, so the bike began to struggle in the softening soil. Finally, the smooth tires lost their grip completely as Michael hit an incline. The heavy machine began to slide backward but Michael regained control and brought it to a stop. He sat for a moment to catch his breath, then killed the engine. Silence and stillness overwhelmed him though his body still vibrated from the long road he had been riding.

Michael laid the bike down and continued up the dirt road on foot. He pulled off his helmet and let it drop to the ground. The dust and grime from his journey were heavy on his skin, making him feel dirty. He wiped his neck with his glove, but the feeling remained. As he continued walking, the road became a trail, narrowing so much that the fresh, pale-green leaves touched both shoulders and caressed his exposed neck. He kept walking, finding that the altitude and the inclining pathway were stealing his breath. He put his hands on his knees to try to recover, but decided instead to cross a nearby stream and rest under the trees.

He stepped into the stream and into the tumult of water that was crashing over and around the rocks. Michael's footing was uncertain, and he struggled with the next steps as the fast-moving water pulled at his legs and his confidence, like the thoughts of a thousand things that needed to be done or made better. All of these things and others pulled at his now-restless mind. He stopped moving as he felt a cough take over his body. He convulsed, losing his balance and falling. The spasm subsided as he was immersed in the cold, soothing stream, but still he felt a burning in his lungs and it was big.

He allowed the water to wash him downstream on his back, bouncing on the rocky bottom. He rolled over to move out of the faster moving water, slowing himself down. He stood, and as the cold water fell from his body, it rinsed off the dust and grime of the road and he felt clean. He walked a few remaining steps to get out of the stream, squishing as he walked with wet, heavy feet. He slowly rose out of the stream bed and sat against a large beech tree, cradled in its bulky, exposed roots. It was far more comfortable than he expected. His shoulders dropped as he began to relax, his breath slowed and became even, and his thoughts once again calmed.

He stared at the rushing stream focusing on a single point of awareness within the moving water. In that single point, he saw beauty, found tranquility, and felt peace. There was a place of stillness within the stream of the great rushing water that held everything that was moving.

"Yes," he whispered in a weary breath. Then, by grace the final veil fell—the veil of thought identification. And as the veil fell away, there was something there but it was nothing distinct and nothing Michael could identify as himself. Michael had come to the place where he ended and everything began. His thoughts seemed very far away and nearly quiet but they did not completely subside; rather he did not identify with them, there was no interest in the story in his mind, there was only happiness. He could still feel burning in his lungs, but there were no thoughts of pain, only gratitude. His breaths were shallow and rapid, but even and steady. The sky steadily darkened as evening arrived, while at the same time, a bright, full moon peeked out just over the horizon and infused the trees with a pale light that mixed with the deepening dusk, eventually overcoming the last bits of fading daylight. The dogwood blossoms reflected the moon's rays, making spectacular pinwheels sparkle in the deep forest with a show of promise, and what felt to Michael as a show of love.

In that moment, for Michael, everything was possible. He pulled his cell phone out of his pocket and looked at its bright glow. It was 9:12. He smiled. He took as deep a breath as he could and then shut his eyes. He was filled with love—there were no conditions and no thoughts. He felt no suffering, only joy.